"Featuring a cursed hero, fabulous secondary characters, a world torn between machines and magic, and a plot that hooks your interest from the very first chapter, *Dead Iron* is a must read."

—*New York Times* bestselling author Keri Arthur

"A relentless Western and a gritty steampunk, bound together by wicked magic. The action is superb, the stakes are sky-high, and the passion runs wild. Who knew cowboys and gears could be this much fun? Devon Monk rocks—her unique setting and powerful characters aren't to be missed!"

—*New York Times* bestselling author Ilona Andrews

"A novel and interesting take on the steampunk tropes, with generous nods to other genres, and plenty of odd but human characters and Mad Science."

—*New York Times* bestselling author S. M. Stirling

"Werewolves, witches, and creatures of both flesh and metal clash in a scarred land stitched together with iron rails—a steampunk world so real I could almost smell the grease and hear the gears grind. Beautifully written and brilliantly imagined, Devon Monk is at her best with *Dead Iron*."

—*New York Times* bestselling author Rachel Vincent

"A magical steampunk history of the Pacific Northwest . . . this is a magnificent tale of Edenic mountains, steam-powered assassins, deathless love, and transformation. Fast-paced, tricksy, turning from one extreme to another, the reader will be drawn ever deeper into the ticking, dripping iron heart of this story."   —Jay Lake, award-winning author of *Green*

continued . . .

BOOKS BY DEVON MONK

————

THE AGE OF STEAM

Dead Iron

Tin Swift

THE ALLIE BECKSTROM SERIES

Magic to the Bone

Magic in the Blood

Magic in the Shadows

Magic on the Storm

Magic at the Gate

Magic on the Hunt

Magic on the Line

Magic Without Mercy

TIN SWIFT

The Age of Steam

DEVON MONK

A ROC BOOK

ROC
Published by New American Library,
a division of Penguin Group (USA) Inc.,
375 Hudson Street, New York, New York 10014, USA
Penguin Group (Canada), 90 Eglinton Avenue East, Suite 700, Toronto,
Ontario M4P 2Y3, Canada (a division of Pearson Penguin Canada Inc.)
Penguin Books Ltd., 80 Strand, London WC2R 0RL, England
Penguin Ireland, 25 St. Stephen's Green, Dublin 2,
Ireland (a division of Penguin Books Ltd.)
Penguin Group (Australia), 250 Camberwell Road, Camberwell,
Victoria 3124, Australia (a division of Pearson Australia Group Pty. Ltd.)
Penguin Books India Pvt. Ltd., 11 Community Centre,
Panchsheel Park, New Delhi - 110 017, India
Penguin Group (NZ), 67 Apollo Drive, Rosedale, Auckland 0632,
New Zealand (a division of Pearson New Zealand Ltd.)
Penguin Books (South Africa) (Pty.) Ltd., 24 Sturdee Avenue,
Rosebank, Johannesburg 2196, South Africa

Penguin Books Ltd., Registered Offices:
80 Strand, London WC2R 0RL, England

First published by Roc, an imprint of New American Library,
a division of Penguin Group (USA) Inc.

First Printing, July 2012
1   3   5   7   9   10   8   6   4   2

ROC REGISTERED TRADEMARK—MARCA REGISTRADA

LIBRARY OF CONGRESS CATALOGING-IN-PUBLICATION DATA:

Monk, Devon.
Tin swift: the age of steam/Devon Monk.
p. cm.—(The age of steam; 2)
ISBN 978-0-451-46453-8
1. Bounty hunters—Fiction.   2. Werewolves—Fiction.   3. Steampunk fiction.   I. Title.
PS3613.O5293T56 2012
813'.6—dc23   2012007897

Set in Electra   •   Designed by Elke Sigal

Printed in the United States of America

PUBLISHER'S NOTE

This is a work of fiction. Names, characters, places, and incidents either are the product of the author's
imagination or are used fictitiously, and any resemblance to actual persons, living or dead, business es-
tablishments, events, or locales is entirely coincidental.

The publisher does not have any control over and does not assume any responsibility for author or
third-party Web sites or their content.

For my family

ACKNOWLEDGMENTS

So many people have given their time and talent to make this book a reality. I want to thank my wonderful agent, Miriam Kriss, for your support and enthusiasm. Thank you to my extraordinary editor, Anne Sowards, for your keen insight and amazing ability to say just the right thing at just the right time. My unflagging gratitude goes out to the fabulous artist Cliff Nielsen for bringing Cedar to life and giving the *Swift* her chance to shine. Big thanks also to editorial assistant Katherine Sherbo and publicists Rosanne Romanello and Brady McReynolds. To the many people within Penguin who have gone above and beyond to make this book beautiful and strong, I just want to say thank you from the bottom of my heart.

While this book was a lot of fun to write, it also took some elbow grease to pull it all together. I want to give a very special thank-you to my brother and brainstorming partner, Dean Woods, for checking in on me every week no matter what, and always asking to read more. I honestly don't know how I would have gotten through the first draft sane without you. You're my hero.

As always, my love and gratitude to Dejsha Knight for your thoughtfulness and support, and for saying this one (so far) is your favorite. Also, a big thank-you to my wonderful family and friends for all your encouragement and help along the way. I couldn't do this without you. To my husband, Russ, and sons, Kameron and Konner: you guys are the best. Thank you for helping me make my dreams come true and for letting me be a part of your life. I love you.

Last, but not nearly least, I want to thank you, dear readers, for giving me the chance to share this world and these people with you once again.

TIN SWIFT

CHAPTER ONE

Cedar Hunt stared down at his blood-covered hands. Glossy and dark, fresh and plentiful, the blood dripped between his fingers, slicking his arms and snicking to the dirt between his boots. More than just covering his hands, the blood tasted sweet and thick on his tongue and coated his throat as he swallowed.

Not the blood of a beast, the blood of a man.

"That's enough now, Mr. Hunt," a woman's voice said, steady and low.

He looked up. Realized he stood beneath a sparse forest canopy, evening light dabbing gold across branches and leaves.

Dabbing gold across Rose Small too. She had on her bonnet, the tips of her hair swinging just above her shoulders to catch that dusky sunlight and wear it in shades of amber. Though shadows lay low over her face, her blue eyes shone through like a sun-filled sky. But her mouth, so often curved in a smile, was tucked down in a tight frown.

She motioned with the shotgun held low at her hip. She didn't have her long-shot goggles on. Didn't have to. Cedar was only a few paces in front of her.

"I'd sure prefer it if I didn't have to shoot you tonight, Mr. Hunt, but by God and glim I will."

"Rose?" Cedar whispered.

Why was the girl pointing that gun at him? They'd been traveling together more than a full month across Oregon and were just into Idaho, he, Rose Small, the widow witch Mae Lindson, his cursed brother, Wil, and the three Madder brothers. He hadn't once come to his senses with any of them standing at arms against him. Not even when the moon had taken him full into his curse.

"Glad you've a mind for talking, Mr. Hunt," Rose said. "Even better your ears are working." She lifted the gun. "But I'll still plug you if you don't step away from that man and head back into the wagon."

He'd known what he had done the moment he'd seen blood on his hands, tasted it on his lips. He'd killed a man. In daylight.

And he'd done it as a man, not a beast, with no thrall of the moon to blame his actions upon.

He looked down. The dead man wasn't very large nor very young. He had the look and the smell of someone who spent most his days riding and hunting bounties on men's heads and most his nights gambling away the noose money.

"Who?" he rasped.

"I'd ask his name," Rose said, "but don't think he'll say. He broke into our camp and tried to kill a few of us, Mae included. You . . ." Her voice faded off. Then she sort of huffed a chuckle. "Never saw a thing like it. And I've seen things. Strange things."

Mae. Of course. He'd never stand idle if she was in danger. But to lose his mind to this kind of rage was not at all like him.

"Did I change?" Cedar couldn't remember the wolf coming upon him. Couldn't remember sliding down that slick, hot stroke of pleasure to stretch into the fur and claws of the beast that the Pawnee gods had cursed him to wear on the three days of full moon.

Reason left him when the beast was in control and his thoughts reduced to hunger, hunt, and killing the Strange. He searched his memory for how the dead man had come to be broken, his blood pouring down Cedar's throat.

Nothing came clear.

"You didn't change," Rose said. "Not in skin anyway. But I'm not sure how much of a man's mind you were in possession of. Didn't use a gun to kill him, Mr. Hunt. You used your bare hands. Broke him once and just kept right on breaking him."

She paused to let that soak in good.

"So," she said brightly, "now you need to be moving on. We want you locked up in the wagon for safekeeping. Yours and ours."

Cedar took one last look at the man. "Someone should search his body. See if he carried a reason to be following us. He was following us, wasn't he?"

"The Madders said maybe for a week or so. They're off seeing if he had company." Rose started walking, her boots crunching through the dry autumn underbrush.

Cedar started walking too, staying well ahead of her trigger finger.

"Don't know as to why he thought killing us was worth the effort," she said. "We don't have much to steal. We aren't causing any trouble."

Then she grinned. "You don't suppose we've gotten famous, do you? Maybe someone heard how we took apart Shard LeFel and his matics? Wrote us up in a newspaper somewhere?"

"Folk are rarely hunted for their good deeds," Cedar said. "I don't think we're famous."

Sure, he had mistakes in his past that might put a price on his head. But Rose had never been outside of the little town of Hallelujah, Oregon, until now. Mae Lindson might be a witch, but she wasn't the sort of person to go about causing harm.

The Madder brothers were a mystery when it came to their moral standings and past deeds. They liked to spin tales fantastical of things they'd done, places they'd been, but none of those yarns pointed clearly to shady doings.

"Could be nothing to do with us," he finally said. He rubbed his thumb over his lips, wiping away the blood there, and resisted the urge to lick it off his fingers.

Core-deep inside him, the beast shifted, letting him know it was still hungry. If there was no Strange blood to spill, it seemed just as happy with the blood of a man.

He straightened his shoulders against the chill of dread that slipped down his spine.

The beast was growing stronger. Hungrier.

"So he was just desperate?"

"Could be," Cedar said. "Saw an opportunity to plunder his way westward. Plenty of folk do it."

"Land pirates?" Rose sounded excited about the prospect.

She'd seen violence. Killed without a flinch men and Strange creatures that crawled up out of nightmares. But even death and much darker happenstances hadn't been able to shake Rose Small's sense of wonder in the world.

Cedar hadn't yet seen a thing that could dim her spirit.

"Just a rustler, more like." He paused. Turned to her. "We should search him."

Rose hesitated. Cedar gave her time to look him straight in the eyes. She held his wild gaze and measured his sanity.

Looking at him like that, when the beast was so near the surface of his reasoning, was something most people couldn't do.

But then, Rose had a bit of the wild in her too. Wasn't a metal she couldn't shape or a device she couldn't jigger with her fast-thinking mind and clever fingers.

"Not that I don't trust you, Mr. Hunt," she said. "It's just . . ." Her mouth tugged a crooked frown. "You tore him apart. With your hands."

"Rose," he said softly, resisting the urge to put his hands behind his back, where she wouldn't see the blood. As if that could hide his sins from her. "Whatever happened, it's done."

She bit her bottom lip and those springtime eyes searched him like she was peering through the shutter of his soul. "I'll keep the gun where it is, just the same."

Cedar walked back to the body. He glanced at the surrounding forest. Didn't see anything out of place. Well, except for the dead man. Not many bugs had found him yet, so it'd been just a few minutes at most since he'd killed him.

Snapped his neck, to be precise.

Cedar knelt and turned the man so he could study his face. A heavy black beard spread chin to temple. All his unwhiskered skin seemed to be covered in grime. His eyes were rolled back in his head and blood dripped a line out the corner of his mouth. Cedar picked up each of his hands. All the fingers were still attached, calluses and scars where you'd expect them to be on a man who rode the range.

He'd carried two guns, one thrown off in the brush about ten feet east, the other still in the holster. The weapons weren't nothing fancy, but they were well tended. He'd been good with his guns.

Not good enough to draw more than one before Cedar had killed him.

With his bare hands.

Cedar searched pockets, coat, and shirt. Handkerchief, tobacco pouch, rolling paper, and a knife. Not a lot else. Not a single coin on him, not a scrap of a letter, not a photo of a loved one.

"You done pawing that fellow to death?" The voice was so near him, Cedar started.

Alun Madder, the oldest of the brothers, crouched down on his heels near Cedar. Cedar was not a small man, but Alun took him on width.

Built like bull buffalos, the Madder brothers were all heavily bearded, wide-jawed, and accustomed to a life of mining, drinking, and brawling. When they weren't fighting, they had an uncanny knack with metal, matics, and odd devices.

Cedar owed them a favor for helping him find his brother, who he had thought was long dead. They'd been true to their part of the bargain, and so he was holding true to his.

Riding east to return Mae to her witch sisterhood before her ties to them and the magic of the coven sent her clean insane. Riding east so maybe those same witches could break the Pawnee curse Cedar and his brother carried. Rose, he supposed, was just looking to see the world wide, though he knew she cared for Mae and wanted to see her set to rights.

And on the way he would uphold his promise to hunt for the Holder, a device made of seven ancient metals cobbled together into a weapon of great power.

The Madders said even uncobbled, the Holder could cause ruin, rot, destruction.

If that was true, then the brothers' priority of gathering it up—wherever it was the pieces had landed—and getting it out of the hands of the innocent was a worthwhile cause.

"You're of a quiet mood, all of a sudden," Alun Madder said. "This man someone you know?"

Cedar pulled a cloth out of his back pocket and wiped his bloody palms and arms until they were mostly clean. He shook his head. "You?"

The miner had a blue kerchief tied tight over his head, but wore no hat. His gaze was on the dead man. "No soul I've ever known. Looks to be a drifter. Found his horse back a ways in the forest."

"Bring it. We can use a fresh mount."

"Already done, Mr. Hunt. I'm not the sort to leave a useful thing"—he gave Cedar a pointed look—"or creature behind. No matter how it falls into my hands." He pushed on his knees to stand and peered down over his thick dark beard.

"As Miss Small was saying, we'd like you locked in the wagon now. Night's coming. We'd rather you weren't out roaming. And besides"—he walked off toward camp—"the witch says she has an idea for easing that curse of yours."

A pang of hope snarled Cedar's gut. "She said she couldn't break the curse unless she had the sisterhood, and days to do it."

"Said otherwise just before you wandered off," Rose said.

"So she's talking?" Cedar stood.

"Oh, she's been talking nonstop since we set camp. Just don't know who she's been talking to."

Cedar followed Alun through the trees to the clearing. There was a little more light here beyond the reach of branch and shadow. The grass was tall and silk-yellow around the stones, bent to the wind, and hushing away at every stray breeze. They'd had the luck of clear weather, but any day now the skies would change.

Storms were coming down from the north Cascade Mountains and Bitterroot Range. Strong enough to bury them in snow. Strong enough to swell little creeks into hungry rivers and trails into muddy bogs. They'd a plan to skirt the bottom of the mountain range and reach Fort Boise, Idaho, by the next week. Now he was just hoping they'd make it far enough into the Idaho Territory by nightfall to reach Vicinity. If the rains hit hard, they'd be locked flat in their tracks for the whole of winter.

Alun strolled over to the hulking wagon he and his brothers drove. The drafts that pulled for them were off a ways grazing. So too the other horses, with a new little roan among them. The dead man's mount. Theirs now.

"Keep going, Mr. Hunt," Rose said from behind, the gun still at her hip. He'd like to tell her she was being overly cautious, but that wasn't true.

More than once he'd pulled up out of a dream of hunt and kill and blood, only to find himself sitting in his saddle, his horse spooking and the other folk in the group asking him what he was stopped and listening for.

He'd told them nothing. But that wasn't true. The beast inside him wanted out. It was making sure it could be heard.

He knew what the Pawnee had planted in his soul and knew how to keep it caged.

Until today.

Mae paced near the fire they'd set between the Madders' wagon and the women's tent. She had a handful of plucked grasses and was braiding them together as she walked and muttered.

Less sane every day that went by. The coven of witches she'd once belonged to was calling her home, and taking away bits of her mind the longer it took her to get to them. He didn't understand witches. Didn't understand why her vows to the coven meant now that her husband was dead, they could drag her to madness unless she returned to them.

But he knew cruelty when he saw it.

"Look who I found just out in the trees, Mrs. Lindson," Rose called out.

Mae turned and studied him across the fire. She seemed to be made of sunset there against the sky. The red firelight burnished her pale skin and yellow hair, catching sparks in her inscrutable eyes, and drawing dusty shadows across her soft lips.

Cedar's pulse kicked up a beat. Since his wife's death, he'd thought he'd never be shed of the pain of grief. Never have reason to feel again.

Until he'd met the widow Mae Lindson.

"I'm gonna take him to the wagon now," Rose said. "And when you're of a mind—"

"No." Mae drew her hand up to smooth her dress, discovered the grasses, and frowned. She let the grasses drop from her fingers. When she looked back up at him, it was with an ounce more clarity.

"Leave your guns and knife here, Mr. Hunt," she said.

Cedar unhitched his gun belt, then his knife. Set them all down easy on the ground. When he straightened, Mae walked round the fire and stopped right in front of him.

He couldn't help but inhale the scent of her, always the sweet honey of flowers. They'd been on the road for days now without much more than a splash in a creek or two to sluice the trail dust. But Mae was beautiful, serene. Looking upon her made his breath catch in his chest.

She took his hand and turned it over like she was looking for a wound.

"This blood," she said. "It's not yours, is it?"

When she spoke, it was as if a rope had been cut free from around his heart. It was a puzzling thing being near her. A thing that felt so much like love, it might even share its name.

Not that he'd said as much to her. He didn't know if there would ever be room in her grief to love another.

"Mr. Hunt?" Mae said. Then, "Are you hurt?"

"No." The beast inside him twisted and dug deep, wanting out. Wanting Mae.

She caught his gaze and held his own hand up so that he would look at it.

"Where did this blood come from?"

He drew his hand gently away from hers. "Man needs burying back a ways."

Rose stepped up a little closer to rub out a stray ember that popped free from the fire. "We can take care of the dead," she said, "after the living are tended and resting in the wagon."

"Are you sure you're not hurt?" Mae asked with a sort of worry he hadn't heard out of her in days.

He pulled a smile into place, hoping it softened his eyes, eased the hard line of his jaw. Hoping it made him look more like a man who still had his reason in place.

"As well as can be, thank you."

"See?" Rose said kindly. "We're all doing fine."

Cedar tipped his fingers to his hat, then strode off toward the wagon, Rose right behind him.

If he stayed near Mae any longer, he'd take her in his arms. Hold her. Hell, kiss her and do the things a man can do to a woman.

Things she would not welcome. Not with her husband's death so fresh in her eyes. Not with the tracks of tears on her cheeks. And the nights, every night, her whispering his name like a prayer.

The clatter of metal on metal rose up from the other side of the wagon, louder the closer he came.

The other two Madder brothers, Bryn and Cadoc, were off just a ways from the wagon, cussing over a chunk of brass and tangle of wood equipped with at least three valves that were sending off thin puffs of steam.

Bryn, the middle born, was taller by a finger or two than Alun, but not so tall as Cadoc. His beard was clipped tight, and he wore a brass monocle strapped over his ruined eye. The lens flashed an unnatural turquoise from under his floppy hat as his wide, nimble fingers used a half dozen tools to tinker with the steam device.

Cadoc Madder didn't much involve himself in conversation unless it was to say something vaguely prophetic. He had on the same denim overalls and heavy overcoat all the Madders wore, the pockets of which bulged with gadgets. Tonight a knit cap sat over the bush of black hair on his head.

Cedar didn't know what sort of contraption they were trying to fire up, but it appeared to require a heavy hammer and wrench—both currently being used to pummel the thing.

Alun Madder leaned against the wagon wheel, smoking his pipe and watching Cedar with a hard gaze.

"Here we go now." Rose motioned the shotgun toward the wagon steps. "A roof over your head and a lock on the door. Cozy."

"You'll need more than a lock," Cedar said. "You know where the shackles are?"

"I think so."

"Find them." He stumped up the stairs and ducked into the darkness of the wagon.

The wagon was so cluttered with supplies, packages, and oddments, it was like stepping into a town bazaar. Nets and scarves and rope hung from the framed ceiling; boxes, bundles, chests, and shelves were stuffed tight to bursting.

The nets could be set out for hammocks, as the Madder brothers were used to traveling in some comfort. To one side of the nets was enough space for a bed. That's where Cedar headed.

He ducked a swinging lantern and stood at the bottom of the bedroll spread on a pile of sacks that had fewer hard edges than most the rest of the wagon's contents.

Wil lay curled on the wool blanket. Even when Wil was in wolf form, his eyes remained the same old copper color and carried an uncanny intelligence. The wolf lifted his head and ears, watching Cedar sit and press his back against the sideboard.

Cedar let his hand drop so Wil could scent the blood, which he had probably already smelled before Cedar had even entered the wagon. Even though Wil seemed able to keep the mind of a man about him while in wolf form, it was plain foolish to bed down near a wolf with unfamiliar blood between you.

Wil sniffed Cedar's hand, then stared past him at the wagon door.

Rose was coming. He could hear the weeping chime of the shackles in her hands.

But it was Mae who stepped into the wagon.

"Mae?" he said. "I thought Rose was bringing the chains."

"She is," Mae said. "I'm here for your curse. To . . . to make it less if I can."

She held a bundle in one hand, just larger than a handkerchief. He couldn't smell what she had wrapped up in it, but Wil whined.

"Do you think you should? Now?"

"Rose saw you kill a man." Mae spread the kerchief out on a crate, revealing the contents. Herbs, a candle, a small bowl, and a bell. Her hand dipped to touch each item, over and over again, as if doubting their reality.

"I suppose she did," he said.

Mae pulled the skinning knife from the sheath at her waist. "I don't think we can wait any longer to . . . ease this."

She straightened her shoulders, but it did nothing to hide the exhaustion threading her. Mae had spent most of the journey dazed in her saddle and staring at the sky through the night.

It tore him up to see her falling apart more and more each day.

Not that she'd complained. Not once. She'd known that leaving the coven would someday set this cost in motion.

"I appreciate your concern, Mrs. Lindson," he said, "but don't you need your sisters' help?"

"What I need, Mr. Hunt," Mae said softly, "is a man with a sound mind." She swallowed and nodded, as if agreeing with herself. Or with the voices only she could hear.

"A lot of land to cover before winter strikes." She nodded, nodded. "Your expertise on the trail and surviving the wilds is invaluable. We are relying on you to see that we arrive at our destination. Safely. As safely as we can."

"Sad day when a cursed man is the sure bet," he muttered.

"Not sad. Not at all. It's a practical thing," she said with a faint smile. "I . . . trust you. And I will need your blood, Mr. Hunt. Water could work, or tears, or sweat, but for what you carry . . ." She studied him as if she saw him clothed in another man's wardrobe. "For that curse to ease, I'll need the blood that carries it."

Cedar stood, took off his coat, then rolled up his sleeve.

In the enclosed wagon, with the warmth of the day still trapped inside, her presence was almost tactile. The scent of flowers, the halting rhythm of her breath, and her gaze that searched him as if uncertain, or afraid, of what she was looking for, fell on his senses like heady wine.

He offered his forearm. "Will this do?"

She nodded, and placed the bowl to catch the blood. "I won't need much. Still—I'm sorry."

He opened his mouth to say he didn't mind, but she had already slid the knife quick and sure through his skin.

A hot sting licked across his arm. It hurt, but not all that much.

Mae set to gathering the drops of blood, her hands sure, as she suddenly became more interested in the blood than in the man who bled.

Cedar forced himself to look away from her, to the wagon door, and the sky and trees beyond.

Rose Small jogged up the steps, shotgun strapped to her back, a smile on her face.

"Found the chains," she declared. "We'll have you tied up and bug snug in no time. Oh." She stopped just inside the door. "Is everything all right?"

"A spell," Mae said. "For Mr. Hunt. For the curse."

"Think you should take a seat, Mr. Hunt?" Rose asked.

"I'd prefer it," he said.

Mae didn't seem to hear either of them. She pressed a cloth against the cut on his arm. "Hold this."

He put his fingers over the cloth, chose a pile of burlap bags for a chair, and sat.

Mae returned the bowl to the crate and then shook out a handkerchief, which she quickly folded.

"Do you need me to tie that over your arm?" Rose asked.

"No. It's nearly done." One of the things the curse gave him was a faster healing time. Already the cut was beginning to close.

Rose shook the chains free to untangle them. "Wish there was another way, Mr. Hunt," she said. "I hate seeing anyone in cuffs."

"I don't much like them myself," he said, trying to put ease in his words. "But it's not as if they do me any harm. Given the choice, I'd much rather the cuffs than your bullet in my chest."

Rose shrugged a little and clasped the cold metal around each wrist. "I would have aimed at your leg, I think," she said, fastening the ankle cuffs.

"And if you'd missed?"

She double-checked the chain that ran from the ankle cuffs up to the wrist cuffs, then latched to the side of the wagon. "I wouldn't have missed." She gave him a smile. "You know that, Mr. Hunt."

He couldn't help but smile back at her. She was right. Rose was a crack shot.

Wil limped over to stand next to Cedar, ears up, head high. He didn't look concerned, wasn't whining or growling. No, if Cedar had to guess, he'd say his brother was just curious about the whole thing.

"I'm going to stand right over there by the door," Rose said, "in case any of you need anything."

She did just that, moving far enough to be out of his reach, but plenty close enough to blow a hole in his leg, or any other part of him, with that elephant gun if she wanted to.

"Mrs. Lindson," Rose said gently as if waking her from a dream, "Mr. Hunt is ready for that spell now."

Mae jerked and swallowed hard. Her gaze pulled away from whatever distant horizon had caught her thoughts.

An absentminded witch about to call on magic was worrisome, to say the least.

"Good," Mae said, wiping her hands down the front of her dress, a nervous habit she'd taken to lately. "Relax, Mr. Hunt." She didn't turn to look at him. "As much as you can."

She crumbled the herbs between her palms, dusting them into the bowl.

Next she lit the candle nub and set that carefully in the bowl. Then she began whispering.

Cedar shifted so the shovel handle sticking up behind him didn't dig quite so deeply into his ribs, and waited. Seemed all the world waited on Mae's words, only moving forward at the pace of her hushed breath that slowly grew into a song.

He lost track of time as Mae's words lifted, fell, and became a second voice for the breeze, a second heartbeat of the world. He vaguely noticed daylight slip away, felt the rise of the moon climbing the sky.

The beast within him squirmed, tugged, wanting free of the bindings, wanting free of the small space of his body, the vise of his will.

Cedar wouldn't let that happen. Wouldn't let the beast take his sense away again. Not so long as he could stand on two feet as a man.

He held tight to his calm, ignored the beast, and let the witch do her work.

Mae held the bowl up to her lips, whispering over the edge, her words coming faster, softer, almost as if she were caught in a thrall. She finally turned toward him, took the few steps across the wagon, her eyes unfocused. Or more likely focused on things Cedar could not see.

Rose shifted against the doorframe. She'd kept the gun holstered and instead held a little bottle with a mix of cayenne pepper, water, and oil. She'd bargained the pepper from the Madders and boiled it to a wicked concentration. Rose said it would stop a man dead in his tracks if he got a face full of what was in that bottle.

Cedar didn't savor the idea of being the man she tried it out on.

"Cedar Hunt." Mae's voice trembled, exhausted as if she were indeed carrying all the world on her words. "Let your debt be paid. Let your ties to those who walk the earth and stars fall away in peace. Let your soul become unburdened, unbound, and return again to the true shape of spirit and flesh."

She blew out the candle and the smoke rolled toward him. He inhaled.

For a moment, he felt lifted, as if he stood beside himself instead of set solid in his own skin. For a moment, the beast seemed a great distance from him, as if pulled away by a retreating tide.

An explosion blasted through the night.

Pain, hot and claw-sharp, dragged him back as if the beast tore into his flesh, muscle, and bone, and clamped down with brutal jaws.

He opened his mouth to yell, to gasp for air.

And the pain was gone.

He sat, shackled, on the burlap. He was not bleeding. He was not injured.

And he was not cured. The beast was still inside him.

The Madder brothers outside the wagon cussed and laughed, congratulating themselves.

Rose stomped back into the wagon. He hadn't heard her leave.

"They blew a hole the size of a barn into the ground. Scared the horses half to death. If we hadn't ground-tied them, we'd have lost them in the night."

"Dynamite?" he asked.

"No, they heated up the boiler so high it blew. Bits of metal and wood everywhere. Such a waste. They think it's a matter of hilarity."

Mae wiped the back of her hand over her eyes and leaned back against the crate, all the strength out of her.

"Did it work?" Rose nodded toward Mae.

"No," Cedar said, "I don't believe it did."

Mae frowned. "It should have. It should have worked. The explosion. Was there an explosion?"

"Nothing to worry about, Mrs. Lindson," Rose said. "It was just a bad turn of luck the Madders are all fired up with stupid tonight."

"The Madders?" Mae said. "That was reckless. Inexcusable. To break the spell . . ."

Cedar watched as her face heated with anger. For a moment, for more than that, he wondered just what an angry woman who also happened to be a witch was capable of doing to a man.

"It's done," he said. "Let it be for now. We all need sleep." He lifted his hands, the chains clinking. "I'll be of no harm to anyone this night."

Mae pressed her lips together, and then her anger was replaced by something more resembling confusion. "I'm sorry."

"Don't worry yourself," Rose said. "After some sleep we'll be coming into new supplies tomorrow. Isn't that right, Mr. Hunt?"

Cedar nodded. "If we want to get over the mountains before winter locks the passes, we'll need to make Vicinity by nightfall."

"There might be herbs we could buy so you could try that spell again," Rose said.

"I don't think . . ." Mae licked her lips and shook her head. "I don't think herbs will help."

"Don't you worry, Mae." Rose took Mae's hands and helped her to the door of the wagon. "There's nothing but bright skies and sunshine for us tomorrow."

Cedar admired Rose's outlook, though he didn't share it. He didn't know what tomorrow would bring. Wil lowered his ears and growled softly at the Madders' laughter.

It was terribly convenient that their device had exploded just when Mae was so close to breaking his curse. A curse that happened to make him hunger to hunt the Strange. A curse that made him an undeniable benefit in the Madders' quest to find the strangeworked Holder.

If Cedar were a suspicious man, he might just think the Madders had broken Mae's spell on purpose.

CHAPTER TWO

Stump Station wasn't much more than a collection of shacks built precariously into the pockets and wedges on the east side of the Bitterroot Range in the Idaho Territory. So barren and out of the way, even the vultures risked starvation.

It was the perfect sort of place to attract those members of society who preferred to remain unnoticed by others. Hard men and rangy women who spent most of their days waiting for the right wind to carry them up to the glim grounds where they could harvest their fortune.

Glim, more precious than diamonds or gold, used to power ships on air, water, or land. Used to heal the sick, cure the blights, turn the tide in wars, and make anything and everything stronger and longer lasting. Glim was even rumored to extend a man's life well beyond his years.

Rare and desired, glim. And as hard to locate as Hades' back door.

Some said glim could be found underground, or out at sea. But the only place glim was known to occur with any regularity was above high mountain ranges, and up higher still. Above the storm clouds, floating like nets of soft lightning, the glim fields were capricious and fleeting. Difficult to find. Deadly to harvest. Most ships couldn't launch that high, last those storms, or lash and land without killing those who flew them.

So it was no wonder glim fetched a pretty price in the legitimate markets, and a king's ransom in those markets less savory.

Captain Hink counted himself among his own kind out here in the rocks. Outlaws, prospectors, glim pirates, soldiers of luck, fools, and the foolhardy, brothers all.

Not that he wouldn't drop a brother at a thousand paces if he jumped his claim, stole his boots, or touched his airship, the *Swift*.

But then, he supposed any of the rock rats who ported, docked, or launched from Stump Station would do him the same.

"Problem, Mr. Seldom?" Captain Hink asked as his second-in-command ducked through the canvas tarp that hung in place of a door in the tumbledown that Hink called home.

Seldom was a wiry-built, redheaded Irish who looked like he'd snap in half if he sneezed too hard. Most people thought he got his name from how often he spoke. But Captain Hink knew he went by Seldom for how many times he'd lost a fight.

Hink figured he and Seldom didn't much resemble each other. Hink scraped up a full six foot, three inches, and had shoulders that took the sides off doorways if he wasn't mindful. Yellow hair, skin prone to tanning, and eyes the gray of a broody sky set in a face that women had never complained about, Hink might have been considered a catch if he'd grown up in the social circles of the old states instead of as the bastard child of a soiled dove.

And whereas Seldom looked old for his thirty years, Hink looked like a man in his twenties, and that was no lie.

Seldom stabbed one thumb over his shoulder, stirring the wool scarves around his neck and jostling his breathing gear, which hung at the wait near his collarbone. "Mullins."

Captain Hink put the cup of boiled beans that passed for coffee up here in the stones down on the edge of the map spread across the buckboard that served as his desk. He leaned back in his chair, enough so his Colt was in easy reach.

He wasn't expecting Les Mullins to come in and shoot him dead. But he wouldn't be surprised if that was exactly what the captain of the big, and recently crashed and burned, *Iron Draught* hoped to accomplish.

Especially since Mullins had had to patch up that old mule of a steamer the *Powderback* to get around.

Mr. Seldom stepped to the corner of the room, and faded into the woodwork like a stick in a stack.

The canvas tarp whipped aside and in strode Les Mullins. Big man, high forehead under stringy black hair and a face permanently burned red from flying too long in the cold upper. He looked mad enough to chew coils.

"Just because I don't have a door," Captain Hink said, "doesn't mean a man shouldn't knock."

Les Mullins smiled—well, more like sneered—showing tobacco stumps where his teeth ought to have been.

"Here's the deal, Hink," he said. "You give me that tin devil of yours, and I won't tie you up like a hog, throw you off this cliff, and drag your broken bits in to the people who will shower me with gold for my trouble."

"Deal?" Captain Hink said. "Why, we haven't even cut the deck yet. How about you get the hell out of my house, Mullins?"

"How about you explain this?" Mullins tossed something onto Hink's desk that landed and rattled like a tin can.

Hink made a big production of leaning forward and picking up the item, even though he knew exactly what it was. "It's a tin star," he said.

"It's a badge," Mullins said.

"So it is."

"Says 'U.S. Marshal.'"

"I see that, Mullins," Captain Hink said. "You thinking of wearing this around so folk respect you? 'Cause it's going to take a damn bit more than a tin star to make people stand up and take notice of the bluster that comes out of your yap."

"What I think," Mullins said, advancing toward the desk, "is that you've been spying on us since you set up nest last spring. Weaseling out our stakes, claims, and buyers. What I think, *Captain*, is that you're the president's man, or near enough it don't matter otherwise. You've come to shut our operation down and to haul us in to the law."

"Shut it down?" Hink brought his hand, star and all, back casual-like toward his holster. "Why would I want to shut down an enterprise in which I make so much money?"

"Don't know the mind of a turncoat dog like you."

Captain Hink weighed that remark for one second. He had a reputation for a bad temper and a quick trigger. Something his mother had told him would get him killed, God rest her soul. So he always gave every statement a full-up two seconds of consideration before he acted upon it.

Then he pulled the knife from his belt and threw it straight and true into Mullins's chest.

Mullins stumbled back. He clutched at the knife with one hand and clawed for his gun with the other. Wasn't much successful with either attempt.

"I sure hope I haven't damaged your talker," Captain Hink said as he stood and sauntered over to the big man, who had stumbled to brace his back against the wall. Not that it'd do him any good. Walls couldn't save men who rode the skies. "Because your story was just getting interesting.

"There's a thing I have a powerful need to know, Mr. Mullins. Where in the world did you get this from?" He held up the badge. "You been sniffing down around the townies? Catch up some poor land lizard with a knack for a tall tale?"

Mullins leveled him a glare and finally got hold of the knife hilt. He pulled it free with a yell and nearly fell to one knee. Didn't much matter, Captain Hink thought. There was no chance this traitor to the states was walking out of his house alive.

"Found me a yellowbelly who knew you, Captain Hink Cage," Mullins rasped. "Said his name was Rucker."

"Rucker?" Captain Hink said. "Name doesn't jostle the memory."

"He knew you," Mullins said. "Knew what you did in the battle of Flatstand. Knew you took more than half your regiment and turned on General Alabaster Saint. Accused him of disobeying orders, profiteering, and holding correspondence with the enemy. You refused to move your men into position, on orders from the president. You cost the Saint the battle, his career, and his eye, you traitor snake coward."

"He tell you any other stories, this Rucker you jawed with?" Hink asked.

"Not after I shot him dead, he didn't."

Hink didn't even wait a second. He clocked Mullins straight across the chin and dropped down over him so he could continue with the beating, as he was the sort of fellow who didn't mind getting his hands dirty to see that a job was well done. Got in one more hit before Mullins pulled his gun.

The cold click of the hammer cocking back soaked through the anger Captain Hink was enjoying and put him right away into a most reasonable and sober mind.

"Don't matter if you're alive or dead," Mullins said. "Just so long as I bring you in."

Mr. Seldom seemed to appear out of the walls themselves. And, just like that, was standing above Mr. Mullins. Then, just like that, Seldom swung the oversized iron marlin spike, slamming the gun out of Mullins's hand. Likely broke up a few of the man's fingers in the process, seeing as how loud he screamed.

"Thought you'd know better than to upset my second, Mullins. You know how he doesn't take well to people trying to plug me." Hink rolled back on his heels and stood, staring down at the bleeding man.

Seldom retrieved the gun from where it had landed, wiped the blood off with one of the scarves hanging to his waist, and tossed the gun to Hink.

Captain Hink caught the weapon, gave it a glance, then tossed it back to Seldom, who pocketed it.

"Won't matter if you kill me," Mullins gasped. "Word's already out. This whole town's coming for your neck, Hink Cage."

Seldom lifted the marlin spike again.

"Name's Hink," Captain Hink said. "Captain, if you can't remember that much. Don't go on and kill him yet, Mr. Seldom. I've still a question or two I want answered."

Hink rolled the tin star between his fingers like a poker chip, then held it with the tips of his index and middle fingers.

"What's this matter to you, Mullins?" he asked as the star caught a shine of light. "Some lander giving you guff about me being a marshal don't exactly stand that it's true. And if so, what do you have to hide you wouldn't want a marshal to know?"

Mullins closed his mouth and didn't do much more than glare and bleed.

"I think this isn't just your business you've got yourself hitched up to, Mr. Mullins," Captain Hink said. "I think you're working for someone. Someone who doesn't cozen to the law. Makes a certain sense, seeing as how we straddle the border of legality, shooting the sky for glim. But more than all that, I think there's a spy in this house who ain't me."

Hink glanced over at Mr. Seldom. "You don't suppose Mr. Mullins knows old Alabaster Saint himself, do you?"

Mullins caught his breath. Not a dead giveaway, but a giveaway nonetheless.

Hink rubbed at his chin. "Let me take a shot and tell you a story, Mr. Mullins. I say there was once a man named Les Mullins. Came from out Kentucky way. Signed up to serve beneath the hardest, blood-thirstiest monster that ever put on a uniform. Followed that monster, oh, let's give him a name—say, General Alabaster Saint—through hell and worse. Les Mullins saw nine out of ten of his fellow soldiers die obeying the general's bloody orders, until the general was tried and removed from command.

"I'd say Les Mullins thought himself damn lucky to have survived. Maybe even thought himself blessed and appointed to continue following General Alabaster Saint's orders long after the battles this United States were engaged in were done and gone. Long after the Saint had moved on to raising his own militia of mercenaries.

"So Les Mullins wants to make himself useful to the general he worships. And he knows what the general wants: glim. Knows the general has plans to bribe, bully, and kill his way into every peak and mountain of this country until he controls every ship and glim field. The man who rules glim and gold rules the world."

Hink paused and nodded toward Seldom. "It's a good story so far, don't you think?"

Mr. Seldom shrugged, focused on flipping the marlin spike: *slap, slap, slap,* as if his palms were restless determined to use it again.

"Let's see," Hink said. "How does this story end? I'd say it ends with General Saint's spy, Les Mullins, getting killed on the floor of a shack in the Bitterroots unless he tells a man named Captain Hink just who, exactly, he's working for and what, exactly, that man wants."

Mullins had gone from bleeding to wheezing. His good hand was pressed over the chest wound as if he could hold the blood inside. Looked like he thought he could hold the words inside too. But Hink would get them out of him. He'd done worse to better men.

"I'll give you a moment to consider my request, Mr. Mullins. Because this is the last time I'm asking you to give me answers. From here on out, I'll just be doing an awful lot of painful taking them from you."

Hink turned back to his desk and took a drink of coffee. His hands shook from a hard anger.

George Rucker had been a friend. The younger brother of William

Rucker, a man Hink served with, and had been unable to save from Alabaster Saint's bloodthirsty loyalists.

Hink had come too late to stop William's hanging, but he'd found young George Rucker and taken him in. Looked after him as best he could, even while carrying out the president's orders. Because Mullins was right about that. That tin star was his. He was Marshal Hink Cage when he wasn't wedged up here with glim pirates, trying to suss out the kingpin of their black market trade.

He'd given that star to George Rucker for safekeeping and as a promise that he would return from this mission to retrieve it from him.

A promise he couldn't keep now because of Les Mullins. A promise that had gotten George Rucker killed.

A shot rang out and the high steam whine of engines catching hot pounded the air. Not just engines. The *Swift*'s engines.

"Captain Hink!" A woman yelled from a good ways off. "The ship. They're on her!"

The gunshot boomed out again, louder. That was the *Swift*'s cannon.

Hink grabbed the map off the table and his shotgun, which had been leaning against the wall. Seldom already had one foot out the door. Hink gave half a second's thought about taking the time, and wasting the bullet, to kill Mullins.

Decided the man wasn't near enough worth either and was halfway down the road to dead anyhow.

He pushed through the canvas and squinted at the onslaught of harsh afternoon light.

There was enough of a tumble of rock and scree on this outcropping that the *Swift* could land and lash, but not so much that any ship bigger than her—and that meant every other ship in the range—could catch hold.

He'd chosen this spot for just that reason.

Mr. Seldom ran quick as a gangly jackrabbit over rock and around wind-twisted scrub toward where the *Swift* hovered, just so high above the ground that a man couldn't catch her ropes with a jump. Not that she had any of her ropes dangling.

Built like a bullet, the *Swift* was one of the smallest airships that carved the sky. Outfitted with the biggest boilers she could bear, she had more power per pound than the North's battle cruisers. She carried a crew of twelve, if needed, and enough water, coal, wood, and glim to get her an eight-hundred-mile range.

But the thing that gave her the edge over bigger, more powerful ships was her skeleton. She was made of tin, which lightened her load considerably and made her sing like crystal glass tapped by a spoon when she hit the cold upper.

All who heard that siren song knew it was the *Swift*. Wasn't a ship that could launch into the storm as quick as she could, wasn't a ship that could ride it out better, wasn't a ship that could fly as fast and true.

Which was all that was saving her tin hide at the moment.

The *Swift* hovered above the heads of two dozen men and women who were unloading shotguns at her belly.

"Get her up, get her up!" Hink yelled. "Who's at the helm?" He ran up alongside Molly Gregor, his boilerman, who had just a moment before hollered him out of the shack.

Molly was a solid-built woman with curves in all the right places and a crop of straight black hair that she shaved short at the temples so as not to queer her breathing gear. He'd never seen her wear a dress a single day in the three years they'd been running glim together.

But even though she had boots, breeches, and a hell of a hand at steam tinkering, there wasn't a man who'd disrespect her. Not if he wanted to wake up breathing the next day.

"It's Guffin," she said, pounding across the rocks beside him. "He was on watch. Checking on that squall headed in from the north."

They were almost upon the mob beneath the ship now.

Molly pulled the nozzle of the flamethrower she had strapped across her back around to the front and struck a match. The slow-burning wick spring-hinged below the tip of the nozzle caught fire. Molly twisted the valve at her belt, readying the mix of oils she'd rigged up to throw a burn a hundred feet.

"Don't set her aflame," Captain Hink said. "And don't burn me neither."

Molly didn't waste her breath on an answer. She rushed past him, clearing a path to the rear of the *Swift* with another blast of fire.

Hink pulled his gun and rushed into the crowd, headed for Jonas Hamilton, the bootlicker who was yelling orders to take the *Swift* down.

"Hamilton, you horse's ass!" Hink yelled. "Get away from my ship."

Hamilton turned. He had a goosed-up Sharps Carbine tucked at his shoulder and took aim straight at Hink's chest.

"Damn it all." Hink raised his pistol and shot Hamilton in the shoulder, just above the butt of the carbine.

Hamilton reeled back, his shot clipping high, but still close enough that Hink heard the buzz of it as it passed his ear.

An explosion pounded rock walls and eardrums alike, and damn near threw Hink to the ground. He stumbled, kept hold of the pistol, trying to see his way through the thick black smoke that filled the air. That smoke better not be from the *Swift* going down, or he'd be skinning these rock rats until doomsday.

A hand reached down out of the smoke and caught hold of his arm and yanked him up hard.

"Rope!" Seldom hollered. The Irish was dangling from the *Swift*'s ladder by one foot and two fingers, looking like a squirrel ready to jump a limb. Since his other hand was helping drag Hink up to catch hold of the ladder, Hink was more than happy to see him.

The smoke was still thick enough it burned his eyes, but the *Swift* was already climbing again. Hink could just make out ragged shadows of those below him picking themselves up from that blast. It wouldn't be long before those guns in their hands were aimed at his head.

"Where's Molly?" Hink yelled over the roar of the ship's fans.

"Boiler," Seldom said as he scurried uncommonly quick up the last of the rope.

Captain Hink put one hand over the other and hauled up the ladder as fast as he could. His crewmen heaved the ladder up while he climbed. Just as he breached the hold and pulled himself into the solid interior of the *Swift*, he heard Molly call out. "Get her up, Mr. Guffin! Get her up fast and hard!"

"He don't know any other way," Seldom muttered.

Hink laughed as the floor tipped alarmingly to one side. He pushed up off his hands and knees and staggered toward the helm.

The *Swift*'s engines popped three hard thumps of steam and power, the awe-inspiring noise of that beautiful steam engine drowning out the crowd and gunfire below, as she took aim for the clouds and let fly.

CHAPTER THREE

Cedar Hunt shifted in the saddle, one hand on Flint's neck to calm him as he scanned the horizon. The Bitterroot Mountains rose up to the north, and the wind that combed the top of those peaks was restless with winter's chill. The rains were coming. From the look of the sky, it was about to break open.

If they were going to get around the mountains here in Idaho and well on to Mae Lindson's sisterhood in Kansas, they'd need more than haste. They'd need supplies.

"Think we'll make Fort Boise soon?" Rose asked, riding up beside him.

Cedar had spent an uncomfortable night shackled up, but the beast had not transformed him in body or mind. Rose had been chatty and happy since finding him still a man, and still a reasonable one at that, when she unlocked him just before dawn.

"Maybe tomorrow, or day after," Cedar said. "Longer if it rains."

A drop plinked down on the brim of his hat.

"Oh, now you've gone and jinxed us, Mr. Hunt." Rose laughed and turned up the collar on her wool coat before tightening her hat's chin strap.

"Vicinity's not too far out of the way," Cedar said. "We can take the night there and let the worst of the storm pass over."

"I'll tell the Madders we'll be in town today. I'm sure they'll be pleased as pigs in a potato patch." She turned her horse and headed back to the big, slow-moving wagon a ways behind them.

Cedar urged Flint ahead of the party. An hour later, he'd made his way through the constant rain, down a deer trail and up a ridge, bringing him to a flat, short valley between hills. Across that flat valley spread a ramshackle collection of maybe thirty or so houses and shacks made of adobe and wood.

Vicinity.

Both a mining town and a trading post, Vicinity was an easy stop for folk taking the trail to Oregon or California.

Peppered with sagebrush and scrub, built without much thought to roads or the whyfors of coming and going, for that matter, the town washed up the hillsides and out to where the valley closed into a V.

There should be a barn they could stay the night, if the townfolk were hospitable, or agreeable to payment or barter. It was as good a rest as they'd have for miles. A lucky port in the storm.

Still, he paused, staring out across the place, listening for the sounds that usually filled a town. There was nothing but the rattle of rain on his hat, coat, and land around him, and the clack of the bit Flint rolled in his mouth.

No other sounds of life.

But there was a scent on the wind. A scent he knew well. It was the smell of the Strange, and it was more. It was the scent of the Holder, some part of it, here, nearly a state away from where it'd gone flying. He'd promised the Madders he would help them gather up the bits of it. Maybe his chance to do so was coming sooner than he'd thought.

The beast within him slammed hard against his will, raging. The beast, the curse he carried, hungered to hunt the Strange, kill them, destroy them. Cedar had no fondness for the nightmare creatures who slipped across this land either. But he held tight to his reasoning.

He wiped some of the damp off his face and peered through the failing light for a glint of lantern, a puff of chimney smoke. The town was as still as a broken watch. It was as if all the people were off to church, leaving not a child, dog, or chicken behind to stir.

That wasn't right. Wasn't the natural way of a town.

They should ride on, ride around this puzzlement. There was death and dying here. And the Strange lurked nearby, maybe the Holder too.

But with night coming on and rain drenching them through, they needed a place to rest. If Vicinity had suffered some kind of sickness or disaster and cleared out months ago, there would still be supplies they could scavenge and a roof and walls against the cold and rain.

Instinct might tell him to run. But reason told him they should check the town first, and ride on by only if there were actual signs of danger.

Cedar clicked his tongue and turned Flint back to rejoin the others.

Bryn Madder was on the little roan, forging the trail, with Rose and Mae right behind him. The bulky wagon brought up the rear, clattering along like a crazy circus sideshow all its own. Cedar didn't know if Wil rode in the wagon or if he had gone out hunting, as was his habit just before sunset.

"Lovely weather we're having," Bryn said when he caught sight of Cedar. The brass monocle over his eye had just a glass lens now. Bryn rubbed the rain off it with the cuff of his shirt. "You find us some place a little drier to stop, like maybe beneath Niagara Falls?"

"Town just up a bit," Cedar said. "Vicinity. Looks empty. Stinks of the Strange, maybe more than that."

Bryn's quick grin split his beard. "Sounds about right. You do have a way of stumbling into the most interesting of predicaments, Mr. Hunt."

He maneuvered his horse—well, the dead man's horse—past Cedar, following the trail like he was clopping along in full daylight. A second later, Cedar heard the click and scratch of a match as one of those green globe lanterns the brothers always carried caught flame.

Bryn tied the glass globe to the saddle, secured so the globe sat snug near his knee. From the clever positioning of mirror-polished metal inside that glass, the globe gave out a brighter and wider circle of light than any lantern Cedar had seen. And since it took such a wee flame to throw that much light, the thick glass wouldn't warm to the touch for a long while.

Rose rode up to him, Mae right beside her. Rose had a lead line on Mae's mule. He didn't know when the girl had decided to do so, but he was grateful for her thoughtfulness. Mae must be deep enough in the thrall of the voices calling her home that she didn't know what Rose had done.

"Did I hear you say the town's ahead?" Rose asked wistfully. "That's about the sweetest thing I've heard for weeks."

"Might be trouble," Cedar said.

"What sort?" Rose asked, glancing at Bryn riding off with a ray of sunshine tacked to his saddle.

"The town looks deserted. And I smell the Strange."

Rose shrugged. "You always smell the Strange, Mr. Hunt. You're made for it. Why, I'd bet if there was a bogey or ghooley in a ten-mile range, you'd know it."

"I would. And I believe there is. So keep your gun handy."

"Always do, Mr. Hunt."

Mae didn't say a single thing. She just sat her saddle, fingers working against each other like she was shucking peas from a pod. Her eyes were glassy, dazed, her lips pale. Full caught in the madness.

One thing was sure. When they made it to the sisterhood, and the witches gave Mae back her slipping mind, Cedar was going to sit down with each and every one of those women. No one should be driven from their good sense because of an old promise. A promise based on fear.

Mae had mumbled plenty during the three weeks on the trail. Pleading to the voices in her mind, maybe pleading to the memories of her past. Saying she wasn't evil. Saying magic didn't so much go bad in her hands as just set things to happening in the most final of ways. Her magic leaned toward curses, the making and breaking of them. Leaned toward vows and binding things and people together.

The sisters had turned that sort of magic on her, and bound her to the soil of the coven. So if ever she strayed too far from the sisterhood, she'd have to return home.

No matter what was in her way—weather, mountains, or madness.

Mae might not complain of the fine cruelty of such a binding, but Cedar wondered if maybe the sisters really didn't want her home. Were maybe working hard to make sure she died trying to get there.

The wagon rattled up, Alun in the high driver's seat. He'd traded his kerchief for a battered sombrero, the wide brim keeping most of his bulk dry beneath it. The pipe clenched in his teeth drew cherry red and the sweet smoke of tobacco rolled circles under the brim.

Cadoc Madder must be inside the wagon.

"Trouble, I hear, Mr. Hunt? Or town?" Alun called out.

"Could be both," Cedar said. "Or the Strange. Vicinity is just ahead and empty."

Alun reached down and pulled a shotgun the size of a small cannon up at his side, resting the barrel across the brake board, where his foot was braced. "Suppose this town has a saloon?"

"Reckon it does," Cedar said.

"Then lead the way! One thing about the Strange, they aren't much for drinking. Should be plenty for us no matter the state of things."

Cedar gave Rose a look, but she already had her gun resting across her saddle horn.

No need to warn her to take care of herself again. Girl had good survival instincts. And that gun of hers had gained a scope and a few other bits he knew weren't attached to it just a day ago.

"You tinker with the gun?" He turned and followed the bobbing green bubble of light on Bryn's saddle, Rose and Mae falling in behind him, the Madders bringing up the rear.

"Just a little," she said. "Last night I wasn't sleeping much and I got to thinking that the shotgun has a heck of a kick, and I could probably harness that energy and use it for a coil, if I had some copper wire and a spring, and a second barrel . . ." She pressed her lips together, then chuckled. "My apologies for rambling, Mr. Hunt."

"No apology needed," Cedar said. "Devising is a skill men hock the farm for. The wild sciences aren't easy for most to comprehend, much less make practical of. You've a gift, Miss Small."

"You're kind to say so," Rose murmured, looking down modestly and fussing with the metal trinkets in her pockets.

Mae was silent, swaying with the saddle, her face tipped up just high enough that her lips and chin caught the fall of rain off the brim of her bonnet.

Cedar caught sight of Wil moving through the scrub, following along cautiously. Wil had been captured by the Strange, used as a slave by them for years. He would know better than to do anything foolish.

Cedar navigated down the muddy path that served as a road into the town. He caught the scent of the Strange on the wind again, and again the odd tang that he'd last smelled on the Holder. Just strong enough to sense before it faded away.

They came upon the first houses set out in a fairly straight row along both sides of the road. The homes looked strong and weather-worthy and hadn't fallen into disrepair.

But there was not a light in a window, not a stir in a yard. The smell of the Strange lay heavy here, like a low fog clinging to the ground, kicked up by their horses' hooves. Bryn Madder paused where the road took a sharp turn to the left, leading into the heart of Vicinity.

Cedar pulled up beside him. The house ahead was situated so that the front door was visible. And so were the man's legs across the threshold.

The man wasn't asleep—held too damn still for that. Cedar smelled death and blood.

"Will you look at that?" Bryn asked. "Terrible way to let the draft in. Maybe we should roust him up, see if he's breathing."

"Maybe we should warn the womenfolk," Cedar said.

"They've seen worse," Bryn said.

That was true. Cedar took point and urged Flint down the road. More houses, none of the doors open, no other sign of people, except for the smell of blood and rot, and nothing and no one at the windows.

The town opened up into an area that had been cleared and flattened, likely for gatherings. They stopped there.

"Where do you suppose all the people are?" Rose asked. "I mean the live ones?"

"There are no live ones," Cedar said.

"That fella laying in the doorway?" she said.

"Dead," Bryn answered.

"Don't think this is a place where wise men shelter," Alun Madder said. "We'd best be moving on through."

"Might be a thicket off east a bit," Bryn suggested. "I'll see if there's anything to stand between us and the rain."

"But we could find supplies here," Rose said. "We need more than what we have to get the horses to Fort Boise."

She was right. They all knew it.

Cedar nodded. "Let's see if we can find a mercantile. Take what's been left behind for ourselves, then check the barns for grain."

"Might as well see if there's liquor at hand while we're at it," Alun said. "For medicinal purposes, Miss Small."

Rose shook her head. "No need to make excuses for me, Mr. Madder. I know you and your brothers polished off the last of the moonshine a week ago. And blew up your still."

"All the more reason to restock," he said.

"Would you help me get Mrs. Lindson into the wagon first?" Rose asked. "I don't think she can sit the saddle for much longer and with dark coming on, I'd hate to discover she'd dropped off in a ditch come morning."

"It'd be my pleasure." Alun swung down out of the driver's seat, dropping to the ground much more nimbly than expected from a man his size, and tromped over to her.

He and Rose coaxed Mae to dismount, then Rose led her carefully through the muck and mud to the back of the wagon.

Cedar stayed right where he was, one hand on his gun, his gaze restlessly searching the streets and houses for movement. The beast within him had gone still. Not because the danger had passed. No— because the danger was near upon them.

"You feel it, don't you, Mr. Hunt?" Alun asked, coming back around the front of the wagon. He'd brought that monster of a gun with him and it rode slung across his shoulder with a wide leather strap so it could rest at his hip, in easy reach.

He took the reins of Rose's horse and Mae's mule from Cedar.

"The Strange?" Cedar asked.

"And more," Alun agreed. "Death."

"The Holder's been here," Cedar said quietly.

Alun's head snapped up like he'd just been slapped. "Are you sure?"

Cedar nodded.

"How? How can you tell?"

"I can taste it on the wind. In the rain." He could feel it in his bones too, just like he could feel the touch of the Strange left lingering in the crannies and nooks of the place. This near to a piece of the Holder, he felt like his bones were tuning forks, resonating with the awareness of that odd device.

"You've a promise to keep us, Mr. Hunt," Alun began, "to retrieve the Holder."

"I'll see it stays kept, if it's near," Cedar said. "But not while Rose and Mae are in this town. Whatever thing drove off the townfolk lingers. Once the women are safe, I'll hunt the Holder."

"Then we best be quickly moving on," Alun said. "See to the womenfolk."

"This woman folk isn't going anywhere," Rose said, striding over from the wagon with a lit globe in one hand. "Unless it's looking for supplies."

"Miss Small—," Alun said.

"I'm sorry, Mr. Madder, but my mind's set on this. We need food. We need blankets. And any coal, bullets, or medicines this place might have stashed. Plus, there is no way in tarnation those two hayburners of yours are going to find enough to forage once we hit the snows."

"This town isn't a proper place for a lady such as you, Miss Small," Alun insisted.

Rose pushed her hat back, the tips of her fingers bare and dirty at the nail though a knit glove covered the remainder of her hand.

"Look in my eyes, Mr. Madder. What you're going to find there is exactly what kind of a lady I am. But since you're in a hellfire hurry, I'll spell it out quick for you. I am a very determined lady. And tonight I am determined to loot this town."

She took the reins of her horse out of his hand, leaving Mae's mule in his keep. Then she swung up into the saddle. "You menfolk can do what you want, but I'm going hunting." She turned her horse into the town.

"I'll go with her," Cedar said. "Stay with the wagon." He clicked his tongue and Flint started after Rose.

"There's Strange afoot, Rose," Cedar said.

"So you've said, Mr. Hunt. We have guns. They don't. Between the two of us"—she paused and glanced off to her left, where Wil was slipping through the shadows between houses—"the three of us," she corrected, "I think we'll manage."

Cedar smiled despite himself. The girl had more spunk than a pot full of peppers.

"I think that place there has a sign on it," Rose said. "Maybe a post office and general store?"

They got close enough that the light from the globe Rose held up caught at the whitewashed letters on the sign, neatly outlined in black. "Brown's General Store," Rose read out loud. "Good place to start."

She swung down out of the saddle and threw the reins over the hitching post.

Cedar did the same, cocking his gun before walking up the step to the door. "Hold the light high, Miss Small."

She did so, the light coming down over his shoulder and dusting off the shadows. He pushed the door inward with only a bit of a creak.

The smell of death hit him hard and full in the face. In the light of Rose's lantern, the bodies of four people lying on the wood floor came clearly into view. A man, a woman, and two young boys. Dead as dead could be.

"Oh, God rest their souls," Rose breathed behind him.

Cedar strode into the room, but Rose hesitated. He heard her pull the shotgun she carried before stepping in.

He didn't see anyone else in the long, narrow room. Nothing was moving, not even a scratching of rats. He crouched next to the bodies and turned the man over so he could see what injury had felled him.

The man's eyes were missing. As if they'd been sucked out like a grape from its skin, leaving clean bloody sockets behind.

He was also missing his thumbs.

"Was it man or animal?" Rose asked, bringing the light with her. She caught sight of the man's face and made a small sound in the back of her throat.

"It was the Strange. Or at least they smell of it." Cedar rested the man back the way he'd been and moved the woman enough to see that she was missing both her ears and her nose. As for the young'uns, both of them had holes where their hearts should be.

"Indian don't mutilate like this. Could be a white man who likes to collect souvenirs." He frowned. "Not an animal, at any rate. I've never seen anything like this from Strange either. The injuries don't add up to the thing that killed them. Well, except for the boys."

The other injuries weren't enough to kill a person right out, and certainly not enough to drop the entire family in a heap, as if they fell dead at the exact same moment.

Was that something the Holder could do? Fall down over a town and kill everyone dead? If that was the case, who, or what, had strolled through town gathering up body parts like they were out picking berries?

The bodies were cold, but no longer stiff. Fresh enough it hadn't been long, but not so long the bodies had bloated. Whatever had dropped them dead had done it within the week.

"They look picked over," Rose said. "Just bits taken."

"Harvested." Cedar stood and looked around the room. Stock and supplies filled the floor-to-ceiling shelves. There was enough food and blankets here to outfit them for the road. They'd just need to find grain and hay for the horses to finish stocking up.

"Looks like plenty here we can take with us," he said. "We can load up and move on."

"We're going to bury them first." Rose's voice was tight, her face set in something more than determination. It was set in sorrow.

"Dig graves?" he asked. "Night's upon us, Miss Small. Whatever or whoever did this to these people could be nearby. I don't think slinging a shovel is going to do us, or in the long run them, any good."

"I won't leave them like this. And you shouldn't want to either, Mr. Hunt. They deserve a decent burial. They deserve to have their souls put to a proper rest."

"I agree they deserve a decent burial," he said. "But it is too dangerous for us to administer it."

"I've heard you," she said. "But there isn't anything about this new land that isn't dangerous. That doesn't mean we have to be the kind of people who turn away from the mercy at hand."

Rose walked to the back of the room, the lantern light swinging shadows and bright at each other like trapeze artists reaching for the catch. She picked up a shovel and then, without a word, walked across the room and out the door, leaving the dark to swallow Cedar whole.

He took in a lungful of it and sighed. The girl meant well, but the last thing he wanted to do right now was dig a grave, much less dig one big enough for four, or who knew how many more. He walked over to the counter and rested his hand there.

A song, like sour trumpets trembling in the distance rose up through his fingertips. He knew that fleeting tune, knew its haunting rhythms and trills. It was the song of the Strange, of one Strange in particular.

Mr. Shunt.

Suddenly, the chill of the night and the dark and death squeezed down around him. They'd killed Mr. Shunt. He'd seen him killed, seen his innards stretched out and pounded to a mash even the crows wouldn't pick over. He'd seen the bits of Mr. Shunt smashed apart by Jeb Lindson, Mae's dead husband.

There was no possibility a man, nor any other creature, could come back together after the taking apart Mr. Shunt had received.

The wind huffed against the rafters, silencing the song as a fresh scatter of rain broke from the sky.

But then, there was no man nor creature like Mr. Shunt. If there was anything in this world unkillable, it would be him.

Suddenly, the harvest made sense. Mae had said Mr. Shunt fell into pieces and sewed himself back together again. Maybe he needed more parts.

But if Shunt were still in the town, hell, if he'd been within thirty miles of the place, Cedar would know. He wasn't here. But he had been.

"Mr. Hunt?" Rose said from the door, her lantern clutched tight in one hand, the shovel in the other. "I think you'd better see this."

"We're leaving," Cedar said, making to walk around behind the counter for the supplies. "Now. Come take an armful."

Rose didn't say anything. Not a peep. Wasn't like her.

He glanced up. She was still standing in the doorway, the shine of light carving out holes of dark against the sweet angles of her face. There was more than just rain falling from the brim of her hat to wet her face. There were tears.

"Rose?" He came out from behind the counter and walked to her. "Rose?"

"I looked into houses. A half dozen houses," she said. "They're all dead." She looked up into his face. "Children too, Mr. Hunt. Little babies missing their feet and hands, all carved up . . ."

Cedar wanted to tell her not to worry about the dead. To tell her that if they left these people behind it was a civilized choice. But that was not true. The place stank of the Strange. And he had seen the Strange do terrible things with the unburied dead.

"We'll do what we can for them," he said. "Give them a grave and a prayer, the only mercy still in our hands."

Rose wiped at her nose and nodded. "We'll need to gather them all up. Maybe in the middle of town? The clearing?"

"That should do," Cedar said. "Let's get the Madders to help. Quickly."

Cedar followed her back out into the rain. They mounted up and tracked back to the wagon.

Alun was leaning at the side of it, the huge brim of his hat and the angle of the wagon blocking rain and wind. He puffed on his pipe while the youngest and tallest Madder, Cadoc, paced about, a strange device in his hands.

The device resembled an ear trumpet. He held it up to one ear, a rope running from the ear trumpet to wrap around the top of a cane in his left hand that he stuck into the ground. He paused for a moment, as if listening through the ear horn, then pulled the cane tip out of the soil and swung it to tap the ear trumpet before spiking the cane back into the wet ground again.

Cedar didn't know what Cadoc Madder was doing, but then he rarely could fathom the man's actions.

"We'll be needing your help," Cedar said. "Bryn's too."

"Are we hunting the Holder now, Mr. Hunt?" Alun asked.

"No. We are hauling and digging," Cedar said. "There's dead in this town. Rose and I have agreed we'll see to their burial before we move on."

Cadoc Madder had stopped pacing. He turned to look at them as if they'd suddenly dropped out of a blue sky and brought the moon down with them.

Alun pulled the pipe from between his teeth and pointed it at Cedar. "What do you think killed all these people? The Holder. It fell into this town, and snuffed their lives out like a wet wick. If a piece of it remains behind, the death will spread, creep to the next town, and kill off the living there. Finding the Holder is a damn sight more important than burying the dead."

"The Strange have been here," Cedar said. "Surely you know what sport the Strange can have with the dead."

"Of course I know! Hang the dead and hang the Strange. If we find the Holder we won't need to stay here to see any of it."

Cedar drew his gun and cocked back the hammer. "Rose Small, myself, and these bullets disagree with you."

Both Madder brothers went stone cold. Even the smoke from Alun's pipe seemed to stop moving.

"No need for guns," Mae said as she came round from back of the wagon leading her mule. "Let us tend those who have been lost." She wore a duster—Cedar thought it might belong to one of the Madder brothers, and though she'd rolled up the sleeves, it was huge on her thin frame. She'd changed her bonnet for a man's hat—again, Cedar guessed it to be one of the Madders'.

He had no idea what she was doing out of bed, nor if she was in her right mind.

"Enough standing and pointing weapons," Mae insisted. "Let's put these people to rest so we can move on and find the Holder." Her voice was clear. Strong.

Alun stared at her warily, as one might a bowl of nitroglycerin left to boil on the stove. "The sooner we're to it, the sooner we'll be quit of this place," he finally said. "Cadoc, fetch up brother Bryn, and bring the wagon and the steam shovel along."

Cadoc swung up into the wagon and started off, the wheels sending a spattering of mud to slap their boots.

Alun turned an eye on Cedar. "I hope you know what it is you're doing, Mr. Hunt. Whole town of the dead is going to take time to bury, and we haven't that to spare."

"You bring out the digging device, I'll gather wood to fire it."

"Rose and I can gather the wood," Mae said. "Unless you'd rather we gather the bodies, Mr. Hunt?"

No. He very much did not want them to be carrying dead bodies around like kindling. He didn't know how long this break of clarity she was experiencing was going to last.

"Keep your guns ready," he said. "Both of you. This night is filled with harm."

"We'll do just that." Rose gave him a look that meant she'd also keep an eye on Mae. "If we need for anything, we'll come calling."

Cedar nodded. Rose could more than look after herself and Mae to boot. Gathering wood, even in the night where wild things crept, was a fair shake better than dragging dead folk into a pile.

Wil skulked out of the shadows, his eyes catching copper from the low light of Rose's lantern. He padded silently over to Rose and Mae and looked up at Cedar. It wouldn't be the new moon for a few days yet, which meant he would remain in wolf form until then.

He'd go with the women to gather wood and watch for danger.

Rose nudged her horse off a bit while Mae swung up atop her mule. "Since we're gathering in the center of town," Rose said, "let's see if there's a woodpile near to it. If not, then we'll check other houses close by."

"Good," Mae agreed.

"Didn't figure you to be the kind of man who endangered the people under your care," Alun said as the women headed off. "Some other reason you're fired up to bury the dead?"

"The Strange are near. The ground stinks of them."

"All the more reason for us to be moving on. Hastily."

"The bodies have been picked apart by Mr. Shunt."

Alun fell into a full-halt silence. "That can't be so," he breathed. "You killed him."

"Jeb Lindson killed him," Cedar said. "Those bodies we found have been gleaned and cleaned. Bits missing. Specific bits, as if just the best of each person was taken."

"You're sure it's not an animal?"

"Yes."

"Savages?" Alun asked.

"No."

"And you're certain it's Shunt?"

"I know that devil," Cedar said. "The smell of him on the bodies. The song of him left in the things he's touched."

Alun just stood there in the rain as if that news rolled like an earthquake under his boots and changed the landscape around him.

"We should look for him," Alun said.

"He's not in the town," Cedar said. "Come and gone, maybe far on as a week ago."

Alun got moving again and Cedar paced him atop Flint.

Finally Alun said, "Dark things slip in this night, Mr. Hunt. You can feel the Strange?"

"Yes."

"They can feel you too," Alun noted. "They know the one man who can track them, hunt them, tear them apart. They know you're here, you and your Pawnee curse. And they don't fear the dark."

"That suits me fine," Cedar said. "Because neither do I."

It didn't take long to reach the center of town. Cedar and Alun got to work moving the dead, starting with the family in the general store, and lifting, or as the circumstance required, dragging the bodies to the clearing.

Cadoc finally returned with the wagon, having found Bryn. After a brief talk with Alun, they unloaded several crates and a boiler out of the wagon. Bryn got busy assembling pieces of a device that looked more suited to pumping a well than digging a grave, while Cadoc and Alun took the wagon farther off to gather up any more people they could find.

It was grim work. Silent work.

Cedar had done his share of digging graves in his life. He'd stood above far too many saying his last farewells. His wife's. His child's.

Many more.

These people were strangers to him, yet the shame of so many lost, stripped and picked over like a feast of convenience, burned a deep anger in him.

He carried a small body toward the pile, each step slower than the last.

The beast within twisted and stretched. It wanted out. It wanted to hunt. It wanted to destroy the Strange. It wanted to destroy Mr. Shunt.

Cedar found it more and more difficult to find a reason to fight that need. A man's hands could do as much damage as the beast. A man's hands could tear a person limb from limb. Why not let the beast take his mind and use his hands for its needs?

"Mr. Hunt?" Rose said. Again, he realized.

He blinked until he could see the world. He'd been standing for some time now.

There was no rain, just the cold exhalation of the night against his skin.

"You can put her right there," Rose said gently.

Cedar looked down. He held a girl in his arms. Maybe two or three years old. Not much bigger than his own daughter had been when he held her, dead, in his arms.

This little girl was cold and gone, a splash of blood on her dress around the hole where her stomach should be. There were no tomorrows left for his daughter. And now there were no tomorrows left for this child.

Cedar swallowed hard and placed her gently next to a woman missing the top half of her skull. He didn't know if it was her mother. He hoped it might be.

"I'm going off for more wood," Rose said. "Mrs. Lindson is going to stay with Bryn Madder to help mind the fire and boiler. Are you all right?"

In the firelight Rose looked softer. Lovely as an angel come to comfort. Cedar knew she had no reason to tell him what everyone was doing.

She must have seen him standing there, frozen with grief and memories, the dead girl in his arms. Her words had tethered him back to the night, eased the beast, and shaken the memory's hold.

Rose was a practical woman. And kind.

"I'll come along with you," he said.

"No need, Mr. Hunt. There's a good stack just behind that house over there. One or two more loads and Mr. Madder says he'll have enough for the digging matic to start working."

Cedar glanced over at Mae, who was working next to Bryn Madder. They had built a fire that could likely be seen for twenty miles.

The boiler was now attached by long metal tubes to the pump device, and Bryn was wrenching wheels onto the base of the thing. It looked like a railroad handcart, with a lumpy brass teakettle the size of a pony bolted to it and a wooden shovel attached by long handles to the front, controlled by pulleys and ropes. Probably a mining matic the brothers had devised.

"I'd prefer to come with you," Cedar said.

Rose inhaled as if to say more, then stopped. She glanced at the dead girl in the pile, then at his hands and coat, which were both bloody enough, the rain couldn't wash them clean.

Finally, she looked at his eyes. Likely seeing the sorrow he could not hide.

"Of course, Mr. Hunt," she said softly. "I'd appreciate your company."

He walked with her to a lean-to that had been built to keep the worst of the weather off the wood stacked up against a house. There wasn't enough room in that small shed for two, so he waited outside.

"Enough firewood here to keep a person warm till next summer," Rose said as she bent beneath the roof eve and piled several pieces into her arms.

"That's true," Cedar said distractedly. The night wind brought with it the sound of crying, the soft weeping of a child. A child close by.

"Have you looked in the house across the way there for bodies?" he asked.

"Not yet. I thought after I gathered the wood, I'd help out finding people."

"I'm going to look inside," Cedar said.

"I'll come with you if you wait," Rose called back.

He didn't wait. He strode up to the back door of the house and tried the latch.

The door opened onto the kitchen. A woman lay on the floor. She was missing both of her arms. Silent. Dead.

In the far corner of the room huddled a child. He'd guess her to be maybe eight or ten years old. Still in her nightgown, bareheaded, barefoot, her cheek tipped onto her bent knees, her hands gently clasping her ankles.

She didn't move. But a soft, wheezing cry drifted from the corner of the room. Cedar put his hand on the doorjamb. No song of the Strange came to him. He took a cautious step into the room.

"Child?" he said quietly.

The girl still didn't stir. But the wheezy sob continued.

Cedar crossed the kitchen, carefully stepping around the mother, and knelt in front of the girl.

"There, now," he said. "It's going to be fine." He placed his hand on her shoulder, hoping he wouldn't startle her.

At his touch, the song of the Strange shot through him like greased lightning, cracking in his skull and stabbing straight through his feet to fuse him to the earth.

The Strange hadn't just touched this girl, they had infested her.

He could feel a tremble, a ticking beneath his fingers.

The girl was not a girl. Or at least not anymore. Now she was a hollowed-out shell. A doll with clockwork innards that ticked, ticked, ticked, slowly winding down while leather bellows wheezed out the last of the air it had been pumping into her lungs.

The Strange had made her. Or remade her.

The girl fell sideways. A metal key stuck out of her back. A small key made of tin that ground to a stop like a music box striking the last tine.

"Mr. Hunt?" It was Rose, come into the room.

"Rose!" Cedar called. "Don't!"

But it was too late. The key stopped moving. Touching the girl had sprung the Strange trap. He'd set off some kind of trigger set deep within her. A trigger that sparked a short fuse.

Cedar was on his feet, running, throwing himself to shield Rose. They tumbled out the door, but the explosion was immense. The kitchen, the mother, and the girl flew into bits. A barrage of flesh and bone and wood rained down around them where they lay out in the mud. His leather duster shielded him from the worst of it.

But Rose was not so lucky. The tin key arrowed into her left shoulder and burrowed in deep. She yelled, and her eyes went wide before they rolled back in her head.

"Rose?" Cedar lifted up off her. She was breathing, fast and shallow, but she did not come to. There was too much blood. Her blood.

He needed Mae. Needed to get that bit of metal out of her. Needed medicines and stitching and herbs.

Cedar swept Rose up into his arms, his heart drumming hard.

A sound behind him made him turn.

Even in the darkness, the mess of blood and flesh from the explosion was startling.

But not as startling as the dead mother who lay on the ground and shuddered. Something—no, not something; the Strange, ghostlike with too many eyes, too many mouths, too many arms—pulled up from the ground beneath her and slipped inside her like a man shrugs into an ill-fitted shirt.

The mother stopped shaking. Then she sat straight up, and got to her feet.

Her ruined face twisted in inhuman glee as she limped toward Cedar. "Hunter," she exhaled.

Cedar had seen the Strange wear the dead once before. Didn't know how they did it. Didn't have time to question. But he knew they were damn hard to kill.

He shifted his hold on Miss Small and drew his gun. He unloaded three bullets straight into the mother's heart.

And still she kept coming.

He couldn't fight with Rose in his arms, and he was not about to put her down. So he strode to the center of the town.

"Madders!" he yelled as he jogged toward the fire. "We have a problem."

As he rounded the last house before the clearing, he saw that the pile of dead bodies they'd so carefully stacked up was now much less carefully unstacking itself.

The dead were rising. Strange slinking down out of the hills and up into bodies to try them on for size.

Vicinity's townfolk rose up with the look of murder in their eyes. And started toward him.

CHAPTER FOUR

Captain Hink leaned out the port door, holding the dead man's grip just inside the *Swift*. Here amid the clouds and freeze, the wind slapped across the tip of Beggar's Peak and chuffed against the *Swift*, making her bob like a cork in a tub.

Not many ships were small enough or fast enough to hide here. It took some tight maneuvering to slip into this notch of rock and snow. But for the ship that could sling it, the tight wedge of stone just north, and the outcropping here, were enough to shelter from the worst of winter's howl.

For a short time, at least.

He'd ordered them to throw anchor and bank the boiler. He wanted quiet and he wanted still. There wasn't a wisp of steam to give them away, not a click of gear or pump of propeller.

Molly had seen to it that even Guffin was sitting still and keeping his mouth shut—no mean feat.

The *Swift* was as invisible as a frog's eyelash.

Captain Hink pressed the brass telescope to the darkened lens of his goggles and closed his left eye to better see the edge of the rocks and cliffs around them. Stump Station was just east a ways. If there was a ship taking to the skies, if there was pursuit, it'd be coming from there.

The rocks were clear, no glimmer, no smoke, no shadow. Hink

lowered the telescope and readjusted his breathing gear over his mouth, and his goggles, making sure the leather buckling both together was secure. The rubber hose that ran from his mouthpiece over his left shoulder and on off into the lines of the ship had plenty of slack, but not so much that it would tangle him up.

They weren't up high enough for the air to kill a man quickly, but blacking out or tripping over a line and taking a tumble from the running board of the ship wasn't going to keep a man's tranklements in one piece either.

A glint off starboard caught his eye. He swung the telescope in that direction, and worked to keep the eyepiece steady in the roiling winds.

The *Black Sledge*, a big steamer, dark-skinned and peaked at the top, bulgy with exterior belly lifts and eight sets of blades driving her on, lumbered up along the ragged edge of the mountain. She was a fully enclosed gondola like the *Swift* and didn't have the ocean-faring open-desk style of vessel dangling beneath her envelope.

She wasn't shooting the glim, didn't even have her nose pointed up, or her trawling arms and nets at the ready. No, she was low and slow. Looking for something. Looking for them.

Hink swung into the *Swift* and shut the door, then spun the latch to keep her tight. He one-fingered the buckle on his breathing gear and let it hang at his chest.

Molly stood at the helm, breathing gear unsecured at her neck. Guffin leaned near the vertical and horizontal rudder controls, scowling like he'd gotten his knuckles rapped by the teacher. He was a slow-eyed and sad-looking fellow with dark brows set too wide and light hair shaved up high off the back of his neck, but left to grow at the top so that his whole head took on a sort of sorry mushroom look.

Mr. Seldom was back among the glim gear, using his pocketknife to clean up a net spread at his feet.

The other member of the crew, Mr. Lum Ansell, a squat,

short-necked man of unknown heritage, was sleeping up against the starboard wall, his hat pulled over his round leather brown face, the brim stopped by the breathing gear latched across his chin. Out of all of them, Lum never seemed to find much use for the breathing gear, no matter how high they flew.

"Listen up," Captain Hink said.

All eyes turned to him. Even Lum shoved his hat back, awake and sharp, his hand drifting to the knife at his hip, as it always did before he was fully awake and taking a straighter sit.

"Looks like we have a cat come prowling," Captain Hink said. "Or more like a bear. Captain Barlow's on the sniff."

"Barlow?" Molly frowned. "What'd we do to stuff his flue?"

"Figure it has something to do with Les Mullins and his idea that I'm Marshal Hink Cage."

Guffin sucked on the tobacco tucked in his lip. "And?"

"And near as I can tell, Les Mullins is doing General Alabaster Saint's business. Since that includes seeing that I'm hung and strung, I'd say that puffer out there is looking to kill me."

"Could be they want our glim stake," Lum Ansell rumbled in his deep baritone.

"Could," Hink agreed. "Except for this." He pulled the tin star out of his pocket.

Molly took in a breath and let it out on a soft curse. She'd met George Rucker, the boy he'd given the star. Hell, all of them had met George.

"So Les Mullins knows you're Marshal Cage," Guffin said. "Think he's gonna hire out Barlow and his big tug out there to take you in?"

"*Black Sledge* has the boilers and the guns for it," Hink said.

Guffin shook his head, that hair of his stirring like a tassel in the wind. "Still don't make no sense to me. Takes money to put a ship up. Your head ain't worth it. No offense, Marshal."

"Well, if it ain't me," Hink said, "I'm still plentiful curious as to why they're flying. No glim in the heavens today, and last I heard, Barlow was pulling lines and headed to Texas to weather out the cold."

"It is strange to find him prowling the west side of the range," Molly said, "at the same time Stump Station happened to empty out to see us off with their guns this morning."

"I say it's time to shut up and hunt bear," Hink said with a grin. "Molly, bring the boiler on line. Guffin, man the rudders. Seldom, strap up the hooks and ready the ropes. And Lum, see that the cannon's set to burn."

He probably didn't need to tell his crew what to do, they fell to it so fast. Ride the windy trail together long enough and people knew what was what and how to see to getting it done.

After all, there was nothing but their skill, hands, and trust in each other between touching the heavens and being crushed by the earth.

Hink readjusted his gear and knew his crew was doing the same. Then he set his feet in the straps bolted to the floor in front of the helm. He didn't intend to take her out hot. No, he'd rather the *Swift* slip up behind the old steamer, and follow in the *Black Sledge*'s wake.

Caution was half of what kept a glimman alive.

The other half was plain foolhardy luck.

The crew of the *Swift* had both, ace-high.

Molly Gregor pushed her goggles over her eyes and strode off to the boilers, shutting the blast door behind her.

Hink waited for the bell to ring, indicating that the *Swift* was steamed and ready to burn sky.

The cord tugged and the bell in the ceiling frame rattled once. The *Swift* was powered to go.

Guffin, Seldom, and Lum all pushed their feet into floor braces. Hink studied the eastern sky, getting a visual on the *Black Sledge*.

There she was, a bulk against the intermittent clouds, coming in and out of sight like a barge slipping through fog down a white river.

"All right, then," Hink said, his words muddled by his breathing gear. "Let's go see what plunder the sky has for us today."

He signaled Seldom to pull anchor, and the Irishman set to releasing the catch and cranking up the line.

Captain Hink let out the throttle. Like a living thing, the *Swift* came awake beneath his feet. He could feel her shudder, feel her lift to the wind, feel her strain to go higher, faster. Built to take the air, the *Swift* pumped up quick.

"Above her," Hink said.

Guffin adjusted the trim and Hink steered her, up and up through the white and gray wall of clouds, until he was well behind the *Black Sledge*, the shadow of his ship pushed behind him by the western setting sun.

The winds were picking up, that squall on the northern horizon headed their way, but not before cooling off between the teeth of the range. If it brought rain or freeze, it'd take as much fuel as they had on hand to fight their way down to a survivable landing.

They were running out of time to get answers.

"Bring her up close," Hink said. He hit the toggle for the bell back in the boiler room, giving Molly the go-ahead to bail it in. "We'll swing by and have a look at where she's lashing for the night."

They maneuvered the *Swift* up close and tight to the *Black Sledge*, bucking riptide winds.

It was hard to get a bead on her with the roil of clouds, but when she veered to the southeast, Hink was right on her trail.

"She's hopping the peaks," Hink said as the big blower chugged along the ridge but didn't fly over. Didn't make sense. If she was trying to move out of the way of the storm, all she needed was a place to hold up—a difficult proposition with a ship her size—or land. And either of those options would be found at lower elevations.

Why would she ride the ridge?

A flash of yellow bloomed out the side of the *Black Sledge* and swept across the peaks below them. Then another flash, and another, like beams of sunlight bursting through the clouds.

Mirrors. Goddamn it all, she had mirrors.

She wasn't hopping the peaks, she was scraping the sky and hills with light. Looking for a flash, looking for a reflection off something metal.

Like, say, a tin ship.

"Back and up!" Hink ordered.

Guffin and Seldom scrambled to work the controls, and the *Swift* jumped to obey. But it was too late. A wide swath of light, bright and hot as summer off a river, swept across the clouds they'd been holding to, and near as much blinded Hink, even through his goggles.

"Son of a mule!" he swore.

Run or fight? The world seemed to pause for a second, to slip away and slow as he thought through the possibilities, spinning through his mind.

The *Sledge* outgunned them, outpowered them. It would be a dead man's gamble to take her on. The *Swift* could outrun her, but running wouldn't answer his questions. Why was Alabaster Saint suddenly going so out of his way to kill him? Who was working for the general, and how deep into the western glim trade had Alabaster entrenched himself?

Answers to all of that might be a thing of national security. There'd been talks of uprisings since the war. There'd been talks of the west, with her mountains and glim defecting from the east with her money and matics. Talks the president was keenly interested in getting to the bottom of.

And on most all of those rumors, Hink had heard General Alabaster Saint's name traded, hand to hand, like coin of the realm. Whatever plans were being made out here in the west, he was fair certain the Saint was a part of them.

"Hellfire," Hink swore, having made up his mind before the mirror's light had reached the tail fin. "Take her on!"

They dove for the *Black Sledge*, pounding sky to beat the devil.

The *Black Sledge* angled up, catching a hard tailwind. Not so much making a run for it as getting up and into more maneuverable sky to avoid being rammed into the ragged cliffs.

"Watch her guns," Hink said. "Seldom, ready the hook and torch."

Guffin pulled his breathing gear off his mouth. "We're boarding her?" He didn't sound so much worried as maybe a little too excited about the prospect of dangling feet in thin air.

"We're taking her down," Hink said.

The racket of the fans pushing the *Swift* drowned out anything else. Hink fought the controls, pushed by crosswinds and updrafts as he gave her full throttle to ram that black bag of air.

Their only chance was speed.

Good thing speed was what the *Swift* had by the bucketloads.

The ship's frame screeched under the strain of the dive, her tin bones singing out like a hundred wet fingers over fine crystal.

The ship vibrated with the sound of it, the song of it. A rise of pride, of power, of fearless joy swelled Hink's chest. He ripped off his breathing gear and let out a whoop and holler. Mr. Lum's deep laughter rolled through the cabin.

The *Black Sledge* yawed to the side, slinging around hard to show the guns that prickled a line down the length of her.

"Ready, Mr. Seldom?" Hink yelled.

"Aye, Captain!" The Irishman set a hook from his belt to the mid-bar above his head, stomped his feet into the floor belts, then opened the starboard rear door.

The gust of wind that rattled the inside of the ship set her to shaking and would have stirred up anything not tied down, but Hink, Guffin, and Lum were hooked tight to the framework by belts at their waist and braces over their boots.

The blast of a cannon pounded the air like a giant clapping the *Swift* between his hands. The port rear fan sputtered before picking up to plumb again.

Hink kept the throttle full open. The window filled with the *Black Sledge*. He could see every stitch and rivet on the big old barge.

The *Swift* screamed out her killing song as the engine pumped thunder and power into her bones. The repercussions of another cannon shot—this one wide—cracked through the air.

Closer. So close, Hink could jump the door and land on the *Black Sledge*'s wing, if he wanted.

"Now!" he yelled to Mr. Seldom. But even as the word left his lips, Mr. Seldom had already let loose the flaming hook.

Guffin got himself settled in to see how many swear words he could fit in a breath as he, Hink, and Lum fought the controls to pull the *Swift* up out of her suicide dive.

The wind gave them hell, but just as Hink was thinking it was time to tell the crew to kiss their boots good-bye, the breeze shifted and nudged the *Swift*'s tail, giving her the air she needed. The *Swift* scraped over the top of the *Black Sledge*, leaving more than a little dust behind.

"Seldom?" Hink called out.

"Dead on, Captain," Seldom yelled.

And then as if in response, the *Black Sledge* shuddered and rocked as she fell away beneath them. A gout of flame took up the port side of her—Seldom's torch hitting dry tinder. They'd go up in a flame if they didn't dump water to put out the fire. Of course, without enough water, there'd be no steam to keep her up or put her down soft. Especially not with a storm looming.

The way Hink reckoned it, Captain Barlow had himself a handful of hard decisions to make right about now.

And otherwise occupied was just how Hink liked the crew of the ships he was about to board.

"Guffin. The wheel," Hink said.

Guffin jammed a staypin in the controls, unlatched his belt line, and with one hand on the overhead bars made his way across the ship to the helm.

Once there, Hink unlatched and left the wheel in Guffin's hands, not waiting to see if he had latched the harness to the interior framework of the ship or kicked boots into the straps.

Hink caught at the framework as he ran to the door Seldom was manning.

"Give me as long as you can," Hink said.

Seldom nodded. "Always do."

Hink unlatched his breathing gear, dragging the scarf at his neck up over his nose, and buttoned it to the leather lining at the edge of his goggles. This high, the cold could freeze a man's face right off.

Seldom unplugged Hink's hose, then latched around Hink's torso the harness that would haul him home. He handed Hink the three-hooks, two rakelike handles with metal barbs at one end and leather cuffs at the other. Hink buckled the cuffs around his wrists and gripped the handles.

"Keep her up, boys!" he yelled. Then Captain Hink stepped out the door and into the brace of wind.

The fall was fast, hard, and at the same time seemed to take forever. Wind blasted his eyes, face, and near tore off his clothes. The *Black Sledge* was just a few stories below him, and if he hit it right, the netting that covered her canvas would be plenty enough for him to catch on to.

Captain Hink hit the ship and swung the hooks in both his hands, which did a hell of a job of tangling up with the ropes.

He grunted in pain as his shoulders bore the weight of his landing and his arms nearly ripped from their sockets. It took him a second to breathe air back into his lungs and shake the dizzy out of his head. Then he was scrambling down the netting, toward the windows.

He hung down off the netting, his harness line still attached to the *Swift*. If this was gonna get done, it'd have to be fast, before the lines fouled and he'd have to cut free.

That is, if he lived long enough to cut free.

He pulled his gun, shot the window, and then smashed the glass out of it with the heavy barbed end of the hook. No return fire, which meant he'd caught them away from the glass, maybe busy, say, trying to douse the flame crawling up the side of their ship.

He pushed in through the broken window. Not much slack on his line left, and he'd be damned if he was going to cut free to go any farther.

The smoke that rolled through the old tub was choking and hot. Captain Barlow was somewhere in that mess, shouting orders. The dim shape of men scurrying to do as their captain told them impressed Hink. Even though Barlow was a snake-bellied traitor, he knew how to run a tight ship.

If the *Sledge* had any luck still on her ledger, she might make it through this little debacle.

They say luck favors the brave and fortune favors fools. Hink decided that he must be just enough of both today. One of Barlow's crewmen was shock-still and strapped to the side bar, likely watching his life march before his eyes. Hink didn't have to take but a step or two before he was in front of the man.

"I'm commandeering your services, sailor." Hink hit him across the back of the head with the blunt end of the hook. The man sagged and Hink took up some swearing as he pulled the extra hauling harness off of his belt and strapped it around the man. He attached a second line onto the rope that was latched to his own harness so they both had a chance to be pulled back up to the *Swift*.

"You better be worth the trouble," Hink muttered as he lifted the man up across his shoulder and stomped back to the window.

Once he'd muscled the both of them out the hole and up the ropes on the outside of the ship, a yell from behind him clued him in that the crew had been stirred up. Then gunshots rang out, louder than the flames, louder than the fire, louder than old Barlow himself. Hink knew he'd better get off this puffer fast if he wanted to keep on living.

He pulled on the rope, three hard tugs in a row, and pushed away from the ship like a kid swinging for a water hole.

The added weight of the unconscious man on his harness near took the breath back out of him as they slammed into the side of the ship. But Mr. Seldom had caught his signal. Hink felt the jerk and pull of the rope winching upward.

The *Swift's* engines changed tone as Guffin maneuvered her up and away from the foundering *Black Sledge*.

Hink glanced up at his ship. She was a shiny beauty, ghostlike and luminescent against the smoke and clouds. Even swinging the waltz on a string beneath her, he couldn't help but smile.

The ground far, far below him twirled as he was hauled upward. The *Black Sledge* seemed to have done some fair good in putting out the fire, and was smoking downward at a relatively safe speed toward a green bowl of a valley cradled between two peaks. They might make it down just fine.

Or they might be stuck in the middle of a range, with little in the way of supplies and a winter storm bearing down.

As if reflecting on his thoughts, the sky flashed with a rattle of lightning, thunder rolling way up above the glim fields. Rain started off in spits that turned into a good hard-driven drizzle. Even at this height, it was still just rain and not ice or snow.

By the time Hink was reaching up for Mr. Seldom's and Molly Gregor's hands to haul him into the *Swift*, he was soaked down to his long underwear and shaking from the cold.

"Who's this?" Molly asked of the man he deposited on the floor.

"Didn't catch his name," Hink said, shivering under the blanket she tossed over his shoulders.

"If you're cold, Captain," she said, "you can work the boilers on the way home." Molly's sleeves were rolled up to her elbows, and sweat trickled down the side of her neck and glossed her cheeks. Every inch of her exposed skin was tanned and dusted with soot from the big engine.

Hink grinned. "Wouldn't want to put you out of a job, Molly."

"The way you handle a boiler?" She scoffed. "We'd be dead before sunrise. Captain," she added.

Seldom finished unlatching the harnesses and ropes between Hink and their guest, and then dragged the man by the armpits off to one side where he could latch him into the straps and framework there and keep him from getting stepped on by the crew.

Hink shoved up to his feet and, holding the blanket around him, walked over to Guffin, at the wheel.

"Heading?"

"Due west. Thought we could bed down in one of the hollows there."

"We got the guts for that, Molly?" Hink asked.

"We'll need to take it slow, but she'll get us there," Molly said. "So long as the storm doesn't kick up too strong."

"Aim us over the ridge, Mr. Guffin," Hink said. "Easy as you can."

"Aye, Captain," Guffin said.

Seldom stepped over to navigation and Lum Ansell kept steady where he was, humming a low song, as was his habit in the air.

Hink walked the planking, trying to pace the warm back into his bones and taking the time to think things through. Who he should have gone for was Barlow, not this ship plugger. For all he knew the man was new to the hills and didn't have a darn idea of why Barlow was looking for him.

"He's coming to," Molly announced. "Want I should put the snore back in him?"

"No, he needs talking to, and I need to do the talking." Captain Hink stopped pacing and stood in front of the man, who had a blanket thrown on him. Likely that was Molly's doing. Sure, the man was a captive and they'd just as soon throw him out to kick the breeze if he so much as spit, but if he froze, they wouldn't be able to chisel any words out of him.

Hink waited for the man to rouse himself enough to pull the blanket up around his chin and tuck his knees to his chest.

"Have a few questions for you, sailor," Hink said. "And if you answer them nice and clear, and nice and true, I won't have my second kick you out of this boat."

He had to raise his voice enough to be heard over the engines and the wind and rain squalling around out there. From the rock and yaw of the *Swift*, it was darned clear they were airborne.

Hink watched as the man scratched the tally of each of those things in his brain.

"I don't want no trouble," he finally said. Well, croaked was more like it. The smoke and the cold had run roughshod over his vocals.

"Then we're of an agreement," Hink said. "No trouble. You give me answers, and I'll see that your boots are planted on solid ground. Here's question number one: who is Captain Barlow answering to?"

"Said his name was the Saint," the man said.

Hink tried not to let his surprise show. The man jumped so quick into telling him the truth, it caught him quiet for a second. Which worked out just fine. The man must have interpreted Hink's surprised silence as an invitation to keep on babbling.

"I don't know anything else, mister. Captain," the man said. "All I know is the cap said there's a general who had a need for us to do our job and do it quickly."

"What was your job?" Hink asked.

"Find Marshal Paisley Cadwaller Hink Cage and bring him in."

"Paisley?" Molly said, smiling. "What kind of pansy-pants name is Paisley?"

Hink did not answer her, though he sent a glare in her direction that would have burned through steel. His mama had her reasons for giving him so many names.

"So once you found this marshal, what was it you were going to do to him?" he asked.

"I don't know," the man said. "Take him to the Saint for the thing he was holding out Vicinity's way."

"Holding?" Hink said, bending down over the man. "What thing? What thing is the marshal holding?"

"Don't know," the man said, cowering back from Hink's questions as if each word was a rock thrown at his head. "Just heard Barlow say something about a holder and Vicinity and Marshal Hink Cage. I don't know nothing more. I swear by it. I don't know nothing more."

Man was half scared out of his mind, that was sure.

"Captain," Molly said. "You might want to step back a bit."

Hink frowned and looked at Molly. She nodded toward his hand.

In that hand was the man's shirt, and in that shirt was the man. Hink had reached out and grabbed him and hauled him onto his feet so he could yell in his face proper. Had done it without thinking, that temper catching hold of his hands and using them before his brain could send in suggestions.

No wonder the man was quaking.

"Sure thing," Hink said. "Sure." He let go of the man and took a step or two back. "Molly, we got anything hot to drink on this boat?"

"Might," she said.

"See to it the sailor here gets something to knock the freeze off."

Molly nodded and headed back to the keg stove at the rear of the ship to rustle up some tea.

Hink took off in the opposite way and came up behind Guffin. "Give over the wheel," he said.

Guffin untethered and stepped back.

"We putting down in a pocket, Captain?"

Hink latched line to the frame and stomped his boots into the floor bracers. "We're cutting over the range."

"Over? Where to?"

"Vicinity," he said. "Before the Saint's devils get there first."

CHAPTER FIVE

C edar Hunt eyed the rising dead piled up in the center of the town. He needed to get Rose to the wagon, then ride out of here before the undead could follow. Only problem was the undead were between him and the wagon, and Rose was bleeding badly from that shoulder wound.

He backtracked, working in the shadows of the buildings and trying to get to the wagon around the other way.

The idea of leaving an entire town full of bodies being trotted around by the Strange set a rod of fear down his spine. How long would they stay in this town, and if they got loose, how many people would die?

The stack of bodies was still unstacking. Some of them slow and awkward, with no hands, arms, feet, or eyes to guide them. They crawled about, moaning and mewling. They might have once been human, but it was clear and sure from the way they moved, and from the unholy sounds coming out of them, that they were human no longer.

Others pulled up quick, catching on to the hows of walking. If not exactly graceful, they were at least steady and growing steadier with every step. First they walked. Then they broke into a jog. Fast. Headed his way.

He shifted his hold on Rose Small, who was still unconscious in his arms, and pulled his gun.

Shot down the two in the lead, but there were more, too many more, behind them. He couldn't fight without putting Rose down. The townfolk paused over the two men he'd shot, they pushed at them, pulled at them. And then the men he'd shot stood back up.

Didn't look like a bullet could kill a thing that was already dead. Leastwise not a shot to the heart or the head.

Cedar swore and started running. He needed an open door, solid walls, and something that could cause a whole hell of a lot more damage than his revolver.

The crack of a shotgun blew apart the night. Cedar jerked toward the blast.

The Madder brothers were driving the wagon hard his way, coming up from behind the undead and rolling over the ones who got in the way of the big iron-rimmed wheels.

Alun sat the driver's seat, snapping the reins to push those big draft horses to full speed. The horses were more than willing to give it to him, dinner plate–sized hooves smashing through flesh and bone just as easily as through mud.

Cadoc Madder stood on the buckboard braced next to Alun. His geared-up shotgun was slung low at his shoulder. He took aim for the middle of the unalives again as the wagon rolled through them.

The flash of gunpowder lit up the night and Cedar's sight went muddy.

When he could blink his focus back, he saw the dead that had just fallen picking themselves up, while others, too broken to walk, still found ways to crawl or drag themselves toward him.

"Don't know what you did, Mr. Hunt," Alun yelled, "but you've angered up a mess of Strange tonight. Never seen them so intent on taking one man down."

"Rose is hurt," Cedar said. "She's bleeding."

The Madders pulled the big wagon up beside him. Bryn was on his horse, and Rose's and Cedar's horses were tethered to the back of the wagon along with the mule.

Where were Mae and Wil?

Before he could ask, Mae leaned out of the wagon, throwing down the wooden steps.

"Hurry," she said.

Cedar was up the stairs and into the wagon fast.

The undead were still coming, still running, slogging through the mud and muck. Not just the pile of people they'd gathered. More townfolk poured out from houses up a ways, places Cedar and the Madders hadn't gotten to yet. Most of them seemed to have good strong legs beneath them, and were closing the distance fast.

"Put her on the bed," Mae said as she found her satchel and started digging for herbs and bandages. Cedar set Rose down as gently as he could. He braced for the wagon to start rolling, expecting the lurch of the drafts pulling fast, but they were not moving.

"Go!" he yelled, not knowing what the Madders were waiting for. "Where's Wil?"

Mae was already bent over Rose, pulling her wool coat open and unbuttoning her dress so she could see to her wound.

"I don't know," she said, her words coming out fast and slippery as if she was fitting them in between a conversation she was trying to listen to. "Oh. Oh, no." She had pulled Rose's dress away to reveal her shoulder, neck, and her chest down to the blood-soaked edge of her shift.

"I need . . ." Mae started. "No, not that. Not those things." She brushed at the air as if pushing away hands that were not helping. "I need hot water. I need herbs to stanch." She looked up at Cedar, her cheeks flushed but her eyes clear, if a bit startled. "I might need tines if there's a bullet in there to be dug out. Can you help me see if it shot her all the way through?"

"It wasn't a bullet," he said, propping Rose up so Mae could hold the lantern closer to her back.

She finished pulling Rose's coat off, then examined the back of her dress. "No blood here, so it didn't go clean through. What hit her?"

"A key. A tin key. About half the size of my pinky," he said. "We ran into the Strange. A trap. Triggered the fuse and"—he hesitated to go too clearly into detail about the girl exploding—"the house blew to bits. Could be wood, metal, or bone in there too."

Mae slipped Rose's dress the rest of the way off her so that she could look at the bare skin of her back.

Cedar supported Rose through Mae's inspection. Why wasn't the wagon moving? What were the Madders waiting for?

"I can't see anything inside the wound. Nothing," Mae said. "All right, lay her down again."

Cedar did so.

"I'll need water," Mae said to herself as she turned to the kettle hung up on the ceiling hook.

It wouldn't be hot. There was no time to stop and make a fire. And still the wagon wasn't moving.

"I'll be right back," Cedar said.

Mae poured the cold water onto a cloth.

He swung out of the wagon, caught hold of the hand bar, and leaned out so he could see up along the side it.

The three Madder brothers were clumped at the front of the wagon, Alun and Cadoc in the driving seat and Bryn on the horse just beside them. They were caught up in what appeared to be a heated argument.

While all around them the undead closed in.

Cedar couldn't hear what they were going on about. And he didn't care.

"Get this damn box moving!" Cedar yelled.

The three brothers looked over at him, not so much guilt on their faces as a sort of determined curiosity.

"We were just having a conversation, Mr. Hunt," Alun said around the stem of his pipe, which was held tight in his teeth. "Involves you, as a matter of fact."

"Do you see the dead coming our way?" he asked.

Driving the wagon through the pile had done some good to slow and muddle the unalives, but they were recovering quickly and would be close enough to take hold of the wagon and the horses in about a minute.

"Yes, yes. But now, about you," Alun said. "You said you could feel the Holder here in town. That still so?"

"Move this wagon and get us the hell out of town."

"As soon as you point us toward the Holder, Mr. Hunt," Alun said. "We'll take a path that rides us close enough that one or two of us brothers can go looking into the house you point at, or the trail you scent. Shouldn't take long."

Cedar bit back a curse. He'd pull his gun, but threatening the Madder brothers never got them to do what he wanted anyway.

"Rose Small needs medical attention. She needs to get to the next town as soon as possible," he said. "To a doctor. Standing here talking about the Holder's only going to get her dead."

"Not if we talk fast enough." Alun gave him a hard look. "You think the Holder is more southerly or easterly?"

"I think the Holder's going to wait."

"That isn't happening, Mr. Hunt." Alun pointed his pipe at him. "You talk, or this wagon's not going anywhere."

Three against one. Rose hurt, maybe dying. Mae doing all she could to stay clearheaded enough to tend her. Wil missing. The dead so close he could count their buttons. Cedar didn't have a lot of luck going his way. Faster to get the Madders to the Holder than to argue them down to reason.

Cedar thought a moment on the draw from the Holder. Strangely, he felt pulled in two directions. One toward the wagon with Mae and Rose, and the other southeast of town.

"Southeast," he said. "Now move this crate."

He swung back around and into the wagon, just as the undead slapped against it with flat palms, as if they didn't know how to crack the shell to get to the meat inside.

Alun called out to the horses, and they were off, jostling hard and fast down the rutted, muddy road. The unalives couldn't move faster than a horse could lope, and soon they had outpaced them.

But they wouldn't be ahead of them for long.

Cedar leaned on the inside doorway of the wagon, keeping an eye toward the darkness, looking for Wil. He reloaded his gun. His rifle was strapped to Flint. As soon as they got far enough out of town and on their way to the next, Cedar would mount up, take the guns and go looking for Wil. The wagon traveled slow enough he should be able to catch up with them soon afterward.

If he found Wil.

"Not well." Mae knelt next to Rose and was pressing something that smelled of comfrey over her wound. "I need to boil water. I need fire. She needs fire, Mr. Hunt."

"She'll get it," he said.

The wagon rumbled along at a bone-shaking pace before pulling up sharp and hard just a short while later. They were on the outskirts of town, near opposite to where they'd first ridden in.

"Mr. Hunt!" Alun yelled. "A word with you, please."

Cedar swung out the side of the wagon again. Only this time his gun was loaded.

"You think maybe the Holder's closer to us now?" Alun asked, completely nonplussed by the gun pointed at his head.

"Move this cart and get us out of town," Cedar said. "All the way out of town."

"So we're close, you think?"

Cadoc Madder cocked back that big shotgun of his and casually aimed it at Cedar's chest. Bryn, atop his horse, had on his shooting goggles. His rifle, also aimed at Cedar, rested across the saddle.

Cedar could kill one, but not three before he was taken down.

"That explosion you heard a while back?" Cedar said. "The one that blew a house apart? Rose and I were in that house when it happened. She's injured, Mr. Madder, and I'm not going to argue away her life."

"Then tell us where the Holder is," Alun said. "Don't know why we can't impress upon you how important it is that we find it."

"More important that a young woman's life?"

Alun sighed and nodded. "Aye, Mr. Hunt," he said sadly. "I'm afraid so."

All three brothers looked more like battle-hardened warriors than crazy miners out on a lark. He'd seen them get this look about them before. Where they suddenly seemed much older, much wiser, and much more world-weary.

"It wasn't the Strange that killed these people," Alun said. "It was the Holder. Or a piece of it at least. We think tin."

"One piece of the Holder—"

"Tin piece," Bryn corrected.

"—killed this entire town?" Cedar finished.

He knew the Holder was a weapon that could do a lot of harm. But this?

"And its poison will spread," Cadoc said softly. "To the forest, to the streams, poisoning, destroying. Then it will reach the next town. And do the same again."

It was a terrifying thought. That a single piece of tin could poison a land. He didn't know if they were telling the truth, but it was clear there was no arguing them out of their hunt.

He put his boot on the edge of the wheel, then dropped down to the ground, landing in the mud. "This way."

He stalked off down the street, following the call in his bones. The wagon rattled along behind him, and Bryn urged his horse up close so he could pace Cedar.

Wasn't hard to find the building where the pull was coming from.

It was only about five buildings down from where the Madders had stopped.

"That's it." He pointed at the square adobe and brick building. It wasn't a house. It was the jail.

"Isn't that something?" Bryn asked. "The jail."

"Might be in a safe," Cedar said.

Bryn tipped his head so he could look at Cedar through his good left eye. "Probably isn't locked up tight. Most folk don't know the value of it when they see it. Could just as much be down the privy hole."

Cedar hadn't thought about that. The Madders knew the Holder was a weapon whether in all seven of its parts, or connected to make it whole. But since each of the pieces had flown off on its own, just one bit of it wouldn't look threatening enough, or likely valuable enough, to note. Well, maybe the bits made of gold, silver, or copper would turn a person's attention, but not the plainer pieces of tin, iron, or lead.

"This the place?" Alun asked.

"Yes."

"Good." He set the brake, then kicked free the coupling on the horses, separating them from the wagon. The gear between the wagon and the horses fell to the ground with a *squish* and *thump*, and the horses whickered and jostled forward a bit. They were unhooked from the wagon, but still harnessed to each other.

"What in the hell do you think you're doing?" Cedar said.

"Taking care of our needs, Mr. Hunt." Alun swung down off the wagon and landed with enough force to shoot mud up to his elbows. "We need the Holder. If it's here, we get it, and all leave town together."

"Mr. Hunt?" Mae said. "Are we stopping now?"

Cedar walked up to Alun and grabbed his shirt. "If Rose dies because of this stop, I'll dig out your guts with my hunting knife. Understand?"

"The day that you and I come to cross odds won't end in both of us breathing," Alun said without an ounce of fear. "Is that day today, Mr. Hunt?"

"When that day comes," Cedar said, "you won't have a chance to ask me, Mr. Madder." He took a step back. "Re-hitch the horses. Now." He turned toward the jail and strode to the door.

It opened easily. Seemed the whole of the town had been left unlocked when the Holder had killed them all.

He placed his palm on the wood of the doorframe. The echo of Mr. Shunt lifted beneath his fingers. Shunt had been here. The song was stronger than he'd felt before, which meant Mr. Shunt had spent some time here. Maybe a day, maybe three.

Bryn sauntered in behind him with a lantern and the big open room shot full of light.

In that light was a wide desk. And on top of that desk were fist-sized clumps of flesh, several piles of bones sorted by size, and a wide, bloody stain blooming out dark across the wooden floor.

"Think this is where the Holder's hid up?" Bryn asked, as if a desk full of body parts wasn't anything of note.

"That way." Cedar pointed toward the hall. Bryn started off and the lantern light stretched bars of shadows across the ceiling. The jail cells must be down there.

"Here we are now," Alun said, coming up behind him. Only it wasn't just one pair of boots Cedar heard crossing the floor.

He turned. Alun was carrying Rose and Cadoc was helping guide Mae, who looked near exhausted on her feet, into the room.

"What are you doing?" Cedar said.

"Giving the witch what she needs to tend to Rose," Alun said. "You didn't tell me she'd been struck by a piece of the Holder, Mr. Hunt. If you had, I would have given a stronger ear to your complaints earlier."

"The Holder?"

Alun laid Rose down on a cot by the wall.

He shook his head slowly. "She should have died from this wound by now. Even a sliver of the Holder will strip a mortal soul from the body easy as shucking corn. There's something more to our Miss Rose Small," he said with something close to pride in his voice. "I think she's got a bit of the old blood in her."

"Old blood?" Mae asked. "What old blood, Mr. Madder?" She had allowed Cadoc Madder to help her sit on a chair near the foot of the cot.

All of them were mostly ignoring the gore-covered desk.

"The sort of blood that still flows in the veins of a few people who walk this land. Rare. A gift from the El."

"El? A people like the Strange?" Mae said.

"As much as light is like shadow, I suppose," Alun said. "There isn't much crossing of their kind to this world, but sometimes, sometimes. Makes me a tad more curious as to who, exactly, her parentage is."

"Will it do anything to help her endure the wound?" Mae asked.

"Oh, I think it will indeed," Alun said. "But we'll need to get that key out of her. Even someone with her strength can't hold up a fight against the Holder for long."

"Can we cut it out?" Cedar asked.

"No. Once a strangeworked thing hooks into mortal flesh, it begins to consume, to spread and devour. But if we can find the piece of the Holder this key came off of, then it will call to itself. Like a magnet to steel. The pieces weren't meant to be changed or altered or broken to bits. But someone has found a way to break this much off. This key. That," Alun said, "is a problem, Mr. Hunt. A grave problem."

"Cadoc," Cedar said, "you can put some water on to boil for Mae."

"Yes," Mae said, perking up. "Hot water. It will help. And I'll need my herb satchel."

Cadoc Madder frowned. "Your satchel, Mrs. Lindson?"

"Canvas thing she keeps at hand," Alun said. "It's likely in the wagon. See to fetching it, will you, brother Cadoc? Mr. Hunt and I will see if the Holder might be found in these walls."

"Her bag of blessings," Cadoc Madder said as he walked to the door. "I know it." He opened the door a crack and looked outside. "Not even a soul to scrape together among them," he noted. "No souls to fly. No wings to rise." Then, shotgun in hand, he went out into the night.

Mae strode to the stove in the corner of the room. "I'll need a kettle, or a pot," she said more to herself than anyone in the room. She pulled the kettle from the back of the stove and checked the flue. There was a pile of kindling in the wood box and Mae stoked the stove, then took the box of matches off the shelf pegged to the wall.

"Mrs. Lindson," Cedar said, "Cadoc Madder will be right back inside and Alun, Bryn, and I won't be far off. If you need anything, call."

She nodded and nodded. "I'm coming. As quickly as I can."

She wasn't talking to him.

"Mae," he said a little quieter, but stepping closer, "did you hear me?"

She blinked hard, then looked up at him. For a moment her eyes were filled with a wild panic, and he could tell her heart was beating fast. She was afraid.

"Mr. Hunt," she said as if just noticing him. She glanced quickly at the room, her eyes pausing on Rose. Her hand flew up to the tatting shuttle she wore on a string, almost like a talisman, around her neck. That touch seemed to calm her, and a bit of color came back to her pale cheeks.

"I'll be fine. I am fine," she said, correcting herself. "It wouldn't matter if I was out of my mind or not. I know the herbs. I can tend to Rose."

"The undead are not far in the night," Cedar said. "Keep your gun ready."

"You'll be in the building?"

"Yes."

She placed her hand on his arm and Cedar caught his breath at her touch.

"Don't look so concerned, Mr. Hunt. I'm well. Well enough. Find the Holder, if it's here. And hurry."

The three windows of the jail, two set high on either side of the door, the other set high on the other side of the stove, were shuttered. Suddenly, those shutters buckled inward, slammed by something heavy from the outside.

Hands.

Cadoc Madder's blunderbuss fired three roaring shots, but that didn't stop the pounding on the shutters.

The undead were out there, close, and they were impatient to be inside.

"Put your spurs to it, Mr. Hunt," Alun said. "I'll hold here."

One of the window shutters near the door burst open, hands and arms reaching into the room. Alun strode over to Mae.

"Excuse me, Mrs. Lindson." He opened the firebox and pulled out a piece of kindling. Then he pulled a bottle from inside his coat pocket and lit the cloth hanging out of it. He stormed across the room toward the door, but looked over his shoulder at Cedar.

"What are you waiting for? I don't believe the Holder's in this room, now, is it?"

"No," Cedar said.

"Well, then." Alun made the shoo-shoo motion with both hands, the flaming wick and kindling stick crackling with small sooty sparks. "On with it."

Cedar jogged across the room toward the hall of cells.

"Fire, brother Cadoc!" Alun yelled.

Cedar was in the mouth of the hallway, and glanced back.

The muddy miner cocked his arm and let the lit bottle fly. It hit hands, arms, and then a huge flare of an explosion seared gold against the night.

Alun laughed and ran to the window. He pushed the scorched shutters together, then put his shoulder to them and pulled another bottle out of his pocket.

Crazy. Plain crazy.

And so was he for traveling with the brothers. Next time, if there was a next time, Cedar would think twice about the promises he made them.

A lantern at the end of the hall washed Bryn Madder in peach light, the stone wall behind him darkened with soot.

"Haven't seen it in crook nor cranny," Bryn said, pushing his goggles up onto his forehead. "You still say it's in here someways?"

"Or was here," Cedar said. "If it's gone, it's left a strong scent behind."

Three cells. Seemed a bit overkill for a town this size. But since Vicinity wasn't that far off the trail leading folk to settle, mine, or otherwise stake their claim out west, he supposed there were times when all three cells might be in use.

The cell doors were open. Another explosion roared out just beyond the walls, and Cedar hurried into the first cell, dragging the fingers of his left hand along the metal bars, listening for the song of the Holder.

"You're a trusting sort of man." Bryn chuckled as he sauntered toward the open door.

"Nope," Cedar said. "Just well prepared." He eased his gun out of his holster and nodded at Bryn.

Bryn grinned, and stopped in his tracks. In the low light of the lantern, his clouded right eye shone gold. "Indeed you are, Mr. Hunt. But you must know that locking you away here would hardly do us any good."

"I don't know the minds of any of you Madders, for how often you change them," Cedar said. "Nor am I certain how you define what is good for any of us."

He paced out of that cell, then into the second one, running his fingers again along the bars. Listening for the song of the Strange, listening for the song of the Holder.

Nothing in this cell. Cedar walked into the last cell.

"We define good in the common way, I suppose," Bryn said. "There's a great good that needs doing in these times. And we're men to see that it gets done."

"Reclaiming the Holder?" Cedar asked.

"That. And more."

"Not sure I'm comfortable putting the Holder in your hands." Cedar ran his fingertips along the bar. "No offense, Mr. Madder."

"None taken," Bryn said much too cheerfully. "It's one of the reasons we are so enamored with you, Mr. Hunt. You are a man of rare morals who sees these things with different eyes."

"Not sure I follow your logic."

"You have made a promise to return a device made of seven pieces—each piece a powerful weapon in its own right, and the pieces together even more devastating. Yet you hesitate in handing it over, not because you want to use the weapon but because you worry that others will."

Bryn sucked on his teeth, while the clatter of another explosion roared out from beyond the walls. "That says something about you, Mr. Hunt. Honorable things."

"Don't know that it's honorable," Cedar said. "Just plain sense."

"The kind of sense that makes for a well-thought man."

Another gunshot roared out, and Alun's voice could be heard over the din. "Are you near done, Mr. Hunt? Brother Bryn? Or should I find myself some bigger bombs?"

"Near on," Bryn shouted out. "It's a cold trail, isn't it?"

Cedar nodded and walked out of the cell. He took a few extra steps to the stone wall at the end of the hall, a wall burned by fire. "Wonder why there's a burn mark here? Not a convenient place to start a flame."

He pressed his fingers against the dark smudge of soot on the wall.

A shock ran through him like lightning striking near his boots. The Holder had been here, and burned here. And over the shock of that knowledge rolled the distant song of Mr. Shunt.

Cedar glanced up. There was a fist-sized hole in the roof. He didn't know how it was possible to propel a chunk of metal through the sky to land a state away, but he was sure a piece of the Holder had burned its way through the roof and landed where he was standing.

"It landed here," he said. "And someone must have picked it up."

"Time's up, gentlemen," Alun called out. "Load your guns."

"It's gone?" Bryn said.

There was a rising noise outside, something that sounded like a matic thumping with full throttle steam just on the edge of Cedar's hearing. He'd heard that kind of noise before, but couldn't place it. A train? A steam wagon?

"It's gone."

"And you're sure?" Bryn stared at the hole in the roof.

"Yes."

"Well, then." Bryn pulled his rifle. "Let's go find out where it went."

Bryn jogged down the hall. Cedar followed.

Alun and Cadoc Madder were stationed in front of the broken windows on either side of the door, which was about to be pounded down.

Cadoc Madder shot grapeshot blasts into the faces of the unalives who were trying to clamber through the window to the left of the door.

"So nice of you gents to join us," Alun yelled as he uncorked a bottle with his teeth and splashed it over the faces and hands of people trying to shove their way in through the window to the right of the door. The shutter was burned and busted into splinters on the floor at Alun's feet, along with four or five unfortunate, and very dead, bodies.

"You find our Holder, Mr. Hunt?" he asked as he waved the burning kindling at the undead at the window, setting hair and skin on fire and sending them lurching back a step or two.

"Saw where it burned through the roof. It was here, landed here, likely a month ago." Cedar strode over to Mae, who had Rose semi-awake and sitting and was trying to wrap a long strip of cloth around her chest to hold down a thick, wet-herb-smelling compress.

"See any indication of where it got off to?"

That tickling at the edge of Cedar's hearing was still rising, growing louder, coming closer. A steam engine pushing hard. But not a train.

"No." Cedar shot the man trying to wedge himself through the window near the stove.

"No idea at all?" Alun asked, taking aim with his shotgun and unbraining three people for his effort.

"Can it walk on its own?"

"It cannot," Alun said.

"So someone took it," Cedar said. "We get the women the hell away from Vicinity, then I'll hunt it down."

Mae finished buttoning Rose's dress and pulled her coat closed. "The women can stand on their own feet." She helped Rose up, and pulled her gun.

Rose looked ghastly pale, but she licked her lips and nodded. Mae's attention had done her some good, but she certainly wasn't up to fighting the undead mob outside.

"I don't suppose you have a spell that might help us out, Mrs. Lindson?" Alun asked.

"No, Mr. Madder. Magic doesn't work to harm people. Not even the undead."

He laughed and madness rode the rise of it. "Oh, magic can do terrible harm, Widow Lindson. To dead and the living alike. But only in certain hands."

"Bryn," Cedar said, "did you see a back door?"

"Nothing by the cells."

"Then we fight, make a path to the wagon," Cedar said. "Mae, take Rose there near the desk. When I yell for you to run to the wagon with her, you do that."

"Wagon's unhitched," Cadoc Madder said as he reloaded his gun, unconcerned about the undead hands scraping the air just inches in front of his face.

Cedar swore. He'd forgotten. If the women made it to the wagon, they couldn't drive it safely out of here. And Rose couldn't sit a saddle to ride out on her horse, even if the horses were unharmed.

"The Holder?" Alun asked again. "Are you sure you have no idea which general direction it got off to?"

Cedar knew, had known from the moment he touched the burned patch where the Holder had smoldered.

"East. It's not near. Not within a day or two. But east. Now," he said, "can we put our attention to getting through that mob?"

"With pleasure." Alun unhooked the hammer from his belt and swung it with bone-breaking force.

The growl and steam of a matic, something big and coming closer, was so loud, Cedar almost couldn't hear the screams and moans of the unalives.

He'd heard that sound before. Not lately. Not in the last few years. But he'd heard it. He just couldn't place what sort of matic it came from.

The window over the stove broke and a woman crawled through. She stumbled across the room toward Rose and Mae.

Mae shot her clean in the head and the woman fell to the ground, twitching.

Cedar stepped up and fired another bullet into her brain.

The Strange that had been inhabiting her pulled up out of the body, a ghost with teeth where its eyes should have been. Insubstantial as fog, it clawed at Rose, but had no more effect on her than a cool breeze.

That was why the Strange wanted bodies. Crossing into this world, they were spirits with no form. They couldn't hurt, couldn't rightly touch the world around them, except for small nuisances—a bite or a pinch. But certainly nothing near to the damage a physical form could provide them.

"Let's blast our way out of here, brothers," Alun yelled. "Put these people to their rightful rest. Mr. Hunt, I suggest you get the women out and away from here. Far and fast as you can. We have ways to find you. You still have that chain we gave you?"

Cedar reached up and touched the necklace hanging around his neck. The Madders had told him it would keep the thoughts of a man in his head when the moon turned him to wolf. And it had done just that.

"I have it," Cedar said. "I won't leave you to these monsters."

"Our paths divide here, Mr. Hunt. I am trusting you to do anything you must to see Rose gets medical attention, understand? We'll find you no matter how far you roam. Believe in that."

"But—," Cedar started.

It was too late. Alun kicked the hinges off the door, which was already buckling with the press of bodies. Six people tumbled into the room and fell down flat.

Bryn and Cadoc shot them till they weren't moving anymore.

Alun rushed out the door with a roar, swinging that big hammer of his, sending body parts flying like a man mowing down wheat.

The thrum of a steamer working hard poured in through the door.

"Nice working with you, Mr. Hunt," Bryn yelled as he pushed his goggles over his eyes and pulled an ax out from under his coat. He followed his brother out into the night. "We'll see you again real soon."

"The Holder wants what Rose has," Cadoc Madder said. "Remember that. The key." He unhooked a wrench the size of a small child from off his back and strolled out after Bryn.

Cedar rushed to the door. The brothers smashed the undead with hammer, ax, and wrench, holding them off the building just enough for Cedar and the women to escape.

The wagon was turned on its side. No way out there. The horses were gone.

A racket of fans grew louder and a flash of light swept across the Madder brothers as they laughed and bashed their way through flesh and bone.

The light wasn't coming from a low angle. It was coming from somewhere up high. The roof? Cedar leaned out a bit and looked up.

The entire night sky seemed to be filled with the bullet shape of an airship. Her fans were working to keep her steady, her nose up into the wind that gusted down from the hills surrounding the town. Lanterns held to what appeared to be mirrors were the source of the light.

And then a rope ladder dropped down, just a few paces from the door.

"Ho there, strangers!" a man's voice called out. "This is the airship *Swift*. If you want a way out of that tussle, grab hold."

Cedar glanced at the Madders.

"Go on!" Alun yelled. "Get Rose medical attention. We'll find you!"

Running was not an option, not with Rose so wounded. No horses, no wagon. They might be jumping out of the griddle into the fire pit, but it was the only way out.

Cedar ducked back into the building. Mae was already helping Rose walk to the door.

"I'll take her," Cedar said, putting his arm around Rose. She leaned against him, weak and heavy, but still standing on her own. "Climb the ladder, Mae. We'll be out of this soon."

Mae glanced outside, and her mouth set in a determined line. She jogged for the ladder, which was now being held by a lean redheaded man standing on the ground. He had a pile of scarves around his neck and breathing gear hanging by one strap at his shoulder.

He steadied the ladder as best he could and Mae started climbing.

"I'm sorry for this, Miss Small," Cedar said. "But I'm going to have to carry you."

"My hero," she whispered with a weak smile.

Cedar picked her up and made fast for the ladder. When the man holding the ladder caught sight of the two of them, he hollered up to the ship. By the time Cedar had reached the ladder a slinglike net had been lowered and the redheaded man held it ready.

"Put her here," the man said. "We'll pull her up."

Cedar set Rose as gently as he could into the sling. She was already groggy from the run he'd taken, and breathing hard.

The man stuck his fingers to his teeth and whistled. Then he gave the rope a tug and the sling cranked upward.

"Up!" The man nodded at the ladder.

Cedar grabbed hold of the ropes and climbed. He glanced above him. Mae was nowhere to be seen, already having stepped into the ship.

"The others?" the man called up.

"Go!" Alun yelled. "Get on out of here!"

Cedar was a half dozen rungs up the ladder, and the man below started up, giving out another whistle.

The ship rose and the rope ladder shifted and swung, nearly clipping the edge of the building. It was dizzying, confusing. The night filled with a roar of fans above him, the yell and cry of the undead below, mixed with the hot stink of gunpowder and the Madders' wild laughter. He thought one of the brothers, maybe Bryn, was singing.

In a night too black, in a town too alive for itself, beneath a ship that was built to ride the skies, not cherry-pick the earth, Cedar climbed.

Halfway up the ladder he suddenly remembered. Wil. He had left Wil behind.

His heart fisted like a lead weight and panic froze him in place.

"Problem?" the man below yelled.

"My brother's down there," Cedar said.

"Which one?" He looked over his shoulder to peer down through the darkness at the Madders.

"Not them," Cedar said.

"Up." The man pointed at the ship. "Up."

He couldn't go down unless he kicked the man in the face, and even then he wouldn't be able to dismount the ladder without killing himself from this height, since all the while he'd been climbing, the ship had been climbing too. Cedar hauled himself up the ladder.

He'd make them land. He'd make them turn around. He wouldn't lose Wil after just barely finding him again.

Cedar topped the ladder and strong hands grabbed hold of each arm, pulling him the rest of the way into the ship, leaving him kneeling on solid wood.

"Welcome to the *Swift*," a man said. Yellow-haired, windburned, he looked to be in his twenties and built like he wouldn't break a sweat wrestling a wild bull to the ground. "I'm Captain Hink. Whom do I have the pleasure of rescuing today?"

CHAPTER SIX

aptain Hink watched the man take in his surroundings with one quick glance. He figured him for a hunter of some sort—a man with one eye always set toward survival. Figured he knew they were glim harvesters just from the way his gaze lingered over their breathing gear.

The man also took note of, but didn't seem to worry about, the rest of the crew: Guffin and Ansell up front flying, and Molly helping the two women, one of whom was injured and being settled into a hammock.

Then the man's eyes slipped back to him. There was something wild in that gaze. Something that made Hink want to have his gun in his hand.

Captain Hink did his own sizing up. Figured he could take him in a fair fight, though he likely wouldn't be walking away afterward.

"My name's Cedar Hunt," he said. "My brother's been left below."

"One of those madmen?" Hink asked. Wasn't every day he saw three men take on a town full of people gone crazy. He'd only once before seen a town rise up so. They'd been bedeviled by the Strange, and there wasn't a one of them who survived the rising of the next day's sun.

"No. A wolf."

Hink pursed his lips and nodded. "A wolf."

It wasn't quite a question. But it was most certainly an observation as to Mr. Cedar Hunt's mental capacities.

"Yes." Not a glimpse of a smile, not a spark of madness. Nothing but sober hard truth in his voice. "A wolf."

Captain Hink tucked his wide hands into his belt. "Don't know that we have fuel enough to stop for him, I'm afraid," he said. "But if he's a wolf, as you say, I'm sure he'll find his way through the countryside without much trouble."

"That won't do," Cedar said. "I won't leave one of mine behind. You'll turn this bird around, or I will."

He didn't reach for his gun. Neither did the captain. But they got themselves into staring and taking the measure of the other man.

Cedar Hunt did not look like a man that took naturally to laughter. No, he looked like a hard man, driven, with too much sorrow lining his face. He came aboard this ship with two women whom he seemed intent on helping out of a tight situation.

There might be honorable intentions in his actions toward the women, but Captain Hink didn't think Mr. Hunt would cry a tear over spilling another man's blood.

He was the sort of man Hink respected. And usually employed.

"You're serious," Captain Hink said.

"Always."

Molly was done getting the injured woman settled and stood right up close to the captain and Mr. Hunt, taking a good hard look at Cedar. Hink appreciated her take on a person's mettle. He hadn't thought it much possible, but she was even more jaded than he as a judge of people.

"It's a pity I can't help you with your brother—," Captain Hink began.

"What's that ring you're wearing?" Molly asked.

Cedar frowned and lifted his hand, looking down at his finger as if he'd forgotten anything was on it. "Gift from a friend," he said.

"Your friend have a name?" Molly asked.

"Gregor. Robert Gregor."

"And where'd you run into this Robert Gregor?" she asked.

"Molly," Captain Hink said, "I don't see as it makes any nevermind."

"Hallelujah, Oregon," Cedar said. "Blacksmith there."

Molly turned to her captain. "We let him look for his brother."

"Like hell we do."

"He's got a reason, Captain, and we let him look before we fly out of here."

"I don't care if he has an entire encyclopedia full of reasons," he said. "Who do you think is the captain of this ship?"

"You are, Captain," she said. "But I ain't running your boilers if you don't turn her around and give the man a chance. And you won't make it over the next hill if the fuel ain't parceled out right."

"Oh, for the love of glim," he said. "Give me one damn reason why you've taken such a shine to him."

"That's a Gregor ring."

Captain Hink looked a little closer at the ring. Seemed to have a bear and the mark of flames behind it etched into the gold. It was indeed Molly's family marking, and looked an awful lot like the ring she wore on her thumb.

One thing about the Gregors. They were a people true to their word, all the way to the last period carved on a gravestone. If someone was wearing their seal, they'd take them in like kith and kin.

It annoyed him to no end.

"Don't much care if it's the ring of the president himself," Hink muttered, rubbing his fingers through his hair, sticking it up before giving it a swipe to smooth most of it down.

He glanced at Molly, who crossed her arms over her chest and stuck her chin out at him.

No arguing with her when she was digging her heels. He growled and turned, striding toward the navigation center, as the ship yawed in the wind.

"Mr. Guffin, Mr. Ansell," he said. "Turn us due west."

"Aye, Captain," both men said.

Seldom just gave him a knowing smile that said Hink had gotten himself whupped by a woman. Again.

"I'll circle over town and give you one chance to spot this brother of yours," Hink said to his passenger. "Because Molly Gregor there has taken a like to you and is vouching for your worth. But that's all I'm going to give you, Mr. Hunt. Stand up here by the windows where you'll have a view. If you can spot a wolf at this height in the dead of night, you've a head full of eyes far better than mine."

Molly nodded, satisfied. "Welcome aboard, Mr. Hunt. Don't mind the captain, he just has a stick stuck up his rudder tonight."

Hink opened his mouth to protest, but she had already strolled off toward the women. The fair-haired petite woman stood next to the amber-haired younger woman who was lying in the hammock. The fair-haired woman was pressing a compress over what looked to be a shoulder wound.

Mr. Hunt strode up to the windows. He got his air legs surprisingly quickly and by the time he reached the window knew how to compensate for the motion of the ship. He'd likely spent some time on a riverboat, or at sea.

That was interesting.

"Molly," Hink said, "how about you seeing to those boilers?"

She glanced away from the woman in the hammock, and the blonde nodded her permission. Well, wasn't that a kettle of fish?

"Aye, Captain." That was all Molly said with her mouth. But with her eyes she was telling him to mind his manners and treat their unexpected guests properly.

They didn't have time for guests, was how he saw it. They had time for hunting down the Saint's plans. That crewman he'd liberated from the *Black Sledge* had said something about a holder.

There were stories of a weapon called the "Holder." Hadn't been proved that it existed, but the president was interested in finding out who, or what, it might be. And Hink was just as interested if General Saint was connected to it.

If Cedar Hunt hurried up not finding his brother, they might be able to lash and land in some hidey-hole before dawn. Maybe check out the surrounding area for men willing to offer a little information on the Saint.

Mr. Hunt leaned up close to the window and slid his goggles down over his eyes, adjusting the lens. Captain Hink hadn't seen that particular sort of lens setup and wondered if it helped him see through the darkness.

Captain Hink glanced out the open door and watched as the town of Vicinity rocked and pitched below, passing by like lumps of stone along a riverbed. They were high enough above the roofs, everything seemed to be a miniature of itself.

That sailor they'd plucked off the *Black Sledge* had babbled all through the night.

Course, could be true that old General Alabaster Saint was on the prowl out these ways. If the *Black Sledge* had fallen under his employ, didn't take much to think there might be other ships, other captains, willing to lend their wings to the general. Especially if he put a stranglehold on how glim was caught and sold. And trading towns near the ranges, such as Vicinity, stood as ideal locations for the Saint's business.

"See anything, Mr. Hunt?" Hink asked as he took out his knife and got to work digging a sliver out of the side of his thumb.

"No."

Hink leaned a bit out the door to gaze at the land. They were outside of town now, just over the western rise of ridge covered in scrub and trees. Close enough to the trees that Hink could reach out and pull off a branch if Guffin were any worse of a pilot.

Nothing moved in these woods. Well, nothing natural. There was the occasional glimpse of the Strange fading from ghostly form to mist to night wind.

Hink shivered despite himself. He had a keen dislike of the things that walked this world in inhuman clothing.

Most men didn't believe in bogeys and ghouls. But he'd spent a lot of the worst days of his life in darkened forests and bloody fields where the dying were going about it loudly and slowly.

He'd seen the things that came to watch. Sometimes with ragged teeth, ragged bone, ragged smiles. Things that found the suffering of mankind as attractive as an opera house play.

Below, a creek ran just north of town, a cold slate ribbon snaking through the night. He didn't see the Strange anymore. Nor did he see a wolf. Looked like Mr. Hunt was on a cold trail.

"Strange things out this night," Hink said under his breath as he went back to picking at his thumb with the knife.

Cedar Hunt grunted as if he had heard his words. Which was near impossible over the *Swift*'s fans and boiler.

"Turn around," Cedar said. "Take us back over the jail, back where the fight's going on."

Guffin and Lum glanced at Hink, waiting his orders.

"Those townfolk wouldn't want a wolf among them," he said.

"Exactly. But that's where he would be," Cedar Hunt said. "Turn us back east straight over the jail."

Captain Hink nodded at Guffin. "Let's get this done and on with," he said. "East, Mr. Guffin."

The ship rolled a bit and felt as if she hovered there in one place as one set of fans pushed harder than the other, spinning her about tight.

"Bring her low, Mr. Ansell. Wouldn't want our guest here to accuse us of leaving an unturned stone."

The prow of the ship tilted down. Cedar Hunt grabbed ahold of the overhead bar to keep his footing, but didn't once look away from the window.

The woman in the hammock let out a soft moan.

Captain Hink frowned, and walked his way uphill toward the women. "My apologies," he said to Mae. "I haven't properly introduced myself. I'm—"

"Captain Hink," the woman said. "Yes. Molly told me. I'm Mae Lindson, and this is Rose Small. Could you hold this binding down, Captain? The knot's come loose."

Hink lent Mae a hand.

The woman in the hammock had her eyes closed. But even so, she looked like a beauty who slept in those old fairy tales he'd been told as a child. Her skin was too pale, her breathing too shallow. Still, the curve of her cheek, the arch of her lips, put a soft thud in his chest in a way only the sight of glim had managed before.

She was pretty, for sure. But not well. No, not at all.

"What's wrong with her?" he asked as Mae tore back the length of cloth so she had a better strip to tie with.

"Caught in an explosion. A bit of . . . of tin is wedged in there."

Hink frowned. "Small wound to be causing so much pain," he said. "Did it blow through the back?"

"No. We checked. It's in there. And it's plenty big enough to kill her, Captain." She paused as if listening to a far-off sound, then shook her head and got back to seeing that the binding was down tight. "It's fine, it's fine," she said. Maybe to the woman, maybe to him. Maybe just to herself. "He isn't looking, he doesn't want it."

"What?" he asked.

"The Hold—"

Captain Hink leaned in closer. The word had died on her lips, and she shot a glance up at him. Fearful eyes lowered, and she set her shoulders as if to remind herself of the weight of them.

"The hole," she said. "That might have been blown through the back of Miss Small's shoulder. You aren't looking for it. Now, if you'd move your hand so I can tug the knot tight?"

"Talk to yourself often, do you?" he asked with his best bar-side smile. "They say the winds do that to a person. You often been aboard an airship?"

"No, Captain. I prefer to keep my roots in the ground. But thank you, for . . ." She looked up, looked around her as if maybe just seeing the place for the first time. "Oh. Thank you for pulling us up and out of that town. Why were you there?"

"We make drops, supplies and such. Doing a run before winter storms wash out the sky trails."

Mae Lindson's eyebrows notched upward. She clearly did not believe him. "Is that so?" she asked, like a schoolmarm catching a student putting a frog in a neighbor's lunch pail.

"Or maybe we've just come back from the mountains and are looking for some supplies ourselves," he said with a wink. "You see what happened to that town, ma'am?"

"We just came through before sunset." She buttoned up Rose's dress, but not so high that it would pull tight across her bandages. Then she buttoned up her coat to keep her warm and decent.

"They were already dead when we got there."

"The townfolk?" Hink asked, not quite knowing what to do with his hand now that he wasn't touching Miss Small. He finally decided to loop his thumb through one of the rigging belts at his hips. "They looked lively enough to me."

"It's a difficult thing to explain, Captain Hink," she said. "Very strange happenings."

"There," Cedar Hunt said. "Can you slow the ship?"

"Captain," Guffin called out.

"Well," he said to Mae, "once we put our feet earthward, I hope you'll save some time to tell me your tale." He tipped his finger to his forehead, even though he wasn't wearing a hat. "Ma'am."

Captain Hink strode away from the women and stopped beside Mr. Hunt, peering over his shoulder at the ground below.

There was a fair amount of movement going on down there. People moving about, but they seemed slower. As the airship paused overhead, they looked up. Well, the ones that still had eyes anyway.

"There's a mess that's gonna need cleaning up come morning," he said.

Cedar Hunt didn't say anything.

"Spot him?" Captain Hink asked.

"No." The word came out more as a growl. The hair on the back of Hink's neck rose up in response.

"Why are you folks out this way?" he asked.

"We're headed to Kansas," Cedar said. "Mrs. Lindson has family there."

Captain Hink nodded. That might be part of the reason. The women didn't look related. Rose Small looked nothing like Mr. Hunt. He hadn't seen a ring on Miss Small's finger. If she and Mr. Hunt were married, Cedar wasn't acting like a concerned husband whose wife just might be dying.

"And you and Miss Small?"

"I'm headed east from there. Miss Small's traveling for education." He glanced over his shoulder, the ruby lens of his goggle giving him the look of a mad deviser. "That sustain your curiosity, Captain Hink?"

"Oh, not hardly," Hink said. "My curiosity has a hearty appetite. Wants to know things like what those mangled folk down there are doing alive, and what came through to mangle them in the first place."

"I don't have clear answers to either of those questions," Mr. Hunt said.

"Mrs. Lindson said you came upon the town at sunset. That's late on the trail this far into the year."

"We didn't kill them." Cedar looked out the window again. "We rode through for supplies. Found them dead. Miss Small insisted we stay to bury them."

"And you listened to her?" Captain Hink glanced at the hammock where Rose tossed restlessly.

"She can be convincing," Cedar said. "There!"

Captain Hink looked out the window again. They were over the outskirts of town near the mill that squatted over the wider end of the creek. Trees, scrub, more scrub.

"I don't see anything," Captain Hink said.

"By the barn. On the edge. It's Wil."

Captain Hink pulled his telescope out of his pocket and put it to use. He finally caught sight of something moving. "Big enough to be a wolf. You sure it's the one you're looking for?"

"That's him. Land the ship."

"That's not going to happen, Mr. Hunt."

"I won't leave him behind."

"And I won't bring a wild animal onto my ship." At the killing glare Cedar gave him, he had to work on not grinning. Meant a lot to him, that wolf. Enough he appeared willing to shoot Hink out of the sky for it.

"Then we are at a very dangerous impasse," Cedar said. "I won't leave him behind."

"Heard you the first dozen times, Mr. Hunt. But the last thing I want on my ship is a beast that could kill us all. So you need to give me a damn good reason to make me change my mind. 'Cause where I stand it'd be just as easy to let you all off, down there into that town, and let fate have at you."

A blast clapped across the heavens, cracking hard as thunder.

"Cannons, Captain!" Guffin yelled.

Hink glanced at his crewman, and then found himself getting grabbed and grappled by Cedar Hunt, who moved faster than a man should. Hink hit the floor with an *oof*, all the wind slammed out of him as an elbow bent around his throat.

The spine-chilling click of a hammer thumbing back filled his ears. As rightly it should, since the barrel of the gun was pressing a cold circle against his temple.

"You already have a wild animal on your ship, Captain Hink," Cedar said. "And I'll blow your head off unless you bring my brother aboard."

CHAPTER SEVEN

It never took Captain Hink long to make up his mind. And whenever a man put a gun to his head, he right off decided that one, the man might not be the friendly sort, and two, he was not going to let anyone blow his brains out.

But before he could so much as make a move to ungun the man, the roar of another cannon splashed a wash of orange over the sky just north of them.

"It's a ship, Captain," Guffin said, not moving from his station.

"Damn it to glim, man," Captain Hink said. "Of all the times to put a gun to my head it's when my ship's under fire?" Another blast thundered off, close enough it rocked the *Swift*. "Let's you and I pick this up after I make sure we don't go tumbling to our deaths."

"Pull my brother up and I'll put my gun down."

Mr. Seldom was already halfway across the ship, a grappling hook hanging casually from one hand. Hink didn't think there was an object, tool, or knickknack Mr. Seldom couldn't make into a deadly weapon. He'd once seen him use a doily to strangle a man.

At a nod from Hink, Seldom would let that grapple fly. High chance he'd knock Mr. Hunt out before his finger squeezed the trigger. High chance Mr. Hunt might be faster with the gun than he looked, just like he was faster in a fight than he looked.

"Days like this I wish I'd listened to my mama and gone into robbing trains," Hink said. "Let's do as he says, Mr. Seldom."

Seldom stopped in his tracks and tilted his head. It gave him a sort of startled-chicken look, but it was clear he thought Hink had gone straight out of his mind.

"I'm of a fine curiosity," Captain Hink explained to his second. "You know how I hate leaving a puzzle unpieced."

Another blast rocked the night, and Guffin started up on his swearing. Looked like he was going to go through it by the ABC's, starting in Spanish.

"Just lower the catch arm, Mr. Seldom," Hink said. "We should be able to scoop the wolf up. If he wants to be scooped."

Seldom rubbed at his face, as if trying to scrub away the stupid of that order. "Aye, Captain."

Man might not say much, but he got his opinion understood.

"You'd be better off taking your gun away from my head, Mr. Hunt," Captain Hink said. "I don't think your brother's going to willingly jump into our net, but it's the best you'll get. There isn't a clearing large enough to land in these hills, except for across and south of town. If you want your brother aboard, you need to come up with something that will lure him in."

Captain Hink felt the squeeze around his throat lessen. He could have broken free right then. Could probably have broken free before that if he'd wanted to waste time on stabbing the man with the knife he kept up his shirtsleeve.

But he had made a promise to Molly that he wouldn't completely kill their guests. And he was pretty sure Cedar Hunt was the kind of man who wouldn't stop fighting until he stopped breathing.

Cedar Hunt's arm loosened and the gun was pulled away from Hink's head.

Captain Hink took a couple steps forward and straightened his coat and breathing gear. "If you broke my gear, you'll pay or replace it," he said. "See to the wolf. Mr. Seldom will help you. And don't get so close he can kick you out the door. He's been of a short temper most of his life."

A blast cracked against the mountainside, the ricochet sharp as the devil's laughter.

"We have a visual on that ship yet, Mr. Ansell?" Hink didn't care what happened between Mr. Hunt and Seldom. He had a ship that needed to keep her skin on her bones.

"What do you see, Mr. Guffin?" He walked up the rocking floor, keeping one hand on the overhead bars for balance.

"Not a *mierda* of a thing, Captain," he said.

"Made it to the M's already?" Hink asked. "Your Spanish is improving, Mr. Guffin. Keep her here. We'll hover long enough to give Seldom a chance at the wolf. Maybe that will also give our cannon-happy companion a chance to go to hell."

"Aye," Guffin said. He pulled levers and Mr. Ansell, who was manning the wheel and humming a deep, slow song, set the rudders and wings in place. The *Swift* huffed and puffed, her fans running slower, as she came to a full halt, resting on her inflated envelope.

Hink scanned the skies, as much as he could see in the night, without lanterns, up against the wall of a cupped-off valley. He pushed away from the front of the cabin and stomped to the back, opening the rear starboard door. Mr. Hunt and Mr. Seldom stood about midway the ship, on the port door. So far, Mr. Hunt hadn't gotten himself booted off the ship.

But both men looked intent as Seldom used levers and pulleys to lower the basket. Huh. Hink would have just tried to snatch up the beast with the arm, but it looked like Seldom had decided the basket—the same device they'd used to pull Rose Small up into the ship—was the better way to go.

Captain Hink was surprised Seldom hadn't insisted that Mr. Hunt ride down and act as bait so he could dump him free a few hundred yards above the ground.

Seldom must have taken some kind of liking to the man. Or maybe he just feared Molly Gregor's midnight wrench-to-the-head.

Captain Hink spun the lock on the door and pulled it open. He latched his rigging onto the overhead bar, then stepped out, one foot on the running board.

The wind was cold, the night made of teeth that bit through leather, coat, and wool, digging down into the meat of him.

The familiar hum of the *Swift*'s fans was absent. But there was another sound in the night besides the *Swift*. Another airship. Captain Hink closed his eyes and lowered his head, much like the praying man he'd never be. He knew the ships that worked the ranges. Knew the sight of them, the smell of them, and most certainly knew the sound of them.

He didn't know who would be fool enough or desperate enough to be running at night. Air at night wasn't favorable to most ships. Neither was seeing the elevation changes of the land. Weren't enough lanterns for running by night to make much sense. And the wet that came along with the cold this late in the season was sure enough to send a ship down like a brick.

The wind stole away his hearing. Then another pounding explosion from the ship's guns roared out. Too big a gun for *Sweet Nelly*, not nearly loud enough for *Brimstone Devil*. Who was out in these parts, wasting money and black powder firing out charges, looking, he knew, to flush them out?

He caught the huff of an engine, working at idle. The wind cut out the sound again, and he shifted his face so the wind was blowing straight into his eyes.

The distant engine caught, then pushed up strong again. Sounded like they had a wet mule in the firebox.

The *Saginaw*.

Captain Smith, who had the worst luck gambling Hink had ever seen, had lost his last boilerman in a five-card draw. He'd ended up taking on that Boston boy, who rode the furnace with the kind of subtlety he must have learned from working in his daddy's slaughterhouse.

But why would Smith be out looking for them? Maybe the crewman he'd plucked from the *Black Sledge* had sent a flare to call up the next passing ship.

Naw, they'd dropped him from high enough, he wouldn't be awake for a day at least.

Hink wondered if Les Mullins had pulled himself off his cabin floor back at Stump Station and talked Smith into a little round-the-mountain look-see.

It was getting to weigh on his conscience, keeping these men at the chase. He much preferred to gun right for them and solve the problem on the clearest of terms—with firepower, or if they wanted the personal touch, fists.

A racket from inside the ship had Hink pulling his face out of the wind.

Seldom was cranking up the basket.

"I'll be damned," Hink said.

In that basket was a wolf. Looked common enough, gray fur with black at the head and tipping the ears. Except it was sitting that basket as easy as a conductor sits a train. Ears perked up, and tongue lolling.

Cedar Hunt said something to it, and the wolf held still until he and Seldom pulled the basket into the ship. Seldom gave Hink one last look—a chance for him to change his mind.

"Let the beast go, Mr. Seldom," Hink said. "You do know we'll kill it deader than Adam if it does any harm."

Cedar Hunt pushed his hat down closer on his head. "There will be no need, Captain. Wil, stay with Mae and Rose."

And darned if the wolf didn't give Cedar Hunt a glance, then trot off to the hammock and the women.

"Buckle up and hold on to your saddles, ladies and gents," Captain Hink said. "We're flying this bird out of here."

He strode to the prow of the ship and clamped his line onto the overhead, then stomped his boots into the floor belts. Cedar Hunt, Mae Lindson, and likely that wolf got themselves settled as Mr. Seldom secured the door and stowed the basket.

Another gunshot bloomed gold and white against the sky, licking across clouds and terrain alike. Coming from the northwest. Hink waited for the next shot, which would give him a better fix on which way the *Saginaw* was drifting.

"Captain?" Guffin asked.

Hink held up one finger for silence, then leaned forward to better scan the sky. Another boom roared out, a little farther north. Good enough—she was drifting back up to the stations on the west side of the mountains. All they had to do was ease out of here east-wise.

"Keep her low and slow, Mr. Guffin," he said. "Due east, easy like."

Captain Hink pulled the bell line and knew Molly would stoke up the furnace. Not that they needed speed now, but if they were seen by the ship, they'd need to be out of there as fast as this tin lady could scream.

The fans changed their song again, and the *Swift* made her way easy above rooftops and trees, hugging the side of the valley as she snuck along to the east.

Half a mile, a mile. Coming on three, Hink started to think they might have done the near impossible and picked the devil's pocket.

"Captain," Lum Ansell shouted. "Captain, sir! We got a hawk."

"Where?" Hink checked the windows for a hawk-class ship. Unlike the *Swift*, which was built for height, and speed in climbs and dives, a hawk wasn't so much built for glim harvesting. Hawks were built for disabling other ships, ripping them to shreds, taking their glim, and scavenging anything of value.

Not a friend of any station, not a friend of any harvester or pirate, hawks weren't nothing but killing crafts, bristling with edges and flame and guns.

"Port side," Guffin said. "She's lighting her arrows."

"High damn it all," Captain Hink said. He gave it a second or two, just enough time to decide if it was the kind of situation to stay and fight, or the sort of thing that a smart man ran from.

He hit the bell three times. "Give me every ounce she's got, Molly Gregor," he said, though he knew she couldn't hear him.

"We're gonna outstrip her, men. Mind your heads and keep your hands on the controls. The road's about to get rough."

"Bad, bad idea," Guffin was saying. He was so against it, he'd forgotten he was cursing by the alphabet and was instead just repeating "bad, bad idea" over and over again.

Seldom jogged back to the cannons, laying the lines so he could load two as fast as possible. Without orders, Mr. Hunt stepped up and took over preparing the port cannon for fire, freeing Seldom to man the starboard gun.

The bell from the boiler room rang a sharp three hits. Molly had her stoked up hot and ready to ride.

"If you've got it, hold it," Hink said.

Then he hit the full throttle. The engine surged like a river breaking a dam, a tornado's worth of roar pushing through her.

The *Swift* shuddered, riding to the edge of rattling apart, shaking so hard and flying so fast, she was screaming. The tin bones she was strung upon screeched like a choir of angels with the devil's hands around their throats.

Captain Hink aimed her up. Straight up. Such a harsh angle that his boots slipped the straps, and he had to do some serious holding on to keep her on the track.

"Captain," Lum Ansell yelled, his bass voice rolling over the scream of the ship. "Captain! The hawk!"

"I see her, Mr. Ansell," Hink hollered. "I reckon she sees us."

The hawk did indeed see them. Hink knew it because she lit up like a bonfire, torches on long rigging poles, on cannons, on heavy artillery arrows caught like a hundred fireflies suddenly warming up at once. The familiar angle of her prow, built just like an anvil, came into view and he knew exactly which ship they were up against. The *Bickern*.

"It's the bloody *Bickern*!" Mr. Guffin said. "We're gonna die."

"Where's your faith in the goodness of my decisions?" Hink yelled.

"You ain't no angel, Captain," Guffin said.

"Damn straight I'm not. For that you can thank your lucky cards."

They were so close to the ship, Hink could make out the full shape and bulk of her. Three times the size of the *Swift*, she was an old northern war vessel revamped for hunt and scavenge. Carried two boilers, and a long open-deck wooden hull that resembled a sailing ship and would do just as well to land on water as on the ground, with that big balloon above her.

He'd heard she'd gone ironsides, but he was close enough to see the nails in her hull, and knew it wasn't true. Wasn't a man who had found a way to put wings on an ironside and get it off the ground.

Still, she was a beast of a ship, and likely carried fifty crew members. But that didn't mean she was slow.

Or that she was a bad shot.

The *Swift* shuddered and rocked as arrows shattered against her skin. The tin-coated canvas wouldn't easily catch fire, but if they shot for her underbelly, here where the cabin was made of wood, they'd be smoking like a ham in a smokehouse.

And if they let loose those cannons, the *Swift* would be in a world of hurt. She couldn't hold up to many direct hits.

Captain Hink ran her straight for the *Bickern*, fast as she would fly. And the *Swift* was the fastest ship in the western sky.

"Mr. Seldom, Mr. Hunt," Captain Hink yelled. "Ready the fire."

Hink pulled hard back and the *Swift*'s nose shot straight up, exposing her belly to the hawk as he yelled, "Guffin, Ansell, hard to port!"

Guffin threw the levers, pulling in the wing sails, and Ansell hammered gears and valves to change the speed of the fans.

A blast of cannons cracked apart the night.

Hink hollered out a whoop. The *Swift* was still in one piece, still flying, turning such a sharp angle toward port that everything not strapped down slid hard across the floor and slammed into the walls.

"Mr. Seldom!" he called. "Fire!"

The ear-breaking racket of the twelve-pound Napoleon filled the ship.

"Hard starboard, hard starboard," Hink yelled as Guffin and Ansell hurried the levers and gears and Hink muscled the wheel.

The *Swift*, that beautiful, graceful ship, spun like a ballerina on toe-tip, cresting the top of the *Bickern*, and leaning down to put the port-side cannon in range.

"Fire, Mr. Hunt!"

The captain glanced toward the man to see if he would follow orders, but needn't have worried. Mr. Hunt handled the gun like a veteran of the field, and the blast and roll of smoke that filled the cabin proved it.

"Right on target," Guffin yelled. "Two direct hits."

"That's all we have time for, boys. Let's bat the stack off her." Captain Hink shot the *Swift* straight up again, counting on speed to get her out of the *Bickern*'s reach.

But the ship rocked like she'd been slapped.

"We're hit!" Hink yelled. "Seldom?"

Seldom was already running, his breathing gear in place as he took the mid-ladder to the top hatch. The slim man scampered out for a climb to get the best look at where the damage was done and if the envelope of air and steam above them would hold.

Hink had his hands full keeping her out of a free fall. "Losing power to the port fans," he yelled. He hit the bell for Molly to beat her on the back—they needed to slow, and slow fast. The ship stuttered as the starboard fans stalled.

"Sails, Mr. Ansell!"

Mr. Ansell had moved from humming to singing. He had a deep, operatic quality to his voice, which Hink would have appreciated if they weren't plummeting to their deaths.

The ship shook as the sails unfurled. Hink clenched his teeth, waiting for the horrifying sound of the sails ripping under the strain of their fall.

Another cannon blast roared out.

Not what they needed. Not at all what they needed.

The *Bickern* pounded up behind them. And so did the *Saginaw*.

The sails held. They could glide her down, but they'd be dead under the other ships' guns before they touched earth.

There had to be a way out of this, a card he hadn't played.

"Looks like we're going to have to finish this fight on land, ladies and gents. Strap in tight, and I'll try to put our back to a wall."

The hills were coming on fast, darkness in the darkness, as he struggled to keep the *Swift*'s nose up and into the wind. He'd come out of worse situations with his bones in order.

Okay, maybe not.

The trees were rushing up awful fast now.

"We need lift," he yelled.

Seldom squirreled down the ladder and hooked gear to the overhead. "Envelope's torn up, so's the rudder and port engine."

"What does that mean?" Cedar Hunt asked.

"It means you'd better start praying for miracles." Captain Hink didn't have time to say more. The ship was making a pained wail, her voice mingling with Ansell's song as she dove toward her final meeting with the Almighty Himself, hot enough to burn feathers.

Cannons shot off again, searing the sky with an explosive round. The *Bickern* didn't want to scrap them, she wanted to end them.

And then the woman, Mae Lindson, stood right up beside Captain Hink, boots spread to take the tilt of the ship, no harness, and not holding on to anything. Just standing there like a copilot looking out across a calm sea.

She was glassy-eyed, as if caught in a fever, half whispering, half singing some kind of prayer as she stared out the windows.

Folks all have a different way to say howdy to death, he supposed, but he'd rather kick death in the eye than go out singing a little ditty.

"Mrs. Lindson, you'd better hold on—"

She reached up and clamped her hand on his shoulder. With a harsh word that wasn't made of the King's English, she wrapped her other hand around the overhead bar. A shock of lightning whipped through him.

Then, all he could hear was the woman's prayer, lifted and harmonized by a dozen women's voices. All he could see was her eyes, soft, brown, warm as the earth turned on a summer day. He tasted wildflower nectar on his tongue, smelled rich honey.

And then he somehow fell all apart and was strung back together by that prayer. He found himself stretched out in a familiar shape, wearing wings and an engine with tin skin that feared no storm nor sky. He wore the *Swift* as if he were a part of it, as if he were the beating heart to a machine that trod the air.

Hink was a questioning sort of man, but he was not going to question this.

She was dying, his ship. Plummeting to her death. He wasn't going to let that happen. Mae Lindson's song that echoed through his veins wasn't going to let that happen.

Captain Hink knew how to trim the wings, he understood the wind as if he had been born to it. And he knew he called out commands to his men. He knew that they answered, just as his own hands fell to the wheel and steered her steady, over a landside he could see beneath him as if he had eyes in his feet.

The gunshots didn't mean anything. He could flick the tip of a wing, and never be touched. But there was only so much the wind could give him. He needed a place to land, a safe place, a hidden place. Somewhere nearby that the other birds wouldn't see.

There was a crack through the mountains that led to a canyon. Most ships didn't bother with it, being too narrow to land in, and nothing in the canyon worth landing for.

It would be perfect. A safe place to make repairs. A safe place to rest.

Hink steered toward the narrow slit in the mountainside, an act of suicide on a bright and sunny day, and a handshake with death at night with a crippled ship.

"You won't make it, Captain," Guffin shouted from somewhere behind the woman's song.

"Like hell I won't." Hink laughed.

The *Swift* pushed her way on, the wind laying the sky on her back, and pushing her belly up, up. Foothills, trees, scraping the hull. Hink gritted his teeth. There'd be more to repair, landing gear fouled. But he could make it. She could make it. All he needed was one good gust of tailwind.

"Wind," he said. "Give me wind."

And it was there for him, wind rising, warm as a blessing, lifting his wings, pushing the *Swift* just a little faster, aiming at the notch in the rocks, as his crew cursed and prayed and the *Swift* beneath him, around him, responded to his every command.

Captain Hink could see the path as clear as if it were lit by a hundred gas lanterns. He steered the little ship straight and true through the crack in the mountainside, and out to the canyon beyond.

The *Swift* tucked wing tight, and slid down, like a feather on a string, toward the little hollow hidden from above by the overhang of rocks.

Easy as thumbing a button through a hole. Hink called orders to ready for landing on the broken gear. Like a blind man on a well-practiced route, he and her crew brought the *Swift* down, a little hot, but without more than a rattle or two before she was set, solid and true, on the earth again.

The prayer, the women's voices, the taste of honey, and the feel of the ship upon him stripped away.

Captain Hink blinked hard to get his bearings.

Mae Lindson was no longer touching his shoulder. She was standing in front of him. No, she was falling, fainting. Hink let go of the wheel and reached out for her, but Cedar Hunt was there, and caught her up before she fell.

For a moment Cedar Hunt stood in front of him, more wolf in his gaze than Captain Hink had seen in the wild beasts themselves. He suddenly wished he had a gun in his hand.

"She saved your life," Cedar Hunt snarled. Then, "Don't touch her."

He strode away past Rose Small in the hammock to the wolf, who was on his feet, ears tipped back and head down, staring at Hink with the selfsame killing eyes as Cedar Hunt.

Maybe they really were brothers.

Hink looked over the crew members. All three men looked a little rattled and were taking a hard pull on flasks of hooch. Mr. Seldom lifted his in a sort of salute toward Hink, then took another generous swallow.

Hink patted his jacket for his own ounce of courage.

"What kind of a cow patty landing was that?" Molly Gregor asked as she stormed out from the boiler room bringing with her the smell of soot and oil and hot wet metal. She took in the sight of Cedar Hunt laying Mae Lindson on the floor and then leveled a blistering glare at the captain.

"What did you do to her?" she demanded.

Hink tugged out a flask of bourbon and took a long swallow. He'd need it to put a calm in his voice.

He knew better than to rile up the Gregor woman, especially after a hard landing. She didn't like hard landings much. None of the crew did. Though a hard landing was a damn sight better than not being around to complain about it.

"Don't know what Mae Lindson did exactly," Hink said. "She

somehow made for bringing the bird down a little easier. I wouldn't have threaded the buttonhole if she hadn't . . ." He paused. "What did she do?" he asked Cedar Hunt. "Was it some kind of witchcraft?"

Molly rolled her eyes, then turned to Mr. Hunt. "You'll have to forgive the captain here. Most days he has brains in his head."

"Now, Molly," Captain Hink said. "That was a question from me to him. Let's let him have his say. Was it some kind of witchcraft?" He nodded toward Rose Small and the wolf before meeting Mr. Hunt's steady gaze. "Mr. Hunt?"

"Yes."

Funny how one word can stick a finger in the world's gears and gum things up for a second or two.

"Huh." It wasn't much to say, but it was all he had in him. He tipped the flask, then walked over and offered it to Molly. She took a nip and handed it back.

"Anything we can do for her?" Molly asked. Heart of gold, that woman. He didn't know if she believed that they had a witch on board. Even if she did, Molly wouldn't let that get in the way of basic courtesy.

"Hot tea," Cedar Hunt said. "Maybe food. But I think she'll be unconscious for a while."

"Well, then," Hink said. "We have work to be getting done. Molly, if you could rustle some grub and tea, we could all use some. The boiler survive the bump?"

"No cracks that I've found yet, Captain," she said.

"Good. Guffin, see to it we're lashed down tight for the night. Ansell, drain the airbags. Seldom, see how bad off the fans and gears are."

"What are you going to do, Captain?" Guffin asked.

"Drink the rest of this flask and tell you to get to work," Hink said.

Molly went back to the galley and the men got moving, though they muttered loud enough to make sure he heard just what they thought of him, his mother, and his orders.

Once everyone was out of earshot, Hink turned to Cedar Hunt.

"Have a seat, Mr. Hunt," he said as he dropped himself into one of the wicker and leather chairs next to a small table. The *Swift* wasn't exactly set up for passenger comfort, but they'd long ago decided that the basic niceties were necessities.

For a moment, Hink didn't think the man was going to oblige his invitation.

Then Mr. Hunt walked over and sat.

Hink handed him the flask. Mr. Hunt took a hard swallow and handed it back.

"Your brother's a wolf, and your woman's a witch," the captain mused. "I find that some of the more interesting things I've seen lately. As luck would have it, I happen to have several hours on my hands to listen to the explanation of who you are, where you're coming from, and where you're going to. And, oh yes, why."

Mr. Hunt didn't say anything, just gave him that hard bronze gaze.

Hink settled in to outwait the man. Because they weren't moving a single step farther along this trail until he knew exactly what kind of trouble he had on his hands.

CHAPTER EIGHT

General Alabaster Saint's sword tapped the top of his boot with each stride as he paced the edge of Candlewick Bluff. The rocky ground beneath him cracked like bones of the dead as he surveyed the lower range and valley of the Big Horn Mountains spread wide before him.

He was waiting. Waiting in the cold dark before dawn, all the men in his militia sleeping, the three airships lashed down and cool in the night. Waiting for a message from his spies.

He'd sent out twenty men. To find Marshal Cage and bring him in. Dead or alive. The same men were told to listen for rumors of the weapon Alabaster Saint most wanted to get his hands on. The Holder.

During the war, both sides had claimed they were in possession of it. He'd found no proof that it was true. But he'd intercepted a man who said Marshal Cage had orders to track it if he could. Which meant the president was interested in the weapon.

And so was General Alabaster Saint.

He had spent years gathering men sympathetic to his cause. Men willing to rise up against the excessive restrictions and regulations on the western glim that the eastern states craved. Men willing to fight for the territory of the west to control all trade and profits made from glim, on both the legal and the illegal markets.

Saint had served his time fighting other men's wars for zero profit.

Now it was time for a visionary leader to join glim harvesters and pirates in a common goal: to control the glim fields of the United States of America and govern the skies under law unconnected with the land beneath it.

A crow shook free from a tree, shadowing black across the gray sky. The general tracked it with the single eye left to him, watching it disappear into the deep of the hills.

This land's war had brought him pain, suffering, and enough grief to choke a man. He'd lost his son, James, on the field, then his wife, Laura, to the grief.

The war had taken both of them from him.

And given him nothing in return. He was done with this land. But he still wanted the sky.

"General?" Lieutenant Foster walked up behind him, his pace altered by the drag of the prosthetic foot he'd worn for the last three years. The lantern in his hand swung a steady beam of light across the rocks and scrub around them.

Lieutenant Foster had been with him the longest of any of his men and had proven himself an unflinching second, unafraid to carry out his every command.

The tales of the Saint's cruelty on and off the field had been passed in whispers between rank and file, building the Saint up into a nightmarish commander. Lieutenant Foster had done nothing to stop such talk. Because none of those tales were quite correct.

Most men, except for perhaps Lieutenant Foster, weren't capable of imagining the sorts of things Alabaster Saint was truly willing to inflict on a man to see that his word was obeyed during the war.

And obey him they did, down to a man.

Until Mr. Hink Cage came under his service.

Charismatic, devious, a man who followed his own caprice, Captain Cage obeyed orders for a year before rising up with half the division and refusing his orders on the grounds that the Saint was not following the president's order to hold the line until reinforcements came.

It was true that the Saint had been acting without orders. It was certainly not the first time. And he had one of the highest mortality rates in the Union army because of it.

Captain Cage had intercepted the president's correspondence, then refused to march.

With one uprising, Cage forced the Saint to call the single retreat in his career.

Publicly shamed, Saint was put on trial for more than disobeying orders. Someone had infiltrated his records and correspondence. Records of the weapons trading the Saint had profited from.

When he stood trial, the man who had spied on him testified. That man was Captain Hink Cage.

The North and South spent five years beating each other into bloody graves. Now the states were one Union again, one land again with a railway to stitch over the old wounds.

But no one had yet claimed the skies.

Lieutenant Foster cleared his throat.

"What is it, Lieutenant?"

"There's a man to see you, sir."

The Saint adjusted the patch over the hole where his left eye used to be and turned.

Foster looked pressed and clean, as if he'd just walked out of a tailor's shop. His dark hair was combed back off his forehead, his face clean shaven except for the precisely trimmed sideburns that reached down to his jaw.

Didn't matter how much mud and blood he was wading through, the man always cut a sharp figure.

"What man, Lieutenant Foster?" Could be one of the spies he'd sent out. But if it were, Foster would have just told him who had returned with news.

The spies knew better than to return without news.

"He didn't give me his name, sir." Foster licked his lips and looked as close to nervous as the Saint had ever seen him. "He's waiting in your office."

"I'm going to need more than that," he said. "Where's he from? What's he look made of? Why's he here?"

"Permission to speak plainly, sir."

Alabaster Saint narrowed his eye. Then, "Granted."

Lieutenant Foster relaxed his bearing just the nth of a degree and met Alabaster's gaze.

"He's tall, lean, and like nothing I've seen before."

"Foreigner?"

"Not a kind I've put eyes on."

"What's your gut say, Foster?"

"He's a killer. A butcher of men. And he enjoys it."

Alabaster Saint didn't see any of those traits as a downfall. Had made a point to bestow his rare praise on Lieutenant Foster for just those reasons.

"And why wouldn't we welcome a man of that stripe, Lieutenant Foster?"

"I think he's out of his mind insane."

Alabaster Saint chuckled, a low, humorless rumble. "All men are insane, Mr. Foster. Just some utilize it better than others."

Lieutenant Foster gave the Saint half a nod, though it was clear he was holding back words of disagreement. That wasn't like him. Foster always told the general what was on his mind.

If other men had spoken with such frankness, Alabaster would have minced their entrails and served them with beans. But not Foster. Alabaster had learned quickly that the man's mind was just as sharp as his uniform.

His insight had turned more than one plan to his favor.

"If you have something to say, Lieutenant, say it," the general said.

"There's something terribly wrong about him. Something Strange. It is my recommendation, sir, to have him on his way as quickly as possible."

"Are you spooked, Mr. Foster?" the Saint asked, amused.

"No sir," the lieutenant said. But his eyes betrayed his words.

Whoever was waiting for the Saint back in his office had managed to put a chill in the veins of a man the general would have bet good money couldn't be spooked.

"Steel up, Lieutenant," the Saint said, as he walked past his lieutenant, "or you're no use to me."

Alabaster Saint strode toward the building tucked far enough back in the rocks and scree that it was difficult to see from the surrounding ground, and, even more important, was nearly impossible to see from the air.

This was his fortress, his stronghold. When he called war—if it came to that—upon the eastern states, this would be his command center.

The only way a man knew of this place was by very careful invitation.

Or so he had thought.

The crunching of Foster's boots over the rubble told him the man had courage enough to still follow him. Good.

Dawn had taken the bruise off the night and was pushing pale blue over the twisted trees and ragged mountain walls. No birdsong rode that light, an unusual omen on so clear a morning.

The house came into view, a large split-log and stone structure that looked like it had sat the mountain for centuries instead of just a few years. The barracks for the men was to one side, a long building with small windows and enough beds to sleep a couple hundred, though he had only half that many pressed into service right now.

To the north of the clearing was the huge shelter for the airships—made of wood and canvas cleverly secured to the side of the mountain to cut the worst of the wind. It wasn't large enough to fly the ships into fully inflated, but once the air and steam was out of them, all three of his pride and joy could nest there together.

The men were waking, smoke from the cookhouse rising to mix with the mist that clung to the crags.

There was a single lantern polishing copper against the window of his office and home. A shadowed figure broke that light.

Even from this distance, the Saint could feel the eyes of the man who stood within that shadow, hidden as if light feared to touch him.

The hair on the back of the general's neck pricked up. Those eyes, that man, were danger. The Saint had no doubt of that. And he knew that dangerous men could be very useful.

He strode up to the door and pulled it open, stepping into his office without taking off his hat. The man stood at the window, his back turned toward him, covered in layers and layers of coats, some of which were long enough to fall all the way to his heels. He wore a stovepipe hat, and a pile of scarves around his neck.

"What's your name, and what's your business?" The Saint paced to the other side of the room and sat at his desk. He always kept a revolver and a sword on him, but his Enfield Rifle-musket leaned against the wall behind the desk. In easy reach now.

The man did not turn. "I hear them," he whispered, low. "The last words on their lips, the last thoughts in their heads."

Lieutenant Foster stepped into the room, glanced at the man, then at the general, and closed the door, but didn't go any farther. His left hand rested on his gun, his gaze on the tall stranger's back.

"Name and business," the Saint said. "Or I'll end this conversation."

"Her name was Laura," the man murmured. "His name was James."

The name of his wife. The name of his son.

Alabaster Saint picked up the Enfield and held it steady at the man. "Who are you? Who sent you?"

"I sent myself."

The man turned. The scarves stacked all the way up his face so that only his eyes, shadowed by the brim of the stovepipe hat, were visible. Those eyes burned with an unearthly intensity, as if the fire of the damned kindled there.

"As to who I am, my name is Mr. Shunt," he said in a tone as soft as a lullaby. "And I have come to offer you my services."

Mr. Shunt lifted his right hand, slowly.

Lieutenant Foster drew his gun.

But all that was in Mr. Shunt's hand was a large black burlap bag.

"My offering."

The Saint eyed the bag, which was misshapen and lumpy. He had no idea what it might hold. "Lieutenant," he said.

Foster walked forward, his weapon still drawn. He held out his right hand for the bag.

Mr. Shunt gave it to him, his fingers graceful, overly long and sharp, each ending in a metal tip.

The Saint had seen Chinamen who like to sharpen their nails into claws, but whatever Mr. Shunt had done to his hands was something else altogether. His fingers shone like metal.

Foster backed away before opening the bag and peering in it. He lifted his head and made sure his gun was on the man for a clean shot.

"Is this a threat, sir?" he asked.

"Not at all," Mr. Shunt said, spreading both long, knob-boned hands outward in a strangely fluid motion. "It is an offer of my good intentions."

"Bring it here," the Saint said.

Foster placed the burlap on the desk, landing it with a meaty thump.

The Saint leaned forward, tipped the edge of the bag, and looked inside.

Body parts. Hands, feet, fingers, ears, and other smaller bits, each wrapped up in cotton gauze tied with a neat bow.

"Is this supposed to impress me, Mr. Shunt?" the general asked.

"No," Mr. Shunt said. "It is to encourage you. I can do many things, General Alabaster Saint. I can even make men's dreams come true."

"I don't recall dreaming about a bag of body parts," General Saint said.

"No, you did not," he said quietly. "Your dream"—he cocked his head to one side, eyes narrowing—"is destruction. Nightmare. Conquest. Ah . . . and then control. Wealth. The skies." Here the scarf at his mouth shifted. A grimace of serrated teeth carved a ragged white smile in the shadows of his face.

"Such sweet dark dreams you have, Mr. Saint," the stranger said.

The Saint thumbed back the hammer on the Enfield. "I'm not a man who dreams, Mr. Shunt. I'm a man who acts. Tell me what you want."

Mr. Shunt plucked at the scarves, pulling them back over his mouth, seeming unafraid of the musket aimed at his chest. "There is a man I wish dead. A man and his brother. If you kill them, destroy them, your reward will be rich."

"I am not a gun for hire," Saint said. "And I am gravely offended by your audacity to think me so. You have climbed this mountain and endangered your life for no good reason, Mr. Shunt. And you have wasted my time."

"I can bring you Marshal Hink Cage."

Silence scraped by on jagged claws. Mr. Shunt did not move, didn't even appear to be breathing. He waited, cold and uncaring as the north wind.

"How?" General Saint asked.

"With these," he opened his hand. Brass blades and needles prickled from each fingertip.

"And that." Shunt nodded toward the bag of body parts. "And this." He reached into his breast pocket and withdrew a small glass vial.

The vial glowed the eerie glim-light green, but the Saint knew glim. This light was too dark. The vial had something else in it.

"What is that?" he asked.

"Glim," Mr. Shunt breathed. "And the dust of strangeworked tin. To repair men."

"Repair?"

Mr. Shunt tipped his head down so that all the Saint could make out from beneath the stovepipe hat was his burning eyes.

"I can give your men back what they lost," he said. "Hands, arms, legs, feet. I can make them strong again, whole again. Stronger than they were. If you kill the hunter and wolf. If you bring me the deviser, the witch, and guards. Then I will give you back your eye, General Alabaster Saint. I will find Marshal Hink Cage."

"You ask me to kill two men, and now you want me to capture prisoners for you? I follow no man's orders, Mr. Shunt."

"Of course," Mr. Shunt said with a formal bow. "Perhaps I was mistaken." Mr. Shunt did not look away. Did not make any indication he was leaving.

Saint leaned back in his chair. He wanted Captain Cage almost as much as he wanted the glim fields. If this crazy rag-a-man could find him, he would be a fool to let him walk away untried.

Better to let him think they could work together, and test his worth.

"Can you prove your claim, Mr. Shunt? The healing of men?"

"Repairs of the flesh," he said. "Yes."

Time to call his bluff.

"Before I agree upon anything, I want you to do so. Lieutenant," General Saint said, "bring me Private Bailey."

"Yes, sir."

Saint took a long look at Mr. Shunt, who stood still as death before him. "If you can repair men, Mr. Shunt, and find Captain Cage, there might be reason for us to enter a business proposition after all."

CHAPTER NINE

Rose Small woke to the sound of men's voices. The voices were close enough she could make out most of the words, but none of them made much sense.

One of the men was Cedar Hunt. She'd recognize his low, threatening tone anywhere. The other voice she was sure she'd never heard before.

It took her a couple tries, but she finally opened her eyes. The ceiling above her arched with scrolling metal beams and joists, over a deep polished wood. She wasn't in the Madder brothers' wagon, though she most certainly was in a hammock. And she wasn't anyplace she could recall being before.

Rose turned her head and winced at the pain digging deep in her shoulder and spreading out like claws across her neck, chest, and back. She'd been hurt?

Last she recalled she and Mr. Hunt were gathering wood. No, that wasn't right. They were doing something more. Gathering up the dead.

Those poor people in Vicinity. They'd been trying to give them a grave. And she'd seen Mr. Hunt holding that little dead girl in his arms, his eyes so lost to sorrow, tears down his face that she didn't even think he felt, she'd taken him with her to gather wood.

That's when he'd heard someone crying. They'd gone into the kitchen and . . .

Something had happened. A shot? An earthquake? Something. She remembered pain, remembered Mr. Hunt holding on to her like he could shield her from bullets, remembered the hard taste of hot metal in her mouth.

And then, nothing.

Now that she'd turned her head, she saw Mrs. Lindson to the left of her asleep on some blankets. She looked pale even in the warm yellow light from the low-burning lantern. Wil was lying beside her, and turned his head to look at her, ears straight up. He didn't seem worried. That was something, she supposed.

Rose took a few breaths waiting for the pain to take itself off to the distance, then turned her head the other way.

She could just make out the back of Mr. Hunt here in the room. He was sitting in a chair. Still had his coat and hat on. The man he was talking to was blocked by him. Well, most of him anyway. She could see one shoulder, and a hand.

Whoever the man was, he liked to use his hands a lot when he talked, taking up a lot of the space around him. She figured he'd be the sort of man who danced with his elbows out.

"When did you meet the Madders?" the other man asked.

"Few years ago," Cedar said. "Knew them as miners. Asked for their help finding a lost boy, and fell into owing them a favor."

"And about that item you said you'd find for them?"

"Yes?"

"Well, I've seen a bit of the land and sky, Mr. Hunt. Might be I've seen what you're searching for. Does your item have a name?"

"It probably has several. They call it the Holder."

Rose blinked hard. She didn't think Mr. Hunt was the sort of man to tell their private business to a stranger. Maybe the man was someone

Mr. Hunt knew from back east or from when he worked in the university. Or maybe the man was holding a gun in his other hand.

One way to find out.

Rose licked her lips and pushed herself up, leveraging her right elbow under her, and pushing back.

From the clench of pain that stomped over her, Rose decided real quick she had overestimated her leveraging abilities.

She moaned, though she tried to hold it back.

Two sets of wicker chairs squeaked, then two sets of boots got louder as they came nearer her.

Well, this wasn't her plan at all. Still, if Mr. Hunt had been under gunpoint, she sure hoped her diversion helped to give him the upper hand.

"Miss Small," Cedar Hunt asked, near now, and clearly concerned. "Easy." His hand pressed gently down on her good shoulder, and she just didn't have it in her to put up a fight. "Do you think you can drink some tea?"

Rose opened her eyes, a little surprised she'd kept them clenched shut so long. Wasn't like her to look away from a situation.

But the pounding at the back of her head and the blur to her vision said maybe her looking away wasn't such a bad idea.

Something soft was being wedged against her back, a pillow maybe or a blanket roll, and then she rested her head, and worked on no more than staring up toward the ceiling until her head stopped drumming a beat.

"Miss Small?" Cedar said again, taking her hand. "Rose?"

Rose tried not to smile. He sounded so very worried. Almost distraught. It was sweet of him.

"Don't worry so, Mr. Hunt," she whispered. Her throat was dry and sour with the hot taste of metal. "Tea would be nice."

He let go of her hand to see to it.

"Does she need anything else?" the other man asked. "Molly has a fair hand with medicine, though we're running low on supplies."

What a nice voice, Rose decided. Deep, with a little music to it, like maybe he hadn't grown up in the Oregon Territory. She liked the sound of it. She hoped he wasn't holding them all hostage.

"We'll start with the tea," Cedar said. "I laced it with a bit of laudanum to take the pain off."

Rose turned her eyes away from the ceiling, catching sight first of the other man. He was light-haired and had a fine face, straight nose, carved cheekbones and a strong jaw that gave him the look of northern people. He was clean shaven, and his mouth seemed more than willing to smile.

His eyes . . . clear gray with a dark ring of blue at the edge, so striking it made her wonder if she was seeing them right. They were the color of storms and blue skies, framed by dark lashes.

Any one part of him might not be extraordinary, but taken all together, he was quite fetching.

Maybe it didn't matter if he danced with his elbows out.

She supposed she might be staring.

She supposed she didn't care.

"Take a sip, Miss Small," Cedar Hunt said. "It will help."

Rose looked away from the man's face and paid attention to the cup Mr. Hunt held before her. She took a sip, placing her right hand under it so Mr. Hunt didn't have to support it.

The tea was weak, but bitter with laudanum. She'd be asleep again soon for sure.

"Where are we?" she asked, the tea having put more of her voice back in her words.

"In the mountains," Cedar said. "This is Captain Hink, and we're aboard his airship."

"Airship?" Rose's heartbeat pumped a little faster, and she glanced again at the metal beams and as much of the room as she could see.

Of course, a ridged skeleton to carry the gondola. Above that ceiling would be the airbags—no, they were called envelopes. She wondered how many boilers she had on her, and how many fans.

"The *Swift*," the man, Captain Hink, said. "She's small, fast, and—"

"Beautiful," Rose said with a sigh.

Captain Hink smiled and pride lit his eyes. "Yes, she is. Have you flown, Miss Small?"

"Only once. But not in a ship." Rose's neck was beginning to hurt from looking up at his eyes, but she found herself not wanting to look away.

She had so many questions. About flying, about the ship. She wondered if they had to use glim to power her like the Madders had used glim to augment the power of the balloon.

But the tea was already starting to make her tired. She reluctantly looked away from Captain Hink and held the cup out for Mr. Hunt so she wouldn't spill.

Medicines were scarce and expensive.

"I'm filled with questions," she said. "But my eyes are so tired. Is Mrs. Lindson well?"

Cedar placed the cup on a nearby shelf. "She will be. She overexerted herself." That last bit he said with a deep growl in his voice. Rose had noticed that when Mr. Hunt talked about Mrs. Lindson, he often had a bit of the wild behind his words. Especially since she'd been so whimsical in the brain lately.

She didn't think he noticed it, but he felt very protective of her. Likely felt more for her than he'd yet admitted to himself.

Funny how a scholar could lose all sense and logic when falling in love with a woman.

She had found it to be most entertaining on the trail so far. Well, except for the day she'd found Mr. Hunt covered in blood with that man dead at his feet. There was a difference between losing your mind when falling in love, and just plain losing your mind.

". . . be in the air before dawn, if we're lucky," Captain Hink was saying.

Rose opened her eyes. She must have slipped off to sleep. The lantern was doused, and there were other voices, farther off, men. Maybe two or three, talking over fuel and lift and steam and something about temperature and rivets and tin.

She heard Mr. Cedar Hunt shift on the floor near her, and got a look at him. He sat, his back to the wall, his hat tipped down to shadow his eyes. Wil sat next to him, his bronze eyes aglow in the darkness, ears twitching to sounds in the ship she couldn't hear. Mr. Hunt's hand rested on Wil's back, and Mr. Hunt was asleep.

The men at the end of the ship sounded like they were bedding down. She even heard the soft breath of a snore muffled by something like a pillow or an arm over a face.

And then Captain Hink was standing above her hammock, looking down at her.

She was startled to see him there.

He appeared just as startled to see her awake.

They held still, caught in a stare they could not seem to break.

He opened his mouth, closed it, glanced over at Cedar Hunt, who as far as Rose could tell hadn't stirred, then finally back at her.

"My apologies," he whispered. "I thought you were asleep."

"I was," Rose whispered back, enjoying his discomfort more than she probably should. He looked like he'd swallowed a prickly pear and didn't know how to get it down proper.

"I didn't mean to wake you." He lifted his hand and showed her the pillow he was holding.

"What did you mean to do with that, Captain Hink?" Rose asked.

"Lee," he said. "Please, call me Lee."

"I'm not sure that I'm on first-name familiarity with you, Captain Lee Hink."

He looked down at the pillow in his hand, then back at her with a smile. "Maybe that's not my first name," he said. Then, "Would you be on first-name basis with a man who was going to offer you his feather pillow?"

Rose held her breath for a second. Was he just teasing her, or had he really come back here to try to give her a little comfort? Why would a stranger do such a thing?

"Is that what you were doing, Captain Hink?"

"Lee," he said. "And yes. I just wanted to see you . . . just wanted to see if you were comfortable."

"Oh, for Pete's sake," a man grumbled from somewhere toward the head of the ship. "Just give the woman the pillow, *Lee*, so we can all get some sleep."

Captain Hink looked like he was trying hard to count to ten before yelling.

Rose didn't want to wake everyone on the ship, most of all Mrs. Lindson. "Yes," she said quickly, "a pillow would be very nice, Captain Lee Hink. Thank you for your thoughtfulness."

He stepped the rest of the way up to her hammock and then seemed to realize there would be a bit of situating to get the pillow under her head.

Rose held out her right hand. "Just don't jostle my left shoulder."

He leaned down. Instead of taking her hand, he placed his palm against her back and helped her sit, while simultaneously tucking the pillow down behind her head.

This close to him, Rose could smell the grease and oil and soot on his clothes. His breath carried the sharp honey-burn of alcohol, all of it made warmer by the very nearness of him.

For a flicker of a second, Rose wondered what it would be like to kiss his lips. And then the very thought of that, with him leaning over her in such an intimate manner, made her busy mind start thinking other things and asking other questions.

What would it be like if he just crawled into this hammock with her? What would it be like if he took his shirt off, if they were all alone on this airship with nothing but the darkness of the sky to shelter them? How would he feel, heavy and naked against her?

She blushed so hard, her head hurt.

"Are you all right, Miss Small?" he asked, pulling back enough that he could see every inch of her blush.

What was wrong with her? Thinking such things. And blushing!

"Fine," she managed. "Thank you, fine."

Captain Hink paused and studied her face, which only made her blush until her stomach stung.

"It's just, I'm not used to a man's pillow . . . I mean, I haven't seen a man's kindness so, um, personal lately." The last word sort of died on a whisper as she realized she was just babbling, and doing more to embarrass herself than to explain herself.

He bit his bottom lip, but couldn't keep the smile from turning into a grin.

"Well." He looked down at his boot for a second as if trying to decide something, then looked straight back at her. "Well."

His eyes were piercing in the low light of the lantern, the angles of his face like something out of a fine art museum. And that half smile curving his lips let her know he knew exactly what she'd been thinking, and approved.

Good God and glim. If she'd been in a more embarrassing spot in her whole life, she didn't know what it was. Still, Rose knew the best way to deal with a man was to step up to the dance. Stand up to him, and match him, move for move. Elbows out.

She raised one eyebrow, and held his gaze, daring him to call her out on her inappropriate thoughts.

"It's a pity," he said softly, "that you've not seen, personal, a man's *kindness*, lately," he said, keeping his smile down to something that looked platonic, though his eyes blazed with mischief. "If I'd known—"

"Good night, Captain Hink," Rose said firmly. She glanced past him to indicate he could just turn that smirk around and get to walking now.

"Good night, Miss Small."

He was still standing there. Still smirking.

She turned her head away and closed her eyes. After what felt like an eternity, he walked away, the sound of his bootheels against wood more and more distant. She opened her eyes again and watched as he moved out of the low lantern light.

The slight bell-tone sound of his palm gripping and releasing the metal overhead bars as if he were in the air instead of on the ground sang a soft counterpart to his retreating footsteps.

How could she have acted like such a fool? Maybe it was the laudanum muddling her mind. Or maybe she could blame it on the pain in her shoulder, which seemed to be getting worse.

The memory of his eyes, the angle of his jaw, that soft smile, the smell and nearness of his body all came rushing back at her and made her skin go tingly with itch.

It wasn't her injury that made her lose her wits around the captain.

It was the captain.

And now he'd had a good old laugh at her expense. She didn't know why it bothered her so much. She usually didn't give a hog's heel for what a stranger thought about her.

But there was something different about Captain Hink.

Maybe it was his airship. Maybe she was the kind of girl who turned into a doe-eyed fool when she met a man who could fly.

Rose considered that for a moment. It was possible. But they weren't flying, and she certainly didn't want to be moving off the ground right now. It was entirely possible it was just the man himself that tightened her spring.

She wasn't thinking straight, that was for sure. The pain was interfering with any logical thought. She needed the tea. She reached out for the cup on the shelf, but that only kicked everything up to hurting more.

She bit back a little groan and decided holding still was much better than trying to reach the tea.

"Would you like some tea, Rose?" Cedar asked quietly.

Had he been awake this whole time?

Of course he'd been awake this whole time. She and the captain had practically had their entire conversation on top of him. He must have heard it all. Every stuttering, embarrassing word.

"Yes," she said, miserable with pain, and now with a whole new kind of embarrassment.

Mr. Hunt got to his feet. He didn't make any noise at all moving in the dark. She'd always wondered about that. He had a way of fitting into his surroundings and taking on the silence of them, much like the natives of this land.

Maybe it was his wolf self that made him like that. Or maybe that was one of the reasons the Pawnee gods had chosen him to carry their curse.

He stood beside her, almost in the same place the captain had been standing. She hesitated to meet his gaze, but when she did, she discovered he wasn't smirking at her. His eyes were kind, searching her face and then taking the measure of the wound on her shoulder.

She didn't think she had the strength to hold out her hand again, but she didn't have to. Cedar Hunt brought the cup to her lips and helped her drink.

The tea was cold and so bitter she almost couldn't swallow it down, but she managed.

"How's the pain?" he asked, replacing the tea on the shelf.

"Not so bad I want to claw out of my skin, but not so good I want to stay in it so much either. What happened, Mr. Hunt?"

"Someone rigged explosives to the girl. The dead girl. I tripped some kind of spark. The whole house went up. And you were hit. I tried to block the blast—"

"I remember," she said. "Do I still have a piece of . . ." Her eyes went wide as she considered what might be embedded in her shoulder.

". . . tin," Cedar said.

"Tin," Rose said, relieved. "Do I have tin in my shoulder?"

"Yes. It's a very small key. The Madders think it's a part of the Holder."

"Oh." She tried to work that through. The medicine was already starting to rub the edges off her brain, sanding her thoughts down to dust. "Do you think it is?"

Cedar nodded. "If we had the device, it would draw the key out quick. But we don't yet. So we'll need to try and dig it out. Mae has the steadiest hand, and she's . . ." His voice tightened up on a growl, but he managed to breathe that down and continue in his scholar's tone. "She's unable to do that just now."

"What happened to Mrs. Lindson? Are the Madders here?"

"She used magic, cast some sort of spell on the captain. She's the reason we landed in one piece. But she fainted and hasn't come to. As for the Madders . . ." Cedar rubbed at the bridge of his nose as if weary from too many hours spent reading a difficult text.

"Last I saw, they were fighting their way through the unalives in Vicinity. Do you remember them rising?"

Rose nodded. She'd likely be nightmaring on it for years.

"The Madders said they can track us and find us. Captain Hink and his crew pulled us out of that mess."

"How . . ." Rose searched for the word. Couldn't quite find it. "Nice," she finally said. Her eyes were staying closed longer and longer between each blink. She didn't think she had much more time being awake. "Thank you, Mr. Hunt," she said softly. "For . . . keeping us safe."

"You're welcome, Miss Small."

For a second, Rose thought she heard a man in the distance curse, and then sleep came and took her to gentler lands.

CHAPTER TEN

Cedar knew Wil would keep watch during the few hours between night and dawn, but sleep did not come easily to him.

They were in trouble. No horses, no supplies, and winter coming on. Everything they'd had, they lost when the crew of the *Swift* pulled them on board. Cedar had some money and his guns. But they didn't even have a change of clothes, a scrap of food, or a spare pair of socks.

He'd been encouraged by Rose's waking and being mostly clear-headed, though in pain.

But Mae hadn't stirred since she'd cast that spell to bring the ship down softly. He didn't know when she would wake, and when she did, he had no idea what kind of condition she would be in for travel.

The captain had assured him that he would take them to the nearest town after the ship was repaired. Captain Hink didn't seem to be a man who'd likely prey upon the misfortunes of others. He'd seemed amiable enough in following Molly Gregor's instructions that they be treated as guests and passengers. But there was something more to him than just a man skimming the western glim fields.

He asked a lot of questions. About the Madders, about the railroad in Hallelujah, and was curious as to any rumors Cedar had heard about men dealing glim in these parts. Many of his questions pointed squarely to the Strange and roundabout to the Holder.

The Madders had said most people wouldn't recognize the Holder. Cedar bet Captain Hink would. Might even have been looking for it. Not that he'd exactly said as much.

Cedar's ability to sense the Holder gave him an edge on those others looking for it. Whether his sensitivity to the weapon was a product of the Pawnee curse in his bones, or pure bad luck, he didn't know and didn't care.

Being able to track it gave him a position of power if it came down to bargaining for their lives.

All he wanted was to get Mae back to her sisters before she was driven insane, and to see if the witches had a way to break his and Wil's curse. Along with that, he felt obliged to see that Rose Small was safe as she found her place in the world.

He hadn't thought much about his future past those things. Maybe he'd find a place in this world where he could start a life again with Wil. Help his brother rebuild a life he'd been cheated out of all these years.

They'd need land, home, and income of some kind.

He could turn back to his scholarly pursuits, or stay outside the hub of civilization and make his living bounty hunting for farmers and ranchers. He could marry.

The image of Mae Lindson came to him. He found himself savoring the memory of her touch as she tended his wounds in Hallelujah, remembered the warmth of her leaned full against him, his arms around her as she wept for her dead husband.

Like counting precious coins, he rolled through the moments he'd caught her, gathering herbs, or gazing at the sky, her face gentle and kind, her voice bent to song. He recalled the sweet sound of her all-too-rare laughter.

He'd been married. Loved his wife well and full. Never thought another woman would pull on his heart.

Mae Lindson called to him like a thirst to water. Not in the same way as his wife. The part of his heart that had loved her had died with her.

He thought, or maybe he only flattered himself in thinking, that some days when Mae was watching him, she was seeing him with the kind of desire he saw her.

He could build a life with her. If she'd have him. If he could still be the kind of man who lived for more than just surviving the rise and fall of the full moon.

The wind outside the airship gusted, and the frame and wood of the ship rocked and creaked a bit. Cedar knew the basic principles behind the steam airships. He'd heard the captain tell his men to drain the airbags—a good precaution so that they didn't get broadsided by a big gust that might send them tumbling in the night even if they were anchored and lashed.

And he'd heard Molly Gregor say the steam boiler was in good condition. But he knew it took more than steam to keep a ship in the air. It took glim.

Glim harvesters kept enough of their take to augment their fuel. But there were men and women who underestimated how much glim they'd need. They were not above stealing glim from other ships, even if that meant shooting the ship out of the sky.

Captain Hink had told Cedar that the two ships that had given them chase, the *Bickern* and the *Saginaw*, were likely pirates out to steal glim and pick over the bones of the crippled ship.

Cedar knew there was more he didn't say, secrets he didn't want Cedar to know.

Wil shifted, his claws scraping the floor. Cedar opened his eyes.

The captain's man, Mr. Seldom, was standing near the far window of the airship, bent a bit so he could see up and out the window. Cedar didn't know what he was looking for. It might be dawn already, but down in this crater, it was still dark as ink. He wasn't sure full noon would send down enough sunlight to sweep the shadows off the rocks.

Wil's ears twitched, and then Cedar heard it too. The far-off buzz and chug of an airship.

He couldn't tell how close by it might be, nor if it was either of the ships from yesterday.

Seldom shifted, his boot scuffing a soft hush against the floor.

Captain Hink rolled over in his cot and sat up.

Hink placed his hand around the nearest metal beam, and held very still. His head was tipped down as if waiting for the slight thrum of a heartbeat under his fingers.

The two men stood that way, without a twitch, for a full minute or so. Then, at the same time, they both moved. Mr. Seldom turned around and bedded back under his covers, pulling the scarves over his nose to keep the early cold off his face.

But Captain Hink looked over at Cedar. He seemed to consider something, then stood. He buckled his coat closed and dragged his scarf over his nose and mouth. He pointed to the door, pointed at the goggles Cedar wore at his neck, then pointed up.

Cedar stood. Captain Hink wanted Cedar's eyes on the sky. Wil took two steps to follow him, then looked back at Rose and Mae and chose to stay behind.

Cedar pushed his hat a little tighter against his head and followed Captain Hink out the door. The captain closed it as quickly as he could, keeping the cold wind out of the room.

The rocky ground was foggy with a frost that made walking a slippery process.

The ship had landed on a small level outcropping of stone that didn't seem wide or long enough for her. Like shooting a billiard ball into the corner pocket blindfolded, the ship's coming to a stop just a few yards from the solid stone wall of the cliffs behind it was amazing. The bluffs above them did a lot to hide the ship from the narrow window of sky.

It was a dizzying, claustrophobic feeling, like standing at the bottom of a well. The darkness of night lay all around them, while just the slightest pink light blushed the sliver of sky high above.

"Heard a ship pass over," Captain Hink said as he marched away from the *Swift*, casting glances at the sky. "Think you can get an eye on it?"

"Might," Cedar said. "Why are they following us?"

The captain clambered up a fall of stones and stood at the top. "Depends on who it is following us," he said. "I've made my enemies. A man who runs glim has no friends. He takes on a crew, and puts his trust in having a ship under his feet that can outrun or outgun his foes."

"Then why pick us up?"

Cedar watched the man shift his stance a bit. The wolf in his blood gave him better than average eyesight, so even here in the dark he could see how the captain paused. Likely he was working out a story to answer that question.

"Truth of it? It was an accident," he said. "I'd heard there might be something or someone I was looking for in Vicinity. When I saw the tipped wagon and angry mob, I got curious. You came pounding out of that jail with two women, one of whom was injured." He was still looking at the sky, but he shrugged his big shoulders. "Seemed the decent thing to do."

"What were you looking for?"

"Mostly same as you, I reckon," he said. "Looking for the Holder. Heard tales of it. Heard it's valuable. I'm a man who recognizes valuable opportunities when they present themselves."

"It's a weapon," Cedar said.

Captain Hink glanced down at him. "You know that for sure, or you seen it with your own eyes?"

"Both."

"A man who's seen the legendary Holder? That's what I call a valuable opportunity."

"Depends on whose hands it falls into."

"True. You suppose you're the sort of man who should be responsible for that kind of a weapon, Mr. Hunt?"

"No. And neither are you."

Captain Hink chuckled. "True. Wait." He held very still, his body as taut as a plucked string. "Do you hear her?"

Cedar Hunt did indeed hear the ship. Coming in from the south. He pulled his goggles over his eyes and peered at the sky. "How many ships know about this bolt-hole?" he asked.

"Too many. And they know the *Swift* can pocket it."

"Do they have charges?" Cedar asked.

"They shouldn't. Glim harvest isn't like shoveling for gold. No need for dropping dynamite when you're digging the skies."

"There she is," Cedar said. The airship skimmed the edge of the chasm, lights flashing from the windows in her sides like stars stuck on a wedge of night.

"Doesn't look like the *Bickern*, too small," Cedar said.

"The *Saginaw*?"

"I didn't get much of a look at her. Distinctions?"

"Narrow hull, three steamer, so you should be able to see three stacks if she shows her rump. She's an open deck, so you'll see sunlight between the hull and the airbags."

"What type of propellers on her?" Cedar asked.

"Quad. Two front, two rear."

"I see fans, front and rear, but I only see one stack . . . no, two." The ship tipped out of sight, but for a bare second he caught the flash of sunlight between the deck and bags. "Open hull."

"It's the *Saginaw*," Captain Hink said. "Hear the cough in her throttle?"

Cedar listened. The ship gave off the strange chugging and hum that all airships emitted. "No."

"Well, I do. It's Captain Smith. Don't know what I did to cook his cockles."

"Maybe he's looking for what you were looking for," Cedar said.

"The Holder?" Captain Hink started down the tumble of rocks, kicking pebbles free. "Don't think so. Most men think that's just a bluff. A contraption to keep men spooked and under the president's thumb."

"The president?" Cedar asked. "What's his part with the Holder?"

"He owns it, Mr. Hunt. Or so much as. This is his country, and to keep the peace, he has the right to control the weapons."

"And what makes you think the Holder's not a bluff?" Cedar asked.

"Besides you saying you've seen it? Records. Drawings sketched out by men learned in the wild sciences. I came across a man once who swore he'd seen it. Said it was headed out west in the possession of a peculiar aristocratic sort of man. A railroad tycoon."

He stopped next to Cedar. "The power a man would carry in the palm of his hand if he had the Holder is enough to take all the states, and the world beyond for the spoils."

"So how well do you know the president?" Cedar asked.

Captain Hink paused. He considered his answer just long enough for Cedar to know he'd hit a nerve. Regardless of what Captain Hink might say, he knew the president. Possibly had served under him. Maybe still did.

"Not well at all," the captain lied cheerily. "But if I get my hands on the Holder, I'm going to march right up the hill and sit down to tea with the gentleman himself.

"We'll need to patch the *Swift* enough to get her to a repair site," he continued. "Old Jack's isn't too far off. We'll have to do it quiet and slow. Crawl the cliffs and stay out of the clears, but we might make it by nightfall."

"Then what?" Cedar asked.

"Then I drop you and yours off at the nearest town, we shake hands and let our paths take us where they may."

Cedar didn't think there were towns in these parts big enough to offer up the mounts and supplies they'd need to make it to Kansas.

There might be a doctor for Rose, but if what Alun had said was true, they'd need the Holder to get that piece of tin out of her.

He'd promised the Madders he'd find the Holder for them. And he planned on doing just that. But he'd also promised he'd do anything necessary to get Rose the medical attention she needed. This was his last bargaining chip for her life.

"I can find it," Cedar said.

Hink had taken three strides back toward the *Swift*, but he stopped dead.

"Find what?"

"The Holder." He'd promised to find it for the Madders, but he had promised no man he'd give it into their possession. Wasn't much promising he'd give it to Captain Hink either. Only that he'd look and find. After that, there'd be bargains to be made.

"I've seen it. I've smelled it. I know what it is. I can find it."

Hink turned around, his head tipped just a little, as if he wasn't clear that he was hearing correctly.

"I'm to take your word on this, Mr. Hunt?"

"If you think it's a valuable opportunity."

"Huh." Captain Hink tucked his thumbs in the rigging gear at his hips. "What would it cost me to hire your services?"

"I find the Holder, and you take us to Kansas as fast as your ship can fly."

"To Mrs. Lindson's family?"

"That's right."

"Are you sure you have your bargain in order?" Captain Hink asked.

"I'm sure."

The captain started off toward the ship again. "Most men would ask for the payment first, and service second."

"I'm not most men."

"So there's a reason you want to find the Holder before taking Mrs. Lindson to her home?"

"Yes."

"And what reason is that, Mr. Hunt?"

"Rose Small will die if I don't."

Cedar was watching Hink in profile as he said those words. The captain had placed his hand on the ship's door. But his shoulders pulled back and his chin jerked up.

"Are you a doctor, Mr. Hunt?" he asked.

"No."

"Then why should I believe your prognosis?"

"Because she has a piece of the Holder in that wound."

"Impossible." He turned. "The Holder can't be broken. Each piece has been constructed so that nothing short of the fires of hell can melt it, no hammer can break it, and no vise can bend it. It's made of Strange elements, Mr. Hunt. It isn't just a tinker's toy."

For a man who had only seen sketches of it, he seemed to know an awful lot about it.

"It's broken into seven pieces," Cedar said, watching his eyes, the pace of his breathing. The Holder meant more to the captain than just a fancy bauble he could bargain with the president for over tea. The Holder was important enough to him that even implying it had been broken, tampered with, possibly destroyed, made him angry.

Not, not just angry. It made him fearful.

He had something on the line in finding the Holder, or in keeping it whole.

"Someone broke it into smaller bits," Cedar said. "This one piece of it, at least. Someone who found this section of it tinkered with it. And I don't think it's an accident. That piece inside Miss Small was meant to kill. I think it was meant to kill me."

"Are you so important that someone would destroy a weapon of that magnitude just to kill you? Isn't a bullet good enough to stop you, Mr. Hunt?"

"I bleed," Cedar said. "I can die. But I don't do either easily."

Hink narrowed his eyes, reassessing Cedar. Cedar waited. Let him make his own conclusions. Cedar had survived fatal wounds, from many of which he still carried the scars. The shift to wolf in the full moon sped up his healing to a remarkable degree.

He was a hard man to kill.

"Yet you'll put the Holder in my hands for a ride on my ship," Captain Hink said. "Not sure I'd trust a man who would hand over that weapon to the first sky rat he took ship with."

"You're not a sky rat," Cedar said. "You're the president's man."

Hink tugged the door open. "Says you." He stepped into the *Swift*, Cedar right behind him.

The relief from the cold was a blessing, even though the interior of the ship was barely warmer than the frigid morning. At least there was no wind.

"Tell me I'm wrong," Cedar said.

Captain Hink held his gaze for a long moment. Then he strode off to the front of the ship. "It's half past dawn, you lazy slacks," he said. "Get up, men, we have wings to mend."

The men were already up, already busy stowing bedrolls and strapping the cots to the walls and overhead storage. They didn't do much more than give the captain a glance, familiar with his moods as only a long-standing crew could be.

Wil, next to Rose's hammock, whined. Rose was awake, though she stared at the ceiling and held as still as she could. Her coloring was off, a strange gray paleness in the shadows of her face.

Cedar walked over to her.

"Mr. Hunt?" It was Mae.

Cedar glanced at Rose, who didn't appear to have heard Mae's soft whisper. She blinked, though, and was breathing steady, if a little shallow.

Maybe Mae could ease her pain with herbs.

He walked around the hammock to where Mae sat on the blankets on the floor. She had one hand on the tatting shuttle around her neck, the other clenched in a fist as if she were trying to hold on to the fabric of this waking world, worried that if she let go, she might slip back into dreams.

"Morning, Mrs. Lindson," Cedar said, kneeling in front of her.

It took her some time to respond. Some time to actually move her eyes away from staring at things he could not see in the middle distance between them to seeing him only an arm's reach in front of her.

"We're not in the sky," she said.

"We landed. Safe. You helped the captain with it. Do you remember?"

Her eyes flicked across his face as if trying to see him through so many other images. "We were falling."

"Yes. But we didn't fall. You cast a spell, Mrs. Lindson. You touched the captain."

"No," she said.

Cedar paused. She sounded afraid. He wasn't sure if she was telling him no, or saying it to the voices of the sisters in her head.

"I didn't touch him," she said. "Tell me I didn't touch him. Please."

He could lie. She would find comfort in it. But he didn't know what kind of spell she had cast.

"I'm sorry," he said. "But you did touch the captain. You were singing. Some sort of prayer. Then he brought the ship down for a safe landing here in the mountains."

She shook her head. "Is he alive? Is he breathing?"

"He's fine." Cedar clamped his teeth down before he said more. Why was she suddenly so concerned about the captain? He was a stranger, a rogue. For all they knew, he could be their enemy. And yet she showed more compassion to him than she had to Cedar in the last few weeks on the trail.

The killing need of the beast rose in him. The need to destroy the captain, to tear him to bloody shreds and leave him for the vultures to pick over. Just the thought of Mae caring for the captain set off a deep fury and jealousy, which he fought back.

No good would come of killing the only man who could repair the ship and fly them out of here.

No good would come of him being angry over Mae's interest in a man other than him.

The beast squirmed under his logic and, finally, relented, leaving his head filled with reasonable thoughts again.

"I . . ." Mae seemed to be trying very hard to pull herself into a calmer state. She relaxed her fist, but did not let go of the shuttle.

"I may have harmed him," she said quietly. "May have bound him to his ship in ways a man's mind cannot endure. I have done worse with magic. Such terrible things." Her eyes were bloodshot, and she was almost on the verge of tears, even though her voice was calm.

"He's clearheaded," Cedar said, still working to push his anger down. "I was just speaking with him outside. He's decided to repair the ship, then go for supplies. He's promised to take us to Kansas. To the sisterhood."

"Are you certain?" she asked.

Cedar gently placed his hand over her fist. "Of his promise? Not at all."

"No," she said. "That he's well. That he's sane."

"Yes. He shows no ill effects of what you did. If you hadn't used magic, I'm not sure we would have landed in one piece. You made the right choice, Mrs. Lindson."

Mae took some comfort in that, and even managed a small smile. "Good," she said. "Good, then. And Rose? Has she shown any signs of waking?"

"Last night, and she's awake now. Can you tend her?"

Mae nodded. Cedar helped her to her feet. She swayed just a little, her hands clutching his tighter. Then she bit her bottom lip and closed her eyes for a moment, setting herself. "What do I have to work with, Mr. Hunt? My satchel at least?"

Cedar bent and picked it up off the floor for her. "What else do you need?"

"I'm not sure. Let me see to her first." She brushed the stray locks of hair off her face and squared her shoulders.

Cedar glanced around the ship. The men were all gone, and so was Wil. He'd heard them head out the door. From the clatter and stomping coming from the roof area, he figured they were already working on repairs.

Captain Hink was in a hurry to leave this hidey-hole, for which Cedar was glad. Too easy to be trapped in such a tight squeeze. If the captain of the *Saginaw* decided to throw dynamite down just to cover his bets, there was every chance he'd bring down the walls and they'd be sealed in here.

And if the snows came, they'd be dead for sure.

Molly Gregor came out of the door at the far end of the ship. She had a teakettle in one hand. "Thought we could all use hot tea this morning. Take the bite out of the cold in this hole."

She didn't wait for an answer, but instead poured a cup for Cedar and Mae, and one for Rose too.

Cedar took it gratefully, and swallowed down the fragrant brew. "Mint?" he said.

"Picked some up when we were last out Chicago way." Molly pulled a cloth-wrapped bundle out of the leather bag at her hip. "I don't suppose you folks have much on you in the way of food and supplies," she said, offering a share of jerked meat and dried plums.

Cedar took some of the jerky and was happy to see Mae take both meat and fruit.

"We left all that we had behind," Cedar said. "Do you know where the captain will be taking the ship for repairs?"

"Probably Old Jack's," she said. "He makes a profit keeping his landing field open and his mouth shut. He'll have food, supplies. Medicines too," she said with a nod to Rose.

"Sounds like a good choice, then," Mae said softly.

Molly smiled, and it softened her blunt features. "It is. The captain might be a blowhard, but he's got a head full of clever."

"How long have you known him?" Cedar asked.

"Too long, Mr. Hunt," Molly said with a grin. "Now about Robert Gregor. How was he when you saw him?"

"He was well," Cedar said. "He and his wife have a son."

"Oh, that's good news! Another addition to the Gregor clan. What's his name?"

"Elbert," Rose said.

That got them all turning back to the hammock. Rose's eyes were closed, and her skin still looked an awful shade of gray.

"Elbert's a fine name," Molly said, glancing a question at Cedar.

"Miss Small had a fondness for Mr. Gregor," Cedar said. "He holds her in high esteem also. Showed her the way around his smithy."

"Did he now?" she asked. "Well, if you've been taught the secrets of metal by a Gregor, you're practically one of the family. Think of going into the smithing trade, Miss Small?"

Rose opened her eyes. Glossy with fever, they still carried a hint of her spunk. "Maybe. Although a boilerman on an airship seems a real fine life too."

"It is," Molly said. "Would you like to help me check over the boiler today?"

"Yes," she said, "I'd love to. Though I'm not sure how much help I can be, with this shoulder."

"Let me tend to it," Mae said. "I have some herbs. Black salve that might give you some ease."

"And while Mrs. Lindson sees to your shoulder, I certainly would like to hear more about little Elbert," Molly said.

The cabin door opened, letting in a gust of wind. Captain Hink leaned his head in, his hand gripping the top of the jamb. "Mr. Hunt. Do you know your way around a hammer?"

"I can do my share," he said.

"Good. We could use an extra set of hands. Molly, when will she be up to steam?"

"She'll be ready to go by the time you get her feathers mended," she said. "Are we going to have all fans on line?"

"Mr. Seldom's never let us down before," Hink said, ducking back out the door. "We'll be in the air before noon. Mr. Hunt?" he called.

Cedar glanced one last time at Mae. She was unwrapping the compress on Rose's shoulder, frowning at what she saw there.

"We'll need more medicines than what I have on me," Mae said. "It looks like an infection is setting in. Do you have any more hot water, Miss Gregor?"

"Of course."

"It's fine," Rose said. "I'll be fine."

But Mae glanced up at Cedar and gave him a slight shake of her head. "As soon as we could be on our way would be best," she said.

Cedar didn't wait any longer. He strode out the door and then shut it behind him.

Morning had chalked clouds across the sky and brought out enough light that it was a fair share easier to see inside this pit.

Still, it was cold and wet, some areas still slick with frost. It was like walking across the bottom of a grave.

"Harbor here for too long and this will be nothing more than a death trap," Captain Hink said. "If those clouds bring rain or snow, we won't be able to launch. The faster we fix her, the faster we fly."

"Tell me what you need me to do," Cedar said.

Hink handed Cedar a hammer. "Take a turn on the rivet work with Guffin," he said. "And pray we don't get rain."

CHAPTER ELEVEN

epairs on the *Swift* were taking longer than Captain Hink Cage had hoped for. Not because the men were slacking. Guffin, Ansell, and Seldom were working as quickly as they could. And quite to Hink's surprise, so was Mr. Hunt, who proved to be a ready hand at all levels of repair he put his effort toward.

"Ever work a ship, Mr. Hunt?" Captain Hink asked as Cedar crimped the seam to align the rivet hole in the tin skin envelope.

"Not an airship." Mr. Hunt hammered the bucktail of a rivet into place. "But I worked the yards as a young man."

"Hup," Guffin called. He tossed a hot rivet off the small forge and up to Mr. Ansell, who sat the other side of the rip tight as a bug in honey. Ansell caught the rivet in an iron cone, then plucked it free with tongs.

Cedar waited for Ansell to set the rivet before hammering it down tight. Cedar leaned back against the rope rigging that let him latch and crawl about the curve of the ship like a man climbing a mountainside.

"I didn't need more than a year before I decided the sailing life was not for me," he said.

The *Swift* had taken more than one shot to the main envelope, and it had taken a good part of the day to mend those tears. They were on the last rip, placing a patch more than doing any final work. The thin sheet of patch metal should be enough to hold her against the winds just so far as to Old Jack's.

"What life did you go looking for, Mr. Hunt?"

Cedar was silent as he pounded another rivet down tight. "The university. Teaching."

"You're a long way from that sort of living," Hink said, shouldering the pulley line to force the strut of the fans into place so Mr. Seldom could set the bolts proper again.

Cedar stared up at the wedge of sky above them, then back at the mostly black walls. "Yes, I am."

"Don't sound displeased about it," Hink grunted, setting his heels to hold the line.

Neither of them spoke for a bit while Hink held muscle on the propellers for Mr. Seldom, and Mr. Hunt hammered another rivet into the patch.

Finally, Mr. Hunt spoke. "There's things about this life I'd never had in the university. Not all of them bad."

"Funny how things work out that way sometimes," the captain said.

"So it is," Cedar agreed.

"That's it, Captain," Ansell hollered as he hooked the iron cone to his belt rig. "She's as tight as we can make her."

"Then tell Molly Gregor to fill the bags. We'll be dragging sky within the hour."

"Aye, Captain." Ansell clambered down the outside of the ship, unlatched his harness from the ropes, then dropped a good six feet to land beside the ship.

Hink just shook his head. Man was unafraid of heights or the falling from them, and seemed most alive anytime he was executing some high-wire stunt. Mr. Ansell was a man born to walk the skies.

"About time," Mr. Guffin grumbled as he got to work on packing gear and setting the small forge to cool.

Mr. Hunt lowered himself down the side of the ship to the ground, then unlatched gear. He might not be as sure-footed as Ansell, but he still moved like he'd been crawling over airships all his life.

Moved through the rocks and tumble like he was born to them too.

Only other sort of man Hink had ever seen be quite so comfortable in every environment he fell upon was the native people.

He didn't know if Mr. Hunt carried native blood in his veins, though his coloring leaned toward it far more than Hink's own yellow and blue.

Cedar glanced off, suddenly still as the stones around him. His hands were held out to the side as if the wind told things to his fingers that ears and eyes couldn't know.

A slight movement in the distance caught Hink's attention. The wolf, Wil, coming this way. It had something in its mouth. Looked like a goat.

The wolf stopped. Cedar wasn't watching the wolf. He was watching the sky.

Hink heard it. The hard chug of propellers pushing over the range. Sounded like she was working against the wind. Maybe against the rain.

It could be raining out there and windy enough that the rain couldn't fall into this hole.

Captain Hink hoped he was wrong, but they wouldn't know the flying conditions until they put their nose over the edge of this rock. And they weren't going anywhere until they were sure that ship out there was gone hunting different ground.

Hink waited. Even Mr. Seldom stopped tinkering with his tools near the fans and leaned back so he could catch a gander at the sky.

The buzz faded off, growing faint, then coming in and out of hearing like she was threading peaks, the echo of her engines soon too quiet to stir the silence.

"Mr. Seldom," Hink said. "Tell me we have wings."

"She'll fly," Seldom said. What he didn't say, what he didn't have to say, was he didn't know how long or how far she would take them.

A drop of rain hit Hink on the shoulder. Another followed. Captain Hink swore as he looped the pulley ropes and helped Mr. Seldom remove the repair braces and tackle. They were going to have to fly her out wet.

Wet, wounded, out of the bottom of hell's well. Low on fuel, heavy on passengers, with airships scouting for their smoke.

Some days there wasn't enough glim in the sky to make this job easy.

"Inside," Hink yelled to Cedar and the wolf. "We'll be launching as soon as Molly can give us steam."

Cedar Hunt took the goat from the wolf and shouldered it as he strode to the ship, the wolf loping at an easy pace by his side. In the shuttered light, Cedar looked taller, inhuman, like a hunter out of legend, or some kind of warrior of old come to put the land right.

It was just a moment, a flicker of a thought. Then Hink shook his head. Those kinds of fool thoughts were the imaginings that had sent him down a life path even his soiled-dove mama hadn't approved.

With wild thoughts, and wilder blood, Hink had been a terror growing up. Some days he wasn't even sure there was enough sky and earth together to give him room to shout.

"Stop dreaming," Seldom said as he slapped Hink on the back. Hard. "You're all wet."

"Wasn't dreaming," Hink said, following his second into the ship. "Was figuring how much money I'm about to lose getting us out of this knothole."

"Money?" Guffin called from up near the navigation. "Whose money are you spilling, Captain?"

"There's only one way she'll fly," Hink said. "Steam and gears alone won't do it down this hellhole. No wind, no launch point. No luck. Nothing but glim."

"We're gonna glim-lift," Guffin grumbled. "There goes a season's profit."

"I appreciate your practical concerns, Mr. Guffin, but the only men glim won't profit are dead men. And I refuse to die in this pit. Mr. Hunt, Mrs. Lindson, and Miss Small, be sure that you're seated on the floor, back against the wall, and buckled tight. Mr. Seldom, see that our passengers are safely secured and have a breathing mask to share."

Hink strode to the rear of the ship to check Molly and the boilers. He braced himself for the heat as he spun the lock and stepped through the metal door. The slap of heat against his skin was thick as in a Sunday bathhouse.

It always surprised him how compact the *Swift*'s boilers were compared to those of other ships. Even so, the engine took up most all of the stern of the ship, making this space a collection of brass and copper, tubes, valves, iron, and rivets. In the right light—hell, in every light—the engine looked like a jewel cut and cast to sit a king's crown.

"How's our fuel, Molly?" Hink asked.

Molly closed the fire box door and stepped back to get a better look at a valve near the steam stack. "You taking her to Old Jack's?"

"Thinking on it." Hink leaned against the corner of the toolbox, and folded his arms over his chest, watching her work the drafts.

"How fast and how high?" she asked.

"I was thinking low and slow."

"Fuel lasts longer the higher we go," she said. "Some reason we need to creep?"

"Think the *Saginaw*'s out there still looking for us. You have any idea why he's on our tail?"

She wiped her forearm over her forehead, slicking away sweat. "Last I heard, Captain Smith had gone up north toward the Big Horn Mountains to winter. I have no idea why he's back this way. You tell Mr. Hunt you're a U.S. Marshal yet?"

"Who says I'm gonna?"

"Why wouldn't you? You trust the man, don't you?"

"Not sure that I do."

Molly hooked the wrench off her tool belt and turned to give him a full consideration. "You don't distrust the man. Seldom told me you let him man the cannon."

"Seldom talks too much," Hink grumbled.

"If my kinsman thought highly enough of Mr. Hunt to give him his seal, then I say he's trustworthy."

"Rings can be stolen, lost in a game of cards, swallowed by a fish. . . ."

Molly stuck her fist on her hip and waved the wrench close enough to his nose that he had to pull his head back a bit to keep from getting hit with it.

"What is it in that head of yours, Lee?" she asked. "You trust the man, maybe even like him to a degree, but you won't cotton to it? Don't you think he's looking after the best interests of those two women he hauled up out of that . . . that nightmare town?"

"There's something about him don't sit right with me is all," he said. "The way he treats Miss Small doesn't have anything to do with it."

"Miss Small?" Molly pursed her lips and shook her head. "I didn't say nothing about Miss Small in particular, now did I? How did Mr. Hunt treat Miss Small? You mean when he gave her the tea to ease her pain after you'd gone over there and made a damn fool of yourself?"

"I was trying to make her rest more comfortable," he started, his voice rising. "And don't put words on my tongue. This doesn't have anything to do about how he treated Miss Small. I don't care how he treats her, or how much she likes him."

"You're sweet on her!" she said, surprised.

"Take that back, Molly Gregor," he warned.

Molly hung the wrench back on her belt, laughing. "I haven't heard that tone out of you since Sally Winkle."

"What tone?"

"The one that says you don't know how hard you've already fallen for a woman." Molly pulled her gloves out of the pocket of her overalls and put them on, her expression daring him to tell her she was wrong.

"I think you might have boiled your brains sitting back here so long," he grumbled. "I have barely spoken to the woman. For Pete's sake, she's barely been conscious. For all I know, she can't tell the difference between me and a fence post."

"Tell yourself whatever you like, Paisley Cage. But that Miss Small is thrumming in your blood, and you won't be quit of her in any easy way."

"I can be quit of any woman I choose. I've proved that often enough."

"Sure you have. The women you've caroused with. But not the few you've loved. Why, you pined for more than a year when Sally turned you down for that city-slicker lawyer."

Hink opened his mouth, then closed it on a scowl. "I came back here asking you to give me fire to fly, Molly Gregor," he said with as much calm as he had in him, "not to waste my time with crazy talk."

She gauged his mood. Read him as easy as one of her dials needling to red. He didn't know why he was always so see-through to the woman. It was a curse.

"You'll have the fire you need," she said. "Which you can thank two women for. Me, and Miss Small."

"What's Miss Small got to do with the fire in my engine?"

Molly's mouth quirked up. "Fire in *your* engine, Captain? Thought I just made it clear why she's got you het up. You like the woman. As for the *Swift's* engine, you can thank Miss Small for spotting a leak I've been trying to chase down since we were stuck in Texas. She's a fine hand at tinkering. Wants to be a boilerman someday, and I think she'd be damn fine at it."

"Because you put nonsense in her head," he groused.

"No. Because she loves steam and loves the sky, glim help her. I want you to promise me you'll tell Mr. Hunt and Miss Small you're a marshal once we hit Old Jack's. I don't like lying to good folk. It's not the Gregor way."

"This ship flies my way, not the Gregor way." Hink tugged a pouch out of the inside of his shirt. He slipped free a small glass vial with the cork tamped tight and waxed. The eerie, beautiful green mist light of glim shone out from the glass. "We've got less than an eighth of the vial," he said. "Make it count." Then he pushed off the toolbox and headed for the door, ducking one of the lower steam pipes.

"Tell them," she said. "Or I will."

"Just give me an engine," Hink said. "And if you can spare some heat to the cabin, I'm sure our passengers—all of them—would appreciate it."

Hink shut the door behind him. Seldom leaned just a ways from the door on the other side, a rope in one hand, tied to nothing.

He was staring at their guests. Well, he was staring at the wolf, who had his ears back and his teeth bared at Seldom.

"Problem?" Hink asked Mr. Hunt, who was standing between Mr. Seldom and the wolf.

"He doesn't like being tied up," Mr. Hunt said. "I think you should hand me that rope, Mr. Seldom." Cedar extended his hand back for the twine, but didn't take his eyes off the wolf.

Seldom didn't look worried. Course Seldom never looked worried. Hink figured the day Death came knocking on his door, Mr. Seldom would just roll his eyes and tell him to wipe his feet.

Seldom placed the rope in Cedar's hand and waited, watching the wolf. Guffin and Ansell up front rested their hands on their guns, but had enough brains between the two of them not to pull their weapons. For one thing, the last thing the *Swift* needed was more holes in her side; for another, it'd be too easy to hurt someone else in this small space aiming for the wolf.

"We're all going to be strapped in," Cedar said as if he were talking to a man, not a beast. "And you're going to be strapped in too. As I understand it, this is going to be a hard takeoff. Am I correct in that, Captain Hink?"

"That's right. We usually launch with wind or a glide. Sometimes a clear runway. But we don't have any of those things. The only way we'll clear the walls of this hole is by glim. And that means straight up. All the crew buckles in."

He didn't know if he was talking to Cedar or to the wolf, but it looked like the wolf was paying close attention to each word he said.

And then the wolf's ears pulled up off the back of his head and he closed his mouth around the snarl he'd been wearing. But those eyes still burned with brass fire. There was a hatred to the beast. A hatred of being trapped.

"Where do you want to be, Wil?" Cedar asked.

The wolf paced over toward the women and sat right next to Rose Small, who was glassy-eyed and leaning on Mae next to her.

Rose put her hand out and patted the wolf's back. "Good choice," she whispered. "Best seat in the house."

Cedar nodded, and glanced from the wall behind Wil to the rope in his hand. "I could rig something up," he said, turning to Hink. "But if you have an extra harness like the one you and your crew wear, I'd be obliged. He doesn't have hands to grip like the rest of us."

Seldom's eyebrows took a turn skyward, but Captain Hink just started walking to the wheel of the ship. "Seldom, get the spare out of the box. I assume you can find a suitable way for your brother to wear it, Mr. Hunt?"

"I'm sure I can manage."

"Good. Be quick with it, and see you tie yourself down tight too. We're done sitting. It's time to catch sky."

Captain Hink latched his own harness to the ceiling bar, his boots snug under the floor straps. He took a breath and a good half minute to settle his mind and his resolve. Flying the ship under bad weather was never easy. Flying her broken, under bad weather and glim, was the sort of thing a man didn't live to brag about.

"Just give me your wings, darlin'," he said softly. "I'll be gentle."

The bell rang three times. Molly had her glim-stoked and ready to go.

"Are we ready, men?"

"Aye, Captain," all three voices shouted.

"Passengers, are you secure?" he asked.

"Aye, Captain," Cedar Hunt called back.

"All steam to the sky," he said.

Hink gripped the wheel, and a sudden awareness slipped over him. The ship wrapped around him like a second skin. He could count the rocks beneath the landing gear, could feel the rattling cold of rain striking against tin. For a moment or two, he imagined he could stretch his arms and feel the sails unfurl.

"Captain?" Mr. Guffin's voice broke the thrall.

He blinked, then rubbed one hand over his face just to remind himself that he was flesh and blood, not tin and steam. His imagination had a way of taking hold of him, but never like this, never this real. And now was the worst of times to be dreaming on his feet

It was a strange thing. A worrying thing. He took another breath to clear his head.

"All go, gentlemen." Hink put both hands back on the wheel. The sense of the ship closing in around him came strong and clear again.

This is what it had felt like when the witch was singing. This is what it had felt like when he'd landed them whole.

Maybe she'd cast a lasting sort of spell. Hink wasn't sure that he liked it. Right now, he'd deal the hand given him, no matter how strange.

The ship wrapped around him, and all the same, he felt himself stretching out as if he were putting her on like a familiar coat.

He was the ship. But he was very much still the man.

And he was going to make the witch tell him what she'd done to him, and his ship, once they hit clear sky.

Captain Hink gave her throttle, just enough to get the propellers up to speed. He could feel the heat and power of the engines beneath his feet and drumming in his chest like a second pulse. And he knew, without needing the ring of the bell from Molly Gregor, that the glim was in the firebox and the heavens were his to claim.

"Trim the sails tight, Mr. Ansell," he called out. "And ready the rudder, Mr. Guffin. We're launching in three . . . two . . . one."

The crew fell to their tasks. Captain Hink tipped her nose up, and let her go. The *Swift* shot toward the sky, the power of steam and glim mixing like a heady rush of whiskey and wine. Hink yelled out in joy. This was what she was built for. This was what he was meant for. Speed, flight, freedom.

Ansell was singing opera. Guffin was yelling about overhangs and rocks and the walls coming too damn close. But all Hink could feel was the sting of rain against his skin, the brace and heat of steam pushing him forward, and the intoxicating rush of flight lifting him higher and higher heavenward.

He didn't need Guffin telling him where the walls were. He could see them, he could feel them, leaning in, rushing by, sharp and cold and deadly. He shot the gap, calling for Ansell to angle the verticals and spinning to skin the air off the walls.

The sky finally, finally fanned open above him, that crack of wide wet grayness spreading out to welcome him as if he were diving upward into a stormy sea.

Through the darkness he flew, through the dragging, clawing rain, with nothing but the hope of light, of air on the other side of the sky if he could just break through.

And then she punched up, out of the clouds, into the cold blue of the sky, sunlight pounding down in flat white light. Higher, higher. She strained for the glim fields that wavered with tantalizing ribbons of soft green light above them.

Hink longed to hit that field, to bathe in the soft whips of glim that shimmered in long, glowing rivers just beyond their reach. He knew that without the trawl set to net, they'd just break through the glim and turn it to a mist that disappeared on the wind.

They didn't have time to harvest, didn't have the gear ready if they did.

And it was too cold up here, too hard to breathe for long.

Hink dragged his breathing gear over his face, and hoped Mr. Seldom had equipped their passengers with masks.

"Look for company, Mr. Seldom," Hink called out. "Give us glide, Mr. Ansell." The sails released and the *Swift* steadied her climb, Hink easing the throttle and hitting the bell to tell Molly to ease the draft.

The *Swift* leveled out. If any other airship was flying right now, they'd be above the clouds. Flight with no visibility among the craggy and treacherous peaks of the mountain range was plain suicide.

And Hink was on the shiny side of positive that none of the rock rats who skiffed these mountains would be fool enough to risk their life flying blind.

Still, Mr. Seldom walked the interior of the ship, breathing tube clattering against the overhead beams as he gripped the bars and took a long, hard look out each window.

He pulled down his breathing mask. "Clear sky," he announced.

"Good," Hink said, glancing at the compass set in the console before him. "We're going down through again in short order. I'm going to hot-flume it over to Turnback Junction, then duck under the clouds at a crawl."

"You want lanterns?" Ansell asked.

"No. I'll bring her in blind."

"Crazy," Guffin muttered, placing his mask securely over his nose and mouth.

"What's that, Mr. Guffin?" Hink asked.

Guffin pulled the mask down. "I said you're crazy." He placed his mask back over his mouth, then pulled it down and added, "Captain."

"And yet you signed on with my crew," Hink said. "Not sure that speaks against your reasoning or mine, Mr. Guffin. Let's take her down easy. Keep your eyes peeled for shadows."

Hink knew his crew hated flying blind, but Hink had always been good at it. He knew this range and could fly it on compass alone.

But he was surprised to discover that even though his eyes showed him flat gray clouds with more gray wisping through it, he knew the shift of wind, and could feel the space around the ship. If there was another steamer nearby, he'd feel it like a hot exhale on the back of his neck.

More witchery. Or maybe the same. Right now, he wasn't going to argue its usefulness.

Guffin had taken to swearing again. Alphabetical, in French. Ansell was humming a slow song.

Mr. Seldom walked up behind Hink and glanced at the compass, then swung back to take a heading on the maps. They were low enough that they were surrounded by clouds. But not quite low enough to be battered against the peaks.

Old Jack's wasn't too far off. All they had to do was pray for a south wind to guide them true.

"Do we need to remain buckled, Captain Hink?" Cedar Hunt asked after a while of drifting level.

"We're on an even keel," Hink said, "but I'd rather you hold tight. Hard winds make threading these cliffs a tricky proposition. Might find ourselves knocked askew with no notice."

Mr. Hunt seemed to take that suggestion with more than a lick of salt. He unlatched and started rummaging through some of the shifted contents near him and the womenfolk.

"Something one of my men can provide you with, Mr. Hunt?" Captain Hink asked, perturbed that he hadn't listened to his advice.

"Just making Miss Small more comfortable."

And that's when Hink realized the soft sound on the edge of his hearing wasn't the wolf whining. It was Miss Small moaning.

"We'll be on solid ground soon," Hink said. "Just a little farther now."

He didn't know why his heart had suddenly sped up, nor why he felt anxious for the wind and glim to hurry and bring them quickly and safely to Old Jack's.

Could be just the thought of Miss Small in pain bothered him. Could be Molly was right about his feelings.

Could be he couldn't afford to worry about that right now. Not flying this kind of terrain.

He poured his concentration into flying. Watching for the rise and fall of cliff and valley, skirting the edge of plains and urging the ship to hold on and hold strong until he got them down safe and whole.

He was so wrapped in the shift of the *Swift's* bones, the drag of rain on her skin, the press and burn of glim and coal, that he didn't even notice Mr. Seldom standing beside him until he put his hand on the wheel.

"Ladyfinger Falls." Seldom pointed.

The glitter of white among the shadow of the cliff was the clear marker that Turnback Junction was just below. Hink nodded. He'd been flying by instinct, flying by feel, more of his thoughts upon the ship around him than on the destination he was headed for.

He could have missed that marker. Could have traveled the wind until there wasn't glim to keep her afloat or land her soft. It was a startling realization.

Lost in a mountain range with winter coming on and almost no supplies was no way to end a flight.

"Mr. Seldom," Hink said, his voice sounding odd, as if he'd forgotten to use it for days instead of just the handful of hours they'd been in the air. "How far out would you think we are from Old Jack's?"

Guffin stopped swearing: Chinese, now, and Ansell stopped singing. Both men looked over at him like he'd just turned into a toad.

He was the captain. He'd never once asked Seldom where he was in the air in all the years they'd run together.

The Irishman didn't hesitate. "Twenty miles due northeast. Don't think the rain's going to let up."

Hink nodded. That's what he'd thought too, but he needed to hear another man's judgment. "Then see to it the torches are ready. And see to our passengers' comfort in any way you can."

Seldom paused a moment.

"Yes?" Hink asked.

"Two bells rang about five miles back."

Two bells meant they were nearly out of fuel. He'd need to coast the *Swift* and make the wind and steam last as long as he could.

"Thank you, Mr. Seldom."

"You losing your mind, Captain?" Guffin called out. "'Cause I'll fly this tub if you ain't right-headed."

"I'm plenty right in the head to know I'd never turn the wheel over to you, Mr. Guffin," Hink said. "We're cutting speed. Earn your keep and mind the gears."

Hink chewed on the inside of his cheek to try to keep more of his thoughts out of the ship, and into the flying of her. Every time he felt his mind slipping, wandering off like it was dreaming itself into the wind, he'd shift his grip on the wheel, wipe his face, or bite at his lip.

Twenty miles seemed to crawl by below. It was heading into evening now, and raining hard. There hadn't been enough sunlight in the whole day to stretch a thimble's shadow.

"We're close enough," Hink finally said. "Seldom, Lum, light the torches and set them strong. There's a hell of a lot of rain. We don't want to be missed."

Seldom and Ansell each grabbed up three torches from the overhead rack near the doors and lit them. Greasy fire that stank of creosote lit up the interior of the ship, flickering glint and glow across the walls.

Then each man opened a door on the side of the ship, latched harness lines to the hand bar and stepped out on the running board to set the torches tight in the exterior clamps.

Three torches on each side was a sign to Old Jack that the ship coming in was friendly, broken, and willing to pay for repairs and shelter.

Seldom and Ansell ducked back into the ship, dripping with rain. They shut the doors tight. All of the crew looked out the windows. They needed to see a torch go up to say they could land. If there wasn't a torch somewhere in the hidden tumble of stone and flats of the maze Old Jack called home, they'd have to move on.

Old Jack only had two ways to greet a ship. A torch to wave it in to land, or a cannon to drop it from the sky.

"There!" Ansell pointed. "Torch at eleven o'clock, Captain."

"Good eyes, Mr. Ansell."

A second, third, and forth torch lit up, creating a square. That was where they'd need to land and lash.

"Reverse engines, men," Hink said. "Bring our lady down soft and easy."

There wasn't much steam left in the boiler. They'd been drafting glim vapors for the last five miles at least. Which meant there was no easy way to put the ship down. But Hink intended to get her rested with the least amount of injury to her, and to those on board.

The wind let off a bit, but the rain was aiming to make it a dangerous proposition. None of Old Jack's landing fields were generous in size. Though the *Swift* was a small vessel, Hink didn't envy a captain of a larger vessel trying to touch down in this port.

With more pitch and yaw than he'd like, Hink tucked the

Swift down, her patched landing gear rolling, then catching at the rocky soil.

"Lash her tight, men. We don't want to dive the cliff by morning."

Guffin, Ansell, and Seldom were already out the door before the ship had more than a heartbeat on the ground. Usually Hink would be right behind them, making sure his ship was secure.

But instead he stood there, transfixed, his hand on the wheel.

The sensation of the ship around him was still there, but not as strong as when he was in the air. He felt Molly dousing the flumes, and the cooling of the boiler and pipes like a slowing heartbeat, as if he were breathing from a hard run and sleep was waiting just around the corner for him.

"Captain Hink," Cedar Hunt said, from close enough that Hink knew he'd been standing there a while, "I think you're wanted outside."

Hink let go of the wheel, one hand at a time, his fingers lingering just a second longer against the smooth wood before he was no longer touching the ship. The feel of her around him, the sensation that he and the ship were tied together closer than skin to bone, slipped away with the contact.

He turned. For a moment, he was just a man again. Hot in his damp clothes, weary on his feet, and much more tired than he usually was after a flight.

Whatever the witch had done to make him aware of the ship, it took something out of a man to endure it.

Mrs. Lindson stood near Miss Small, who sat, her eyes closed, at the rear of the ship. The wolf was untied and pacing in front of them.

He didn't see Molly.

The rain spit like gravel against the ship, and over that, he heard his name.

"Captain Hink, you'll come out of your ship with your hands up, or I'll blow that bucket out from under your feet."

Hink would know that rusted voice anywhere. It was Old Jack.

"Do you want me to go with you?" Cedar asked.

"No need," Hink said, unbuttoning his coat and pulling a small bag that might hold tobacco or coins out of his pocket.

"I just need to make between Old Jack and I, an understanding." He drew his revolver, then strode out the door.

CHAPTER TWELVE

G eneral Alabaster Saint paced in front of the tent. Mr. Shunt had insisted that they erect a space for him apart from the barracks, the mess hall, the hangar, and General Saint's quarters.

They had done so, and just after dawn Mr. Shunt had set about his task.

Private Bailey was the first man to enter that tent. He screamed for an hour. At the end of that hour, he had been carried out, weak and exhausted. And with a new hand attached where before there had been nothing but a stump.

A hand that worked as if it were his own. Except for the dull silver stitchwork around the wrist, and the slightest clicking sound when he curled his fingers into a fist, it would pass for a living thing.

"Does it please you?" Mr. Shunt asked from the shadows inside the tent door.

"Will he survive it?"

Mr. Shunt spread his hands. "Some will not. The strong become stronger."

"Will he survive it?" Alabaster Saint asked again.

"That one?" Shunt narrowed his eyes and lifted his head as if he could see through the walls of the barracks where Bailey rested. As if he could see all the way through the man to the nightmares beneath his skin. "Yes." He exhaled.

"I will be pleased when all the others are done."

General Saint turned on his bootheel and strode off to his office. "Lieutenant Foster, to me," he barked.

Foster fell into step behind the general.

A third of the Saint's militia had been crippled from the war. Men who held a grudge against the war made for excellent fighters against the standing rulers.

The general waited until Lieutenant Foster had shut the door before turning.

"I do not trust that man," the Saint said, pacing. "You will see that there is a gun on him at all times."

"Yes, sir."

"Report to me when he has finished his task."

"Yes, sir." Lieutenant Foster turned toward the door, then hesitated. "Sir? I suggest you put Sergeant Pearson on duty."

"Why is that, Lieutenant?"

"To allow me to be repaired next."

Saint frowned. "Plainly, Foster."

"I'll let him have at my foot. By the time he's through the men, I'll be out of my cot to hold a gun to his head while he repairs your eye."

"Did I say I was going to let him repair my eye, Lieutenant?"

"No, sir."

Foster did not move, did not shift his steady gaze. He knew Alabaster as well as any man who walked this earth. He knew just how much the Saint would sacrifice for the chance to have his vision back full again.

"Fine. Tell Pearson to stand your place," Alabaster said. "You've just earned yourself a ticket to the front of the line, Foster."

"Yes, sir."

"Dismissed."

Foster opened the door. The hoarse yell of the soldier under Mr. Shunt's mercies carried on the thin morning air.

Foster tipped his head up and smiled slightly before shutting the door behind him.

General Saint finally settled behind his desk and scanned the map spread out across it. Twenty spies, and still no message. If Mr. Shunt could find Marshal Cage, then they would have no problem capturing him, nor any hesitation in destroying him. All they needed was a scent to go on.

The low rumble of an airship coming up from the south slipped past the edge of his hearing. He waited until the fans came closer, the echo off the mountains rolling so that it sounded like four ships were arriving instead of just one.

A knock on his door rapped out.

"Enter."

A young soldier walked into the room. "Airship coming in, sir."

"I can hear that, Private. Who is it?"

"It's the *Powderback*, sir."

That was one of Les Mullins's ships. He'd sent Mr. Mullins out to gather information on Marshal Cage.

"See that she sets anchor. Bring Mr. Mullins to me immediately, but any remaining men with him are to stay on the ship."

"Yes, sir." He stepped out and Saint heard the rousing of men ready to catch lines to hold the ship steady.

He pulled out his pipe and tamped in tobacco, lighting it and waiting for Mr. Mullins to arrive. Got through a bowl before a knock on the door was quickly followed by the same private stepping through and holding the door wide.

Two soldiers carried a litter. And on that litter was Les Mullins. The parts of him outside the blanket were bandaged. The parts of him that weren't bandaged were pale and sweat-slick.

"Do you have news for me, Mr. Mullins?" Alabaster asked.

The man swallowed hard as if trying to set his words rightways in his throat. "Marshal Cage. Found him."

"Where?" the Saint asked.

"Stump Station. Down in the Bitterroots. Running glim."

Alabaster leaned back in his seat and puffed on his pipe. "Glim? Wouldn't think he had the guts for it."

"Payment," Les Mullins said.

"Your payment?" Alabaster sat forward, the wooden chair crackling as he shifted his weight. "Of course, Mr. Mullins."

He strolled over to the man.

The bandages around Les Mullins's neck and chest were brown with dried blood. His head was wrapped too, both of his eyes going black.

"It appears you have made a poor acquaintance of someone, Mr. Mullins," Alabaster said. "Who left you in this condition?"

"Hink Cage," Mullins growled.

Alabaster stared down at him. "Then I will give you your reward. After you bring Hink Cage to me. Until then your word is no better than a rumor."

"My blood's your proof. He shot me and that damn Irish broke my hand. They would have finished the job if that raft of his hadn't been shot at."

"Raft?"

"He's flying the *Swift*. You want him, find the fastest ship in the western sky. He'll be on it. Now, give me my damn pay."

The general ignored the rancor of his tone. He paced to stare out the window that faced the dock where three airships waited.

He did indeed want Marshal Cage. The man had disgraced him, and stood trial against him to end his military and political career. And now Cage was working for the president, spying on the glim trade.

Marshal Cage was a dangerous man to leave wandering these hills while the Saint built his network of glim harvesters, trade posts, and militia who would join his rebellion against the east.

He did not want the president's eyes prying into his plans.

"Unfortunately your services are inadequate and incomplete, Mr. Mullins. I sent you to bring him back with you, which you have not done."

"Like hell," Mullins wheezed. "You wanted to know where he'd hid himself, and now you do. I'll take my money."

"What you will do, Mr. Mullins, is allow my doctor to tend to you, free of charge, of course. After that, you will attend to one last mission. You will travel with six of my men and follow Marshal Cage's trail. You will find him and bring him to me. Alive. Upon completion of that task, I will pay you. Very generously. A full glim stake in the fields above the Cascade Range."

The Saint waited. He knew the man wouldn't say no. Knew that glim, and the profits that could be made off it, was a powerful motivator to a man like Les Mullins.

"You drive a hard bargain," he said.

"Take him to Mr. Shunt," the Saint said to the soldiers. "Tell Shunt I want him on his feet by nightfall."

The men picked up the litter and hurried out.

"Not you, Private."

The soldier stopped at the door. "Sir?"

"Tell Captain Dirkson I want to see him."

"Yes, sir."

The boy left the office and the Saint returned to his desk.

The Bitterroots. Near enough there was a good chance they'd catch his trail. And if he was making a point of bragging that his ship was the fastest in the skies, surely there would be more men who would point to where he'd been seen.

It was a stroke of luck that General Saint would not let slip through his fingers.

The private was back shortly, knocking on the door.

"Come," he said.

"Captain Dirkson, sir." The private held the door and a man walked in past him.

Dirkson was a burly man with a square plug of a face, small eyes, and a nose broken flat into the shape of a shovel. He was a force on the battlefield, unafraid and merciless.

"Captain Dirkson," the Saint said. "I want you to choose six men to accompany you on a mission to locate Marshal Cage and his ship, the *Swift*, in the Bitterroots. You will take Mr. Les Mullins with you, once the doctor has seen to his wounds."

"Yes, sir," he said. "And when I find Marshal Cage?"

"Bring him to me. Breathing."

"Yes, sir."

"Dismissed."

Dirkson turned and walked out into the silence of the morning.

"Is there anything else, sir?" the private asked.

"No, Private, that is all."

But before the private closed the door, the Saint saw Lieutenant Foster being helped out of Mr. Shunt's tent. He looked pale. Other than the sweat that soaked his shirt, he was sharp as ever, not a stitch out of place.

He saw the general looking at him, pulled his arm away from the man who was helping him keep his feet, and stood unsupported.

Alabaster gave him a short nod, which he returned.

Good. The men would soon be repaired, and now Cage would be brought to his knees before him without Mr. Shunt's help. That changed the game a bit.

After Mr. Shunt mended his eye, General Alabaster Saint would have him killed.

CHAPTER THIRTEEN

edar Hunt waited just inside the *Swift*. Captain Hink and his men were on the ground, out in the hard wind and drizzle. Negotiating with Old Jack was what the captain had said he was doing.

Sounded a lot more like arguing.

"Two days at the most," Captain Hink was saying. Again. For the hundredth time.

Cedar rested his shoulder against the doorway. He intended to keep to the shadows unless it looked like Captain Hink had gotten in over his head. Or if he suddenly decided his passengers were part of his bargaining chips.

"Beds, hot water, supplies for repair, and restocking our larder and needs." Hink went down the list. "We'll pay in glim dirty, or gold pure, either way you want it. Half now, half on lift."

"You'll leave in the morning," the man said in a ruined voice.

Cedar expected he'd taken a blast to the throat, or maybe had a habit of drinking kerosene. Whatever he'd done to his voice, or had done to it, it had left it sounding like the rasp of a saw against metal.

Old Jack was white-haired, white-bearded, and bent so bad at the shoulders that he had to tip his chin up to look out from under the brim of his hat.

But Cedar could count the glimmer of four cannons mounted

in the rise of cliff that took up three sides of the landing field, and the four silent Negro boys who stood behind them.

He could also count the one very bright Colt in Old Jack's steady hand.

"It will be two days, you know that, Jack," Hink said, his patience going sour. "She's shot full of holes, and I have a young woman in need of a bed and medical attention."

"The young woman have a name?"

"I suppose she does," Hink said. "Don't think that much matters in our price. You know how it is. I don't ask what you've got stashed here in this labyrinth of yours, and you don't ask me what, or who, I have stashed in my hold."

Hink's men shifted slightly. Not making a big deal of it, but enough that anyone would know they had their hands on their guns.

This was the line in the sand. Well, mud. Cedar knew if Jack crossed it, they'd be in for a fight. He didn't like the odds of facing down cannons with a ship that didn't have fuel to fly.

Finally, Jack took his finger off the trigger.

"Medicines will cost you twice as much as last visit," Old Jack wheezed. "And you know why."

"I told you I'd make clean on our last dealings." The clink of coins under cloth shook in the cold night air. "This takes care of our previous meeting." A second clink rang out, this one a little louder.

Cedar heard Guffin's whispered curse.

"And that," Hink said, "is a generous thank-you for extending our credit. For two days."

"Two days," Jack said. "No longer. Medicine still puts you back double, food isn't cheap, but it don't have bugs. You want hot water, boil it over your own fire. Follow me this way."

"Good doing business with you," Hink said. "Gentlemen, let's see to a bed that's both warm and dry tonight. Except for you, Ansell. Stay with the *Swift*."

"Aye, Captain."

"Seldom, please follow our proprietor."

Seldom strode off behind Old Jack, silent as a ghost in the wind.

Hink walked up to the ship, and paused short of the door. "Didn't see you there."

Cedar moved away from the threshold so the captain could step in.

"We've a bed for the night and the next, Mr. Hunt," Captain Hink said, pulling a satchel down from the overhead rack and filling it with maps and other oddments. "Old Jack can't much be trusted, but we've paid him to keep his mouth shut, and keep his hands to himself. We won't be robbed or shot in our sleep."

"Don't mean he won't rob us or shoot us when we're awake," Ansell rumbled, walking in behind the captain.

Cedar glanced over at Mae, who stood stiff, her hands clenched at her sides. She looked as if she'd been frozen in ice; only the slight movement of her lips, as if she were whispering, betrayed her.

Rose still sat on the floor, a blanket tucked tight around her, her fingers twined in Wil's fur. Her eyes were open, her hair stuck down by sweat. She was watching Cedar, and more so, watching Captain Hink as he moved about the airship.

Mae was sleeping on her feet, and Rose was unable to stand but conscious. He didn't know how they'd get either of them to walk to a bed through the rain and cold and rocks.

"Maybe we'll stay in the *Swift* tonight," Cedar said.

"What?"

"The women and I might best stay the night here," he repeated.

Hink had finished filling the satchel and slung it over his shoulder. He turned and looked first at Cedar, then Mae, and finally Rose.

Something about how he looked at Rose made all his edges go a bit softer, as if seeing her hurt like that took the steam out of him.

Rose gave Hink a small smile. She didn't do anything else but blink slowly. Her breathing was even and calm as if she were holding herself very still against a pain that would bite to the bone if she shifted even an inch.

"I'll bring a wagon," he said. "Old Jack has a steam muler wagon that gives an easy enough ride. And it's covered to shelter against the rain."

"Didn't see any structures out there," Cedar said. "Where are we bunking?"

"Down in one of his catacombs—and those have elevators if we need it, though going more than a couple turns into the mouse run he's burrowed through these rocks will get a man lost for good."

At Cedar's look, he continued. "There's a half dozen big rooms he carved out for paying guests. Big enough each can hold a ship's crew. Back in the day, they say he was commissioned to make this place livable in case the war took such a bad turn that the president himself would need a place to hole up. They used it as a base to tamp down the Indian uprisings for a bit, then lost interest in the place after the war was settled.

"But no one told Old Jack to stop digging. There's plenty of space in this mountain for us, Mr. Hunt. And the main rooms are heated and free from hard drafts. Ask Molly here, if you need a second word."

Molly had just strolled in from the boiler room and quickly took in the situation. "We can get us all there comfortable," she said. "The medicines at his disposal would do Miss Small here a long bit of good. And I think Mrs. Lindson could use a rest too."

"Yes?" Mae asked as soon as she heard her name. She shook her head slowly and then her eyes came to focus on the room around her. "We've landed."

Cedar didn't like his choices. Stay out here in a crippled ship under cannon watch for the night, or step inside the spider's web of tunnels carved in the cliffs by a man no one trusted.

Not for the first time, he wished he still had his supplies, his horse, and a steady horizon in front of him.

"Mrs. Lindson," Cedar said, stepping over to her. "We're going to be staying here in the mountains for the night."

She nodded. "Of course," she said, her hands smoothing down the front of her coat and skirt. "And Rose. We'll need to see to her."

"I'll get that wagon," Captain Hink said.

Cedar heard the huff of a small matic coming closer. Then Guffin stuck his head in the doorway. "We thought we'd spare the ladies a walk, Captain."

"Very thoughtful, Mr. Guffin," he said. "Molly, see that Mr. Hunt has the assistance he needs." The captain gathered up the bag he had packed and one extra that looked near empty, then stepped outside.

Cedar walked over to Mae, and Molly did the same.

"Can you walk, Mrs. Lindson?" Molly asked gently.

"Of course," Mae said. "Yes, of course." She took a step, then drew her hand out to the side as if trying to feel her way through a dark room.

Cedar caught her hand and her elbow.

"Oh," she said, a breath of relief shuddering out of her. "Mr. Hunt. There you are. Could you show me to the door, please?"

"Right this way." Cedar gave Molly a look and she nodded.

"I'll wait until you're back to help with Miss Small."

Cedar took two steps and Mae followed like a woman suddenly gone blind, her steps hesitant even though there was nothing in her path.

"There now, you're doing fine," Cedar said softly.

"That helps," Mae said, keeping her chin up.

"What helps?"

"Your voice. I can hear you. As if you're right here next to me."

Cedar winced at that, but kept his tone calm. "I am next to you, Mrs. Lindson. Right here. And we're near across the floor of the airship on our way to a wagon and a dry bed. Heard there might be a hot bath at the end of it all, if that pleases you."

"A hot bath." Mae actually smiled. "I can't think of anything more lovely at the moment. Thank you, Mr. Hunt."

"Haven't drawn the bath yet," Cedar said. "Might want to hold off on your gratitude until we see if the tub leaks."

"I wasn't thanking you for the bath." With what seemed to be a great effort, she tipped her head up and met his gaze. "I was thanking you for not losing me."

"Losing you?"

"To the . . . all the chaos. I would have understood if you simply left me. I haven't been much benefit, haven't been . . . well."

He nodded. "We all have times when we aren't . . . ourselves. No need to worry, Mrs. Lindson."

"Mae," she said.

"Pardon?"

"Please. Call me Mae."

It might be the slide from sanity, or that she was having a rare clear moment. But Mae reached up and brushed her fingers gently down the side of his face. "Always so grim, Mr. Hunt. I'd like to see the day there's joy in your eyes again."

They were at the door now, and the wind caught at the tendrils of hair around her delicate face. Cedar swallowed hard against the rise of need in his chest. Swallowed again so he could speak.

"And in yours, Mrs.—Mae," he said. "Now, let's see to that wagon."

"Who?" she asked, searching his face. "I said I'm coming," she added in a whisper.

Her eyes were unfocused again, the voices of the sisters taking her mind away.

It was like watching the clouds smother the light out of the sky.

He hated it. Hated what the sisters were doing to her. Chipping her away and hollowing her out. If they didn't get to the coven so those witches could break this spell on her soon, there'd be nothing of her left.

"This way," he said, not knowing if she could hear him.

They stepped out of the ship to the muler. It was a much more modern matic than Cedar had expected. Even in the poor bit of light splashing over it from the lanterns, he could see it was a sleek buggy in the front, with a wagon bed attached at the back. The wagon bed was canopied by oilskin buttoned down on three of the four sides, leaving only the back open.

If he had to put a guess to it, he'd say it hauled heavy but delicate materials, though for the life of him, he didn't know what those might be out this far from any civilized place. Maybe nitroglycerin for Old Jack's blasting habit.

Guffin and Captain Hink waited near the front buggy, Hink's eyes on the door to the *Swift*.

Guffin slipped into the buggy's seat and Captain Hink came around the back of the wagon to help Cedar get Mae settled under the canopy. A lantern hung from the ceiling inside the wagon, the light revealing a bench along one side, and a cot along the other. The floor was smooth, and covered in a clean canvas that smelled surprisingly of herbs, as if it had been boiled in chamomile.

"I'll stay with her," Captain Hink said, "if you want to help Molly with Miss Small."

Mae sat on the bench, her eyes closed, her hands folded in her lap. She was in no state to look out for herself. Cedar hesitated.

"Go on ahead," he said to the captain. Wil would be there beside Rose. He wouldn't let anything happen to her.

Captain Hink studied his face for a moment, then nodded. Cedar didn't know if the captain thought he didn't trust him with Mae or did trust him with Rose.

"Miss Small," Captain Hink started. "She's . . . well, I want you to know you can trust—"

The rumble of engines rolled over the thrashing of the wind.

An airship. Close enough it must be landing.

"God blast it," Hink muttered.

"More trouble?" Cedar asked.

"Maybe not. But the way my luck's been running?" He plowed off to the *Swift* and it wasn't but a moment later that he and Molly appeared in the door, Wil a shadow skulking behind them.

Cedar had expected the captain and Molly would be helping Rose walk. But instead, Captain Hink had picked her up in his arms and was carrying her, wrapped in her blanket, his own coat draped over that to keep the worst of the rain off her.

Molly walked next to him, a duffel slung over her shoulder, her tool belt bulky beneath her long coat.

Cedar helped Hink ease Rose into the wagon and up onto the cot. Molly slipped in next and tucked a rolled-up blanket under Rose's shoulder.

The captain knelt at the back of the wagon, frowning at the women. Cedar knew he was listening to the fans of the airship, to try to get a read on which bird it was.

"Let's go," Cedar said.

Captain Hink nodded. "I'll sit the controls with Guffin." He swung out of the wagon, and a moment later, the muler's engine puffed up and started rolling.

The buggy shook a bit at first, then it seemed to glide. Cedar hadn't seen a smooth trail in the rocky outcropping. And he hadn't seen rails. But the way the buggy was rigged up made for much easier travel than he'd expected.

Mae didn't say a thing throughout the ride, and Rose only whimpered now and again when a particularly hard bump jostled her.

The sound of the wind died down and then even the clattering of raindrops on the oilskin stopped. There were no windows in the buggy, but they'd gone under cover.

"Where are we now?" Cedar asked.

"In the muler shed next to our accommodations," Molly said.

"Do we all stay in one room?" he said.

"Of course. There's privacy and there's privacy, Mr. Hunt," Molly said. "But in these catacombs, we'll want to stay in eyeshot of each other. Person can get lost in Old Jack's place. Get killed too. By taking the wrong turn in the tunnels, or forgetting to add an extra copper to whatever it is Jack's selling."

"Are there other guests here?"

She shook her head. "Didn't see any ships except for the one coming in."

"Can you tell which ship it is?"

Molly rubbed at the short crop of hair above her ears, smoothing back the stubble there, her eyes tight at the corner as if she were squinting to read a distant sign. "Might be the *Constant*, or the *Dawn Breaker*." She listened for a moment more. "But I don't think so."

The buggy rolled to a stop and the hiss of steam being vented filled the air.

"This is our stop," Molly said.

Cedar opened the buggy door and helped lead Mae out.

"I'm fine," she said.

"Good," Cedar said. "We're headed to our room for the night." He held her hand as they walked out into the unremarkable and dimly lit cavern that housed two more mulers, both silent and cold.

Mr. Seldom was across the way a bit. He leaned in a doorway. Bright yellow light spilled past him to orange up his hair and paint his shadow on the rough floor.

Cedar and Mae headed that way, walking through the door past Seldom, who gave them a nod before they stepped into the room beyond.

Bigger than a barn, it really was a hollowed-out hole in the stones. Stone ceiling, walls, floor all worked smooth and painted in whitewash, with lights set up and about in such a way as to make the place look comfortable. A fire crackled away in a carved hearth, so well vented he didn't even smell the ash or smoke. A stack of supplies, hooks with pots, and a hand pump with a bucket and a large washtub all took up that side of the room.

The main of the room was set with tables and chairs and, surprisingly, a shelf with a few books and map tubes piled on it.

He didn't know if there were sleeping rooms, but there was plenty of floor space to put out a bedroll.

"Just a little farther and we'll have that dry bed," he told Mae.

"Cedar," Mae said. "Mr. Hunt?" She squeezed his hand.

Cedar looked down at her.

Mae's eyes were bright. Clear. Her cheeks were flushed as if she'd just woken too quickly from a deep dream.

"I'm fine. Truly. It's much . . . quieter here." She looked around, taking in her surroundings, then took in a good deep breath.

"Maybe it's the stone," she said. "I'm feeling much more myself. Let me help. Where's Rose?"

"In the buggy," Cedar said, a little stunned by her complete turn-around. "Are you sure?"

Mae smiled, an aching hint of happiness before sadness, or perhaps fear, took it away again. "I think we should embrace our luck as it comes, Mr. Hunt. And right now I am . . . feeling much better. Are there medical supplies at our disposal?"

"We'll have to ask the captain about that."

"Ask the captain about what?" Hink asked as he strode into the room, his hat in one hand so he could shake the rain off it.

Molly and Seldom had found a litter from someplace and gotten Rose upon it. They were carrying her across the room, Wil walking at her side, his ears up, nose working the scents in the room. He stared at Cedar, and then followed Rose as Molly and Seldom took her through a doorway on the far side of the room.

"Where are they taking her?" Cedar asked.

The captain put his hat under his arm and opened his satchel. He dug out his flask, took a swig from it, then walked it over to Cedar. "Beds back that way. Enough bunks for us all." He handed Cedar the flask, and Cedar took a long swallow.

It was good bourbon.

"Do we have medical supplies, Captain?" Mae asked.

Hink's eyebrows shot up and he looked from Cedar to Mae, then took another pull on the flask.

"We will," he said. "As soon as I pry them out of Old Jack's greedy fingers. What exactly do you think you'll need, Mrs. Lindson?"

Mae glanced off the way Rose had been taken. "I'll need to see her first. But something to take the pain. It'd be best if it didn't knock her completely out. Am I to assume we have only a modicum of safety here, and that we will be leaving as soon as possible?"

"That's about the gist of it," Hink said. "I'm pleased to see you're feeling better, Mrs. Lindson."

"Thank you, Captain," she said. "Let me check on Miss Small. Then perhaps I could accompany you to speak with Mr. Jack about medicine?"

Hink shot Cedar a quick look and Cedar nodded. "Of course," the captain said. "Rather not pay for something we'd throw away."

"Very well. I'll be back in a moment."

Mae headed across the room, steady on her feet, and as near as Cedar could tell, clearheaded.

"Isn't that something?" Hink said. "Or maybe it's not. She come and go like that a lot?"

The captain pulled out a chair and folded down into it with a grateful grunt.

"She's usually very clear," Cedar said. "Days have been hard lately."

"Ain't they always?" Hink took one last drink from the flask, then tucked it back into his coat.

"Molly didn't recognize the ship," Cedar said.

"Seldom's putting his eyes on it. We'll know soon."

"Bad kind of hole to die in," Cedar noted.

"Haven't yet met a hole I wanted to die in," Hink agreed. "Ansell's putting fuel on board before he beds down. Coal. And he has the barrels out to catch the rain. If we need to crack the sky, we'll have power."

"Will the ship hold together for flight?"

"Not far. And this is the last friendly, well, relatively so, resupply station that has what we'd need for repairs. If you want to get those women to Kansas, we'll need the day, maybe two."

"I don't know that Rose has that long."

Hink looked up at Cedar. The captain's eyes were sober, tired. None of them had snatched more than a handful of sleep. And the captain looked like he'd been riding too hard for too long well before they'd fallen in together.

Cedar lowered his voice. "There is some chance the Holder would heal her, set her to rights."

"I'll get her medicines," Captain Hink said, "which you'll pay me for. We'll patch the *Swift*. If you have some clue as to where the . . . device . . . ," he said, avoiding using the word "Holder," "is, then I'll take you to it. But there just isn't any more I can do at this point, Mr. Hunt. Picking up you and yours has put me behind, shot holes in my ship, and made a general mess of the life and dealings of both myself and my crew."

"Our paths could part here," Cedar said. "We're grateful for your help out of Vicinity, and for putting us down to earth again. But there isn't any reason we must continue on together."

"Other than you owe me for those things." Captain Hink leaned forward. "We had a deal, Mr. Hunt. And I'd be sorry to see what would happen if you stepped back on it."

Mr. Seldom strolled into the room, his hard-soled boots somehow silent on the stone floor.

"So who's our company, Mr. Seldom?" Hink asked.

"*Coin de Paradis*," he said.

"Heard of them?" Hink asked.

He shook his head. "Northern from the look of her. French, from the sound."

"How northern?" Cedar asked.

Seldom shrugged. "Pacific-rigged. Sleds for ice."

"So she can ride the sea and the mountains," Hink said. "Must be a regular delivery barge to Old Jack."

"You don't think she's a glim ship?" Cedar asked.

"Not in a specific way," Hink said. "Glim ship's not going to be rigged to take the storms over the ocean, and won't much care about landing in snow since pulling harvest in the brace of winter is just a quick way to catch a bad case of dead."

He continued. "There ain't a ship out there that would take the cold upper with the weight of extra equipment. So if she's rigged Pacific and ice, she's bringing supplies over and through on those conditions. I'd wager she's come down from Fort Vancouver at least. Maybe up the Alaska territory. Old Jack has a hunger for things only got from exotic shores."

"How many in the crew?" Cedar asked.

"Ten or less," Seldom said.

"They tied down yet?" Hink asked.

Seldom shook his head. "Lashing on the south pad."

"In that case, find us all some food, won't you, Seldom? Something hot with meat in it."

Seldom walked off out another door that must have been a larder and came back with a pot, which he set on a hook over the fire, and a pan he set to the side. Then he was gone again and back with supplies wrapped in brown paper and canvas.

He pulled his knife and got busy working up some food.

"Been here a time or two," Cedar noted with a nod toward Seldom, who was moving around the kitchen like he grew up here.

"Sat out the tail end of winter a season or two back," the captain said. "Us and four other crews. Got to know our way around the living quarters, but not much more. The tunnels Jack blasts in these mountains don't have a map, except for whatever he keeps in his noggin. And every blast does as much to close down a tunnel as open another.

"Don't go wandering off, Mr. Hunt. And for glim's sake, don't let Mae or Rose or that wolf of yours get out of eyesight."

The scuff of approaching footsteps and low murmur of voices put a change in Captain Hink.

He gave Cedar one last nod, then leaned back, shifting his wide shoulders so one arm slung over the back of the chair, flask open in his hand. He smiled, and looked just a little drunk.

Which he most certainly was not.

Cedar eased back, but made no attempt to hide his manner. Friend or foe, he'd deal with it squarely.

Eight people walked into the room. Two women, one slender and tall as the men around her, wearing a proper skirt and corset, an umbrella clasped in her kid-gloved hand, the other shorter by at least a foot, uncovered hair hanging in two yellow braids, skirt split for riding. A lady and her maid? What were they doing all this way out in the hills? On an airship?

He scanned the men, looking to see if there was a husband or a father in the mix.

They were scanning him back. Four of the men had on gear that resembled the coats, vests, and harnesses Hink and his crew wore around as easy as tuckers and suspenders.

Cedar would count them as crew to the ship.

The man with the wild brown curls and impressive handlebar mustache might be the captain, and the other man, a quiet-looking fellow wearing a wool check suit, a bowler hat and sporting a carpetbag in one hand, didn't quite fit in with Cedar's notion of a crew. Maybe a passenger. Maybe a salesman.

"You must be Captain Hink." The mustachioed man strolled across the room toward Hink with an easy roll to his gait and surveyed the place like he was inspecting a crop ripe for the picking.

"Oh, I'd say 'must' is a rather strong word, Captain. . . . Have we made acquaintance?" Hink didn't stand. He just peered up at the man, who stopped next to their table.

"I've seen your ship," the man said. "The *Swift*. Not a faster ship in the sky, nor a sharper man behind the wheel, they say. I am Captain Beaumont of the *Coin de Paradis*."

"Pleased to make your meet," Hink said, offering a hand but not budging from his chair. "Supply run?"

"Just so. I'm afraid I miscalculated the storm. And you?"

"Repairs mostly. Headed southwest to sit out the winter."

"And your crew?" Captain Beaumont asked.

"Boots off. Except my second there, rustling pots. You're welcome to join in the victuals if you want."

"No, thank you. It's been a long day in the sky and I must see to my passengers being settled properly."

Beaumont's crew spread out across the room, rucksacks over their shoulders as they headed toward the room where Rose and Mae had gone.

Guffin appeared at the door, picking at his fingernails with a knife. Wil paced out to stand beside him.

"Occupied," he said. "Take the next door."

At the sight of the wolf, the crewmen took a couple cautious steps back, then tromped off to another door down a ways.

The two women and the bowler-hatted man exchanged a startled look, glancing between the wolf and Cedar.

The tall woman finally spoke. "Captain Beaumont," she said in a surprisingly rich French accent, "if it would be no bother, I would very much care for a hot meal."

"Not at all, Miss Dupuis," the captain said smoothly. "Please, make yourself comfortable." He held his hand out toward an empty table as far across the room from Cedar and Captain Hink as possible. "Unfortunately, I cannot join you. I'd best speak with the proprietor before we turn in to settle our bill."

"Of course, Captain," she said. "Good evening."

The captain gave her a slight bow. Cedar supposed he would have too. She was the kind of woman that made a man feel like he should kiss her hand.

"Well, then," the blond woman said, "I'll help with the food." No French accent from her. If anything, she seemed to have a healthy dose of the South in her words.

"Thank you, Joonie," Miss Dupuis said.

Joonie marched off and tried to strike up a conversation with Seldom as she checked the larder. Seldom responded with barely discernible shrugs and an occasional pointing of the knife.

The man with the carpetbag, who had been staring at Cedar this whole time, seemed to gather his wits, and he strode over to pull a chair out for the lady. He moved smoothly and efficiently, like he was used to being in front of people.

A statesman? Lawyer?

"Could I get you some water, Miss Dupuis?" he asked quietly, but not so quietly that Cedar's keen ears couldn't pick it up. He fingered his vest pocket, withdrawing a pair of spectacles and placing them on his nose.

"No, thank you, Mr. Theobald," she murmured. "Please, be seated."

From how quickly the man obeyed, it was clear who among the passengers made the decisions.

And from the lowered lashes and slight smile she gave him, it was just as clear that he was more than her traveling companion. Much more.

Interesting, but ultimately nothing that concerned him. He was just about to get up and see if Rose and Mae were settled, when Mae walked back into the room. The passengers, all of them, including the blonde flipping flapjacks, looked over at Mae.

Cedar watched the strangers. Joonie noticed his gaze right away and went back to minding her pans. Mr. Theobald was slowly slipping the lenses of his spectacles down over one eye, holding a book open in the palm of his hand, but not reading it. The last person Cedar had seen wear a contraption like that was Bryn Madder, when he was trying to make sense of Cedar and his curse.

But it was Miss Dupuis who stared straight at him, watching to see if he had any reaction to Mae walking into the room.

Cedar shifted in his chair to see Mae, who was walking their way.

His heart clutched in his chest, and heat tightened his skin. Every time he saw that woman, the need for her struck him near dumb. More than that. The wolf in him twisted and pressed. Wanting out. Wanting to protect. Wanting her.

Cedar swallowed hard, pressing the beast down deeper and holding tight to the thoughts of a man.

Mr. Theobald took in a sharp, quick breath, and his fingers stopped snicking lenses into place over his spectacles.

Cedar knew he was looking at him. He could smell his fear.

It was all he could do not to turn and stare at the man until he backed down.

"Hello, gentlemen," Mae said once she was at their table. "We have company?" From the tone of her voice, she really wasn't sure if she had missed seeing them there before, or perhaps she was unsure if they were really in the room.

"Ship's crew came in," Cedar said quietly. "Supplies. The captain is off talking to Jack."

"Oh," Mae said. "I see." She paused and smoothed her hands over her skirt, then rested them on her hips. "I believe you and I need to speak to Mr. Jack also, Captain." Then she noticed the flask in Hink's hand, and her eyebrows went up.

"If you are prepared to speak on our behalf," she added.

The captain took in a deep breath and held it as he made a big lot of noise over standing up and away from that table.

"Why, of course, I'm prepared to speak. Shall we?" He offered her his arm, which Mae took.

Cedar clenched his hands into fists and worked on not imagining clocking the captain for that smile he was giving to Mae.

"Keep the pot hot, Mr. Seldom," Captain Hink called. "I have a feeling I'm about to work up an appetite."

They'd get medicines for Rose, he told himself. That's all he was talking about.

Captain Hink had proved he could be trusted so far.

The captain wasn't drunk, and yet he was acting like it. Who was he trying to fool? Beaumont? His passengers?

He wasn't going to send Mae off on her own with him. Cedar strode over to where Wil stood in the shadows just inside the doorway to the sleeping quarters. He looked down into his brother's copper eyes. "Watch Mae for me," he whispered.

Wil padded out into the room, then through it with grace and speed.

"My word!" Mr. Theobald said.

Joonie reached for something that was not a spatula.

Mr. Seldom caught her hand before she could pull whatever sort of gun she had hidden in her skirts.

"Flapjacks are burning," was all he said.

But by the time she looked back out in the room, Wil was gone.

Cedar strode over to the table where Mr. Theobald stood, the lens over his eye a hard red. He still smelled like fear, but he was steady on his feet, his hand tucked in one pocket, where no doubt he had some kind of weapon he felt confident using. His expression held more than a little bit of curiosity.

For a brief moment, that look reminded him of the Madder brothers.

Miss Dupuis sat straight-backed and proper, as if she expected tea service to arrive at any moment.

"Though we haven't been made full acquaintance," Cedar said to Mr. Theobald, "I'd be obliged if you kept your hands off your weapons around that wolf of mine. I wouldn't want him to think you meant to harm him."

He said it quietly. But it was a threat.

Miss Dupuis smiled, the curve of her full lips not quite showing her teeth.

"Where are my manners?" Mr. Theobald said, his voice smooth, friendly, and inviting in a way that was hard to resist. "I am pleased to introduce Miss Sophie Dupuis, Miss Joonie Wright, and I myself, Otto Theobald. We are traveling east to Miss Dupuis's father's estate before the winter sets in. And whom do we have the pleasure of speaking to?"

"Cedar Hunt," he said. "Most recently out of Oregon. Good evening, Miss Dupuis, Mr. Theobald. May your travels be smooth."

"Please," Miss Dupuis said. "Sit with us, Mr. Hunt. Join us for our meal. Joonie is a wonderful cook."

Mr. Theobald looked at him expectantly. As if he had a rack of questions he was hoping Cedar would hang answers on.

"No, thank you, Miss Dupuis, Mr. Theobald. Perhaps tomorrow. I have other matters to attend."

"We understand," Mr. Theobald said. "I'm very pleased to make your acquaintance." He held out his hand and Cedar shook it.

The look on Theobald's face changed to something more like stunned respect, which didn't make a lick of sense.

He certainly was an odd man. Cedar couldn't quite get a bead on him.

"Ma'am," Cedar said, nodding to Miss Dupuis, who gave him a soft smile.

"Good evening to you and yours, Mr. Hunt. I do hope we'll have a chance to catch up tomorrow."

Cedar walked to the bedroom. The sleeping quarters were a barracks that could bunk about a dozen people. Cots were lined up against the walls with empty shelves and coat hooks beside them.

Rose was settled in on a bed toward the end of the room. Molly sat on the cot next to her.

"Smells good out there," Molly said. "Captain set Seldom loose on the griddle?"

"He did. How is she?"

Molly sighed. "Sleeping, I think. Or fainted. As comfortable as we can make her. Mrs. Lindson is hoping there's some herbs in Jack's stores that will help." Molly paused, and looked over at Rose, who was pale and still. "That infection's gone worse in a terrible short time," she said. "I don't know how long she'll hold against it."

"She's strong," Cedar said, stepping over to see her more clearly.

"I can tell she is," Molly said. "You said my kinsmen thought kindly of her?"

Guffin, who had been lying on a cot toward the front of the room with his hat over his head, groaned and sat up. "I'll leave you two ladies to your gossip. My belly's chewing on my spine anyway." He left the room.

Cedar sat on a bed next to Rose. "Yes, he did. Had her at his side since she was a young girl, I'm given to understand. She's got a bit of the wild sciences in her, and Mr. Gregor had a way of making her see that as a good thing."

Molly smiled. "She was whispering in her sleep. Something about matics and cogs and gears. Thought she might lean toward devising."

"She's handy with those sorts of things." He wondered if he should put something in Rose's hand, a device, a whimsy, so her busy fingers would be comforted, but he had nothing to give her. They'd lost everything they owned in that damn town.

Cedar ground his teeth until his anger became nothing more than frustration.

No trail was easy, but trying to get Mrs. Lindson to her coven had proved to be more than difficult. It was quite possibly going to cost Rose her life. Most likely had cost the stubborn Madder brothers theirs.

That wound Rose carried should be his. He'd had some time to think about the windup dead girl, and who might have such a terrible mind to set such a trap. Most of the Strange he'd killed over the years didn't do much more thinking than an angry animal. They certainly weren't the sort to pull together complicated traps.

But there was one Strange man who was more than up to this sort of trickery: Mr. Shunt. Shunt had done terrible things back in Hallelujah. Pieced together walking, killing bodies for the Strange to inhabit. Pieced together other horrifying killing contraptions.

And since he'd felt Mr. Shunt's presence and known he'd been there in Vicinity for more than a day or two, he was of the mind that Mr. Shunt had meant for that girl to kill him.

Cedar should be the one suffering right now, not Rose.

Molly stood and stretched. "Anger won't fix her, Mr. Hunt," Molly said. "And it won't do you a lot of good either, I'd wager."

Cedar glanced up.

Molly shook her head. "Don't know why you're so riled, but I'd like to suggest you take that temper and stow it. This isn't any kind of place to lose your head."

"So the captain has told me. How many men does Old Jack have out here?" he asked.

"Just a handful. But it ain't men you need to worry about. Old Jack is fond of explosives and doesn't mind rearranging his living quarters, if you get my drift. Course there's always people coming and going. Suspicion is something of a hobby among glimmers."

"The passengers out there?" Cedar said.

"I heard. French ship. *Coin of Paradise* or some such?" At his look she grinned. "Got to keep your ear to the ground in this business. I've heard of Captain Beaumont. Doesn't run glim, but likes to think he's better than us that do."

"Do you know his passengers?" he asked.

"Nope." She strode toward the door. "But I'm going to make my meet over a plate of food before Guffin and Seldom clean the pot."

She paused at the door. "You should do the same, Mr. Hunt. Full belly makes a clear mind."

"Thank you for your concern, Miss Gregor," he said. "I'll wait a bit."

She nodded. "Suit yourself."

She left the room and Cedar took off his hat. He ran his hand over his head, then scrubbed his face. He was suddenly bone-tired. The smell of bacon fat sizzling in the pan and the low murmur of voices conspired with the darkness and warmth to make him want to just lie back and sleep for a week.

Instead, he leaned his head against the wall, and kept watch over Rose.

CHAPTER FOURTEEN

Mae Lindson walked with the captain. She thought it gallant that he offered her his arm, although it could simply be that he had noticed she'd been out of her senses the last couple days and didn't want her wandering off.

"What sort of medicines do you hope to wrangle tonight, Mrs. Lindson?" Captain Hink asked.

"Almost anything," Mae said truthfully. "I still have my satchel, and my black salve, but I have nothing to ease her pain except a small bottle of laudanum. She'll be out of pain, but deep asleep. And if she's asleep, it will be much harder for us to travel quickly if we need to."

"I know just the thing. There's leaves from South Africa Jack likes to bring in and bargain off. Coca. Good for pain, good for energy," Hink said. "Will you need bandages or sutures?"

"Clean bandages would be wonderful. There's no need of sewing anything up yet. We haven't removed the fragment. Maybe yarrow if he has it. That should help with fever and infection."

The stone passage took a turn and suddenly they were on a wooden floor with wooden walls. After all the natural round and unevenness of the caverns, and before that, the curved edges of the interior of the *Swift*, seeing square wooden corners was suddenly strange and refreshing.

Mae took her hand away from the captain's arm and he gave her a sideways look. "Don't know if I've said it to you, Mrs. Lindson, but the tunnels in these mountains can confuse a bloodhound. I think it's in your best interest not to wander off alone, or at all, for that matter. As you saw back there, we have us company of another crew."

"Thank you for worrying about my welfare, Captain," she said. "But I can take care of myself."

"If you're on my ship, you're mine to look after, Mrs. Lindson. That wasn't a request. It was an order." He gave her a smile. "Hate to have that man of yours blaming me for misplacing you."

"Man of mine?" she asked.

"Mr. Hunt."

"I'm sorry, Captain, but you're mistaken. Mr. Hunt is simply our trail guide."

"I see. Is that how you think it is?"

Mae set her shoulders. She was used to people thinking she was prone to impropriety. But she didn't want the captain to make assumptions that were not true.

"What I think," Mae said, "rather, what I *know*, is Mr. Hunt helped both Rose and myself through a rough patch a short while ago when my husband was killed. He and I have an agreement and vested interests in reaching Kansas before winter. And that is all."

"Doesn't look like that is all when he sets eyes on you, Mrs. Lindson."

"You are misreading our relationship, Captain, and I'd be obliged if you let the matter rest."

He pressed his lips together. "You'll forgive my manners, I hope," he said. "Living on the edge of the sky doesn't do much to keep a man sharp on his niceties. But if I had a word left to say on the matter—"

"I most certainly hope you do not," Mae said.

"I'd just say you ought to give him another look." Captain Hink's smile was wide and friendly. "It wouldn't be the first time I've seen an agreement and vested interests be the beginnings of something else altogether."

"Are you always this irascible, Captain Hink?"

"No, I'm usually much worse."

Mae smiled despite herself. "You certainly are sure of your charms, Captain. I'm not so sure I'm convinced of them."

He stopped and Mae paused, waiting for him to refute her claims.

"If, for some reason, things between you and Mr. Hunt are no longer in agreement, I want you to know I'll see to it that you and Miss Rose reach whatever destination you choose."

"And I'm to take your word at your honor?" she asked.

"I wouldn't suppose you would," he said. "But that's the truth of it. And if you'd rather take Molly Gregor's word, she'll vouch that when I promise such a thing I don't turn away from it until I see it done."

Mae could see he meant what he said. She just didn't understand why he would be so willing to go out of his way to help them. Men who harvested glim were not the sort who went about tending to the troubles of others.

"It's a kind offer," Mae said slowly. "And I will keep that in mind. But you don't have to worry yourself. If Mr. Hunt decides not to fulfill his promise, then I am sure Rose and I will find our way just fine."

They started walking again, the sound of boot against the wood echoing off the bare walls.

She couldn't hear the sisters' voices here, not since the buggy had brought them deep inside the mountain. Mae didn't know if it was because the mountain blocked their song, or if she dared hope that they were done singing, calling, pulling, dragging her home.

She'd never once been so close to insanity as the last month on the trail. It frightened her. When the sisters were calling her, it was all she could hear, and their faces were all she could see. The longer she denied her return, the louder and more constant their voices became. She couldn't escape them, waking nor asleep.

It was only when Cedar Hunt spoke to her that she could navigate her way through the overwhelming noise and visions. Or when he touched her that she could feel the world solid around her.

And here, where by the grace of the Goddess, she was free of the voices for however a long or short time, she realized how very far gone she had been. If not for Cedar, if not for Rose, she wouldn't have even made it this far on the path the sisters forced her feet to follow.

It was a chilling horror to know that her mind was slipping away. Even more frightening to realize these might be her last lucid moments.

But if this was all the time she had left, she'd tend to Rose. With herbs and with magic. Bind health to her bones, curse the infection. She had enough herbs in her satchel to work the spells and blessings needed. She didn't know why that hadn't occurred to her before.

It wouldn't remove the piece of the Holder, but it would help her stay strong.

"Didn't mean to set you silent," Captain Hink said.

"Not at all," Mae replied. "I was just going through the things I'll need to tend Rose."

"Well, I hope your list is done and checked. This here is his office."

The hall branched off to the left, heading back into the mountain, she assumed. Right in front of them was a metal door that looked like it belonged on a bank vault.

"Old Jack likes his privacy." Hink stepped up and pulled on a chain beside the door. Mae thought she heard the clatter of a bell on the other side.

Soon bolts slid aside and gears clicked as a chain tightened.

And then a young, dark-skinned man opened the door and stepped aside so they could walk into the room.

Hink nodded for Mae to cross the threshold first, and she did so, the captain right on her heels.

The room was a stockpile of bags, crates, and shelves. It looked more like a general store, though it was the largest general store she'd ever seen, reaching two stories high.

She paused, unsure of where his office might be in the mess.

"Straight on," Hink said. "There's a door down that way. His office is beyond it."

"Perhaps you could lead?" she asked.

Captain Hink stepped up and around her, avoiding knocking over a precarious stack of clay jugs.

He dusted his hands as if he'd found spiders there. "Place knows how to put a chill up a man's spine," he said. "Never know if something bumped is just the sort of thing that explodes."

The door shut behind them with the snick of latches, bolt, and locks.

"And I hate that damn door," he muttered.

Mae glanced over her shoulder. The servant stood next to the door, giving her a cool, disinterested gaze. If they wanted to get out of this room in a hurry, there would be no way to get through that much metal.

She suddenly realized she didn't have a gun on her.

But that didn't mean she couldn't take care of herself. Whereas magic was usually the last thing she would turn to in time of trouble, it seemed easy to think on it now, to want to use it, like an itch beneath her fingertip.

In her hands even good spells went wrong.

Like what she had done to the captain.

"Captain," she said quietly as they wove their way between a pile of burlap and a row of barrels that smelled like lime, the servant following at a polite, but easy firing range behind them.

"Mm?"

"I'd like to apologize for . . . for what happened on the ship. What I did to you."

That got him to stop full up and turn toward her. He was wide enough that doing so completely blocked her path. "What are you talking about, Mrs. Lindson?"

"I . . . I worked magic on you, Captain."

A slow smile slid up his mouth and she caught a sparkle in his eyes. "Did you now?"

She'd seen this before. For all that folk always seemed to want to burn any woman who might be accused of being a witch, they'd just as soon not believe that magic was real.

"Yes, I did. And I am sorry. I haven't been in my right mind lately. I never would have done that if I'd been clearheaded. Or if we hadn't been about to crash."

"Hold on now," he said, camping back a bit on one foot. "You mean to tell me you think you cornered that landing?"

"No. You did that, Captain. You and the ship. Tied together as close as heart and vein by the spell I cast on you."

He narrowed his eyes. "There some reason why you're going to apologize for us hitting the earth with our bones unbroke?"

"Not for that, no. Of course not. But you are bound, Captain. Tied to the ship. And I'm not sure how I would go about unbinding you, though I'd be happy to—"

"Why don't we just let it be as it is," he interrupted. "We're on the ground, we'll be repairing the ship come daylight and flying her out dawn after next. I'm sure whatever it is you think you've done will have passed by then."

Mae opened her mouth to tell him he was wrong, but another man was walking from the far end of the room toward them.

"Come to speak to Old Jack, Captain?" the man asked.

He had a wild head of dark hair and a neatly trimmed and greased handlebar mustache that stretched from ear to ear.

"Captain Beaumont," Hink said, "I don't believe you've been introduced to Mrs. Lindson. Mrs. Lindson, Captain Beaumont and his crew landed to pass the night here."

"How do you do?" Mae said, nodding to the gentleman.

"My pleasure, Mrs. Lindson," he said. "Captain Hink, I had no idea you were traveling with such captivating passengers. I do a bit of passenger service myself, Mrs. Lindson. Where is it you're headed?"

"Toward family, Captain."

"Southwest," Hink added, though that was not the truth. "Could have sworn I already mentioned that."

The captain smiled, the mustache shrugging over his lip. "Ah, and perhaps you did. It's been a very long day. The details fly from me like leaves on a breeze. Good evening to you, Captain Hink, Mrs. Lindson."

"Good evening, Captain," Mae said.

Hink started off again. "And to you, Beaumont."

The man squeezed past crates of walnuts toward the door. "Come, boy," he said to the servant who had been following them. "See me to the door."

Mae watched as he walked away. Captain Hink obviously didn't trust the man, since he'd told them they were headed southwest, when Kansas was really southeast of here.

Captain Beaumont obviously didn't trust Captain Hink either, since he'd asked Mae where they were traveling. Likely, he had been trying to catch Captain Hink in a lie.

As far as Mae knew, there was no reason for Captain Hink to think their destinations were worth hiding. Which meant that Captain Hink might want to hide his own doings from the man.

Were all airship captains so distrustful?

Not for the first time, she wished they hadn't stopped in Vicinity. Wished they'd just ridden straight through and on down to Kansas. It'd still be many miles left to go on horseback. A month at least, but they wouldn't be tangled up with glim pirates, reclusive miners, and the sorts of men that other men felt warranted lying to.

"Coming, Mrs. Lindson?" Hink asked.

"Yes." She caught up to his long-legged stride. He knocked on the polished rosewood door carved with an image of elephants and tropical trees.

More bolts and locks snicked and clicked, and the door opened again.

But instead of letting them in, Old Jack stepped out. "Why is it a man has to be bothered every damn second? What do you want, Captain Hink?"

He shut the door behind him, but not before Mae caught a glimpse of another servant in the room. The room seemed relatively sparse, but the servant was leaning out the window and lighting a wick that burned a strange green-yellow color.

That was all she saw before the door shut firmly behind the hunchbacked old man.

"This is one of my passengers, Jack," Captain Hink said. "And she's in need of a few medicines to tend the woman who's injured in our company."

"Medicines? Yes, yes." He shuffled past them both toward one wall covered in wooden shelves and drawers and filled with bottles, jars, boxes, and parcels. The sweet, dusty scent of dried herbs was stronger here, as was the smell of beeswax and oils.

"Tell me what ails the girl," he said, stopping short in front of the first of the shelves, "and I'll tell you what I have to soothe it."

"I just have a short list to fill," Mae said.

Jack craned his head up so he could see out from under his bushy eyebrows. "Then get on with telling me the list."

"I'll need yarrow and clean cotton for bandages. And I'll need something for the pain that won't put her to sleep."

"I've got the first two." Jack tottered along the line of shelves and reached down for a packet of clean cotton cloth. "Bandages." He set them on the top of a hutch filled with small perfume bottles.

"Yarrow, yarrow . . . that's right over here. Haven't had a bundle for a while." He pulled a thin metal stick out of his pocket, no bigger around than a cigar. Then he tugged it straight. The brass stick stretched out three feet long. He pointed the clamp on the end toward a jar on one of the higher shelves. He hooked the jar down and set it next to the bandages.

"As for keeping someone awake and out of pain, I'm not sure there's much for that. You can have your pick of whiskey, laudanum, or Bateman's Drops." He opened a small door on his apothecary hutch.

"No coca leaves?" Captain Hink asked.

Old Jack shook his head. "Bartered them off for a case of champagne. Have a bottle of Peruvian coca tonic left." He withdrew a slim green bottle.

"Knew a glim runner who used it once," Hink said to Mae. "He didn't have complaints."

Mae held out her hand and Old Jack passed her the bottle. She studied the label. "There's three dosages worth here." She considered the long road ahead and that they had lost nearly all their supplies in Vicinity. "Better this and two bottles of laudanum, if you have them."

"Said I did, didn't I?" Jack pulled down two bottles. "They ain't cheap. We're coming into winter and I won't have new supplies until the winds calm in spring."

"You just had an entire ship of supplies dock tonight," Hink said. "You can't tell me Beaumont didn't have a stash of patent medicines on board."

"I can and I will," Old Jack said. "You can pay me for what I'm selling, or you can find some other trading post to do your business."

Hink exhaled in the sort of way that made it seem like he was counting down from ten to one. "You know I landed on nothing but fumes. If you're expecting me to pony up a fortune, you're hitting the wrong rock."

Old Jack licked his lips, his sharp eyes narrowing for the haggle. "You said you'd pay in glim or pay in gold. I want both."

"I think you may be misinterpreting the word 'or,' Jack."

"And you're misinterpreting my ability to give a damn, Hink."

"No. I never thought you cared about anything but your own skin.

That and robbing folks like me blind. I can give you glim in the morning if the *Swift* flies, or gold today. But I ain't about to give you both."

Jack sucked on his bottom teeth, then slid a glance at Mae.

Mae gave him an even stare, as if the act of negotiation bored her, instead of showing how frustrated she was. They needed this medicine. Rose needed it. But they had to rely on Captain Hink's ability to haggle right now.

He was going out of his way to see that Rose had what she needed. Mae didn't know how she would repay him. Didn't know if Mr. Hunt had already negotiated some kind of payment.

And she was not about to mess it up by looking desperate.

The men were shaking hands. Mae realized, with a start, that she had been too lost in thought to notice that the negotiation was drawing to a close.

"If you'll excuse us," Captain Hink said, the bundles and bottles in his hands, "we'll take our leave."

Old Jack gave Mae one last hard stare, as if expecting her to say something or do something.

"Good evening," she said.

"See them out," he yelled to the servant waiting a respectable distance behind them.

The servant headed toward the door, and Hink reshuffled the packages in his hands and started walking. Old Jack headed straightwise to his office.

"I'll expect the money on my doorstep in the morning," Old Jack said as he lifted the latch on the carved door. "Or that ship of yours becomes my goods."

"Didn't put her up as collateral," Captain Hink said. "Don't make me straighten your facts with my fists, Jack."

"Gold or the ship, either fills your debt."

"You touch the *Swift* and it will be the last thing you fondle," Hink said. "I'm not blowing steam. You send anyone for my ship and I'll kill him dead."

Captain Hink wasn't looking at Jack as he strode across the room, but Mae glanced back at the old man.

His office door was half open, his hand still on the latch. Through the windows on the other side of his office the odd green-yellow light flooded the room, and poured out in a wedge around his feet.

"Do not threaten the bear in its den, Captain Hink Cage," Old Jack said. "The bear always wins." Then he stepped into his office and slammed the door behind him.

Hink's jaw was set so hard, the muscle at his temple bulged. He stopped in front of the metal door. For a moment, Mae thought he might just turn on his heel and take up a fight with Old Jack. But instead he blew out a breath and waved at the door.

"Go ahead," Hink said to the servant. "Open it up. Seems there's a bear loose in these parts."

The servant worked the locks and chains and bolts, then pulled the door inward smooth and easy as if it didn't weigh a thing.

Mae and the captain walked out into the hall.

"I hope you didn't promise him too much, Captain."

"That penny-squeezing thief would pick my pocket by way of my tailpipe, if you'll pardon my language. I didn't give him a nickel more than those medicines were worth."

"But your ship . . ."

"My ship isn't a part of my debt." They walked a short way. "He was just blustering because I didn't have any glim to throw at his feet, the greedy pig."

"Your kindness hasn't gone unnoticed."

"Oh?"

"I am grateful for your assistance," she said, "though I must admit I don't know why you've gone out of your way for us."

"Haven't gone that far," he said quietly. "Was headed over Vicinity when you fell into trouble. Picking you up wasn't any bother. I'd have put you down somewhere of your choosing before now, but your man—"

"He's not my man."

Hink waggled his eyebrows. "—convinced me that our interests align." He walked a little farther until his bootheels were no longer thudding on wood, but once again fell soft and muted against the dirt and stone hall.

"What interests, Captain Hink?" Mae asked softly so as not to have her own words echo back at her.

"Your man says he can find the Holder. That's something I'm very much interested in. So do you know if he might be telling me true?"

Mae thought it over. She had a foggy recollection of Cedar telling her he had spoken to the captain about the Holder. And that they'd made a deal.

"I have only known Mr. Hunt to be an honest man. If he gave you his word, his word is good."

"Then I see this, us traveling together for a bit, as a sort of . . . partnership, Mrs. Lindson. Where we both benefit from the other's well-being."

"That's good to know, Captain," Mae said. "And I'm sure Rose will be much more comfortable for your willingness to see things in such a light."

Captain Hink smiled, and it didn't take much to see that it was the mention of Rose that had put that smile on his face.

"Do you know her well?" he asked.

"She and I have been friends for many years." Mae didn't offer any more information. If the captain was interested in Rose in more than a passing manner, then he'd need to be specific about his inquiries of her.

There was still a bit of a scallywag manner to him. She wasn't sure that she liked the idea of encouraging his attentions in Rose.

"She heading to family same as you, Mrs. Lindson?"

"She left her family behind."

"So she's looking for brighter skies? Man with a ship could show her every corner of these bright heavens."

They were nearly back to the large common room again. Mae could smell the meat, potatoes, and flapjacks. Her stomach clenched. She hadn't eaten a full meal in some time. Still, she stopped and turned toward the captain.

"Rose is ill, Captain Hink. She's going to have all she can handle just holding on to the earth. If she has the fortitude to recover from this . . . to live . . . then maybe you can ask her if she's looking for the sky."

The captain's face became blank, his eyes dark. He was a man who had seen death; that was very clear. Mae expected it of a person in his occupation. But what she did not expect was the startled sorrow reflected in the depth of his steady gaze.

"Well, then," he said softly. "Let me know if I can do anything else to help."

Mae nodded. "I will, Captain. I will."

And then they stepped into the room, the captain pulling the flask from inside his coat and taking a long draw as he paced toward the hearth where Seldom leaned.

Mae crossed instead to the sleeping chambers, to do what she could to keep Rose alive.

labaster Saint refused to lie back on the table. "If it can't be done sitting, then it won't be done."

Mr. Shunt's mouth crooked up and his black-tipped tongue flicked over his bottom lip. He held an artful tin cup, carved with hypnotizing intricacy, between his finger and thumb, his other fingers stretched wide. Blood covered his fingers, gathering in a slick rivulet down his wrist to soak into the wetted lace of shirt and coat cuff.

There was blood everywhere in the tent, enough that his sleeves dripped a steady *tick, tick, tick* of it to the damp ground.

Shunt seemed unconcerned about the blood, though he was a difficult man to read. He still wore coat and hat, and in the poorly lit tent, shadows shrouded his eyes.

But when he smiled, those serrated teeth were easy enough to see.

"Yes," Mr. Shunt said. "Sitting would be most"—he pursed his lips and took a sip of the water from the cup—"satisfactory."

Lieutenant Foster stood in the corner of the tent behind the general, his gun an easy draw at his side. He shifted a bit at Shunt's leer, but didn't pull the weapon on him.

The general had been pleased to see Lieutenant Foster walking under his own power, without any hint of a limp. And now Foster stood, calm and clear-eyed, not showing a hint of recent pain.

Just a handful of hours ago, Lieutenant Foster had been helped off the table in this tent and taken to his cot. A few hours after that, he had washed the sweat and blood off his skin, combed his hair, and put on a fresh uniform.

So he could shoot Mr. Shunt straight through his greasy heart if need be.

"How long will this take?" the Saint asked, removing his uniform jacket and shirt. He left his undershirt in place.

Mr. Shunt had used up nearly all the day to get through the rest of the injured men. He had worked meticulously and methodically, never hurrying.

It was almost as if he savored his work, like a fine craftsman at the bench.

If he didn't have a part in the right size or shape, he'd pieced together bits of bone, tendons, metal, and leather until he had created a functioning replacement. Every piece was stitched with thread that seemed to spool directly from his razor-sharp fingertips. And every incision he sealed with a smear of glim and tin.

A quarter of the men hadn't made it through Mr. Shunt's ministrations. But that was a small price to pay for the rewards reaped by the others.

Of course, Mr. Shunt had seen to it that the freshly dead had not gone to waste. He was as unflinching and clever of a field surgeon as the general had ever seen, and harvested fresh bone, muscle, and flesh at the last rattle of a man's breath. These he wrapped in clean cotton to add to his supply, or straightaway put them to use.

The Saint did not trust him, did not like him, and did not want to be in debt to him. But he wanted an eye. Wanted the sight that Marshal Cage had taken from him. Wanted two good eyes to see when Marshal Cage suffered in kind.

Six of his most loyal men stood in the cramped tent. Well armed, well rested, three of them having had parts and pieces replaced.

If Mr. Shunt did anything beyond their agreement, he would be dead. Instantly.

The general pressed his shoulders against the chair. Mr. Shunt seemed unconcerned of the men in the room. Unconcerned of the Saint. He sipped water and watched Alabaster over the brim of the cup.

On the table between them was a line of bloody instruments: bone saws, fillet knives, awls, and crimping tools. Just off to one side, nearest Alabaster, was a square piece of white cloth. And in the very center of that cloth was an eye. The yellowing orb had been soaking in glim and tin. Moist and sticky green-gray, the globule looked like it was eaten by rot, even though it was whole, and perfectly round.

Slender bloodred tendrils attached at one end of the eye and curled like mealworms against the white cloth.

The Saint lifted the patch from over the hole in his face and tossed it on the table next to the eye. "Let's get on with it, Mr. Shunt. There's people we'd both like to see dead."

Mr. Shunt placed the spectacular tin cup on the table as if he were handling fine china and then glided over to the general. He bent and leaned in so close to study the hole where Alabaster's eye had been that the Saint could smell the oiled leather and bitter stink of him.

"Yes," Shunt whispered, his fingers probing gently around the eye hole. "Such hatred you have for him. And he for you. Joined in nightmare, drenched in blood. Beautiful."

And then he reached over and plucked the eyeball off the cloth, delicately dangling it by its red strands. He turned back to Alabaster.

There was not even the faintest hint of humanity in his shadowed features.

"If you cannot hold your head still, General Alabaster Saint," he said. "I will steady it for you."

He withdrew the small vial of glim and tin and flicked the hinged cork off with his thumb. Then he tipped the vial, his thumb over the mouth to catch a small pool of the odd green and silver mixture.

He recorked the vial, keeping glim balanced on his thumb. Then pressed his fingers across the top of the general's head and poised his thumb in front of the general's empty eye socket.

"Now you will know pain."

The general set his teeth and inhaled through his nose. He had been tortured, maimed, and worse. He was no stranger to pain.

And he'd be damned if he was going to yell in front of his men.

Mr. Shunt shoved his thumb into the general's eye hole.

The agony was staggering. Alabaster held his breath against the moan building in his chest as time dragged from one tick to the next.

Mr. Shunt took his time scraping his thumb inside Alabaster's eye socket until the scarred flesh was raw and alive again.

And all the while he hummed and smiled.

Shunt drew his bloody thumb out of the hole, allowing Alabaster a small reprieve from the pain. Not for long. Not even long enough for Alabaster to release one breath and inhale the next.

Shunt forced his head back, clamped it still, and was over him again.

The general's chest clenched in fear. His neck was exposed to a madman with blades for fingertips and no humanity behind those eyes.

It had been many long years since Alabaster Saint had feared any man.

Mr. Shunt was not any man.

Monster. Nightmare. Madness. Alabaster's head squirmed with memories of every horror he had endured, every failure that had brought him to his knees.

The general wanted a gun in his hand, a knife in Shunt's throat. He wanted out from under the vise of Shunt's grip, out from under the damp heat of his breath, out from under these memories that choked him.

But he did not move, did not twitch. He met that man's burning gaze with his own.

"Enough," the general gritted out. "Just get this done."

Shunt's lips hitched up. "As you wish, Alabaster Saint."

The world dissolved under a torrent of pain, battering every last nerve in his body.

Agony drummed through him, thick, constant, hammering, scraping, burning. He blacked out more than once, only to have the sharp horror drag him back from the terror of his dreams.

There was no escape from Mr. Shunt's methodical, vicious mercies. No escape from Mr. Shunt, who followed him into his dreams and was there, tearing him apart when he passed out, and there, laughing, when he woke.

Finally, the general came to. Drenched in sweat and so wrung out from the pain that he didn't have air enough to yell. His throat was raw. He couldn't remember screaming, couldn't remember anything except Mr. Shunt's laughter and the endless pain.

The echo of agony still rode the edge of nerve, skin, and bone.

Every heartbeat hurt.

Mr. Shunt straightened away from the general, his long, knobby fingers clicking down one by one to tuck into his palm like feathers on a wing.

Alabaster blinked, trying to focus. The room seemed too far away and too close all at once. It was nauseating.

"General?" Lieutenant Foster said from over his shoulder. "Are you well, sir?"

Alabaster unclenched his fingers from around the base of the chair seat, his knuckles swollen and sore. He ached. Every damn muscle ached.

He glanced over his shoulder at Lieutenant Foster and realized he could see, clearly, out of both eyes.

He had spent years carrying half a world of darkness with him wherever he went. And now, finally, the world was whole and his to see again.

To own, earth and sky.

He licked the salt from his lips and tasted blood there. "Perfectly well, Lieutenant," he rasped. "See to Mr. Shunt's payment."

The lieutenant nodded once.

The six men in the tent all pulled their guns and leveled them at Mr. Shunt.

Mr. Shunt held very still. Except for his head. That he turned, almost unnaturally far, first one way and then the other to assess the men and the weapons aimed at his person.

"You, Mr. Shunt," Alabaster said in his ruined voice, "have done us a great favor. We intend to thank you for it."

Mr. Shunt folded his hands together in front of his breast and tipped his head down. "Are you sure you want to do that, General Alabaster Saint? Have we not an agreement already?"

"We got what we wanted, Mr. Shunt. I can't say the same for you."

Shunt hesitated, as if weighing that statement. Then he smiled.

"These stitches, these gifts are mine to give," Shunt said quietly. "And mine to take away."

One of the soldiers behind Shunt lifted his gun, aiming at Shunt's head.

Shunt couldn't see him. Shouldn't be able to see him, since he stood well at his back.

Mr. Shunt flicked one finger and the soldier's hand shook. A guttural scream started up out of the soldier's throat. His eyes bulged in terror and pain.

The stitches around the man's wrist slithered out of his skin, leaving a track of bloody holes behind. And then his hand, the hand Mr. Shunt had given him, crackled, wet and gristly as it separated from the man's arm, and fell to the floor with a thump.

His gun fell to the floor with it.

The man was still yelling, couldn't seem to stop yelling. He buckled to his knees, grasping at his stump that gushed blood.

"You have entered *my* agreement." Shunt's whisper could be heard, impossibly, over the soldier's screams, as if he sat in Alabaster's ear and murmured there.

"You will be useful to me, Alabaster, or I will no longer offer my kindness." He flicked his hand again and the soldier writhed on the floor, limbs thrashing uncontrollably.

"Or mercy." Shunt flared his fingers outward.

The soldier fell apart at the seams. It was as if each joint, each crease, each piece of his body suddenly separated, tied by different strings that had all, violently, been tugged.

The soldier was nothing but a quivering pile of flesh, bones, and meat in a bloody stew. No more a living thing than the sweepings of a slaughterhouse.

To their credit, the remaining soldiers did not fire on Shunt, did not move, did not say a thing. They awaited their commander's decision.

"What game do you play, Mr. Shunt?" the general demanded.

"One with few rules," he answered, "and high risk. To you. You are now a part of me, General Alabaster Saint. A part of my . . . kind. Held together with glim and strangework.

"My finger is pressed on the knotted string that binds your flesh together. And if I lift my finger . . ." Shunt opened his hand.

Alabaster's new eye squirmed and pulled against its roots, lancing pain through his skull. Agony bloomed in his joints, fired down every inch of his spine. He held his breath, tightening muscles to hold his shifting bones where they belonged.

Shunt chuckled. ". . . you will come apart like a straw doll." Shunt closed his hand and the sensation was gone.

"Fire!" Alabaster ordered.

The thunderous roar of guns unloading at point-blank range shook the tent and sent splinters flying through the smoke and flames.

Mr. Shunt rattled from the impact, one arm blown completely off, the rest of him crumpling to the ground.

"Lieutenant Foster," Alabaster growled in the thick stench and smoke of spent gunpowder, "finish him."

The lieutenant strode out from behind the general's chair and stood above Mr. Shunt. He unloaded his pistol into the back of the strange man's head.

Blood, black as oil, seeped from the holes peppering his body, mixing with the fresh ruby wetness that covered the floor.

Then, from within those holes, small brass clamps and bits of dull metal flickered like metal snake tongues, stitching up flesh quick as a blink.

Mr. Shunt stood in a fluid rush. Before Alabaster could react, the man was behind him, his remaining hand vised around the general's throat.

"I am not so easily killed," Shunt hissed. "Not by men like you."

Mr. Shunt's arm crawled across the floor, leaving a black, bloody trail behind it.

The soldiers in the room didn't move, transfixed by the disembodied limb wriggling over to the hem of Shunt's coat, where it then grabbed hold of the wool and clawed its way upward, slipping into the sleeve and refastening itself in place.

"So easy to unstring you, Alabaster," Shunt hissed. "So easy to unstring all your little soldiers. And since you will not play my game—"

The men lifted their guns again, but Alabaster held up his hand. "Wait," he groaned.

The men lowered their weapons.

"You want to play?" Shunt cooed. "My game. My rules: kill the hunter, kill the wolf. Bring me the deviser, and bring the witch. Both alive. If you wish to see the next season turn."

"I agreed to kill the hunter and wolf. That was all," Alabaster said.

"Then leave the witch behind. It is your suffering, not mine," Mr. Shunt said. "And a short suffering it will be. You didn't think my gift would last, did you, Alabaster Saint?"

He squeezed Alabaster's throat, then let go, the razor tips of his fingers scratching delicately across his cheek.

"What do you mean?" the general asked.

"My gifts will not last. Without the witch's spells, her binding of life to living, you will die. Soon, soon. Days, weeks. All of you dead."

He clucked his tongue. "Poor men of dirt, bones of ash. So weak and frightened."

He strolled out from behind Alabaster and offered him a wide, jagged smile. "Your grave hungers for the taste of you. If you do not kill my enemies, if you flee . . . I will pull the knots on your strings. Piece by piece, you will all fall down."

The general pushed up onto his feet, holding the edge of the table and locking his knees. "I will not be threatened, Mr. Shunt," he said. "And I will not bow to blackmail."

"I do not threaten, Alabaster Saint. I make dreams come true. You took yours willingly. I gave you everything you desired. Dark wishes."

"The witch for your bones, the deviser for mine." He opened his coat and revealed the hole where his chest should be. In that ragged space was a terrible work of blood and bone and eyes and hands and mouths and things that should never be strung together. All of it moving, grinding, pumping.

In that strange work, dead center, was a gold and crystal clockwork dragonfly. So beautifully fashioned, Alabaster couldn't help but be caught by the glory of it.

"This vessel," Shunt said, "will fail me without the witch's blood, without her magic, without her binding. But it will last many years beyond you and your men. Decades. The deviser can make me new again. I want her. I want them both. Now. And you want them now too."

He bared his teeth and spat. His spittle landed on the table in front of the general's hand and burned into the wood.

"Now."

Mr. Shunt walked around the table and lifted the beautiful tin cup. He took a sip, his eyes fluttering closed for a moment before he began picking up the instruments of his torture, the instruments of his craft, one by one, as if no one else were in the tent with him.

He drew a cloth over each bloody blade, rubbing it clean and humming like a child with his favorite toys.

"General?" Lieutenant Foster said quietly.

"Out," Alabaster barked. "All of you."

Everyone left the room except for Foster, who lingered near the door.

Alabaster straightened and took a moment to don his shirt and coat, thinking through his actions. If what Mr. Shunt had said was true, he and a third of his men were at death's door.

He refused to give in to the reaper so easily.

"We don't know where the hunter and wolf are, Mr. Shunt," Alabaster said. "It could take us a lifetime and more tracking these wilds for a man, and still leave him unfound. If you want him killed, you had best tell me where he is. You know. Don't you?"

Mr. Shunt said nothing for a long stretch of silence. Alabaster buttoned his coat and waited. For all that Mr. Shunt had proven to be an unholy monster, in doing so, he had given a shred of advantage to Alabaster.

Shunt was failing. Dying. Perhaps the strange man was failing faster than he admitted.

Finally, Shunt inhaled a breath that sounded like leather bellows pulling full.

"In the air. In the sky," Mr. Shunt whispered. "This—" He reached into his pocket and Alabaster readied himself for a gun.

But all that balanced in Shunt's palm was a small wooden coin with a tiny tin hole in the center of it.

"Money?"

"A compass," Shunt said. "A beacon. To the hunter, the wolf, the deviser, and the witch."

He stretched out his overly long arm. The same arm that had just crawled about on the floor under its own power. Shunt waited for Alabaster to take the coin from his palm.

The general set his jaw. "And what will I owe you for that coin?"

"The coin is my promise," Shunt said. "It will show you the way to the deviser. Like a tin lock to a tin key." He gave a dry chuckle, as if that statement were a great amusement to him.

His hand remained steady, palm flat, as if offering a treat to an animal.

Alabaster Saint took the coin. It was cool, light wood with a tin plug in the center. In the middle of that was a ragged little hole. Just like a key would fit.

"This is what will happen, Mr. Shunt," the general said. "I will kill the hunter, kill the wolf. The witch and deviser will be under my hold. When you have reversed this evil you have brought upon us, then I will give you the witch and deviser to do with as you please. Do you understand the order of things here on my mountain, Mr. Shunt?"

Shunt had gone back to polishing his instruments. He paused, a corner of bloody cloth pushed between the teeth of a saw.

"Of course, General," he murmured. "I am but a servant to your every wish."

"See that it remains so, Mr. Shunt."

He walked out of the tent, resisting the urge to pull his sword to see if Mr. Shunt would remain ticking without his head attached. Watching him die would almost be worth the gamble on whether or not his life really balanced on finding the witch and the deviser.

Almost.

"With me, Lieutenant," he said.

Foster strode up behind him. It was an odd thing to hear the even rhythm of his pace, the slight drag of his prosthetic gone.

Just as strange as to be seeing the world again clear and sharp from two strong eyes.

General Saint had no intention of giving up these gifts Mr. Shunt had given them. But he'd be boiling in hell before he let another man rule over him.

"Have Les Mullins and Captain Dirkson left to find Marshal Cage?"

"Yes, sir. Several hours ago."

"Good. Take this coin, and man the *Devil's Nine*. Find the witch and deviser and bring them to me."

"What about the hunter and wolf, sir?"

"If you find them, leave them behind. Alive. If Shunt wants them dead, he'll have to do it himself."

"Yes, sir."

Lieutenant Foster turned toward the shed to ready the scout ship, leaving the heavier armed ships behind for General Alabaster Saint and the troops if they needed them.

"Sir?" Foster asked before he'd gone more than a step or two.

"Yes?"

"What about Mr. Shunt? What will you do with him?"

"I will break him to my will, Mr. Foster. Follow the compass, and set a flare when you've found the witch and deviser. Then we will discuss Mr. Shunt's fate when we have what he most wants in our hands."

CHAPTER SIXTEEN

Rose Small dreamed she was swimming in tea and honey. It was a lovely dream, warm and comforting.

"Rose," Mae's voice said as she drifted. "Wake up. You need to drink this."

She wanted to tell Mae she didn't need anything to drink. She was surrounded by tea. Then something cold and wet pressed against her forehead, and her lips, making her very thirsty.

All the tea around her tasted like dust.

"Wake up, Rose," Mae said again. "Time to wake up."

It took Rose several tries, but she finally lifted her eyelids.

Pain rolled through her back and chest, and made her stomach sour. She was cold, hot, and raw from the top of her head, hurting the most down the left side of her face, shoulder, and arm. She bit her lip but could not stifle a moan.

Mae sat next to her. She leaned in and Rose could see her better in the low light of the room.

"Hey, there now," Mae said. "This will help the pain. Just take a couple drinks."

Mae held the cup to Rose's mouth, which was good. Rose didn't think she had enough strength in her whole body to lift even one hand, much less support a whole cup.

The tea came on bitter and green at first, and then was sweet and strong with the hot burn of alcohol.

"Water?" she asked after taking down as much of the tea as she could. She didn't want to cough, didn't want to jangle her body so harshly, but the burn of the tea was too strong in her throat.

Mae pulled the cup away, then held another at her lips. Rose swallowed several gulps of water until the fire in her belly cooled and her throat soothed.

"I'm going to change the compress on your shoulder," Mae said softly. "I have a new stock of medicines, and it's going to help you feel better."

The warm numbing of whatever Mae had put in that tea was already spreading sweetly through her. She felt more awake, and although not completely out of pain, it was at a much more tolerable distance.

"That helped," Rose said. "I've never tasted anything like it."

"It's coca leaves," Mae said. "From Peru."

"Sounds fancy," she said as Mae spread a greenish-black paste onto a clean cotton cloth and then poured what looked like tea over the top of the cloth.

Mae whispered something, and the words made Rose's head itch and her nose tickle. She wondered if Mae's words held magic, or a blessing.

Rose always did like the idea of Mae having magic at her fingertips. Seemed like such a handy thing to keep around.

"Is that helping yet?" Mae asked.

"The pain is better," Rose said. "We're not on the airship, are we? With Captain Lee Hink?"

"No," Mae said, pulling the covers down to Rose's waist.

From the coolness, Rose suddenly realized she was mostly naked.

Mae gently slipped Rose's shift out of the way so she could place the compress over her shoulder.

Rose sucked in a breath and blew it out between her teeth to try to keep from screaming. But it was only a few breaths more before her shoulder stopped hurting so. And then a few breaths after that Rose actually felt . . . well, not better, but not quite so torn up.

". . . so we are in a mountain, a cavern, carved out by the man—Old Jack," Mae was saying as she gently lifted and turned the cool wet rag on Rose's forehead. "Who has us as his guests, but only through the generous and constant payment of Captain Hink."

"Is he here still?" Rose asked.

Mae's hands stilled a moment and then she looked down at Rose and smiled. "Captain Hink? Yes, he is. And he's asked after you."

"The captain?" Rose asked. "The airship captain?"

"That's the one," Mae said. "He's out in the main room eating a meal. Everyone is out there—his crew, Mr. Hunt, and a crew from another airship."

"Another airship?" Rose said as a flush of warmth spread out to the tips of her fingers and toes. "How wonderful. Could you help me sit? I'd like to see this place."

"I don't know . . ."

"Please? I feel so much better right now. I'd like to see this place. I'd like to see everything I can."

"Let me get a few things." Mae walked a little ways off.

Rose turned her head to watch and pain bit down hard enough to make her stop breathing.

She was still under a lot of hurt. But at least she could see a few cots lined off in one direction. The walls were unhewn stone, dark, with clever shelves chipped into them and lanterns set here and there. It almost made the place look like a night sky broken by stars.

"What mountain are we inside, and how did we get here?" Rose asked.

Mae came back with a blanket rolled in her arms.

"We are north of the Bitterroots. I'm not clear as to our exact location. Captain Hink said this is Old Jack's place. Jack takes in airships for supplies and repairs." Mae reached down and quick as a wink lifted Rose by her waist and tucked the blanket behind her to prop her up a bit.

It hurt, and Rose let out a whimper, but got over it quick enough.

"How exotic," she said.

"I think it's damp, dark, and not nearly as warm as I prefer," Mae said. "But it's like nothing I've ever seen. Apparently, Mr. Jack has blasted a labyrinth of tunnels and rooms in the hills.

"I have been informed, in no uncertain terms, that I am not to go wandering off down any random tunnel just because my curiosity takes hold of my feet. Apparently, if I do, I'll lose all sense and be lost forever."

Rose smiled. "Sounds like you. Always with a whim in your eyes."

"Well, there's some truth to that. Lately." She paused and took some time to make sure Rose's blanket was tucked in properly.

Rose stretched the fingers on her good hand, touching Mae. "You've done fine. More than fine. I saw you on the ship. We were going to crash. You . . . you gave us a blessing and saw that we landed properly, didn't you?"

"I wasn't in my mind. I don't think I should have . . . I didn't ask the captain if he wanted . . ."

"I'm sure he wanted to see us all back to land safely. You did right by us. Thank you, Mae."

"It's done," Mae said. "If I can undo the harm, I will. But not until I return to the sisters."

"Do you hear them here? The sisters?" Rose asked.

"No." Mae frowned. "It's something about these mountains. The silence is thick. Not that I'm complaining. The spell set on me to return me home is . . ."

Rose would have said "punishing," but Mae just set her shoulders straight a bit and said, "Insistent."

"And we're not flying," Rose said. "Did we stop to supply or repair?"

"A little of both, I suppose," Mae said. "You haven't had a bite to eat in far too long. Let me see if there's something left for you." Mae patted her hand gently and made a motion to move.

"I'm dying, aren't I?" Rose asked.

Mae stopped as if she'd suddenly been caught by ropes.

"No."

"I never did think you lied very well, Mae," Rose said softly. "I can feel it. The thing that is inside my shoulder is digging under my skin, twisting. I can taste it in the back of my mouth. Like hot, sour ashes."

"You are not dying," Mae insisted. "We need to get you to the sisterhood. I'm sure they'll have a spell, a magic, a way of helping you heal, of keeping you strong. Many of the sisterhood are far better with herbs and tinctures than I am—why, sister Adaline alone is an amazing healer."

Rose studied Mae's face. "You are the strongest witch to ever come out of that coven," she said gently. "It's why they fear you, you know. Why they are tugging so hard on the reins to get you to turn back to them. They know how powerful you are, Mae."

"Rose . . ."

"If you can't break this pain, send healing to this wound, then I hope you don't mind me saying so, but I can't think of another witch capable of doing more for me."

Mae's eyes were sad, but there was that determined set to her. Rose had seen her plenty of times like that before. Times when Mae refused to give up on someone she cared about.

"I'd like to know," Rose continued, "as one friend to another. Am I dying?"

Mae hesitated, before she nodded once.

"Yes. You are not well. But there is more than just the sisters or my skills to hang our hopes upon. The Madders told Cedar that if we find the Holder we'll be able to extract the tin key in your shoulder. And I am positive that once we remove the key, you will mend up and be good as glim again."

Rose managed a smile even though she didn't think Mae believed what she was saying. Still, hope was hope, and it did the soul good to hold to it. Even if it was a lie.

"Rest while I get you some food. You need to keep your strength up." Mae patted her hand once again and then walked out of the room.

The tea and compress had done a welcome job of pushing the pain far enough away that Rose didn't much care about it. Though she probably should. It was strange to think that right here under the cover of a mountain she couldn't find on a map, she might be living one of her last days.

She drew the fingers of her good hand along the rough blanket edge, wishing she had something to touch, to turn, to keep her hands and her mind busy and away from dark thoughts.

There were so many things she had wanted to see—the big cities, New York, Philadelphia, Paris. There were people she'd wished she had met, family out there, somewhere she'd run out of time to find. And so many things she had wanted to experience. Flying her own airship, falling in love with a man who loved her back, adventures.

She took a deep breath and let it out slowly. Probably wasn't going to have any of those things now. The look on Mae's face had told her what she suspected. She had only a few days left, and likely she'd spend each of those getting weaker and weaker.

Such a thing. Here she had set off on the trail looking forward to each new wonder she would discover, all the while not knowing she was just riding hard and fast toward a meeting with her death. Wasn't at all how she'd expected her life to turn after leaving Hallelujah.

The sound of footsteps stirred her from her thoughts.

"Didn't think you'd be awake, Miss Small," Captain Hink said as he strolled toward her cot.

Well, she could be certain of one thing. It wasn't just the low light of the airship that had given the man a handsome swagger. He was just as good-looking now as then.

"Mrs. Lindson woke me to see to my shoulder," Rose said. She realized that her shoulder, neck, and a good portion of her chest were bare except for where bandages wrapped around them.

She was sitting half naked in front of an airship captain. It was such a thing she'd only secretly dreamed about. But not like this. In her dreams she'd been bathed, fresh, and certainly not wounded.

The captain's gaze roamed briefly over her bare skin before lingering on her bandage and then returning to her eyes. "It's nice to see you feeling good enough to be sitting," he said as he walked off into the shadows of the room a bit, then returned with a chair into the warm wash of lantern light.

He put the chair next to her cot and sat there, next to her. "Sorry for the landing. Not the smoothest flight I've ever offered a passenger."

"Oh, no, it was wonderful."

"Wonderful?" he asked. "That medicine Mrs. Lindson gave you must be clouding your memories a bit. Maybe I ought to give it to all my passengers." He smiled and it put light in his eyes, and an ease in all the rest of him.

Captain Cage was wide at the shoulder, with hair the color of gold and a face that looked like it would fit in just fine with those heroes of Nordic myths. He looked like he hadn't shaved in a few days, which only gave him a sort of devil-may-care air, which she should not find so heart-stoppingly handsome.

But he was. And so far, had been kind to her too.

"I'm just sorry I couldn't enjoy it," Rose said. "I've always fancied what it might be like to pilot an airship, to harvest glim."

"Well, I can tell you just what it's like," Captain Hink said. "Have you ever ridden a horse so fast it's taken your breath away?"

Rose nodded.

"It's like that but with more power. Steam train will almost give you the feel of it, except instead of barreling down a track, you're shooting for the sky, with no rattle of the earth in your bones, and nothing but the soft green fire of glim burning in the sky around you.

"Up there, glim seems so strong and real. You think maybe you could lean out the window to feel the drag of it across your fingertips, taste it on your tongue, or catch a whiff of fragrance. But there's no sensing it that way, no sense to it at all. Glim is a feast for the eyes only, though some say they've heard it ring like an angels' chorus of bells on the wind."

He shrugged and slouched in the chair a bit, relaxing into this. "We catch it with nets." He spread his arms out wide. "Long-armed outrigging that drags through the sky, gathering glim on the strands, like pollen on a bee's butt. Those strands draw the glim down to finer threads, where it collects like liquid in large glass globes. Can't box glim up in too small a spot. It's always looking for a way out, a way back to the sky, I reckon. Keep too tight a hold on it, and it will burst its cage.

"I've always thought glim and those who harvest it are much the same in that way. Too much of the need for the open sky in them. But then, I suppose you've heard all about how glim is got. Didn't mean to rattle on."

"No, it's fine. More than fine," Rose said. "I've heard some of how it is harvested, read about it in the papers. But that's all. If you don't mind, Captain—"

"Lee," he said.

"If you don't mind, Lee," Rose said, liking the sound of his name on her lips, "I'd love to hear more."

"More about glim," he asked quietly, "or more about me?"

Rose held his gaze steady, glad she wasn't blushing from that look he was giving her. A look she was giving him right back. "Both."

He nodded and leaned in a little closer to her. "I'd be happy to oblige you on both accounts, Rose."

She liked the sound of her name on his lips too.

Mae stepped into the room. Captain Hink leaned away, but his smile, and the heat in his eyes, did not dampen as Mae walked over to the bed.

"Captain Hink," Mae said. "Thank you for keeping Miss Small company. I hope you haven't tired her out too much before her hot meal."

"Not at all," Rose said. "He's been telling me about glim."

"Has he?" Mae said. "That's certainly an interesting subject."

"Just so," Captain Hink said. "Of course, not much is known as to the whys of glim: why it gathers above the mountains, why it has such restorative powers, or even where, exactly, it comes from."

"Doesn't it come from the storms?" Mae set a plate down on the crate next to Rose's cot and turned with a bowl and spoon.

"It's not known, really," Hink said. "I've gathered glim on a clear day just as often as above some of the worst lightning storms the range can cook up. There are men with better minds who have tried to argue it out. Haven't heard they've agreed on an answer yet."

"I'd love to read up on the theories," Rose said.

"Not until you eat something." Mae picked up the bowl.

"Let me give you some room for that." Hink stood.

"No, that's fine," Mae said. "It's no bother."

"Nonsense. I take up more room than a man ought, and I'd rather not be in the way of Miss Small's meal." He stepped around the chair and Mae took his place, settling in next to Rose's bed.

"Think you can try some broth?" Mae asked. "Mr. Seldom is a surprisingly fine cook."

Hink chuckled. "I don't keep him on the ship for his conversational prowess. Ladies." He tipped his head in a nod.

"Are you leaving?" Rose asked. She really wasn't hungry, and wasn't hurting enough to ignore the sheer restlessness rolling through her.

She wanted out of the bed, out of the room. Wanted to explore this mountain, or maybe go see the *Swift* again while she was awake, aware.

"I have a few things to see to," the captain said. "Ship repairs being one of those things. I'm thinking if we get all hands on her, we can fly out by the end of the day tomorrow. Dawn next, the latest."

"That would be a very good turn of events, Captain Hink," Mae said. "The sooner we can be on the road again . . . well, I suppose sky again, the sooner we will set right our troubles."

"I most certainly hope that is so," he said.

"So," Mae said, after Hink had left the room, "are you feeling strong enough to do this on your own, or would you like some help?"

"I think if you place the bowl on my thigh, I might be able to handle it."

Mae helped her to get situated, and Rose took a spoonful of the soup. The broth was rich and filled with meat and had soft salted dumplings in it. If she'd been in better health she might have enjoyed the meal very much. Right now, she just wanted to get out of the bed and follow Captain Hink to watch him inspect the ship.

She could learn so much from him. Might even learn how to fly. Molly had seemed happy with her help on the boilers. Maybe she'd let her help again.

If she had time. If she lived.

In answer to those two grim thoughts, Rose applied herself to the broth. Once a person stopped eating, it was never long until they were in the grave. And she was not going to lie down to rest easily.

After she had determinedly gotten through half of the soup, she gave the spoon and bowl over to Mae in exchange for a cup of water lightly laced with brandy.

"Never drank so much in my life," Rose said.

"Just to keep the pain at bay," Mae answered, tidying up things.

Two of the men from Captain Hink's ship sauntered into the room and dropped down on cots. They didn't even take the time to undress or shed their boots and harnesses before they were snoring softly.

Molly Gregor showed up next, and tromped over to Rose's bed.

"Well, don't you look perky?" She smiled, and dragged her breathing gear off over her head. "I suppose the menfolk will sleep up on that side of the room, so us fine ladies can retire in relative modesty here. Not that I'm much used to modesty, traveling with those yokels."

She held her breathing gear and goggles in one hand, then looked around, trying to decide where to drop them. She finally took the cot that was set somewhere between the men's cots and Rose's. She dropped the gear at the head of the bed, then sat. She unlaced her boots and sighed.

"I do get tired of the boots," she said, staring down at her stockinged feet as she wiggled her toes. "Now." She got up and watched Mae fuss about with blankets and such around Rose's bed.

She gave Rose a wink. "Is there anything you might need my help with, Mrs. Lindson?"

"What?" Mae asked. "Oh, no, thank you, Miss Gregor."

"Molly," she said. "Please use my given name. Friends and crew always do."

"Thank you, Molly," Mae said. "I can't see anything else that can be done tonight. And Captain Hink said we might be flying out to-morrow if the *Swift* is in good repair, so I think sleep might be the best course for us all."

"He said that, did he?" Molly asked. "Man seems awfully sure of the work he hasn't even started on yet."

"Is the ship badly damaged?" Rose asked.

"Oh, no worse than she's been before," Molly said. "We'll fix her up so you wouldn't even know she'd taken a hit. Whether it will take a day, or maybe two, is more my doubt."

"But the captain said—," Rose began.

"Yes, my dear, I know the captain." She gave Rose a look. "And I know the sorts of things he says."

"Oh, I didn't mean to say that you didn't," Rose said.

Molly closed her eyes for an extra moment, and a kindly smile curved her lips. "You haven't said anything to bother me, Rose—may I call you Rose?"

"Yes."

"Good." Molly strolled closer and then glanced over her shoulder toward the men in the room, listening for their snores.

Satisfied that they were sleeping, she said, "I just think the captain very much wants to see you and all of his passengers safely to your destination as quickly as possible. He has a way of promising the moon when his heart's in it. And just between you and me? When his heart's in it is when he always manages to come through."

"Is it?" Rose asked, searching Molly's face. Molly didn't carry a heavy resemblance to Mr. Gregor. For one thing, her hair was iron black, whereas the blacksmith's wild hair was fire red. But there was something to the arc of her cheek, the square of her chin, that reminded her very much of her good friend.

"Is what?" Molly asked.

"His heart . . . in it?"

Molly's eyebrows quirked down just a bit, but she was smiling. "Are you asking me if the captain is concerned about the safety of the people who travel with him, or if he's concerned about you, Miss Rose Small?"

"Both," Rose said quietly. Yes, she should be much more modest about these sorts of questions. After all, she hardly knew Molly Gregor. But if she didn't have much time left to her life, Rose figured she would live it as forthrightly as she could.

"Any passenger he agrees to have aboard the *Swift*—and those are few and far between—the captain has always seen to their safety and comfort. But you?" Molly unbuckled the tool belt around her hips and slung it over one shoulder. "He's particularly interested in your safety and well-being."

"Oh," Rose said.

"And just in case you didn't understand that, he likes you, Rose, though he's barely said more than three words to you. I'm not one to tell the captain who to associate with, but I do want you to know that my loyalties will always fall at his side. Treat him kindly."

Rose just nodded. It might be the medicine and the pain, but it didn't seem like Molly was threatening her. It almost sounded like she was encouraging Rose's interest. Maybe glim runners had a different sort of values when it came to a woman's attraction to a man.

"Good night, Rose Small," Molly said as she walked off toward her cot. "And good night to you, Mae."

"Good night, Molly," Mae said.

Mae came over to Rose and tucked her blanket in around her. "Cold?"

"No."

"Pain?"

"Still bearable. The tonic helped."

Mae smiled. "Good, then. Get some sleep. It's nearly midnight and I think we'll all want our wits in the morning."

"Mae?" Rose asked, catching at her hand before she turned away. "Thank you for taking care of me. I'm sorry I'm . . . well, I'm sorry I'm such a burden."

"Nonsense," Mae said. "You've certainly looked after my well-being when I've needed it."

Mae turned down the wick on the lantern next to Rose's bed. Rose could hear her footsteps as she took to her own cot and settled down upon it, taking off her shoes but not her outer dress.

Molly turned out the lantern next to her bed, and the room was filled with the kind of ink black found only in the deep of caves.

"Mae," Rose whispered.

"Yes?"

"Do you think it wrong for someone to want . . . happiness? When things seem so dire?"

Mae was silent for a bit, then said, "We all deserve happiness, Rose. Our lives should be filled with it whether the days are dark or sunny.

Happiness doesn't beg permission. It just walks across our threshold, sets itself down beside us, and waits for us to notice."

"I suppose that's so," Rose said. "Thank you."

From the sound of Mae's breathing, she slipped into sleep quickly. Molly was snoring softly, and so were Hink's men.

But for Rose, sleep was fleeting. To try to work herself down into slumber, she closed her eyes and imagined herself at Mr. Gregor's blacksmith shop, naming each tool on the wall, in the order they were hung, and repeating what they were used for.

She'd gotten through most of the crimps and hammers when she heard footsteps at the doorway to the room. Not Mr. Hunt. He had a way of stepping so that it was difficult to hear his heel set down.

No, it was the captain, Hink. Her heart picked up a pace and she opened her eyes. She was used to the dark, but he obviously was not. He stepped over the threshold and walked a way into the room. Then he plucked a lantern from the hook on the wall and lit it, turning it low so that only the barest hint of yellow rimmed the blue edge of the wick.

He carried that with him, pacing by the foot of the beds, past his men, past several empty cots, then past Molly's bed, where he stopped.

Holding his lantern up a bit, he scanned the rest of the room. Rose didn't close her eyes, enjoying too much the play of softly lit shadows on his face.

She didn't think he could see that she was awake. She wondered if he would come closer, wondered if he would sit down next to her.

But after a moment of assessing both Mae and Rose in their cots, he turned his back and made his way to the far end of the room, where he set the lantern back on the wall hook, glowing there like a lone star lost in the night. Then he eased down onto a cot without even bothering to take off his hat.

She wondered where Mr. Hunt was, wondered where Wil was. Mae hadn't mentioned them.

Her curiosity was sated just a few minutes later. Mr. Hunt and Wil came into the room, both of them together on six feet not making as much noise as one man alone on two.

Mr. Hunt didn't seem to need light to navigate the night. He moved through it naturally and silently, pacing across the room to where he finally settled in a cot between the other men and the women.

Wil made a slow and careful inspection of the boundaries and contents in the room, then set himself by the door, facing outward.

Rose closed her eyes and listened to the breathing around her. She wished she could be sleeping peacefully like the others, but her thoughts were still racing.

She tried to return to imagining Mr. Gregor's shop, but her mind was crowded with Captain Hink. She imagined his smile, the hard angle of his jaw, and the low roll of his voice. She imagined they were alone on his ship, flying over the green blanket of trees that was interrupted only by fields and mountains and embroidered streams.

She imagined he was showing her how to fly the ship, how to know the feel of the engines, how to sense the stretch of wings.

Then her imagination wandered onward to other things. The taste of Hink's lips as he kissed her, the heat of his skin, the touch of his hand against her body. Would he want her that way? Would he smile between kisses? Would he hold her gently or with possessive strength? Would he, even for one moment, love her?

Those were things she wanted to know. Things she might never have the time to learn.

She hoped Mae was right. Hoped happiness knew how to find its way into a person's life. And she hoped if happiness found her, she might have at least one kiss, one loving moment, before she had to lay down this life.

CHAPTER SEVENTEEN

Hink was having a hell of a time trying to sleep. He heard Cedar come into the room with that wolf of his. Listened to him check in on Mae and Rose.

Mr. Hunt was nothing if not a protector of the women. Hink found that commendable, though right now he'd prefer if Mr. Hunt would mind someone else's business.

He lay still, wishing sleep would drag him down already, but there was too much on his mind. He'd checked the *Swift*. It wouldn't take much, maybe half a day to repair her, less than that to supply her.

He'd paid his gold to Old Jack and signed the billing of what he could take from Jack's stores. If luck would land on his side, they'd be out of this bear trap by tomorrow evening.

The things Mae Lindson had told him about Rose stuck and rubbed, no matter how he turned his thoughts around. Rose was dying. And the longer it took him to get his ship in the air, the less of a chance that there would be a way to see to it that she didn't die.

Hink was itchy with the need to be doing something. To find the Holder or Alabaster Saint for the president, to get Rose to someplace that could mend her—hell, to get himself and his crew on a range of mountain that wasn't filled with folk bent on wanting to see him and his ship dead.

But no matter how much he tried to tell himself it was all the crashing and being shot at that had set his nerves on edge, he knew that wasn't so.

It was Rose Small.

He'd only spoken to her twice. But there was something about her, something behind that knowing smile and innocent eyes. Yes, she was a pretty thing, but he'd seen plenty of pretty women when he was growing up in a bordello. And he'd seen plenty of pretty women since then.

There was something about her. Even fevered, in pain, she stirred him. Made him wonder what her laughter sounded like. Made him wonder what would catch her temper, and what would tease her toward forgiveness.

Mae said she was looking for family. And Rose had seemed intense, rapt, when he'd been talking about the ship, about glim.

The sort of woman who wanted to travel, who found things around her wondrous even when it was just as clear how equally dangerous they were, was rare in this world.

Molly said he had fallen for her. He hated it when that Gregor woman was right.

Still, there wasn't anything he could do about his feelings. Not right now.

He rolled over, and punched at the blanket roll under his head. The cots were loose strung and about as comfortable as sleeping on a swayback horse. He thought the stone floor might put fewer kinks in his back.

Didn't seem to be bothering the others. Seldom and Guffin were snoring away, and Molly too, though more softly. He could pick out Cedar Hunt's breathing and wasn't fully convinced he was asleep. Mae, though, was still and breathing evenly. And Rose . . .

She made a small coughing sound in the back of her throat as if she were thirsty.

Then he heard her shifting, likely trying to get to the cup of water near her bed.

Mae would help her.

He waited for Mrs. Lindson to move. Nothing. Waited a bit longer.

Rose made that sound again, then caught at her breath as if waiting for a pain to pass, or trying to keep a coughing spell at bay.

Surely Mae heard that.

When Mae still didn't move, Hink shifted a bit in his bunk, then sat. His eyes had adjusted to the light and he could see Mae was curled on her side. Her eyes were closed. Everyone else looked lost in the land of dreams, so Hink made his way over to Rose's bed.

He wasn't bringing a pillow this time. No, he'd do his best to avoid talking to her, for that matter. She had a way of making him feel doubtful, clumsy. Except for when he was talking about his ship. Nothing made him feel awkward when he was talking about the *Swift*.

Mr. Hunt didn't stir as he passed. Neither did Molly or Mae.

He paused below Rose's cot. She had her hand over her eyes. Maybe she was sleeping. She coughed again, a dry hack, and he could see her throat working to get moisture.

Hink came up beside her bed. "Rose?" he whispered.

She didn't answer.

He tried again. "Miss Small, do you need some water?"

Rose lowered her hand. Her eyes were wide with surprise, but she nodded. "Please," she barely rasped.

Hink took the cup from the shelf and sniffed it. Didn't smell like booze or tea. Just to be sure, he took a very small sip. Stale, but water.

"Here." He held the cup out and she took it, raising it up to her lips. But her hand was shaking so badly he was afraid she was going to knock a tooth out.

Hink wrapped his hand under hers, helping her bear the weight of the cup and steadying her trembling.

She drank the cup dry and then let him take it away and replace it on the shelf.

"Was that enough?" he whispered.

She nodded.

He just stood there staring at her. Like a boy who was tongue-tied and slow.

"I suppose I should go," he said quietly. "Unless you need anything else?"

"No." Then, thinking twice, she said, "Yes. I mean, yes, if it's not too much of a bother."

"Not at all," he said. "I was already up. Can't seem to sleep tonight."

"Neither can I," she said.

"So what is it you need?" Hink asked. "Medicine? Mrs. Lindson?"

"The sky."

"What?"

"I feel . . ." She licked her lips as if trying to work out the words before she said them. "I feel all cooped up here in this stone, here in this bed. I feel like I've been on my back, sick, for years. It hasn't been years, has it?" she asked.

"Just a couple days, I'm given to understand," Hink said.

"I'd like to see the sky. The stars, if they're out tonight."

Hink considered the wisdom of such a thing. She could catch her death of cold out in the mountain air. Even moving her out of the bed might make that shoulder wound of hers worse. He was fairly certain Mrs. Lindson would be set against it. And if Cedar Hunt caught him taking Miss Rose for a midnight stroll, he was fair certain the man would happily string him up by his own tendons.

"Please," Rose said.

Hink nodded, and let out a breath. "I don't think you're up for walking and I don't have a pony hid away in my pocket."

That earned him a quick smile, and his heart took to a happy thumping.

"I can walk some," she said. "As far as I can go, I want to. Need to."

"How about we save your walking for outside the caverns. I'll carry you."

"I . . ." She glanced at his face, and he knew it was set in a determination that made it clear he was not going to take an argument on this.

"Very well. Thank you," she whispered.

Hink figured some of the folk in the room must be awake from all their whispered words. Well, maybe not Guffin or Molly, but Seldom slept like a snake—with both eyes open.

And he figured Mr. Hunt wouldn't have slept through all that.

Still, he reached down and lifted Rose, blankets and all, into his arms as carefully as he could.

She wrapped her good arm around his neck and moaned softly against the pain of movement.

At that sound he instantly stilled. "Are you sure? I could set you back in your bed."

"No," she said. "I'm fine. Please."

He started across the floor. To his great surprise no one stirred. The wolf at the door even let him pass by.

Maybe luck was slipping this one his way.

"How about we go catch us a bit of sky, Rose Small?" he asked as he made his way down the corridor that led to the flat rock just before the landing pads.

"You don't know how happy that would make me," Rose said, her voice breathy on a whisper.

Hink smiled, but didn't say any more for fear of tripping over his words. He liked the idea of making her happy. More than liked the feel of her in his arms.

And for the moment, for the first time in a whole lot of years, there was nothing more important to him than seeing that Rose Small got what she wanted.

CHAPTER EIGHTEEN

Cedar Hunt watched as Captain Hink walked out of the room carrying Rose. He had heard everything they said. He didn't know why Rose was so set on asking Hink for help. She was sick and hurting. He didn't want Hink to hurt her more.

He sat up.

To find Mae also sitting. She was looking at him.

Cedar walked over to her, careful to move quietly so as not to wake the others.

"I'll see that he brings her back," Cedar said.

"No," Mae said.

"No?"

Mae wrapped a blanket around her shoulders but didn't bother putting on her shoes. She stood and started walking off, catching his hand and drawing him with her through the room and out a ways down the hall.

Hink was already well out of sight, and even Cedar's keen hearing didn't bring to him the sound of his footsteps or voice.

"He's taking her outside," Cedar said. "I'll just follow and see that she comes right back in."

"I don't think she'd want you to do that, Cedar."

"Doesn't matter what she wants. She's sick. She needs someone to look after her. This isn't the kind of place to just let her wander off with a man, alone."

"She wants to be with him," Mae said. She pulled the blanket around her a little tighter, then leaned against the wall. "She knows she's dying."

"She's not going to die," Cedar practically growled.

Mae gave him a long, cool look, as if gauging the heat on a pot. "She knows there is a strong possibility her wound is fatal," she said. "You can't deny the truth of that. Rose isn't a dreamy-eyed girl. She has a very practical streak about her. I think we should let her have this."

"Have what? A stranger we barely know carting her off in the middle of the night when she's sick and helpless? I know the sorts of things a man like him can do."

"Cedar—," Mae started.

"She's dear to me, Mae," he interrupted. "Both of you are . . . dear. I won't let her catch harm."

"It's not harm she's looking for. It's companionship." Mae tipped her head back and closed her eyes. "She just wants, for once in her life, to know the touch of a man."

"She's wounded."

"She's dying."

Cedar held very still. He heard what Mae was saying, but he couldn't seem to take his eyes off her bare neck, off the delicate curve of her lips, the flutter of her eyelids as she sighed.

His blood rushed hot under his skin and he could feel the heat tightening his muscles. He wanted her, wanted Mae. Not just the man in him, but the beast too.

Deep within, the beast turned, pressing to be released. Pressing to be with Mae, to taste her. To claim her.

Cedar jerked his head back and stepped away until his spine scraped against the other side of the hall. He pulled his arms to his side, each hand in a fist. His heart was pounding too hard, and it was all he could do to keep his breathing calm.

"It's against my better judgment," he said huskily.

Mae smiled just slightly, her eyes still shut. "Mine too, Mr. Hunt. But these are dire times. And we all must do that which we can to find our happiness among the ruins." She opened her eyes. Studied him.

Cedar couldn't know how she saw him. Maybe his anger. Maybe his desire. He tried his best to calm himself, to calm the needs clashing within him.

Mae's expression shifted from amused to puzzled. Then her eyebrows slipped up. "Oh," she said.

"Mae—" He took a step, his hand out. To explain. To make an excuse for his thoughts. To tell her he understood her husband had just set to the grave and she needed time. Time to grieve. Maybe to tell her he would wait. Forever for her, if need be.

But she did not move. Just held his gaze as if she could see right through the whole of him, as if she could see his soul.

And did not find it lacking.

So he took a step closer. Still she did not move. Did not say a word. Did not look away.

She was breathing a little more rapidly. He could almost feel the beat of her pulse thudding beneath her smooth, pale skin as if it were his own. He wanted to run his fingers along the curves of her body, wanted to taste her, bury himself in her heat.

He took another step. And then he spread one palm against the wall behind her, needing the cold, rough rock to remind him this wasn't a dream. Wasn't a promise for anything more than this.

And this was simply now.

"Mae," he said again. He stood so tight to her, she had to tip her face up to meet his eyes. If either of them moved just an inch, they would be touching. He held himself steady, straining to give her even that much space. "If you say no . . ."

She shook her head. Then, quietly. "I'm not saying no."

Cedar leaned down and slipped his hand around her waist so that he could draw her the last fraction of distance toward him.

Even through the layers of her day dress and wrapped in a blanket, she was soft, warm, supple in his arms. He pulled her up closer against his chest, hips, thighs. She melted there, as if savoring, hungering for the sudden, needful contact.

Cedar did not remove his palm from the wall. He didn't dare chance it. For if he did, he would gather her up, and take her away. To a land of his choice, a place where he could guard her, keep her, love her.

The beast in his mind keened for that freedom.

But Cedar was not about to let the beast, his curse, have any sway over his thoughts, his body, his desires. Mae, for this single moment, was his. He wouldn't let anything take this moment away from him.

He lowered his head, heard her breath hitch in her chest, then tasted the sweet tea and honey of her exhale on his lips.

With more gentleness than he thought he could contain, he brushed his lips across hers, wanting more, so much more, and telling himself that this brief touch, this trembling knowledge between them, might be all they would ever share. All she was willing to give him.

The tiniest sound escaped her throat, and her lips softened, opened, welcoming him into her warmth.

Cedar shifted his attention to her mouth and slid his tongue to stroke slowly along hers. Fire licked his belly, tightening him with need.

It had been years since he had kissed a woman. Years since he had touched a woman. Years since he had cared. So long, he had been sure he would never love again.

Mae's hands dragged without hesitation along his ribs, then up his back, where she clutched the fabric of his shirt in her fists.

She gave herself to the kiss, to him. Her lips, her tongue, urged him to explore. And offered him pleasure in return.

Cedar gave to her willingly.

He would give her so much more. Anything she asked for.

But soon, far too soon, Mae placed one hand on his chest and pressed there. He knew he had to let her go. Had to break this kiss.

Their only kiss.

With one last lingering touch, Cedar reluctantly drew his mouth away from hers.

She was on tiptoe, one hand still tucked up behind his back, the blanket around her held in place only by his arm across her back. There was no light in the hall. But Cedar didn't need light. He would know her, see her even if he were a blind man.

"I think," she breathed, her hand on his back still holding strong as if she wished she would never have to let go, even as her palm on his chest pushed him away. "We need time. Some. Time. When my mind is clear. When I'm myself again. After the sisters' call is gone. Then."

She was searching for understanding in his eyes. Her cheeks were flushed, her lips wet and swollen. He knew he needed to put her on her feet. Needed to let her free.

It was the last thing he wanted to do.

Mate, the beast within him whispered.

The truth of it resonated through him.

Cedar closed his eyes, inhaling the scent of her one last time. And then he carefully set her back on her feet. Once he knew she was stable, he pulled his arm away. Lastly, he drew his palm away from the stone wall, and stood there, too empty for the world full of wants that warred inside him.

Mae straightened her dress, straightened the blanket around her, not looking at him.

He could not look away from her.

He thought she'd walk back to her bunk. That this was done.

But instead, she reached out and touched his hand that was loosely fisted at his side.

"It's been a long road," she said, "and it will be longer still ahead of us. I don't want to walk it without you. Don't want to arrive at the end and find you gone."

"You won't," he said simply.

Mate.

Mae nodded, then headed back to the sleeping area, leaving Cedar in the cool echo of the hallway, alone.

CHAPTER NINETEEN

Rose loved the feel of the wind on her face, loved even more the heat and strength of Captain Hink's arms around her.

He had paused just outside the blind of rocks that hid the doorways to the caverns from the open landing area.

It was dark out, but not raining. In the shift of clouds over the deep ink sky, she could make out two ships crouched on the landing flats. The larger ship was a hulking silhouette that looked like a wooden frigate, the inflatable envelope above it lashed by lines to the ship's hull below. There were no long, spindly trawling arms sticking off it. Instead, alongside the bottom of the hull were long, wide sleds that looked a little like extra large canoes attached to the vessel.

In comparison to that ship, the *Swift* looked tiny.

It was the first time Rose had really seen her from the outside. Built lean and narrow like a bullet, she was a smooth gray ghost with her pointed nose tipped ever so slightly up, as if she were yearning for the sky. The horizontal sails on her side, which were tucked in tight now, made her look even more like the bird she was named after. The only thing to spoil that look was the glim trawling arms extending straight up along her sides, the netting clicking and clacking as it rattled against the metal arms.

"There she is," Captain Hink said. "My everything."

"She's beautiful," Rose whispered with a sigh.

"She is. And fast. And strong."

"Can we go to her? Go aboard?" Rose asked.

"You sure I haven't worn you out yet?" he asked.

"No. Not at all. I'd love to see her. While I'm awake."

"Well, then, welcome aboard, m'lady." Captain Hink strode toward the *Swift*, every step jostling Rose and making her shoulder ache. But even though she hurt, the closer they came to that ship, the more her spirit lifted, the more she felt alive and happy.

"How long have you had her?" Rose asked.

"Oh, near three years now. Bought her from a pilot named Charity Senders. Her husband and she had built the *Swift* themselves. He had the deviser knack. The boilers, for one thing, are brilliance. Small, powerful. And making her out of tin skin keeps her light and tough. Not a single other ship out there like her. No place in this world."

Rose smiled. She watched his face as he talked about his ship, and there was a light there, a joy that couldn't be hidden by the night. Lee Hink loved this ship.

There was something about that kind of dedication in a man that made her like him all the more.

"Did Mrs. Senders retire?" Rose asked.

"Near as I know. Her husband was ill. Black lung. She decided to stay the ground to be with him for however long he still breathed." He paused. They were so close to the ship now, the inflated envelope blocked out most of the sky above them.

He shook his head as he looked up at the *Swift*. "Takes a certain kind of love to give up a ship like this for someone," he said. "I'm not sure that I'd have the will to do the same."

"Maybe you just haven't loved deeply enough, Captain," Rose said.

He put one foot on the threshold and slipped a hand free to turn the door's latch. "Likely you are correct, Miss Small. Not a lot of time for love when you're riding the skies."

He pushed the door open.

"Problem, Captain?" Ansell called out from the nose of the ship, his gun in one hand and knife in the other.

"Just taking a stroll, Mr. Ansell," Hink said. "No need to stay awake on our account."

"Aye, that, Captain." He stowed his gun and rolled in his cot so his back was to the rest of the ship.

Captain Hink stepped fully into the ship. "Shall I set you on your feet, Miss Small?" he asked quietly.

"Please."

Rose held her breath as he adjusted his hold on her and let her feet touch the ground. Her stomach roiled at the movement and she broke out in a cold sweat. But that couldn't dampen her joy. She was determined to see the ship, all of her, or at least all of her that she could before either fatigue or pain made her pass out.

"Tell me about her," Rose said, looking around.

"What do you want to know?" he asked, watching Rose as she held on to the metal bars and slowly walked toward the rear of the vessel.

She looked over at the captain, a big smile on her face. "Everything. I want to know her like a friend."

He paused, studying her. The intensity in his gaze near took Rose's breath right out of her chest.

Then he smiled, just so much that it curved his lips. It was an intimate sort of smile. As if he was intending to take his time and show her pleasure she had never known before.

"Let's start in the boiler room," he said. "It's always a bit warmer there."

Rose realized she was shaking. From the cold, yes, and the pain, and the effects of the coca leaf. But also with excitement. She was standing in an airship. With a handsome captain.

If she weren't aching and cold, she might think this was a dream. A pleasant one at that.

Captain Hink paced up near her and wrapped his arm around her back, helping to guide her to the back of the ship. "This way."

He opened the blast door, then turned a small gear, which struck a spark against flint. The burnt sulphur smell tickled her nose, as light caught across a network of glass globes around the metal rafters of the room.

Rose stopped full and put her hand to her heart, unable to speak. The lights were beautiful, catching flame in the burnished copper and brass of the big iron boilers.

Pipes, flues, and tanks filled the room, mahogany and teak adding their own beauty among the valves and compasslike gauges, even more lovely than when Molly had brought her back here.

"I've never imagined," she began. "Well, I've imagined, but I was wrong."

"Thought it might be a bit fancier?" he asked, turning his shoulders so he could walk into the room, his thumbs tucked in his belt.

"No. She's more wondrous than I'd hoped. I can't seem to make my eyes big enough to take it all in." She smiled, and found Captain Hink smiling right back at her.

"Molly has a cot here." He pointed to the snug bed in the corner of the room. "Why don't you sit before you lose your knees?"

"You don't think she'd mind?"

"Molly? Might be a bit hardheaded, and Lord knows she doesn't listen to orders well, but she has a heart the size of the seven seas. I hear Gregors are built that way."

Rose got herself over to the bed and was out of breath from that much activity. "I knew a Gregor," she said, puffing a little. "He was just the same."

The captain strolled to a boiler, and out of habit touched it, checking for heat, before leaning back against it.

"So this is the heart of the ship," he said, looking around the room. "Molly's the pulse that keeps it beating. Up front, I stand as the brains.

Seldom is my navigator, that makes him the eyes. And Ansell and Guffin, I suppose, are her wings. We run a small crew, but we like it that way. Less chance of us stepping on top of each other and wanting to finish our disagreements with guns."

"How long have you been harvesting glim? Three years?" she asked.

He looked down at his boots and shook his head. "That's about right."

"What did you do before that? Transport? She seems a small ship for that."

Captain Hink took a deep breath and then started walking toward her. "I haven't told you all the truth, Miss Small. Plainly, there hasn't been time."

He sat himself down beside her. So close, his shoulder brushed against hers. He rested his arms out over his knees, and loosely carded his fingers together.

"I've been running glim for three years. Several years before that I was a soldier in the war. And since the war, I've also been working for the president of the United States."

"You're a statesman?" she asked, confused. Didn't make any sense for a statesman to be out in the wilds hopping skies for glim.

But then, Mr. Hunt was from the universities back east, and had been a teacher before hard times fell upon him. Maybe Captain Hink's story was the same.

"Not so much a statesman. I'm a lawman. U.S. Marshal."

"Really, now?" Rose said.

He tilted his head to get a better look at her. "You don't believe me?"

"I just think if a fellow were trying to impress a girl, being an airship captain, a glim pirate, *and* a U.S. Marshal just might do the trick, unless maybe you'd like to add doctor, lawyer, or war hero for good measure."

She was trying not to smile but couldn't help it. He looked so confused.

"I suppose war hero might be true too," he said, "or not, depending on whose side you believe. But I swear on my sweet mama's grave. I was a U.S. Marshal long before I took to flying or harvesting glim."

"Yes," Rose said, keeping her expression serious. "Of course you were."

He frowned and blew out air. "It's"—he gestured with his hands, as if trying to catch a fleeting thought—"true," he finally managed.

"Then why don't you wear a badge?"

"I have a badge."

"Can I see it?" she asked solemnly.

He dug in the inner pocket of his coat, hesitated a moment, then drew his fingers out. In his hand was a tin badge shaped like a star.

"Oh," Rose said. She really had thought he was teasing her, trying to impress her. "So should I call you Marshal Captain Hink now?"

"I'd rather you not. And it would be Marshal Cage if you did."

"What about 'Lee'?"

"That's one of the names I answer to."

"How many names do you have, Captain?" Rose asked.

Hink hesitated. "I'd hate to tarnish your opinion of me, Miss Small."

"Over a name or two?"

"Not that, as such." He took a breath as if bracing for something, then let it out. "I have one name for each man who might have been my daddy."

Rose pressed her fingers over her mouth. "Oh, I didn't mean to pry."

"Not at all. I had it coming." He grinned wickedly at her.

"My mother was a woman of some *adventure*, if you understand what I'm saying. Wonderful woman, and I loved her very much. But she once told me she wasn't quite sure which of her suitors had fathered me. So she gave me a name from each of them, in case they ever came back to claim me."

"Your mother was a . . ."

He raised one eyebrow and nodded encouragingly, as if daring her to use a word to describe his mother.

"She was alone to raise you?" she asked.

From his look, that was not at all what he had expected out of her. She liked being able to surprise him.

"Some other adults lent a hand now and then, but yes. She raised me alone."

"And did your father return?"

"No."

"So how many . . . names do you have?"

"Four."

"Four?"

"Lee Cadwaller Hink Cage."

"That's an impressive list."

"It's done me no harm."

He stared a little too long, then finally turned his gaze back to the star in his hand.

"Don't normally have to reveal all my secrets just to get a woman to kiss me. A well-timed smile usually does the trick."

Rose's face warmed from that comment, but she tried not to let it show. "I can't imagine those were all your secrets, Captain—"

"Lee," he said.

"Lee," she repeated. "Surely there's one or two surprises left to you."

"Might be at that," he said softly.

Then he repocketed the star, and before she could come up with the next thing to tease out of him, he was shifting sideways to her, one hand firmly at her back so she could lean against it if she needed to, the other gently brushing a strand of her hair from her cheek.

And then, without asking, without a word, without permission, he lowered his mouth to hers.

Rose stopped breathing. Stopped thinking. She'd been cornered by boys and kissed before. It was always rough, not always innocent. But she'd never had a man do this.

Lee held her lips with his own in a sort of embrace, moving slowly, as if showing her the steps to a dance she should follow. She moved with him, and shivered when his tongue dragged delicious warmth along her lower lip.

And then she paid no mind as to what came first and what came next. She opened her mouth to him, wanting that warmth inside her. He tasted like bourbon and something pleasantly richer.

The heat of his mouth sent flames over her skin and she wanted to stretch into that feeling. His lips were soft, but insistent. His stubble scratched along her cheek and only made her want more of his skin, more of his body against hers.

He seemed willing for that too. His hand slid along her thigh, cupping the outer curve of it before he slid his palm over the crest to rest upward on her hip.

That wasn't where she wanted him touching her. That wasn't the only place she wanted to be touched.

She couldn't seem to get near enough with these layers of clothes between them.

Unthinking, she lifted her left hand, her wounded shoulder.

Pain shot white-hot through her, stealing her breath, vision, and body.

When the pain and white pulled away, leaving her aware of her body again, of her own skin and thoughts and breath again, she heard her own screams.

She clamped her teeth together, trying to breathe instead of moan. The pain was getting less. Of course it was getting less. She'd be fine. Just fine. In a minute.

And beyond the rattling of her thoughts, was Lee's voice.

"You'll be fine, Rose," he was saying in a constant string, as if reciting the words of a hymn. "Almost there now, and we'll get your medicine, nice soft bed, blankets, and sleep. This will all be a dream, a bad dream, but you're going to wake up, and you'll be fine, Rose."

She tried to focus on the world around her. Black. No glittering brass or deep rose-colored wood of the boiler room. And it was cold. They were outside again. He was carrying her back to the cavern.

She rested her head against his shoulder and closed her eyes. His words fell around her like a gentle net, holding her close, keeping her there, anchored in her own thoughts, in her own skin, away from the clawing pain.

Distantly, she heard the sounds of other voices. Mr. Hunt's low growl, Mae being calm as ever. She wanted to tell them not to fuss over her so, but by the time she got the words together, she was lying down on the cot again, and Mae was urging her to drink as much as she could out of the cup she held to her lips.

Rose drank the cup dry. "Thank you," she whispered.

"I'm going to repack your shoulder as soon as that starts working," Mae said. "Don't worry. You'll be asleep soon."

Mae moved to set the cup to one side and she could see Cedar Hunt and Lee Cage both standing at the foot of her bed, facing each other, and neither one of them looking happy with the other.

She didn't know what they were all worked up about. Yes, she was wounded and the pain had been something awful. But she didn't plan on giving up breathing anytime soon. There was too much of life she still wanted to see in the time she had left. Too much of it she still wanted to feel.

"Take your discussion outside, please, gentlemen," Mae was saying. "Rose needs a little rest now."

Rose didn't know if they did what Mae said or not, for she was falling down and down into darkness and was asleep before she could hear what either of the men answered.

CHAPTER TWENTY

Cedar paced outside in the afternoon sunlight, taking a short break from helping with the repairs on the *Swift* to get a drink of water. He'd been in to see Rose and Mae. Rose hadn't woken since Captain Hink had brought her back to bed, clear out of her head with pain.

Being around Mae, who was helping organize the supplies for the ship and taking care of Rose, just made him restless.

What they needed was for this ship to get off this rock, get moving, and get them as near to Kansas and the coven as they could be. They needed to hunt the Holder, and he needed Mae in her right mind. Permanently.

The wind shifted, coming down from the northeast. Cedar paused, lifting his face into it. There was a feel to the air, the slightest scent of the Holder.

It was just a moment, almost too faint before it could be acknowledged.

And maybe he was wrong. Wishing for something he wanted so badly did not make it true.

Still, he waited for that faint song to rise on the wind, the faint scent to return, but there was only silence and the stinging smell of snow.

Miss Dupuis strolled out of the caverns toward him. She wore a chocolate brown and plum dress, cinched in tight at the waist with ruffles beneath the hem giving the skirt shape. A hat sat jauntily to one side of her head, and her hands were covered by close-fitting brown silk gloves. Cedar hadn't seen a woman in such formal wear since his days back east.

Her man, Otto Theobald, and her woman, Joonie Wright, were not at her side.

"Good afternoon, Mr. Hunt," she said, stopping beside him, her eyes cast to the *Swift*, where Captain Hink hollered at his crew to work faster. Beyond that, the expansive *Coin de Paradis* had her envelope fully inflated, looking like she'd leap to the sky at any hard wind.

Cedar thought that might be true if it weren't for the ropes knotted around metal hooks jutting up out of the rock that kept her tight to the earth.

"Afternoon, Miss Dupuis. Will you be leaving soon, I suppose?"

"No."

Cedar gave her a look. "You'll be staying here, then?"

"No. Or rather, I hope that isn't the case. I was wishing to have a moment to speak with you, Mr. Hunt, but you have been a busy man."

"Not doing anything now," he said.

"Yes. Good. Would you be willing to take a short walk with me?"

Cedar glanced at the ship. The *Swift* was nearly ready to fly again in his estimation. Cedar and the others had been working since Captain Hink had roused everyone out of bed before daylight. The crew had put themselves to the task of repair with a single-minded determination.

Pounding rivets and hauling metal and timber had done Cedar's temper some good. Enough to entertain a short walk.

He figured what little needed yet to be done on the ship was more suited to Captain Hink's and the crew's expertise.

"Of course." Cedar motioned with his hand for her to walk with him, and started off down the path that led around the bend in the terrain.

"I'm afraid I haven't been completely forthcoming with you, Mr. Hunt," she said. "There was a very specific reason Captain Beaumont brought myself and my companions here through the teeth of a storm."

"Oh?"

"Yes. We came here with great haste because you were here."

Every nerve in Cedar's body flashed cold and a rush of wariness swept through him.

"Oh?" he said again.

"We are of a joint acquaintance, you and I," she said. "The Madder brothers. Perhaps you know them, yes?"

"We've met," Cedar said.

"They informed me, all of us, that they were looking for you. With great need. I believe you owe them a favor."

"Did you speak to them recently?" Cedar asked.

"Yes."

"So they found their way safely out of Vicinity?"

"Yes. But they had to see to some repairs of their equipment and knew it would cause a delay. So they sent messages to locate you."

It didn't come as a great surprise that the brothers had found a way to send a message to people who had airships at their disposal. There seemed to be no pot the Madders wouldn't stick their clever fingers into.

"Messages to whom?" he asked.

She paused, and stared out across the dark peaks of mountains that stood like fortress walls in the distance, cotton-topped with mist.

"We are here to see that the Strange do not take over this new world," she said.

"You hunt the Strange?" Cedar asked.

She turned her gaze back him. "We search for them. Sometimes we find them, or find the people they have harmed. There are very few in this world who can see them. Fewer still who can hunt them."

She slid a smile his way. "Theobald, myself, and Joonie can see them. You, however, can hunt them, or so I am told. That is a very rare gift. So rare that the Madders sent us to find you. Any of us who could travel quickly."

"Find me? For what?" Cedar asked.

"A gift such as yours? You are our ears, our eyes, and our teeth. You can destroy the Strange where we simply try to control their spread, close their trails, break their weapons. You can find the Holder, as if it were a fresh blood trail, and keep it safe from Strange hands. You are one of us, Mr. Hunt. And we want you to join our cause."

"I don't know what you think you know of me, Miss Dupuis, but I am no one's servant. I neither follow nor pledge to any man's cause."

"You carry upon you a curse from the gods of these lands," she said with a nod. "I can see the beast within you, as can Mr. Theobald. You have given your pledge to find the Holder for the Madder brothers. Will you turn from that now?"

Cedar wondered if he already had. He'd promised Captain Hink he'd find the Holder, just as he'd promised the Madders he would find it. But the weapon could be given to only one man. And he didn't know whom he should trust with it.

"That agreement is between me and the Madder brothers."

"They are great men," she said. "Steadfast in this fight. But these times have been . . . difficult. We have lost so many."

She searched his face, perhaps looking for sympathy there. He had none to give her.

"The Madders may prefer secrets and riddles," she said, "but I prefer to be clear. I am going to ask you plainly, Mr. Hunt. Will you join us? Become a protector of this great land, this great world and see that the rising tide of Strange is turned back?"

The wind rose, pushing at his back, and drawing Miss Dupuis's carefully coifed hair into ribbons around her face. Far off, a hawk circled the shadows of trees, calling out once before it climbed higher.

He didn't know enough about the group of people she wanted him to join to make a decision in their favor. His promise to the Madders would stand. He'd find the Holder. But that didn't mean he wanted to spend his life killing Strange for those who could not.

"I have my own path to walk, Miss Dupuis, my own . . . family to keep safe. The very last thing I would do right now is leave them behind. I cannot travel with you, nor join your cause. The curse I carry is no gift, no matter what the Madders think. And I will not live my life beneath its demands. Thank you for the walk. Good day."

Cedar turned to stroll back to the landing area. Did he believe that Miss Dupuis and others could fight the Strange? Yes. But that fight had never been his choice. The "gift," as she called it, given to him by the Pawnee gods was a curse that had nearly killed his brother, and destroyed both of their lives.

He would be free of it if he could.

He owed the Madders a favor, and had given his word to Captain Hink. He would see those things through. Find the Holder, then bring the Madders and Hink together to discuss just where the weapon should be kept.

But first, the Holder would be in his hands. And he would use it to cure Rose. Then he would take Rose, Mae, and Wil to the coven, where their curses would be put to rest once and for all.

And if that happened, if his curse were broken, he wouldn't be the kind of man Miss Dupuis or her cause would want among them any longer.

Something crackled under his boots. Glass.

He stopped, looked down, and took a step back. Green glass rolled away from his boot, roughly in the shape of a teardrop the size of his head. He had broken a globe. He bent, picked up the remains. It stank of gunpowder and oil. He looked around from his crouched position to see where it might have fallen from.

A flash of light caught his eye. From this angle, he could see through a slot in the cliff face along the way he had come. Miss Dupuis stood a ways down the path still. Over her shoulder, where it wouldn't be noticed until at least another turn in the path, burned a green-yellow light, bright enough to hurt the eyes, even in the afternoon.

He knew what it was. Globes, like the one he had broken at his feet, coupled with mirrors which were set up across the peaks, catching and shooting that light to more and more mirrors scattered across the peaks to the east. Those globes were carefully shrouded so that no light was reflected here at the landing area.

It was a signal system that stretched for miles.

But for what. Or who?

Cedar left the glass behind and jogged to the ship. He strode over to Captain Hink, who was cranking a wrench against a bolt to secure the trawling arm.

"Captain," Cedar said to Captain Hink's back, "a word with you?"

"Don't need my hands or eyes to listen. Speak up, Mr. Hunt."

"What's the signal light for?"

Hink grunted as he squeezed the last turn out of the bolt. "What signal light?"

"A flare, burning in a glass globe and reflecting off mirrors across the peaks."

Hink froze. Then, "What color was it?"

"Green and yellow."

"Son of a bitch," Hink swore. "Get the women on the ship, now. Get what supplies you can grab. I'm going to go beat the hell out of Old Jack."

He pushed past him, but Cedar grabbed his arm.

"What is the signal for?"

"It tells whoever Jack's made a deal with that he has the person they're looking for. He must have lit it last night sometime. Whoever wants me, or you, or hell, maybe Captain Beaumont over there, is close enough to see the signal and is on their way here. With guns. Get the women on board. Now."

Hink pulled his arm out of Cedar's grip and broke into a run. "Molly

Gregor," he yelled, "fire that boiler. We've been spotted and we've been flared. Tell Beaumont's crew!"

Hink's crew scrambled like a kicked hive of wasps. They secured nets, outrigs, and set the slip on the lashes as fast as they could.

Cedar ran back toward the cavern and passed Molly Gregor as she was running toward the ship. "Make it quick, Mr. Hunt!" she shouted.

Cedar rushed through the halls, taking the turns by memory to their sleeping quarters. Wil looked up from where he had been dozing as Cedar pounded into the room.

Mae had a satchel stuffed and slung over her shoulder, her coat on, and a hat securely in place. She was grabbing up the blankets they had brought in from the ship.

"We need to go. Now." He rushed over to where Rose was sleeping and gathered her up as carefully as he could into his arms.

"What's happening?" Mae asked as she hurried to the door.

One thing about Mae, she knew how to ask questions on the go.

"There was a signal set off. A flare. Captain Hink thinks someone is coming here. Either for us, or for the people aboard Captain Beaumont's ship."

"Who?" Mae asked. "Who would be coming here for us?"

"I don't know," Cedar said, "but the captain says that light was fired last night, and whoever's on the way will be armed."

Mae didn't say anything more. They jogged through the tunnel until they hit fresh air.

The landing pad was a study in chaos. Beaumont's crew hauled supplies into their ship, as did Hink's men. Great gouts of smoke filled the air above, blocking what sunlight there was and making the entire scene more confusing.

Wet flues coughed up so much smoke and steam that the landing area and all those working or running about on it were obscured.

Wil ran straight for the *Swift*, not needing his eyes to know where she was anchored. Cedar and Mae were right behind him.

Cedar was glad Rose was unconscious. He could get her to the ship quickly or he could get her there painlessly. And they didn't have time for painless.

The rumble of turbines and fans firing up clogged the air along with the shouts of voices, and banging of metal, rope, and wood as the ships prepared to fly.

But above all that, up in the sky, a high whine was growing louder.

Cedar wasn't the only one who heard it. Seldom paused and tipped his face skyward. Captain Hink was nowhere to be seen, though Cedar could hear him cussing out Old Jack somewhere back toward the doors to the living area.

Whatever ship it was coming in above them, whatever threat it might bring, Cedar wanted Rose and Mae out of the line of fire. He stepped up into the *Swift*.

"You think the hammock, or should we strap her in?" he asked Mae.

"Better strap her in. Here." She spread one of the blankets out on the floor, and then shook the harness loose from its place attached to the wall where they had last sat.

Cedar got on his knees and eased Rose down onto the blankets.

"Hold her up a bit," Mae said. Cedar did so, listening to the ruckus outside while Mae slipped Rose's arm into the straps and buckled the harness over her chest.

The crack of a gunshot rang out, and the repeated shots of return fire.

"Hold tight," Cedar said, "and stay with the ship." They needed the crew on the ship, in the ship now, giving her fire to put her in the sky. Molly was aboard, back behind the blast door trying to drum up the boilers. But the rest of the crew were outside.

Cedar ducked out the door, intending to hunt Hink's men and haul them in by the scruffs of their necks if that's what it took to get this ship out of here.

In the short time he'd been in the ship, the chaos of people rushing about had turned into a standoff.

Old Jack and all his men were lined up behind the rock blind, near the doors to the living chambers, guns drawn. Up on the top of the cliffs, his men were scrambling to man the cannons. If they fired those cannons on them, or worse, on the ship, they would cripple her and strand them all here.

Captain Hink, Ansell, Guffin, and Seldom stood side by side in front of the *Swift* as if their bodies alone could shield the ship from harm.

Standing behind them were Miss Dupuis, Mr. Theobald, and Miss Wright, weapons the likes of which Cedar had never seen before, drawn and facing off Old Jack.

"You snake-belly, backbiting pissant," Captain Hink yelled. "Who did you sell me out to?"

"Ain't yours to know. Yet," Old Jack yelled back.

The big boilers and fans of the *Coin de Paradis* caught hold and puffed out steam. Then the fans picked up and threw so much wind and dust and smoke around, it was impossible to see half a foot in any direction.

"Fire!" Old Jack hollered.

Jack's men powdered the air with shots, bullets lost to the sound of the fans angling for the climb. Hink and his crew fired back, taking scant cover from the few crates of supplies still scattered out on the field.

"The ship!" Captain Hink yelled. "Seldom, Guffin, Ansell. Out, out! Get her out before they fire the cannons."

The men ran for it under the clamor and god-awful racket of the *Coin de Paradis*'s slow launch. Cedar didn't know why the ship was so loud. But what he did know was there was an ax strapped next to the *Swift*'s door.

He grabbed the ax, stuck it in his belt, and drew his gun, wishing for his rifle. He jumped out of the *Swift*, Wil right beside him, and fired at Old Jack and his boys so the crew could make the ship.

But Captain Hink, Miss Dupuis, and her companions were pinned against one side of the landing pad, concentrating their fire at the cannon stands, to keep Old Jack's men from firing on the crew and ship.

"Get to the ship!" Cedar yelled. "Dupuis, Theobald, Wright. Get to the *Swift*."

But Miss Dupuis and her crew did not budge. "We stay with you," she said.

Captain Beaumont's ship cleared the landing pad, lifting up straight at Old Jack and his boys. Old Jack used the ship as cover, and by the time the last board on the ship's hull had scraped the wall of rocks, Old Jack was gone.

But his men had made the cannons, and let loose a blast straight at the *Swift*. It missed, but not by much.

Cedar ducked behind the corner of stone where the captain and others were huddled, just as Captain Hink ran out into the middle of the landing pad, waving his arms and airing his lungs in full shout. ". . . backstabbing devil! Don't you go hide in that hole of yours and leave them out here to fight for you. And you!" He yelled up to the men on the cannons. "Stop shooting at my ship!"

Through the dense shifting smoke, another shadow loomed over the field.

Cedar looked up just as a new gout of gunfire ricocheted off the cliff walls, throwing sprays of dirt and rock like someone had tossed dynamite.

Hink ran for cover. "Fly!" he yelled, throwing his hands up twice, as if by will alone he could push the ship into the air. "Get the hell out of here!"

For a moment, Cedar didn't think Ansell, Guffin, Seldom, and Molly were going to do what the captain said, didn't think the *Swift* would take to the air. She had a few holes in her, but hadn't yet been hit by a cannon.

"That's an order!" Hink added.

And then, so fast that Cedar had to suck in a hard breath, the ship was up and screaming over the edge of the cliffs, rocketing to the clouds.

The looming shadow passed across the landing pad, and as the smoke cleared, Cedar craned his neck to see the sky. A ship was coming in for a landing.

Easily as big as the *Coin de Paradis* but built with a closed deck and plenty of portholes with cannons set to fire, she rose up from the cover of the mountain peak, turned into the wind, and bore down on them.

Old Jack's signal must have reached its intended party.

"It's Les Mullins's boat," Hink said as he, Cedar, Miss Dupuis, Mr. Theobald, and Miss Wright pressed their backs against the rock wall. Wil was there with them too. Not a lot of cover, but it was either stand out in the open flat with an armed ship homing into view, or take a chance in the mazelike tunnels of Old Jack's place. Tunnels Jack and his men knew like the insides of their eyelids.

"Who's Les Mullins?" Cedar asked.

They were all busy reloading their weapons, and glancing up at the ship closing down on the field, while the singing cry of the *Swift* beating against the wind to make her retreat filled the air.

"He's a man I should of killed when he was in my sights. Works for a general who wants me and mine dead."

"Which general?" Miss Dupuis asked.

"General Alabaster Saint," Hink said. "Heard of him?"

"Yes," Miss Dupuis said, pumping the shotgun in her hands. "I have. Dismissed from command for trading weapons between the North and South, among other offenses." She glanced at Cedar. "He is in league with the forces you and I were speaking of earlier, Mr. Hunt. Dark forces."

"The darker, bloodier, plain crazy hell on earth thing the Saint can find," Hink said, "is what he's going to be in league with. Never saw a more bloodthirsty insane rabid demon in my life."

"What does he want with you?" Cedar asked.

"He wants me dead." Captain Hink holstered his gun and picked up a modified Smith and Wesson. "I served under him. Mutinied. Saved a hundred and fifty men's lives that day, and got the Saint discharged for disobeying the president's direct orders. He's wanted my head ever since. The feeling is mutual."

The shadow of the airship had passed over them now, and the ship itself was coming into position just to one side of the landing pad. It wasn't moving in fast, whether due to the shifting winds or smoke, or if they were waiting to see if the cannons were manned, Cedar wasn't sure.

"Well, that's some good news," Captain Hink said. "They're looking for us."

"And how do you define that as good news, Captain?" Theobald asked.

Hink grinned at him over his shoulder. "Son, so long as the *Swift's* in the sky, we all have a chance of getting out of here. I know Les Mullins. He's got a gut wound from our last meeting and a crew who'd just as soon kick him out of the boat as take a bullet for him. We shoot, we put a few holes in that ship, and Mullins is gonna turn tail and run."

Cedar lifted his head. There was a scent on the wind, a song he could feel in his bones.

Wil snarled.

The Strange. He narrowed his eyes and searched the ship's portholes. Steely-faced men stood there, rifles, shotguns, and flamethrowers at the ready.

Theobald pressed his spectacles closer to his face, glanced at the same portholes Cedar was looking at, and swore. "I think we'll need more than guns for this fight."

The men staring out of the ship were not human. Well, not all of them.

They were strangeworked.

Just like the things that had nearly killed Mae, Wil, and little Elbert back in Hallelujah. Just like Mr. Shunt.

"Why do you say that, Theobald?" Captain Hink asked.

Cedar's heart thumped against his ribs. "Those aren't men."

"What?" Hink asked. "Of course they're men. I know his crew."

"They aren't men," Cedar continued as Theobald got busy unpacking things from his carpetbag and handing them to Miss Dupuis and Miss Wright. "They stink of the Strange."

Hink took a moment to give Cedar a long look. Then, "Strange. All right. So they're not men. Haven't met a thing that breathes that can't be unlunged. Take the ship first. Fans, and rudder, don't aim for the envelope. Unless we have fire, a few rounds of bullets won't take her down. And if we ground this beast, be ready to aim for the head of anything that crawls out of her belly.

"We clear on that?" he asked.

"Yes, Captain," Miss Dupuis said, latching a contraption of brass and tubes and gauges that fit over her shotgun, like a second weapon.

"Aye, sir," Theobald said, adjusting his goggles and shrugging a belt of bullets over his shoulder, that fed into the chamber of the blunderbuss in his hand.

"Aye," Miss Wright said, winding a coil of wires up her left arm and sliding her gun into a fanned-out device of brass and copper that looked like a dinner plate–sized shield with tubes and wires rolling around it.

"Mr. Hunt?" Captain Hink asked. "Are you in agreement?"

The beast pushed against Cedar's bones. It wasn't the full moon—wasn't even close. The new moon should be tonight, complete blackness in the sky. But he couldn't think. Couldn't just think as a man ought to. The hunger, the need, the scent of the Strange drew a hard, killing thirst up through him.

His grip on logic, on the thoughts of a man, was slipping.

The beast thrilled and tore at his mind. Taking. Ruling.

Kill, it whispered. *Destroy.*

Cedar strained to push that desire away. His sanity was sliding with each breath.

He growled, and pulled his goggles into place, his crystal-sighted Walker heavy in his palm, and the need to spill blood and tear bones from flesh rolling through him in a hot wave.

"You have me," Cedar rasped, answering Hink, answering the beast within him. And promising the ship full of strangeworked men, coming down hard over the landing pad now, doors open, guns rattling through the air, that he would be their end.

Distantly, Cedar was aware of the captain and the others firing at the ship.

He didn't care about the ship. Didn't care about the bullets spraying through the air. Didn't care about the cannons locked and loaded, fuses lit.

He ran. To the ship, to the strangeworked crew, Wil beside him, ahead of him.

All the world seemed to slow to a dream landscape. He could sense the heartbeats of the strangeworked men in the ship. He could hear their sour song, hungry to devour this world, tainted with the nightmare singsong stitched together by Mr. Shunt's thread.

The song, the beat of hearts, the blood he could almost taste in the back of his throat were so clear, they made Captain Hink's yell, the gunfire behind him, the gunfire ahead of him seem like the softest hush of wind through leaves.

Cedar's world was filled with the scent of the Strange. All his reason for breathing was their death.

He was running, close enough now so he could see their faces clearly, the flat hatred twisting features into snarls of malevolence. The ship wasn't near enough the ground, still, three of the strangeworked men jumped from it.

Their legs should have shattered. But they landed cat-light, and were running, guns firing, straight at him, each with a flamethrower at the ready on his back.

Cedar didn't pause. Ax in one hand, gun in the other, he shot the first Strange in the head, then pivoted and hacked the second man through the neck.

They both fell.

And they both stood up again. But not for long. Wil was on them, tearing out throats, breaking necks.

Cedar laughed. He licked the blood off his lips, shifted his grip on the slick ax handle, and lifted his gun. He took aim again and fired.

CHAPTER TWENTY-ONE

Captain Hink realized all the shouting in the world wasn't doing a thing to stop Cedar Hunt from charging straight into enemy fire.

He'd seen that sort of thing on the battlefield before, where a man goes fool-headed and doesn't know when to retreat.

But there was something about Mr. Hunt that he didn't expect.

He moved fast, far faster than a man should, and seemed to have an uncanny awareness of where the bullets were headed and when to duck them.

The wolf beside him was the same. They moved and fought like two creatures with one mind, faster than their enemies, always knowing where their enemies would be and how best to take them down.

Before Hink could even get more than a few cuss words out, Cedar and the wolf had killed three men.

Except then the three men got back up again.

Holy hellfire. That was something Hink had never seen on the field before.

But Cedar Hunt just laughed and found himself a flamethrower. And then got serious about his butchery.

More men were jumping out of that ship. Men Hink recognized. Men who shouldn't be walking without crutches. Men with hands where stumps had been.

They weren't Mullins's men. No, the ship's crew stayed on the ship, and turned the guns on the field.

It didn't matter how fast Cedar Hunt was. Didn't matter that the wolf moved like shadow and smoke. They were going to be killed.

More gunfire rained down from the cliffs above them. Jack's men had turned out the Gatling guns and were aiming them at anything that moved.

Theobald stood side by side with Miss Dupuis, that gun of his shooting out grapeshot that caught anything it touched on fire, while Miss Dupuis unloaded her shotgun, sending out bullets that exploded on impact.

They were a coolheaded couple who looked like they'd seen their share of battle at each other's sides.

But it was too much. Too many bullets. Too easy to die. And Hink wasn't about to get himself shot and let Mullins finish him off for good.

"Out!" he yelled. "Get in the tunnels. There's a door that way you can bust in."

"What about Mr. Hunt?" Miss Dupuis yelled.

"I'll get his attention. You get running!"

Captain Hink bolted toward the stone stairs that led up to the main cannon. He was exposed, halfway up the stairs, but out of range of the Gatling guns, which couldn't fire straight down on him since they were set back too far in the hole cut into the cliff.

Almost there, almost there, he panted as he ran the stairs.

Something hot bit through his leg and he fell forward.

Son of a bitch. He was shot. If that bullet came from Mullins's gun he was going to dig it out and make the jackass eat it.

Hink got back on his feet and took the rest of the stairs, cussing his way through the pain.

The cannon was unmanned. Likely the boy had been shot and tumbled to his death, or had hightailed it when he saw Mullins's ship come up with her guns.

Hink got busy, checking the cannon, clearing the barrel, adding the powder, tamping, and dropping the ball inside.

It was slow work for one man. But Captain Hink was a determined man who had no problem doing the work of two when he put his mind to it. He glanced down over the battle. The ship still hovered there, letting loose round after round of ammunition, while Cedar and the wolf seemed to have come enough to their senses that they'd taken cover behind a scree of stones.

Hink could make out six dead men on the ground, pieces and parts of them tossed about, and on fire. Cedar must have gotten the hang of that flamethrower.

Miss Dupuis and her crew were scurrying from one scant cover to the next, working their way away from the landing pad toward the opening into the mountain.

"Burn in hell, Mullins." Hink took aim and lit the cannon's fuse.

A chest-thumping explosion reverberated across the cliffs and sent sharp echoes over the horizon. The shot struck true. Right down the port side of the ship, knocking out her fan and blasting her hull into splinters.

Before the chunks of ship had a chance to hit the ground, Cedar Hunt was running.

Toward the damn ship.

He got up under her belly, and caught one of the netting ropes.

With the flamethrower strapped to his back, Cedar overhanded his way up that rope. When he was close enough, he stopped, triggered the flamethrower, and shot a blast of oil and fire twenty feet out, setting the ship on fire.

The ship he was hanging from by a thread.

The man was crazy, that was clear sure. But he knew how to cripple a foe.

Cedar slid down the rope, then let go. The ship rocked wildly, trying to stabilize without her port fans. Cedar was thrown more than thirty feet, but he tucked and rolled, taking the fall like a tumbler.

And then he stood up, looked around the field. The wolf, his brother, loped up next to him. As the ship above burned and wailed, Cedar Hunt and that wolf glanced first at Miss Dupuis and her people nearly in the tunnel, then up at Hink.

Cedar was bloody, burned, dirty. And yet he stood there as if he felt no pain. Like a warrior out of legend.

Likely he didn't feel the pain. Hink had seen that on the field before too. Sometimes it took a man an hour or more to realize how he'd been broken, and what he was missing. And that discovery came on sudden and unpleasant. Some men never survived it.

Captain Hink cupped his mouth and yelled, "Inside. Tunnel!"

He didn't wait to see if Cedar heard him, but the man had damn good ears.

The relative silence from the Gatling guns' reloading wasn't going to last.

He wondered if Mullins was going to try to land that fiery barge. As if in answer, a huge explosion hit the field, throwing Hink to his knees and nearly sending him tumbling down the stairs.

Dynamite. Old Jack was done horsing around with his guests.

Since he'd likely been paid by all the parties involved, he meant to kill them all. Old Jack never took a side in a conflict, other than taking as much money as he could fist, and saving his own hide.

Ears ringing, Hink got up, and got moving. Didn't care about cover. He wanted speed. Every step down that staircase was agony, his leg getting heavier and heavier. But he pounded on, down the stairs, across to the hole in the mountain. Dupuis and her people were gone, hopefully already inside the mountain.

Just a few more yards, and he'd be there. Just a few more yards.

An arm came out of nowhere and grabbed hold of him by the waist, tugging his arm over a shoulder.

Cedar Hunt had somehow caught up, even across the distance of the field.

"Don't need help," Hink panted.

But Cedar kept hold of him, and half ran, half carried him despite his complaints.

Man was inhuman. The strength of him, the calm of him, the speed of him. And even though Hink had seen that on the battlefield too, to have him up close like this, the wolf guarding their rear, and then running ahead to make sure the path was clear, as if the wolf had a man's mind in an animal's body, sent a certain kind of dread through Hink's belly.

Cedar Hunt had said the men they were fighting weren't really men, but men worked up by something Strange. Hink agreed.

It was also clear that Mr. Cedar Hunt was not really a man either. Or not just a man. Same as the wolf was not just a wolf.

They were stuff of fairy tales and legends, or at least the bloody ones.

He was suddenly very glad to be on the same side of the fight as Cedar Hunt and his brother and wasn't looking forward to a day in which that was no longer true.

They were nearly at the door now. Joonie Wright stepped out just enough to let loose a couple shots at the gunners who had reloaded the Gatlings. That copper shield device of hers wasn't shooting bullets. When the hammer of her gun hit, the shield let out a blast of lightning that cracked across the air and dropped the Gatling gunner flat.

"Get inside," Hink ordered.

She moved aside so he and Cedar and the wolf could enter the hill.

This was not the hall where they had been staying. As a matter of fact, it was halfway across the landing field and to the south of where they had been. Three tunnels led off in three directions. The only light came from Theobald's foldable lantern that he'd pulled out of that carpetbag of his and lit.

"Let's get moving," Hink said.

"How badly are you hurt?" Miss Dupuis asked.

"The leg. It's fine."

"Broken? Shot?" she asked.

"Shot. And I said it's fine."

He pushed away from Cedar, who still had hold of him, and nearly collapsed.

"You might say the leg's fine." Miss Dupuis motioned to Theobald to come closer with the lantern. She knelt down in her skirts so she could get a better look at Hink's thigh. "But your leg says otherwise."

Hink was going to argue, but her man had placed the lantern on the floor and put his arm around Hink so he wouldn't fall while Miss Dupuis probed at the wound with no remorse.

"She has quite the hand with battle injuries," Theobald was saying, his voice carrying that smooth rhythm to it that drew attention away from everything else. "It's how we met, as a matter of fact. I'd taken a terrible shot to the chest. She nursed me to recovery."

"Did she make you hurt like the blazes too?" Hink ground out.

"She did. But you can endure," Theobald said, and it annoyed Hink to no end that he found himself wanting to believe that every word the man said was true.

Miss Dupuis checked the front and the back of his thigh. "I think it went clear through. You are a very lucky man, Captain Hink. Any lower and that would have taken your kneecap right off."

"If this is what lucky feels like, it ain't all it's talked up to be."

Cedar was standing watch at the door. "Men. Headed this way. Guns. We need to move. Quietly. Wil, choose a tunnel."

"Do you think it's wise to follow an animal into this hill?" Theobald asked.

"He's more than an animal, Otto," Miss Dupuis said. "He carries the same gift as Mr. Hunt."

"You," Cedar said over the top of their conversation, "can do anything you want. Surrender to the men on their way in here and beg for mercy if you like. Maybe they're not interested in killing you."

"No need to worry," Miss Dupuis said. "We follow you, Mr. Hunt. Do you have bandages, Theobald?"

"I have something that might work." Theobald pulled out a clean neckerchief. "Will this do?"

"Very nicely, thank you," Miss Dupuis said with a smile. A sort of intimate smile, from Hink's perspective.

Huh. Maybe these two were quite a lot more than traveling companions.

He grunted, and exhaled on a curse as Miss Dupuis bound his leg tight. Woman had some muscle behind her.

"Now," Miss Dupuis said, standing and drawing a derringer out of a pocket cleverly hidden in her dress. "What is our plan, gentlemen?"

"Can that . . . ," Hink started. "Can Wil find a way out of here?"

Wil stood in the far right tunnel entrance, sniffing the air.

"I don't know," Cedar said as the sound of gunfire rang out behind them. "But what's left of Mullins's crew isn't going to give us much of a choice."

"I hate tunnels," Miss Wright said as she swiftly unwrapped the coils from her arm, and handed those and the shield device to Theobald to pack in his carpetbag along with the harness that had attached to Miss Dupuis's shotgun.

"Too dark, and too many echoes," she said with that soft Southern accent. "I can't hear a blasted thing." She tossed Miss Dupuis her denuded shotgun.

"Now, I'm not arguing it's a certain kind of risk navigating these tunnels, Joonie," Theobald said. "But I trust Mr. Hunt and Wil will see us through."

Joonie shook her head. "You say those pretty things, but then we still get shot at, Otto."

He grinned at her. "And yet we always win, don't we?"

"So far," she agreed.

While they'd been talking, Cedar Hunt had been staring out the door.

"Dynamite," Cedar yelled. "Get back!"

They ran for the tunnel Wil had chosen. Theobald, who had the sense to snatch up the lantern, was somewhere in the middle of the group, Miss Wright and Miss Dupuis at the front behind Wil. Captain Hink and Cedar brought up the rear.

Theobald lifted the lamp, and wild light dragged the rock walls.

They couldn't run, because they couldn't see that far, but Hink sure as hell wished they would get moving a bit faster.

The blast sounded like the world cracked itself in half. Rocks rattled down from the ceiling and a huge push of warm air and dust rushed into the tunnel, turning the lantern light muddy.

Hink covered his head and pushed his back up close to one wall.

It took a while, but the crackle of stones rolling to the ground eventually quieted.

"Everyone okay?" Hink asked.

"I think so," Miss Dupuis said, coughing. "Otto?"

"Right here, Sophie. And apparently still in one piece," he said.

"Joonie?" she asked.

"I'm fine," Miss Wright said. "And the wolf, Wil, is it? He's next to me and seems uninjured."

"Can't go back," Cedar said, peering through the dust the way they'd come in. "Sealed off."

"What do we do, Mr. Hunt?" Miss Dupuis asked.

Cedar walked past Hink, past Theobald and Miss Dupuis. "We go forward."

"To where?" Joonie asked. "The bottom of this mountain? Shouldn't we just wait until dark and dig our way out the way we came in?"

"Don't think so," Captain Hink said. "Men with guns are gonna camp right on the other side of that rock pile waiting to shoot anyone who sticks their nose out. Old Jack ain't gonna ask if you're friend of foe, he's just gonna kill you."

Hink pushed off the wall where he'd been leaning to take some of the weight off his bad leg and started after Cedar Hunt. "We got any other light besides the one?" he asked.

"Might be something up here," Cedar said from a ways down the tunnel. "A couple crates here on the wall."

"Still got that ax on you, Mr. Hunt?" Captain Hink asked.

A crack of steel breaking wood was answer enough. "Could use the light, if I may," Cedar said.

Theobald handed the lantern to Miss Dupuis, and she handed it up until Hink took it and stood next to Cedar, peering down into the crate.

"Canteens, buckets, blankets," Hink said. "No food. Pans, though. Bust open the other one."

Cedar took a few steps down the tunnel and broke the next crate.

Hink looked over the contents. "Lanterns." He picked one up, gave it a shake. "It's got oil. Looks like there's three of them. Light them all just to make sure they're wicked proper, then take what supplies we can carry. Mr. Hunt, do you think Wil can do some scouting for us?"

"He already is."

Hink glanced off where he had seen the wolf just a second ago, but he was gone, silent as the night. "He have a good nose for fresh air?" Hink asked quietly.

Joonie might be worried about being trapped, but Hink was more worried that the air would run foul.

"Yes. And he'll find daylight, but it could take time," Cedar said. Then, to the others, "If anyone else has a way, or device we might use to track out of the tunnels, now would be a good time to suggest it."

"I have a compass," Theobald said.

"You have paper and ink to record our headings in case we need to backtrack?" Hink asked.

"A man in my line of work always keeps paper and ink," Theobald said cheerily.

"What line of work is that exactly?" Hink asked.

"Oh, I'm a man of many trades, but mostly I am a speaker and man of politics."

He got busy digging in that bag of his, and produced a journal, a fountain pen, and a compass, which he strapped to his wrist like a watch.

"Everyone have a light?" Hink asked.

"Yes, Captain," Miss Dupuis said. "I believe we are all ready."

Cedar started off down the tunnel, moving easily over the sandy floor littered with stones, at a pace Hink could match. Except for Theobald calling out change of headings through the twists and turns, they didn't talk for a long while, each of them busy minding feet and head.

Wil showed up after a bit.

"Any luck?" Cedar asked.

The wolf couldn't speak, or so Hink supposed. But somehow, Cedar seemed to understand what the animal was trying to say.

"Branches off up here," Cedar said. "Be careful."

Hink was starting to really feel the leg wound. Each step was a little harder than the last. He knew he couldn't walk these tunnels all night. He'd need a rest soon.

They took the left branch of the tunnel where Wil waited patiently for them. Then there was more walking. Some uphill, some down, and enough turns and branches that Hink was very glad Theobald was keeping close track of their meandering.

Just when Hink was about to tell Mr. Hunt his leg was going to completely give out on him, a gush of cool air washed into the tunnel.

Wil was some ways down that tunnel, whining softly.

There wasn't any light up ahead, but the breeze had to come from some kind of opening to the outside.

"We're facing east," Theobald said.

"East sounds good to me." Hink was going through his memories of flying over Old Jack's mountain.

Not a lot of ships traveled here, and Old Jack had the guns to keep it that way. Still, he'd drifted the *Swift* silent on no engines over Jack's on a full moon once.

"If we're any sort of lucky," Hink said between the brief moments of putting weight on his bad leg, "we'll be somewhere near a clearing. Plenty of valleys between most of these peaks."

"And then what?" Theobald asked.

"I'll signal for the *Swift* to come get us," Hink said. "If she's anywhere within twenty miles and the sky is clear, she'll be able to spot us."

"You have a signaling device on you, Captain Hink?" Miss Dupuis asked.

"All airship crewmen carry one. Or should." He grunted up the uneven floor. "They'll be looking for it."

And then the light from outside, even though it must be late evening, carved a blindingly white hole in the tunnel ahead and just slightly above where they stood.

It hurt to look at it, and Hink covered his eyes until he could bear the sight. Pretty soon he lowered his fingers and looked at the pile of stones that appeared to be the only way to climb out.

The tunnel opened wider here. Big enough you could drive two Conestogas and their teams of oxen side by side through it if you had the mind to.

Cedar stood at the bottom of the rock pile, his hands on his hips, his face tipped up, the wolf pacing silently behind him. He was thinking a route up those rocks.

"I'll climb it first," Cedar said. "Then I'll help anyone up who might need it."

Hink looked around and found himself a rock of suitable size for sitting. "Sounds like a plan to me." He pulled the flask out of his jacket and took down the last swallow of bourbon. It didn't do much to ease his pain, but it cleared the dust out of his mouth.

Cedar clambered up the stones, reached the top in short order, then threw his shadow across the bright as he looked out to see where they'd ended up.

Didn't take him much time. Not nearly enough for Hink to catch his breath. But he'd rather be breathless and out in the open sky than stuck down this bunghole.

Cedar retraced his route down the rocks and brushed off his hands as he walked over to where they were waiting.

"It's a clearing. A valley," Cedar said. "Sky's clouded, but no rain. I didn't hear anything in the air, but I didn't wait very long."

"The *Swift* will be silent," Hink said. "Either anchored and watching, or set to drift and watching. Don't worry. She's out there."

Hink stood and cleared the groan out of the back of his throat. "Go on up ahead of me. The leg's going to slow me a bit on the climb."

The others headed to the rockfall. Wil was already halfway up the stone tumble and Theobald was shortly behind him, helping Miss Dupuis and Miss Wright along the rough spots.

Hink put off climbing until they were nearly at the top, then limped over to the stones. This was not going to be any kind of pleasant.

He sighed and took the first step up. He hated caves, hated being on the ground, hated worse being underground. For just this sort of reason. Give a man the sky, and he could soar in the heavens. Stick him in a hole and all he did was crawl over rocks.

He cussed and sweated his way through the climb, and when Mr. Hunt offered him a hand about a third of the way from the top, he did not let pride get in his way of accepting.

Finally at the top of the pile, the cave opening slanted up a bit. He'd need to hike that, shoot the flare, and keep an ear out for the *Swift*. He took a breath, steeling himself for the rest of the walk.

Cedar came up on one side and put his shoulder under his arm.

"Getting pretty tired of you picking me for your dance partner," Hink said.

"Don't get shot next time."

"Next time?" Hink said. "I don't believe Old Jack will ever let us cross his dirt again."

"No great loss," Cedar said. "A man who can call a ship full of Strange is a worrisome thing."

"You sure that's what those men had been afflicted with? Strange?"

"They stink of it," Cedar said. "They stink of the only . . . man I know who could have done that sort of work."

"He got a name?"

"Mr. Shunt. Strange walking in flesh. Nightmare. Haven't found a way he stays dead yet."

"Like the men out there with too many holes in them getting back up?"

"I doubt they'll stitch back together now," Cedar said. "Can't say the same for Mr. Shunt."

"You have caught the attention of an odd sort of creature, Mr. Hunt," Hink said. "I've seen a few in my days, but none so dead set on killing a man." They stopped a ways out from the opening to the tunnel, and Cedar let him go. "This should do."

Not quite dusk yet, and the clouds were taking on a clay-colored darkness. The wind was unsettled, blowing up over brush, going dead, then rushing down over the tips of the peak. It wasn't raining or snowing, but the heat of the day was gutted and gone.

Both men scanned the sky and listened.

Hink thought he heard an engine, but it didn't sound like the *Swift*. Could be any number of ships out this way looking to land at Jack's for supplies.

Could be Old Jack had signaled in more than just Mullins and his crew. Could be a fleet of ships, a fleet of Alabaster's ships hovering in dusk's arch.

"You hear that?" Hink asked.

"One engine?" Cedar said.

"It's not the *Swift*."

Cedar nodded, his gaze still on the sky.

"Flare's going to let everyone in the sky know right where we are," Hink said.

"Going to be night soon," Cedar noted.

Not approving or disapproving. This was Hink's call.

"It's worth the risk," Hink said. "Jack knows these hills. He knows where we got sealed in, and he'll know where we're bound to pop out. Could be aiming his guns on us right now."

"Then stop talking and fire the flare, Captain," Cedar said. "Your ship is carrying people I've made promises to. Promises I intend to keep."

Hink couldn't help but smile. Cedar didn't seem the smallest bit concerned that they might be inviting another firefight down on their heads. "You are a reckless and fearless man, Mr. Hunt," he said. "It's a wonder you're still alive."

Cedar drew his gun and pulled his goggles over his eyes. "No wonder to it," Cedar said. "Just skill."

The captain laughed. "Miss Dupuis, Mr. Theobald, Miss Wright, be prepared to run if the *Swift* comes over. But don't go jumping like a fish on a hook at any rope that lowers. We might have unfriendly vessels looking for us. Are we of an understanding?"

Miss Dupuis pulled the shotgun off her shoulder. "Perfectly, Captain."

Hink drew the flare gun from where it was holstered low on his hip. He took aim straight up, and fired into the clouds.

A bright orange-pink flame burned a trail up and up, then blew open like a Chinese firework.

The sound of an engine grew louder. Whatever ship was out there, they'd seen the flare. And they were on the way.

CHAPTER TWENTY-TWO

Mae was trying not to listen to the sisters. Ever since they had run out of Old Jack's mountain, the voices had come back in force. Furious. They no longer sang, but screamed for her to return home, clawing at her sanity, stabbing at her mind.

She didn't know how she had endured it before.

When Mr. Guffin had told her they were anchored and she could take off her harness and step away from the wall, she just shook her head. The need, the push to be home at the coven, was so strong she didn't trust her own feet.

It would be too easy to listen to the voices that told her to come, walk, run to them. No matter that there was nothing but hundreds of feet of empty air between her and the ground—if she weren't harnessed, she just might step out into the wind.

The sisters' voices had come on so gradually since Jeb's death that she hadn't realized just how much of a torment they had become. Her marriage vows to Jeb had taken the place of her vows to the sisters. But now that he was dead and that vow was broken, her earlier vows, made of magic and blood, were demanding her return.

And she knew the sisterhood wasn't so much calling her home as calling for her death.

They feared her magic. Feared the curses and bindings, oaths and vows she so easily drew upon.

They feared her. Probably always had.

Once she returned, if she returned, she would ask them to break this binding that tied her to the soil of the coven.

She should have never let them throw such ropes around her, but she had been young and afraid of her own abilities. They had told her the bindings would hold her safe, like a net. A way to assure that she never fell into using magic for ill causes. That she never harmed anyone.

Even though magic could easily lean toward dark results in her hands, she had only wanted to use it for good, for love, for mercy. And the sisterhood could not tell her she had ever done so wrongly. Not without admitting that what they were doing to her now was also wrong.

Rose was awake, silent, lying on the hammock and staring at the ceiling. Her color was so pale and gray, it was almost as if her skin were turning into tin. Even her lips had a bluish cast. But when Mae brushed her hair back from her forehead with shaking fingers, she blinked and smiled.

"Have we seen the signal yet?" she asked.

Mae had to hold her breath against the screaming in her mind and focus on Rose's lips to understand the words.

Signal? Oh, yes. They were waiting for a signal from Captain Hink so they could find him and Cedar and those other people. So they could rescue them. If they were still alive.

"Not yet," she said. "Soon. I'm sure soon."

Rose swallowed and closed her eyes. Mae knew she wasn't sleeping. She'd offered to give her another dose of the coca leaf tonic, but Rose had refused it. She didn't even want the laudanum, afraid it would put her too deeply asleep again.

All she had allowed Mae to do was change the dressing on her wound.

Her shoulder was hot, and still weeping greenish-yellow fluid. They needed to find the Holder, and remove the key buried in her.

Even if they removed the tin, Mae wasn't sure if it would be enough to save her.

"There!" Guffin said. "The flare. See it?"

Ansell and Seldom both scrambled to the windows. And so did Molly, who had been whittling on something that looked like a whistle while waiting for the engines to be needed.

"We want steam, boys?" she asked.

"Bring her up, Molly." Seldom was already jogging to the wheel while Ansell and Guffin took their places on either side of him.

"Hold tight, ladies," Molly said as she opened the blast door, releasing a billowing wave of heat into the cabin. "We're on our way!"

Rose opened her eyes. "Are we flying?"

"Yes," Mae said. "We're flying."

They had strapped Rose into the hammock and tied cross lines from the hammock to each wall so it couldn't swing too far to either side.

Mae made sure the blanket was tucked tight around her.

"Can I have the tonic now?" she asked.

"Of course." Mae helped Rose drink the tonic straight from the bottle. "Just a sip," she cautioned.

"Up anchor!" Seldom called.

"Aye," Ansell answered. He worked the winch and cranked the anchor free.

The ship swayed in the breeze, but seemed to drift for only a moment before the fans were on and the sails were set.

"We'll have them soon," Mae said, to herself, to Rose, to the sisters screaming in her head as she rubbed her hands down the front of her dress, wiping her palms. "We'll have them and then we'll be on our way. On our way soon again. Soon. And then," she said, speaking just to the scream of the sisters voices in her head, "I will break this tie between us."

The roar of the fans turning against the wind and the huff of steam clearing the flues drowned her soft words.

CHAPTER TWENTY-THREE

Captain Hink scanned the sky, his gun in his hand. Everyone was spread out among the boulders outside the opening to the tunnel, weapons drawn, waiting for the *Swift*.

But all he could hear was the engine from another vessel, bigger, heavier. A vessel he did not know.

He cussed and kept a sky eye. If he didn't hear the *Swift* soon, then they'd all take cover back in the tunnel and hope the other ship didn't get a hard read on that flare.

And while they were at it they could hope Old Jack hadn't happened to see the flare light up the eastern sky, and wasn't willing to send his boys around to do some more shooting.

They were trapped. He was wounded. And unless they wanted to run through the mountain range on the turn of winter with no provisions other than a few blankets and lanterns, there wasn't anything else they could do but wait for the *Swift*.

There was the chance the ship wasn't headed toward them, but was coincidentally stopping off at Old Jack's to resupply. Hink had never met a coincidence he was willing to bet his life on.

The engine grew louder, but the peaks threw the sound around and broke it up so bad that for all he could tell, there were two or three ships out there.

"Two engines," Cedar said from where he stood with the wolf not too far off from Hink.

Hink tipped his head. "Either you're full of wishing, Mr. Hunt, or you have damn sharp ears."

"I gave up wishing years ago," Cedar said. "Is it the *Swift*?"

Hink took a breath and held it, straining to hear the familiar fans of his vessel. She'd be coming in fast, or at least he hoped to hell she was coming in fast for them.

Every time he thought he had a bead on it, the wind changed and snatched away the rumble of the fans, and all he heard instead was Theobald sneeze, or the brush around them rustle and scratch.

Cedar Hunt had said he heard two engines.

There. Yes. Hink could make out the pulses of two different ships. One wasn't the *Swift*.

But he would bet his bottom dollar the other was.

"Two ships," he said, loud enough the others could hear. "One's the *Swift*. I'd say she's coming from the . . . south?" He glanced at Cedar.

Cedar nodded.

"She'll land if we have time. If not, if that other ship decides to take a swat at us, or worse, tries to shoot us dead, then we might want to do a running board. Ever done that?"

Miss Dupuis shook her head. "Explain. And we'll follow."

"If she lowers ropes, you can catch them and hold on, they'll winch you up. If it's a ladder, get on and climb. If it's the nets, hold still and let them bring you up. And no matter what it is that you're holding on to, for glim's sake, hold tight. The winds can knock the skin right off you.

"If there ain't any time to pull us up, they'll fly us out of range of the other ship, then take us aboard. It'll be cold, and breathing might not be a lot of fun, but you'll survive if you don't let go."

"Isn't there anything else we can do?" Theobald asked.

"Sure," Hink said. "If you get fired on by a ship that isn't made of tin, shoot back."

The wait was nerve-racking. The rattle of fans grew closer and closer until it was all that filled the air. Hink thought the *Swift*'s engines sounded louder, stronger than the other ship's.

She might be closer. Seldom was a fine pilot in his own right. He knew how to skim the sky. Maybe he'd slip in before that other vessel.

But as the ships neared, Hink began to wonder if he'd have to set off another flare. He waited, hoping the *Swift* was closer than the other ship, hoping she'd got a good read on where they were tucked in.

He knew from experience it was difficult at best to wave down an airship. If they wanted feet off the ground, he'd have to shoot another light to guide them in.

Hink stood, aimed straight up. Mr. Hunt looked over at him, and whispered something to Wil, who was crouched tight by his side, and looking . . . different somehow. It was like the wolf was suddenly tired, all the steam out of him, without enough strength to even lift his head.

Hink hoped he wasn't injured.

"Make fast for her," Hink said. He squeezed the trigger and sent another wild orange and pink flare into the sky, blooming like a flower against the muddy sky.

"On the ready!" he called out.

He'd been right. The ships hadn't caught tight to their location.

But now a ship homed into view. Twice as big as the *Swift* and painted red on her belly, the vessel was all one piece with an attached gondola, like the *Swift*, nets and lashes attached to her, but no trawling arms. She lifted up over the peak to the north, then nosed down toward them, tail in the air, like a kid bobbing for apples.

Nosing down revealed all the guns and cannons strapped to her. She wasn't just coming in to Old Jack's to resupply. She had seen their flare and was coming for them.

Crouched beside rocks, they weren't under enough cover to resist an aerial attack. And those guns had a hell of a lot more range than their firearms. As soon as the ship leveled out and swung broadside, they'd be easy pickings.

Then they'd be dead.

"Do you know her?" Miss Dupuis asked.

"Not yet," Hink said. "Turn, you bitch," he whispered to the ship. "Let's see your true colors."

The ship swung to the side and her shadow drew a net of darkness across the valley, rolling over scrub and stone.

"The *Devil's Nine*," Hink said, a mix of dread and hatred rising hot through his veins. She'd gotten her name for how many cannons she carried. "That's Alabaster Saint's ship," he yelled to the others.

The ship was still too high to shoot, but it wouldn't be long before those cannons opened up.

They were about to be blasted into little bits.

If they had been spotted. There was a chance, not much of one but some, that the men aboard the ship couldn't see them huddled in the shadows of the stones with the failing light of day.

Hink's heart beat hard and even. Time to make choices.

Run while they were still out of firing range? Or stay still and hope they searched the next valley?

"Steady," Cedar said, thinking along the same lines as him. "The ship is full of Strange. We bolt and they'll chase us through that tunnel and tear us to shreds. We can't outrun them."

"I can't," Hink agreed. "You and your brother could."

Cedar looked over his shoulder at him, his eyes the color of burnt copper. "We stay together."

"Hold," Hink said to the sound of shifting rocks behind him.

"Captain," Miss Dupuis said, angling a spyglass to the sky, "there's another ship."

Hink craned his neck to see sky around the *Devil's Nine* and squinted against the clouds.

Another ship. Coming in high and fast, sweet and slick as a silver needle glowing bronze as she sang through the clouds.

"The *Swift!*" he yelled.

She was coming in too damn fast.

At first he thought Guffin was at the wheel, overshooting the valley. But then the *Swift* tucked wing and turned, pulling around so hard you could hear the sails pop. She powered up above and behind Alabaster's ship. That was one of Seldom's moves.

The *Swift* dropped dozens of Old Jack's glass jug firebombs that they'd smuggled along with the coal they'd loaded when they first landed.

Half the bombs hit the ship and started her on fire. The other half hit the ground and also ignited flames.

Hink let out a belly laugh. There wasn't a situation in the world Seldom couldn't cure with an explosion and burning something to the ground.

And it was always a delight to see.

The wet brush caught quick from the oil and flame, and sent off a horrible amount of smoke that worked as a screen to keep them hid from the *Devil's Nine*.

But getting them out of this wallow relied on whether Seldom had had a fix on him and his companions before mucking up the visibility.

Gunshots rang out. Cannons. Nine in hot succession, hard enough to make his molars ache.

The *Devil's Nine* was aiming to blast the *Swift* out of the sky.

But the *Swift* was already on the fly. The cannon shots rocketed through empty air as the *Swift* gunned it west, much faster than the other ship. She dove hard, and headed straight for Hink.

The *Swift* was running at speed, her trawling lines and nets lowering for them to catch, her nose aimed straight toward the mountain behind them.

"She won't pull up in time!" Hink yelled, getting on his feet. "Run for her, or she'll miss the lift! Run!"

He didn't have to yell twice. Miss Dupuis, Theobald, and Wright were already running straight into the flame and smoke toward the ship, weapons holstered but not out of reach. Cedar was pounding dirt for the ship too.

And so was Hink. The heat from flames licked at his clothes and the smoke skinned the inside of his lungs. Every step sent a sharp flash of pain through his leg, but he kept on. The net dipped down, as low as the trawling arm could reach.

The *Swift's* fans roared, flattening the smoke into heated whips.

Miss Dupuis jumped for the netting, caught and started climbing. Miss Wright leaped after her, found good footing and started up. Mr. Theobald was only seconds behind them.

Cedar bent down. Hink lost sight of him for a second in the smoke. When he came into view again, he had Wil across his shoulders. The wolf seemed to be unconscious. Had he been hit?

Cedar reached up, leaped too high for a man with over a hundred pounds of animal on his shoulder. And then he paused and held one hand down for Hink.

Hink jumped for it. Grabbed rope with left hand and both boots, right hand gripped by Cedar Hunt, who didn't even grunt from the impact, even though he was still supporting the wolf, and holding on to the net with only one hand.

"You clear?" Cedar yelled.

"I got it!" Hink yelled. Cedar let go of Hink's hand.

The trawling arms were lifting, which meant the nets were billowing out beneath them, and the speed of the wind at this angle holding them all tight to the ropes.

Hink didn't try climbing. Once the nets reached horizontal, he knew he could mostly crawl his way in.

Bullets cracked through the smoke and fire, and another set of cannon blasts broke the mountain into echoes. Hink held on, waiting for the nets to go horizontal, smoke digging tears out of his eyes.

Then the *Swift* shook like a wet dog. She'd been hit. Hink could feel the pain of it in his chest as clearly as if he had been shot. So clearly that he looked down at his shirt to make sure he hadn't taken a bullet.

He was whole, but the *Swift* was not. The *Devil's Nine* must have doused the fire Seldom had started in her. And now her cannons were about to blast the *Swift* into brittle bits.

A voice yelled out over the noise of fans and winds. "Cage!" the voice boomed. Not one of his crew, and not coming from the *Swift*. No, that voice was coming from somewhere below them.

Hink looked down.

He hadn't expected an angel. He didn't get one. Nope, all he got was a demon.

The *Devil's Nine* hovered beneath them, every damn gun, cannon, and harpoon on that ship aimed their way.

"Marshal Cage. Come aboard, or we'll fire."

They wanted him.

They didn't want his ship. They didn't want his crew or Cedar Hunt and his brother. They didn't want Rose. And if they gunned the *Swift* out of the sky they'd all die.

He had to buy them time. He had to buy Rose a chance at seeing the skies again with her own wings.

"Take care of her," he whispered to the *Swift*.

"Marshal Cage!" the amplified voice from below yelled out again. "Surrender!"

Hink didn't intend to surrender. Not his ship. Not his crew and passengers. Not Rose.

He twisted his head and looked down at the *Devil's Nine*. He'd hit her nets if he dropped now.

"Captain!" Cedar yelled.

Hink looked up at him. "Get them the hell out of here!"

Then he pushed off of the net and spread wide so he could catch at the *Devil's* ropes and rigging.

He hit her envelope with all the grace of a drunk knocked sprawling to a barroom floor. Instinct curled his hands, arms, legs around anything he could catch hold to.

A long, sickening slide made him wish he'd taken up a god to pray to, and then he stopped, the ropes pulling taut.

He was still on the *Devil's Nine*, though he'd slid down the envelope so that he was dangling by both arms off the side. No graceful way out of this. He figured he had about a minute and a half before the captain tipped the *Nine* and he spilled brains all over the hills.

Of all the places he'd thought he would breathe his last, it certainly wasn't on these damn rocks or on somebody else's damn ship.

Hot, sharp pain cut through his arm, bad enough that he was sure the bone had broken.

But the *Swift* shot into the sky, barely clearing the mountain range, pulling up with a beautiful scream. He couldn't make out anyone on board, but he was glad they'd had the sense in their skulls to get his ship out of danger while they had the chance.

The ropes tugged. And four men came scrambling over the netting like spiders over webs. Fast. On hands and feet. Hungry for the kill.

Death or capture? Hink held on. So long as there was a chance of breathing left to him, he intended to take it.

The men caught up to him at once. One of them pressed a cloth over his face, while the two others caught his arms. The last one punched a fist in his bleeding leg.

Hink yelled, but never heard the end of it, what with the passing out he was intent upon.

He came in and out of consciousness as he was harnessed, carried, lowered, then dropped to a solid surface. Just glimpses of moments in which he should have been fighting, or planning an escape, and instead couldn't do much more than take in a lungful of air before going black again.

But when someone slapped him around and stuck smelling salts up his nose, he came right on up out of his terrifying slumber.

Swinging a punch.

But his arms were tied up over his head. His feet were spread wide and tied up too. Mouth gagged. Chest strapped down. Trussed like a pig, but on his feet, which wasn't much good, as the pain of being unable to take the weight off his bad leg was enough to drench him in a hard sweat.

He was inside a ship. Not the *Swift*. From the smoke and the grind of the engine, he knew it was the *Devil's Nine*.

Which probably meant Alabaster Saint was nearby.

What he couldn't figure was why the Saint hadn't already skinned and roasted him.

"Awake, Mr. Cage?" a man's cultured voice asked. Not Alabaster. "You will be pleased to know your ship is out of range. We could have decimated her, but she is of very little interest to us."

Hink knew that voice. But the pain, and whatever extra breaks and contusions the crew had decided to treat him to while he was unconscious, teased the memory from him.

On top of that, the pain in his chest he'd felt when the *Swift* got hit was still gnawing away, burning hard as if his skin were on fire. His broken arm throbbed dully.

No use trying to talk. The gag held his tongue in place. So he waited.

Finally, the speaker strolled out in front of him.

Neat, thin, dark hair combed back and not a wrinkle in his sharp uniform. Lieutenant Foster, Alabaster's right hand.

"We both knew this day would come, Mr. Cage. My apologies for the limited degree of my hospitality. If it were up to me, I'd be breaking your bones, one by one. But the general has given me strict orders to bring you to him whole. So he can give you a . . . proper welcome. And you know I am a man who always follows orders."

CHAPTER TWENTY-FOUR

Cedar hauled himself into the *Swift*. He had watched Captain Hink drop to the ship below. The captain hadn't let go expecting to die, nor had he been shaken off. No, the captain had jumped.

Fool. The ship was filled with strangework—Cedar could smell it, could taste the oil and sour of their sweat on the back of his tongue.

Hink may have thought he'd survive the fall, but he had to have known he'd never survive if they captured him.

The crew was struggling to pull the *Swift* up and over the edge of the mountain. The ship had taken a hit from the other airship and was listing, struggling to hold a true heading. Coupled with the angle and the speed, the mountain range was coming up so close that Cedar would be able to reach out a hand and touch the stones in a minute or two. That is if they didn't just plow into it.

"Up, damn you, up, up!" Guffin yelled.

Seldom, at the wheel, never flinched or hesitated. He angled that ship up the edge of the peaks, cutting so close that the netting where Hink had just been clinging a moment before caught on the outcropping of brush and rocks.

"Net hung!" Cedar yelled.

Seldom didn't change course. The trawling arm snapped in two, as the *Swift* screamed to the sky.

Leaving the captain. Leaving the *Devil's Nine* behind.

"Did he make it?" Guffin yelled out. "Captain. Did you make it?"

Cedar stood in the door and turned, one hand clamped tight on the overhead bar.

"He jumped." Then Cedar saw Wil curled in the corner, wedged between some crates that were strapped down so he wouldn't slide across the floor. He looked sick.

"What the blazes?" Guffin rushed to the window and looked down. Cedar wasn't sure he could see anything through the smoke and the speed of their ascent.

"Did you see him land?" Guffin asked. "Did you see him hit?"

"He landed on the other ship. Grabbed hold of the rope." Cedar crossed to Wil, knelt, and ran his hands over him. No blood. He wasn't hurt.

Wil lifted his head, held Cedar's gaze for a moment, then dropped his head to his paws again.

"Then the captain is still alive?" Miss Dupuis said. "Are we going to leave him behind?"

"He told me to get you all out of here," Cedar said, pulling a blanket from overhead and tucking it around Wil.

"Like hell we leave him behind," Guffin said.

"He'd want the ship safe," Ansell said.

Seldom reached up and pulled the line that set a bell ringing back in the boiler room.

Molly came stomping out just a moment later, her coat thrown off, in nothing but her breeches and short sleeves. "Can't believe we pulled out of that one, boys!" she said with a huge grin. "Can this lady fly, or can she fly?"

Then, "Where's the captain?"

"Jumped," Seldom said. "We save the ship and save these people, or we go save his skin."

"Why can't we do both?" Mr. Theobald asked. "We can fight with you. We won't be a detriment to your efforts, as you've seen."

"There isn't enough time for both," Cedar said. "We don't know where they're taking him. Rose doesn't have much time left. Neither does Mae, and the ship is damaged."

"I'm not leaving the captain behind," Molly said. "Rose is a lot tougher than you think she is, Mr. Hunt. She'll weather a little longer."

"You don't know that," Cedar said.

"Why don't we ask her?" Molly said. "Let her choose."

Cedar didn't even know if Rose had come up to conscious thought since he'd carried her onto the ship.

"Now," Seldom said. "While the *Nine* is still in range."

"Ask a woman on the edge of death how long she can endure?" Cedar said. "There's no reason in that statement. We take her and Mae to Kansas. Now. And pray we reach our destination while both women are still breathing."

"No," Rose said.

Even over the rush of wind outside, her soft voice carried.

Cedar moved to stand above her. He held his breath against the sound of surprise that choked his throat.

Rose's skin had turned a pale silvery tone, like the satin shine of tin. Her lips were blue-gray with just a hint of blush to them, and her eyes, once blue and soft as summer, were dark as winter clouds.

It was the Holder; must be that bit of tin inside her causing the change.

But when she turned her gaze on Cedar, her eyes were very clear. Very sane. "I know I'm going to die, Mr. Hunt," she said. "And I know Mae's near out of her mind. But I won't turn this crew from their captain on account of me."

"Rose—" he started.

"I might live the day, or another. Or none. But Lee has years ahead of him. If we can find him."

Cedar bit back his argument. He could overpower her. For a wild moment he considered overpowering every person on board, tying them up, and flying the ship to Kansas himself.

But going to Kansas wouldn't be the same as finding the Holder. And if he didn't find the Holder, Rose would die.

Rose gave him half a smile. "Whatever you're thinking, don't do it, Mr. Hunt. You don't have to look after me anymore. Please promise me you'll look after Captain Cage. He risked his life to save us all. He risked his ship. More than once. It's time we take a risk for him."

Cedar put his hand around hers. She might look like she was slowly turning into cool metal, but her hand was warm, soft, and very human. "I will never stop looking after you."

"We don't know where the Holder is, do we?" she asked.

It pained him, but Cedar answered her true. "No."

Rose knew, they all knew, that only the Holder would be able to remove the little tin key that was killing her. And they didn't even know that for certain. But the Madders had said it would work.

With a world of maybes between them and finding the Holder, and still not knowing if it would do any good if they found it . . . he knew it made sense for Rose to accept she had little time left.

Cedar, however, wasn't always a logical man.

"Can you find him?" Cedar asked Seldom.

"The captain?"

"General Alabaster Saint."

"I can find him," Mae said quietly.

"The general?" Cedar asked.

Mae cleared her throat and wiped her hands over her dress before grabbing on to the wall of the ship for support. Her eyes were glassy, unfocused, but her voice was strong. "Captain Hink. His heartbeat is in this wood, in this ship, in the binding I cast on him and cast on the ship. The *Swift* knows where Captain Hink is, and I can guide her to him."

No one said anything. Too shocked at her admission, maybe not even believing that she had cast a spell and bound a man to a ship. Or maybe not believing that Mae was anything more than a woman gone mad.

But Cedar had seen the strength of her magic. He knew what she could do. Knew that though she might be losing hold of her sanity, she had not lost hold of what her magic had done to Hink. She wasn't lying. If anyone could track the captain, it would be Mae.

"We'll find him, Rose," Mae said, though she was staring straight ahead, staring blankly at the middle distance. "You'll see him again. I promise."

"Perhaps you should sit yourself down, Mae," Molly said.

"She can do it," Cedar said.

"No one can do that," Molly said.

Cedar gave her a look. The beast shifted just beneath his skin, its hatred and hunger threatening to swallow his reason. There was no time to argue with her. Rose was dying. And Mae was hurting.

"Yes," Cedar said, knowing the raw power of the beast hovering just behind his eyes, just beneath his words. "She can. Follow, or get out of my way."

Molly's hand slipped down to the gun at her hip.

Cedar didn't move. If he had the breath in him, the reason in him, he'd tell her Mae was a witch and damn good at magic. But it was all he could do to keep the urge for blood in his control.

"Stand down, Molly," Seldom said. "If she can find our captain, we follow."

Molly shook her head, switching her gaze from Cedar to Seldom and finally to Mae.

"Then let's find the captain," she said. "Before Alabaster hangs him up by his guts."

Molly stomped back into the boiler room and shut the blast door.

"Ansell, see to the repairs," Seldom said.

"Aye, Mr. Seldom." Ansell picked up a toolbox and scrambled up the ladder to see what he could do above.

"Heading?" Seldom called out.

Mae didn't say anything. Just stood, swaying slightly, breathing a little raggedly as if she kept forgetting how often she should be filling her lungs.

Cedar ducked under the line that held Rose's hammock from swinging too hard. He stepped up to Mae, stopping just short of touching her.

He could smell the scent of the herbs she'd been using on Rose's shoulder, a watered honey and green odor that blended with the fragrance that was all her own. A fragrance that stirred him to his bones.

"Mae," he said, holding his own desires firmly in check, "we need a direction. Where is Captain Cage?"

"Flying."

That wasn't going to help much.

"Which direction is he headed?"

There was a long pause. Finally. "Southwest. Running fast. Above the ridge."

"Southwest," Cedar called to Seldom.

Mr. Seldom corrected course and brought the *Swift* around.

"A compass direction won't be enough," Guffin said.

"More west," Mae said.

"More to the west, Mr. Seldom," Cedar relayed.

Seldom corrected course again.

"Yes," Mae said. "Steady."

"Hold that heading steady," Cedar called.

"Aye," Seldom said.

Guffin took a reading of the compass. "Ain't nothing but mountains and Indian territory that way. She know how far?"

"She's following the captain," Cedar said. "As far as he goes is as far as we go."

"Aye that," Guffin said.

"And what," Mr. Theobald asked, "is our plan once we catch up with this ship?"

"You find out what weapons we have at our disposal," Cedar said. "Then we'll talk plan."

"Aye, sir," he said with a slight smile. "Miss Dupuis, Miss Wright. Would you help me take inventory? Captain Seldom, permission to check the stores?"

"It's first mate," Seldom said. "Granted."

Mr. Theobald and his companions got busy counting the munitions they had on hand. All Cedar wanted to do was pace, but he was afraid he'd miss some whispered change of direction from Mae.

He finally leaned one shoulder against the wall of the ship and simply watched people do their jobs.

To his surprise, Mae's hand slipped down between them and caught at his fingers. Her hand was trembling, cold.

He wrapped his arm around her, pulling her into the heat of his body as she shuddered. It was almost as if the frigid wind beyond the ship was wrapped around her.

Cedar quickly unbuttoned his coat and shrugged out of it, put it around her, and then drew her close to him again.

Mae leaned into him and doggedly kept hold of the ship with one hand too.

"We can't lose him," Mae said.

"I won't," he said. "I won't lose anyone."

He held her tight as the airship scorched the sky.

CHAPTER TWENTY-FIVE

Hink measured time by how long he could hold out against the pain before he cussed or moaned.

Lieutenant Foster's men made it easy by coming past him every once in a while and hitting him in the face, the stomach, or his bad leg. He'd hoped one of them might have the guts or the hate to knock him clean out, just so he could slip the pain unconscious, but they were good soldiers.

They knew exactly how much he could endure. And doled it out.

Mr. Foster didn't have a lot to say, which was fine with Hink, since he'd always thought the man to be a piss-proud lick finger who couldn't blow his own nose without asking Alabaster Saint to hold the hanky.

But on the other hand, if Foster was the chatty sort, he might have some kind of idea where in damnation they were taking him.

Not that he supposed he'd get out of it alive anyway, but if the chance fell upon him, he'd like to know which direction to run.

The uneven drone of the ship's damaged fans filled his head. There wasn't a window anywhere in his eyesight. They'd thrown him below-decks, but made sure he was trussed up well out of reach of any of the supplies down there with him.

And there were plenty of supplies.

Along with three guards who kept their guns leveled at him.

He knew one of those men. Couldn't much recall his name, but he'd been part of the mutiny Hink had led all those years ago. Chickened out of it halfway to Chicago. Heard he went back begging to Alabaster for forgiveness. Heard Alabaster had accepted him into the new army he was mustering.

Course, he cut off his ear first.

Wasn't a man who'd served under the Saint who had walked away from the last battle unscathed. So Alabaster Saint made sure the man carried a wound just like the rest of them.

The general enjoyed his torturing almost as much as he enjoyed just plain killing folk.

Hink thought maybe he could get a little conversation out of the soldiers, but he was still gagged and, frankly, not feeling his best.

So he did what he could to breathe, and hurt, and memorize the faces of the men who inflicted that hurt on him.

The Saint might be top cock at torture, but there was no man who could match Hink when it came to revenge.

With no water, and no relief, it was a long damn ride before the ship fans altered in sound.

They were heading into the wind, changing course. From the tip the floor suddenly took, they were coming down to land. He half hoped his gun company would find themselves something less useful to do and give him a moment to gather his wits.

Instead, they stood watch over him as the ship went through the various stages of anchor, catch, lash, and landing, and was walked to whatever dock or port had been readied for her.

Then one of the soldiers walked up to him and hit him so hard in the side of the head, he heard his neck crack before he went out.

CHAPTER TWENTY-SIX

Mae didn't know how much longer she could last. Staying connected to the spell she had worked between Hink and the *Swift* took all the concentration she could muster. It would be too easy to slip into believing she was a part of the ship, to feel the pump of steam like hot blood driving her wings, to flinch from the icy cold of the night sky.

Between that and the sisters' whipping voices, she might completely lose all hope of remaining herself, of knowing her skin was her own, her mind was her own, and her will was her own too.

If it weren't for Cedar, who held her, the warmth of his body, the heat of the anger burning within him, helping her focus on her own bones and breath, she would be nothing, her mind torn apart and left in scattered ribbons on the wind.

He was a rock holding her to the earth.

He was a heat refusing to let death's cold claws slice her apart for good.

"Mae," Cedar said. "Where is he?"

It seemed to take forever to make her mouth move, to lift her tongue and carry the words from thought to breath. "South more. East soon."

At the edges of her awareness, she heard his voice carrying her words. So much stronger, with so much more life and power than she had left in her. She knew people were moving about the ship.

They were talking about repairs. They were talking about weapons. She'd heard firebombs and cannons, dynamite and guns. But there was no fire in those words. Whoever had said it was worried, the words thin and tenuous, knowing that would not be nearly enough to win. To save Captain Hink.

She felt the connection between Hink and the *Swift* tug. Hard. Down.

"East," she said. "Landing. He's landing."

Cedar carried her words again, and the *Swift* shifted joyfully closer to Hink, to the captain she searched for.

"You can let go," Cedar was saying. "Mae. Mae. Let go of the ship. We see the landing area. We see the ship's lights."

But Mae could not seem to sort his words out from the sisters' screaming for her return, could not divorce herself from the taut shiver of awareness, the almost inhuman hunger between the ship and Hink.

She heard his words, but they were just another rattle of noise that threatened to suffocate her screams.

Someone clamped a hand over her mouth. And then someone tore the ship away from her.

No, someone tore her away from the ship.

And that someone was Cedar.

Mae came to her senses, her mouth covered by Cedar's palm, her body pulled up against his so hard, not even her feet were touching the ground.

It was that, the complete disconnection from the *Swift* that finally cleared her head enough for her to realize that she had been screaming.

Everything and everyone around her was silent, staring at her.

Even the ship was silent.

They'd cut the steam. She was gliding in.

But Mae didn't know where.

"Easy now," Cedar was saying. "Quiet now. You're safe."

Mae nodded and Cedar nodded back, his eyes searching hers and apparently liking what he saw.

"I'm going to set you on your feet," he said, "but I won't take my hand away until I know you're all right. Understand?"

She nodded again.

Cedar shifted his hold on her and gently set her down on her feet again.

She didn't feel like screaming.

"All right now?" he whispered.

One more nod.

Cedar removed his hand. "We're coming in silent to see the structure below. As much of it as we can in the dark."

"The captain?" Mae asked, trying to get her thoughts and her mouth working in unison again.

"The ship is there," Cedar said. "Unless you think they dumped him overboard on the way?"

"No."

"Then he's there and we're going to go in there and save him."

Mae brushed her skirts to straighten them. The sisters' voices still swirled in her mind, but at least she wasn't tied so tight to the ship. "I'll need to give Rose medicine."

"Rose stays with the *Swift*," Cedar said. There was no room for argument in his words.

"Yes," Mae said. "But I want her awake, at least. In case . . ." A hundred possible things that could go wrong rolled through her mind. "In case she needs to be," she simply said.

Cedar let go of Mae's hand. Mae hadn't realized he was still holding on to her.

"Be quick," he said. "We'll drop down and go in after him, and the *Swift* will stay steady as long as she can. Then Ansell is going to get her, and you and Rose, out of the range of fire."

"Only Rose and me?" Mae asked as she found her satchel strapped to the wall and dug through it for the coca leaf tonic. "Everyone else is going down there?"

"You, Rose, Wil, Theobald, and Joonie stay on board. Molly won't stay behind, and Theobald says he knows the basics of running a steam engine. Ansell flies, Miss Wright can navigate. That's the smallest crew that can stay on the ship. Seldom, Molly, Guffin, me, and Miss Dupuis are going down."

"If Ansell and Miss Wright are flying, who's going to man the cannons?" Mae asked.

"Miss Wright can handle one if need be."

"And I'll handle the other," Mae said.

"Are you sure?" he asked.

She found the bottle of tonic and then looked Cedar straight in the eye. "I think I'd find some deep satisfaction in blowing something to bits right now."

He gave her a quick, animal smile that made her go hot and needful inside. The memory of his mouth against hers, his body hard pressed along every inch of her flashed quick through her mind.

She had lost her husband. She'd never thought she would feel again. It frightened her to think that Cedar, that any man, could take the place of Jeb. But there was something about Cedar. Every time he looked at her, she was reminded that she was alive, strong. And still had a long life ahead of her.

A life she did not want to live alone.

"Be careful," Cedar said, shaking her out of thoughts that had nothing to do with cannons or rescuing Captain Hink.

"I will be."

Cedar turned away.

Mae opened her mouth to say something more, to tell him. . . . She didn't know what she should tell him. That she cared for him. That he had made a place for himself in her heart without her even knowing.

But then he was gone, leaned at the door next to Mr. Seldom, scanning the earth in the darkness and planning their attack.

CHAPTER TWENTY-SEVEN

Hink came awake strapped to a table beneath the stretch of a canvas tent. On the one hand he was glad to have missed the fun of being packed like fresh kill out of the ship and into wherever it was that he was now.

On the other, the first real fingers of horror were sliding down his skin along with his cold sweat.

He didn't know where he was, but he was bound, and General Alabaster Saint was likely on his way.

They'd taken the gag off. That was something. But then, he knew Alabaster liked to hear a man beg.

The sound of boot soles over stone and dirt somewhere off over his right shoulder caught his attention.

He turned his head that way.

A tall man in a long coat and stovepipe hat stood in the corner of the room with a doctor's bag open on the table in front of him. He was drawing knives, saws, and clamps out of the bag, inspecting them, before setting them down in a neat, straight row.

Even though Hink didn't say anything, the man paused, and swiveled his head so that his eyes, lost in shadows of the hat and scarf around his neck, fixed on him.

"You," he breathed, a strange sound that made the word seem foreign on his lips. "Have touched the witch."

Hink had no idea what the hell he was talking about and opened his mouth to say so.

The man skittered across the room. Fast. So fast that Hink didn't have time to close his mouth before the man was above him, his fingers stuck between Hink's teeth, prying his jaws open.

Hink yelled a bit, trying to shake the man's fingers free from his mouth, but the man just clamped his other hand down over Hink's forehead and pressed down to hold him still.

Then the man leaned in so close, Hink felt the spiderweb tickle of his scarf brush against his cheek. Something inside that man was ticking, clicking like a cog with a broken tooth. Whatever it was that kept that man together, it wasn't of God's design.

He was Strange. Like Mr. Hunt had said the other men were. Made of bits, made of something rotting, something ticking.

The man ratcheted Hink's mouth open a little more, then placed his face so near Hink's lips that Hink could taste his moist, hot exhale. The man sniffed at Hink's mouth, then inhaled deeply.

"You are sweet with her," he cooed. "Sweet with her magic." He lifted away just enough to peer down into his eyes. "Shall I bleed her magic out of you?"

"Mr. Shunt," a voice said from somewhere near Hink's boots. "Step away from my prisoner."

Hink knew that voice. General Alabaster Saint.

Mr. Shunt held still, making his decision. Then he slipped his fingers out of Hink's mouth, revoltingly slow, stroking the inside of his cheek, the side of his tongue and finally his lip as he pulled his fingers away. He straightened and licked Hink's spittle from his fingertips.

"Your prisoner," Mr. Shunt said. "And the witch? My witch. Where is my witch?"

"I have ships out looking," Alabaster said as he paced nearer, but not near enough Hink could see him yet. "You'll have your witch soon enough. And the heads of the hunter and wolf. For now, leave me."

"Will he scream?" Shunt asked.

"Yes," General Alabaster Saint said, stepping up nice and close now, so Hink could see him, and his two eyes, one flat brown, the other the color of old tin, but both of them working. "He will."

Shunt gave the Saint a nod and Hink heard him retreat to the corner of the room but didn't hear him leave. Of course his heart was pounding so hard in his ears, he was surprised he could even hear the Saint's words.

"After all these years gone past," the Saint said, "you and I are finally at the table of negotiation."

Hink kept his mouth shut. He knew he wasn't getting out of this in one piece.

"Nothing to say?" the Saint asked. "As I recall, you always had a smart mouth. Testified against me on every charge. Had me dismissed from my command, from the army. Dishonored. All for trading weapons, profiteering, and disobeying orders of retreat. So many things you had to say about my character then. And now? Silence.

"Perhaps you fully realize your situation. You know I intend to make you pay for all you have taken from me, Mr. Cage."

"Marshal," he said.

"Marshal Cage," the general agreed. "The president's man. Charged to speak with his law and act on his honor. When you die, Mr. Cage—for I am going to kill you—it will almost be as if I am killing the president himself. Such pleasure."

"What about that spook?" Hink asked. "You his man now?"

The general pulled his pipe out of his pocket and tamped tobacco into it with his thumb. "You talk too much. Assume too much. You think I'm threatening you, when I am simply stating facts. I'm going to kill you, Cage. But not before you beg at my feet."

"The witch," Mr. Shunt whispered from the corner.

The general's eyes flashed with anger.

He and the abomination didn't get along. Good. That might be something Hink could use to his advantage. And if he survived this—not damn likely, but still, he wasn't the kind of man who gave up—he'd want as much information on the general's plans as he could get.

"I require silence from all my subordinates, Mr. Shunt," the general warned.

Mr. Shunt folded his fingers together. They made an eerie clacking sound, as if he was more metal and bone than flesh and blood.

"I require the witch," Shunt said, quiet as a beast stalking prey.

"If," the general replied, his voice rising, "you will not fall in line, then you will be escorted out. This is my land, my rule. Do you understand?"

There was a pause. Hink had tried his bindings while the men postured, but there was no slack in them. Alabaster's men knew how to keep prisoners kept.

"I understand every piece of you," Mr. Shunt said.

It was a threat. Hink held his breath, waiting for weapons to be drawn. Hoping they would be.

"Then you understand my need to destroy this filth," the general said.

To Hink's surprise, Mr. Shunt gave a sort of hissing laugh. "Yes."

Whatever hope Hink had of finding a way out of this hell was crushed with that one small word.

Alabaster paced away. Hink could just make out the table forge in the corner of the room. It smelled hot.

"You took my men, Mr. Cage," the general said. "You took my rank. You took my career, and my eye." There was a pause while he scraped coals, and then there was the pop of his lips sucking flame into the pipe tobacco.

"I never forget those who die for me," he said, "and I never forgive those who don't."

The scrape of metal tongs stirring coals filled the tent.

"So now you have a choice, Mr. Cage."

Hink strained to hear anything beyond the tent, anything that would tell him where he was. But all he heard was the scratching of something metal stirred in the hot coals, the puff of Alabaster's pipe, the *tick* and *click* of Mr. Shunt, and the rush of the wind outside.

"Do you want me to dig your eye out of your skull?" General Saint asked.

He turned and paced over to Hink, standing above him. "Or do you want to do it yourself, Marshal Cage?"

Sweat rolled down Hink's neck and he swallowed hard. The general gripped a pair of tongs in his hand. Clamped in those tongs was Hink's tin badge. It was red-hot, the wicked points of the star dusty white and smoking.

Hink had no weapon, no plan. He'd told his crew to run and they damn well better have run. He was tied down in his enemy's parlor.

There was no bargaining with the Saint. No forgiveness and no negotiation. Hink knew the general wasn't offering him a choice so much as just wanting to watch him squirm.

"How about your man, Mr. Shunt?" Hink asked. "Aren't you going to offer him a go at me?"

"This is between you and me," the general said.

"Then hand me that poker," Hink said. "And you'll have my answer."

The general puffed on his pipe and smoke curled up around his head, like some kind of devil come elbowing up out of hell.

"I disapprove of your tone, Marshal." The Saint leaned over him. The heat from the poker lashed a hot shadow over his face. "Struggle. It will make this all the more memorable for me."

Hink was breathing hard. He clenched his teeth, steeling himself for the pain.

"I'm going to push this through your eye. Then I'm going to stir it in the coals and push it through your other eye. After that, we'll see how long you can stay alive while I cut off every other part of you, bit by bit.

"But first, let me make it clear to the world just whose man you are." The general pressed the hot star into the center of Hink's forehead.

Hink screamed as his skin crisped and burned, pain flaying his nerves.

The Saint removed the star and turned to place it back in the coals.

Blood dripped down into Hink's ears and eyes, and the rancid smell of burned hair and meat choked his throat.

"Marshal Cage," the general said, puffing on his pipe. "Now no one will forget exactly who and what you are."

Just past the rattle of his own heartbeat, the Saint's words, and the sizzling metal dropping wet into the coals, Hink heard a sound. It was the hum of an engine in the sky.

He knew that engine. He could feel that ship in his blood.

The *Swift*. She was coming for him.

The general turned with the star in tongs again. "Now, I will have your eyes."

Hink smiled up at the Saint. "Go to hell."

"After you, Marshal Cage." General Alabaster Saint clamped his teeth on the stem of his pipe and then stabbed the poker down.

Hink screamed as agony burst through him and swallowed him whole.

CHAPTER TWENTY-EIGHT

Cedar knew it wasn't much of a plan. But they'd drifted over the base, seeing what they could make out in the darkness, then fired engines low, just long enough to put them in a position to strike.

Captain Hink was somewhere down there. Mae knew that for sure. Cedar didn't doubt her instinct. He just didn't know how they were going to extract a man from a well-guarded and well-armed hold.

"Three ships," Molly Gregor pointed out before they glided the last turn around the ridgetop. They'd have to fire engines to set into place, and when they did, everything needed to happen fast if they were going to have any chance to get out of this alive.

"All tied down," she continued. "Double boilers. Won't be able to stoke them and get them up into the sky faster than the *Swift* can run."

"We hit the hangar first," Cedar said. "Take out the ships. That should keep them busy. We'll go in under the chaos, quiet if we can. Shouldn't take long to check each of the structures for the captain."

"Teams of two," Seldom said.

Cedar nodded. "Molly and Miss Dupuis, Seldom and Guffin, and I'll go in alone."

"I don't think that's wise," Miss Dupuis said. "You should have cover. Molly and I will go with you."

"We need to cover as much ground as quickly as we can," Cedar said. "Three teams."

"I go where you go," a familiar voice said.

Cedar spun and looked at the shadows of the ship by the crates.

Wil, his brother, stood as a man, a blanket wrapped around his shoulders covering him to his knees. His hair was wild and brushing past his shoulders, and he was in need of a shave, but he smiled. "But I'll need pants first."

For a wild moment, Cedar wondered if Mae had somehow broken his curse. But then he remembered the new moon was tomorrow. The curse made it so Cedar changed to wolf form for the three nights around the full moon. Wil, however, changed to man form for three nights around the new moon.

Cedar had hoped they would have made it to the coven by now. He had lost track of the moon over the last few days.

"Wil," Cedar said, crossing the ship to him.

"Holy blazes," Guffin said. "Where the hell'd you come from?"

"Wil is my brother," Cedar said. "The wolf. His curse lifts around the new moon." He put his hand on his brother's shoulder and Wil smiled.

"It's good to see you," Wil said.

"And you," Cedar said. Then, to Guffin, "He'll be walking on two legs until dawn."

"I'd rather walk with pants on," he said. "And a gun, if we're going on down there to save the captain."

Wil and Cedar had spoken while on the road, Cedar staying up the nights so he could spend every moment asking Wil about the years they'd been apart. Those talks had been rushed and far too few. But Wil had told him that even in wolf form, with the instinct of the beast full upon him, he could understand plain English and more or less think like a man.

Guffin wasn't moving. No one was moving.

"Outfit him," Seldom said to Guffin. "We need all the guns we can get."

Guffin shook his head and muttered his way back to his trunk, where he dug out a spare pair of breeches, shirt, and boots.

"Here." He handed the clothes to Cedar. "I understand he's your brother, Mr. Hunt, but I ain't willing to get all that close to him."

Cedar took the clothes and handed them to Wil. They didn't have time for niceties or further explanations.

"Unarmed, naked, and a man, I'm a threat," Wil said as he moved off to one side to shuck into the clothes. "Yet when I was clawed and fanged, you didn't complain that I watched you while you slept. What kind of people you traveling with, brother?"

"Good people," Cedar said, missing this, missing Wil's sly humor and wit.

Guffin opened his mouth, closed it, then just shook his head again and set himself to rechecking the weapons he'd already checked a dozen times.

"There's a lot of strangework down there," Wil said.

Cedar nodded. "I know."

"But all we're there for is pulling out the captain, right?" Wil shoved his feet into the boots, then bent and tied them tight.

"That's right." Cedar knew what Wil was really asking. If he would be able to keep his head, keep his reason about him when he was dropping down into a hive of strangeworked men.

"Rose doesn't have time for us to clean the place out," Cedar said. "And Mae . . ." He looked over at her. She was standing by the cannon, one hand resting on the metal barrel, oblivious to what was happening in the ship around her.

"I won't lose her just so I can kill a few strangeworks."

Wil nodded. "Then let's get this done."

Cedar handed him his Walker and a pouch of bullets. "We spend as little time as we can searching, and pull back fast."

He turned to the rest of the group. "Search your building, then head for the ship. One of us is bound to find the captain."

"Keep an eye skyward," Seldom said. "Ansell will fire a flare when the captain's on board. Ready men?"

Everyone called out their affirmatives.

"Mr. Ansell," Seldom said. "Tell Mr. Theobald to bring her on line."

"Aye, sir," Ansell said from the pilot's position.

The big steam boilers chuffed, fans catching and roaring. And the *Swift* came singing out of the mountaintops down toward General Alabaster Saint's stand.

Cedar checked his harness as Wil was strapping his on. Heavy rope attached to the belt of each of their harnesses was tied around one of the metal support bars of the ship.

Ansell would bring them in as low as he could. They'd jump out on ropes, and unlatch so the ship could climb to get out of range.

The ship tore toward the ground.

Seldom was at the cannon, having loaded it with some kind of devised artillery they'd liberated during the escape from Old Jack's. Guffin told Cedar they were the same kind of charges they'd dropped on top of the *Devil's Nine.*

Which meant it was going to blow through the hangar and catch everything inside it on fire.

"Ready?" Ansell yelled.

"Ready," Seldom yelled back.

"We're coming over it . . . now!"

The *Swift* pulled up hard, her nose sticking into the air and wings snapping to catch her suicide dive.

Cedar held tight to the overhead bar as ground, sky, ground sped past in a wild blur.

Seldom didn't say a thing. He waited, spotting the structure and holding his fire until he had his aim. Then he let the cannon fly.

The head-breaking explosion of cannon fire rattled the ship and set her tin bones ringing in response.

Ansell slipped the ship sideways like a sled on ice. "This is your stop," he yelled. "Jump for it. I'll hold as long as I can."

The explosion from their firebombs was massive. The *Swift* bobbed like a boat on the sea from the concussion of air and heat coming off the hangar.

The hangar wasn't just going up in smoke, it was a raging bonfire burning down to dust. Whatever munitions, oils, or compounds they kept stored in the place were touched off. From the successive rumbles and blasts, a lot of gunpowder, and probably a goodly bit of dynamite, had been packed in the place.

Miss Dupuis was the first over the side of the ship, and Molly Gregor was right behind her. Then Guffin took the jump, and Seldom after him.

Wil was at the door. He quickly double-checked his harness, then jumped from the ship, letting out a whoop that was swallowed by the explosions.

Cedar was last. He shoved himself out of the ship, and felt the sickening free fall twist his guts like a fork through stew before the line caught and nearly knocked all the wind out of him. He dangled for a second, getting his bearings as to what was up and what wasn't.

Mr. Ansell had a good eye for distance. Cedar was maybe six feet off the ground. Wil pulled the lever to unlatch the rope, hit the dirt, and stood right back up. The others already had weapons drawn and were running toward the buildings as smoke—so much smoke and fire—rose up and further fouled the night air.

Cedar pulled the lever on his harness, relaxed for the landing and came up out of a roll.

Wil had his gun drawn and motioned toward the wooden building.

Cedar slipped a shotgun off his shoulder and they started at a jog toward the structure.

Men were yelling. Gunshots clattered through the night. Smoke and flame turned the compound into chaos as the *Swift* fired down into the crowds.

Cedar jogged beside his brother, who was grinning with anticipation, opening and closing his left hand as if thrilling in the sensations of being a man again.

And then the wind shifted, carrying with it the scent of the Strange.

No, a Strange.

Mr. Shunt.

Cedar stopped, turned on his heel. The world slowed. Then he ran toward that scent, Wil pounding step-in-step beside him.

Mingled with the foul odor of Mr. Shunt was the scent of Captain Hink, his blood, his pain.

But not his death. Not yet.

The soldiers were quickly realizing the assault they were under, and turned to guns and cover, taking aim at the *Swift* and abandoning the ships in the hangar.

Molly and Miss Dupuis were pressed up against the shadow of the low, long building that was probably a barracks, shooting, reloading, shooting, as they made their way toward the door.

Seldom and Guffin were lost to the smoke and flashes of gunfire. A separate explosion rocked the building behind Molly and Miss Dupuis.

Seldom must be that way.

Cannons from the *Swift* aimed at the artillery shed. The world flattened into a silent roar of red as the munitions blew a hole in the hill.

Blood everywhere, screams in the darkness. Men dying. Strangework pulled apart as if the strings had suddenly been cut.

And then another cannon fired. Not the *Swift*. This was a much bigger gun.

The hillside bloomed with a white-hot flash as the Saint's heavy artillery aimed at the *Swift*. The *Swift*'s fans roared, carrying her higher, but not out of range. Not nearly out of range yet. She'd been repaired, as much as they could do in the air, but she wasn't up to full muster.

The scent of Mr. Shunt was stronger. Cedar's mouth watered. He wanted to taste that creature's blood. He wanted to tear him into so many pieces there wouldn't be enough of him left to smear the sole of a shoe.

Wil beside him laughed as they tore across the rocky ground, Cedar only half a step behind him.

Shunt was in the tent just ahead. Hink was in that tent. That, Cedar knew for sure. What he didn't know was if there were more men in the tent, more prisoners.

They rushed into the tent, fingers on triggers.

The world went slow, so slow around him. And the scene in the tent clicked like the flash pan of a camera in Cedar's mind.

Three tables. Covered in blood. Low light from lanterns glossing the hooks and blades of surgical tools, a pile of discarded body parts and bones stacked in one corner.

In the middle of the room, strapped down to a table, Captain Hink. Unconscious, his face a gory mess, still breathing.

Two men in the corners. Strangework, but not Shunt.

Behind those men, the doorway Mr. Shunt must have just run out through.

Son of a bitch.

Cedar leveled his shotgun and blew the man on the left off his feet. Wil took aim with the Walker and plugged the other man right between the eyes.

Both men tumbled to the ground. But they were Strangework. They'd get right back up again if Wil and Cedar didn't tear their throats out.

No time.

He'd come to save Hink. That was his promise to Rose. That was what they were all putting their lives on the line for.

He drew his knife and cut Hink's straps. He tossed Wil the shotgun and caught the Walker Wil threw at him in trade.

Then Cedar leaned down and pulled the captain across his shoulders.

Captain Hink was not a small man. Cedar snarled under the weight of him. Walking out of here was not going to be a pretty thing.

Wil came up beside him. "You got that?" he asked.

"For now," Cedar said. "Go."

Wil pushed through the tent flap and back into the night.

There were enough buildings on fire now that it was easy to see the row of soldiers, all aiming weapons at them, standing just a few yards away, blocking their route to the ship.

Mr. Shunt stood behind them, tall and ragged and far too alive.

A burly man paced forward. He was in uniform, wearing the rank of a general, a sword at one side, gun at the other. His eyes were strangely mismatched in the wavering light, so much so that one seemed to be nothing but a metal ball with a black hole in it.

"Well, then, I see Mr. Cage has his uses after all," he said. "Mr. Shunt, is this the hunter and wolf?"

"Yes," Shunt hissed.

"Where," the general asked, "is the witch?"

Cedar couldn't fight with Hink on his shoulders. Twelve men held guns on them.

Shunt stood behind them, letting the strangework bodies guard his own. But even with all the flesh and fire and blood between Cedar and Shunt, Cedar could smell his fear, he could hear the ticking of whatever he was using as a heart, each tick minutely slower than the last, and he could sense the Holder. Singing the high, slow song that set the hair on his arms rising.

It was near here. No, it was near Shunt.

"Tell us where the witch is, and we will let you go," the general said.

"Do you think us stupid, General?" Cedar asked.

The general opened his mouth. But whatever he was going to say was cut short.

"You half-cocked piece of crap," Molly Gregor yelled from the shadows. "Get the hell away from my captain."

A bolt of lightning shot out across the soldiers, missing General Saint, but dropping a half dozen men to the ground and throwing the entire stand off into a scattering of chaos. Miss Dupuis had Joonie's lightning gun.

"Fire!" the general yelled.

His men lifted their weapons.

Like a house of cards collapsing, everything seemed to fall in quick succession.

Three men turned to fire on Molly and Miss Dupuis. Cedar could count the bullets, could see Molly duck out from cover into the spray, her rifle steady as she took aim at the general's head.

"Molly," Cedar yelled, "no!"

Three men aimed at Cedar and Wil.

Wil was faster, taking out two with two bullets: throat and eye.

Cedar ran, Hink still over his shoulder, weighing him down, firing as he pounded for cover, not at the man aiming at him, but at the soldiers aiming at Molly.

Miss Dupuis was behind Molly, grim and calm, the lightning gun spent and the revolver in her hand blasting shot after shot.

Cedar couldn't stop the bullets heading to Molly. Miss Dupuis couldn't pull her away in time.

Molly pulled the trigger on her rifle to kill General Saint.

She shuddered, bullets tearing through her. She fell. But got one shot off.

Her bullet sped toward General Saint's head.

And blew right through the middle of his forehead and out the back of his skull.

He crumpled to the ground.

The *Swift* was too far gone to help. Every soldier in the compound was running over here with loaded guns.

Where were Guffin and Seldom?

They would not survive this. None of them.

They didn't have guns enough, didn't have cover enough, didn't have time enough.

But Cedar wouldn't leave Molly here to die alone.

As each foot fell, as Wil fired beside him, matching his pace, taking out men, he knew the escape they ran toward became more and more unlikely with each heartbeat.

They had lost this fight before they had jumped rope off the ship.

Molly lay on the ground, facing the sky, bleeding. Miss Dupuis had had to fall back for cover, and couldn't get close enough to drag Molly toward her.

Cedar caught a glimpse of Seldom, pinned down by gunfire behind a stack of crates.

Seldom looked across the smoke and fire, saw him with Hink across his shoulder. Cedar met his gaze. He didn't know if the captain would make it. Didn't know if Molly still breathed.

Even across the bloody field, Seldom seemed to understand.

"What are you thinking, brother?" Wil asked, his shoulder set tight against the sideboard of the wagon they had ducked behind.

"I'm going to set Hink down. Then I'm going to go get Molly."

"Good plan," Wil said. "But mine's better." Wil ducked around the wagon and ran for Molly.

Cedar starting swearing and took aim on the men who rose up to fire on his brother.

He had six shots and made them all count.

Wil bent, smoke shifted to cover his exact whereabouts. But he'd have to stand to get Molly out of there. And he'd be an easy target.

"Damn hot-blooded idiot," Cedar cursed. "I will not watch you die again."

He shifted so he could lower Captain Hink.

The roar of an engine right over his head drowned out the sound of gunfire and threw chunks of debris everywhere. Then that ship let loose a glass globe. Pretty. Familiar. Green with a silver cap to it.

When that globe hit the ground it shattered. Wasn't anything more than instinct that made Cedar close his eyes and turn away. Good thing he did too. The flash of light that exploded from the globe was unholy bright white tinged with the strange green of glim. The combination was so bright it blinded.

Men cried out, unable to see, unable to shoot.

Cedar squinted, his vision foggy and fouled even though he'd had his eyes screwed tight.

Walking across the field, with another green globe in one hand and a tinkered blunderbuss in the other, dark goggles firmly over his eyes, was Alun Madder.

Above him hovered a wooden airship that resembled a child's top with fans stuck out every which way.

Bryn Madder leaned out the door of the thing and cranked a Gatling gun into the crouching soldiers.

Cadoc Madder was standing in a basket that had been lowered from the ship, laying down fire in the opposite direction.

They were all wearing dark goggles and were likely the only people on this rock who still had clear enough vision to shoot.

Alun looked over at Cedar. "Evening, Mr. Hunt," he yelled over the gunfire. "Got a message from Captain Beaumont you might be in the area. Have you found the Holder for us yet?" He smashed the globe into the ground and another painfully blinding light flashed out.

Men screamed.

Cedar growled at the pain of the light, even through his eyelids. "Can't find something blind," he yelled.

Alun laughed. "Don't expect you'd need your eyes for that. Still . . ."

Another flash went off, and this one wasn't just light. This one was dynamite. Cedar's ears cracked with the sound, and rocks and dirt slammed through the air.

Then Alun was beside him, his hand on his arm. "I'll get you to the basket. Then we can talk about your promise to us aboard ship. Shall we?"

"Wil," he said. "He's got Molly."

"Already have them on the way to the basket. The men with Miss Dupuis too. You're the only one left out here worth saving, Mr. Hunt. You and whoever that is you're wearing as a neck warmer."

"Shunt's here." Cedar jogged blind, with only Alun's rough hand on his elbow guiding him forward.

"Did you kill him?"

"Not yet."

"Maybe you'll get your chance. First, you'll need eyes. Step up."

Cedar lifted his foot and stood up onto a wooden platform.

"Mr. Hunt," Cadoc Madder said by way of greeting. "Good night for flying. Find the Holder?"

"Don't have it on me," Cedar said.

"Not a yes, nor a no," he noted.

"Make her fast, brother Cadoc," Alun said. "They'll be finding their eyes, and their trigger fingers any moment now."

The floor beneath him jerked, and the wind rushed by his face as some kind of pulley system lifted them up to the ship.

It took a surprisingly short time to be level with the interior of the ship, and the light inside made it easier to see.

"I am so pleased you were able to find us," Miss Dupuis said.

"Got your message by way of Captain Beaumont," Alun said. "He passes his regards to you."

Seldom and Guffin helped Cedar get Hink off his shoulders and set down onto the floor next to Molly.

"Where's the *Swift*?" Cedar asked.

"She's anchored on the other side of the ridge," Alun said, as he helped secure the basket, and stomped off to the front of the vehicle. "Busted up pretty bad. Don't know how long she'll stay in the sky."

"We need Mae," Cedar said. "She has medicines that might help Molly and Hink."

"Molly's gone," Seldom said softly.

Cedar closed his eyes a moment, and swallowed against the sorrow. She had been a fine woman. It had been her word, the Gregor word, that had convinced Captain Hink to help them.

He had thought he could get to her in time, but he had failed her.

"I'm sorry," he said.

"What we need," Alun said as he guided the ship, which moved a lot faster, and seemed to take much sharper turns than most ships, "is the Holder, Mr. Hunt."

"I think Shunt has it," Cedar said.

Wil, who was taking a swig out of the canteen Miss Dupuis had handed him, put the canteen down and gave him a hard look. The same look Miss Dupuis and all the Madders were giving him.

"Are you sure?" Wil asked.

"Smelled it on him. Heard its song."

"You hear it?" Wil asked.

"Don't you?"

"No. Not really. It's more like . . . a feeling of heat or cold, and that strange glow each piece gives off."

"You think they glow?" Cedar asked.

"Think nothing," Wil said. "They do glow."

"Sounds like each of you has your own way of tracking Strange objects," Alun said. "I don't care how it's tracked, I just want it found. Now."

"Take us to the *Swift*," Cedar said.

"Is the Holder on the *Swift*?" Alun asked, his words hard with challenge.

"Not all of it. Not yet."

"Sounds like you have a plan, Mr. Hunt?"

"Might. But we'll need the *Swift*."

"Then you'll have her. Hold fast. I'm going to open her up."

The Madder brothers scrambled to hold tight to bars and ropes, and the rest of the crew did the same, as Alun Madder worked the levers and gears of his strange flying device and blasted them through the night sky at breathtaking speed.

CHAPTER TWENTY-NINE

Mae pulled her hands away from Mr. Theobald, wiping his blood on her dress. She had done everything she could for him. Everything she could think of doing through the yelling of the sisters' voices, through the rattling of gunshots, the boiler being shot in half by the cannon, taking Mr. Theobald's life.

Joonie had helped her drag him out of the ruined boiler room where they'd suffered the most damage. Mae tried to tend his injuries, but he was missing a great deal of the right side of his torso.

She whispered a prayer for his soul's gentle passage.

Joonie was on her knees, crying beside him. Mae placed her hand on Joonie's shoulder in comfort for a while, then stood.

She walked over to Mr. Ansell. "Are we going down, Mr. Ansell?"

"The envelope will hold for a few hours at the most," he said. "We have no boiler, so no steam. Throw the anchor, Miss Lindson, or we'll be crushed against these mountains."

Mae made her way to the anchor and pulled the linchpin, releasing the anchor. They seemed to drift for a long time, too long, before finally, the anchor caught hold and stopped them.

"What about the others?" Joonie asked, picking herself up finally and wiping her face. "We've got to go back and get them out of there."

Ansell turned, his round face grim. "We don't have power, Miss

Wright. We don't have steam. We can't go back. There is nothing we can do to help them. So we wait for them to find us in the next couple hours. If not, we'll let air out of the envelope, slow as we can, bring the ship down, and walk out of these hills."

"But Rose—," Mae started.

Ansell just pressed his lips together, shaking his head, and turned away.

Rose couldn't walk, and the three of them couldn't carry her. If they brought the ship down, she'd have to be left behind.

They were no longer the rescuers. They were in sore need of being rescued.

"Mae?" Rose said softly.

Mae jerked. She didn't know how long she'd been standing there, the sisters' voices filling her thoughts, but Ansell was now sitting staring out the fore windows and Miss Wright was staring out the aft. Someone had pulled a blanket over Mr. Theobald and moved him to one side of the space.

Mae rubbed her hands down her dress and walked over to Rose, her boots strangely loud in the quietly rocking ship.

"I'm here," Mae said.

Rose opened her eyes. "Maybe I could help," she said. "Fix the boilers?"

Mae took her hand. "I don't think there's anything we can do. Any of us, right now."

"Ship coming," Joonie said. "Straight over from the compound."

Ansell jumped up and jogged over to peer out the window. "What kind of thing is that?"

Joonie bit her lip and shook her head. "Nothing I've seen before. Wait. That's glim light in glass. A single globe high. It's okay, Mr. Ansell. That's a friendly ship."

"Lots of people can get their hand on glim," Ansell said, pulling a gun down from the overhead storage.

Joonie put her hand on his arm. "It's a signal among the people I work for. Miss Dupuis knows it."

"You think she's aboard?"

"She must be."

The sound of fans grew louder as the ship neared.

"There!" Joonie said. "That's Mr. Hunt."

Mae's heart lurched. She didn't realize she'd been holding her breath, wondering if he was alive.

"We're coming aboard!" he yelled, from where he hung half out of the craft.

Ansell strode over to the door. "Is the captain alive? We lost the boiler."

"He's alive," Cedar yelled. "Stand back while we secure the ship."

Ansell got out of the doorway. A cannon boomed, and ropes fell like rain around the ship. No, not rain, it was a net with weighted bolos on the edges catching at the ship.

Clever.

Ansell stepped up to the door and latched the net onto the hooks worked into the frame. Then he tied two extra lines from the netting to bars inside the ship. The net formed a sort of rope walkway between the two vessels.

Mae shifted so she could see out the door. Cedar Hunt strode into the room, bloody, burned, but whole, and Mae felt as if she'd just seen the sun rise.

Then Bryn Madder strode in behind him, his tool belt and pockets bulgy with metal and devices, his goggles strapped across his forehead. "Heard there's a blown gasket or two?" he said. "Mind if I take a look?"

"Back that way," Cedar said.

"You know him?" Ansell asked, eyeing the bull-shouldered short Madder.

"Yes. And he'll treat the ship right, Mr. Ansell." Cedar paced over to Mae.

"And the captain?" Ansell asked.

"He's still breathing, but hurt badly," Cedar said. "Mae, can you help him?"

"The captain?" she asked. "I can try. Of course. But I won't leave Rose. Cedar, we can't leave her behind."

Cedar's eyes went hard. "Who said we're going to leave her behind?"

"I . . ." Mae looked around the room. Someone had said it. Surely they had. But she couldn't remember. There were too many voices in her head, too many words screaming at her, pulling at her.

Cedar's hand gently touched her face. ". . . need you to stay with us, Mae. Just a bit longer."

She blinked hard, trying to focus on him. His touch, his words. "I'm fine," she said. "What do I need to do?"

"I need you to tend to the captain."

"Bring him here," she said.

"Mae, the ship isn't steady. It'd be better if you came over to the Madders' craft. Better if we all boarded their ship."

She heard him, his voice a low rumble beneath the sisters' constant shriek. But he wasn't listening to her.

"Captain Cage needs to be here," Mae said, not sure that her voice was rising above the sisters'. "He needs to be on the *Swift*. He's tied to her. Bound because I bound him, tied him. His ship's dying. He's dying."

Ansell muttered something, but Cedar must have heard her and understood. "I'll bring him. Stay here with Rose."

Then Mr. Alun Madder was suddenly strolling across the ship toward her.

"How's Miss Small?" he asked, looking genuinely concerned.

"Fine as wine," Rose whispered.

Alun looked down at her and gave her a smile. "Just lying around when there's a ship to be flown? That's not like you, Rose."

"I offered to fix it," she said slowly, her words falling off at the end of each breath. "Mae said no."

"And you listened?"

"Just haven't argued yet," Rose managed. Then her face screwed up in pain and she bit her lip, her moan thin and high. Even the blood that trickled from her lip was tinged with gray.

"Mrs. Lindson," Alun said, "if you have a way of making Mr. Hunt find that piece of Holder, then now's the time for him to do so. She won't last the hour."

There was a ruckus of boots and grunting as Cedar, Wil, and Seldom carried Captain Cage into the ship and laid him down on the blankets near Rose's hammock.

Someone had taken the time to wipe most of the blood from his face, but there was no hiding the hole where his right eye should be, nor the burned star in his forehead.

"I'll need my satchel," Mae said, walking over, then kneeling next to the captain. "Someone check his limbs and torso for wounds." She ran her fingers over his neck, his head, and then looked at both his ears.

He had lost the eye. His face was burned, bruised. But he still had one eye, his tongue, both ears, and his nose.

Seldom split the buttons on the captain's shirt and spread it open. His entire chest was bruised and knotted, with black, green, and sickly yellows spread out across his skin.

"Bullet hole in one leg," Seldom said. "Broken arm. I don't see blood except his face."

"That's good, thank you, Mr. Seldom." She took her satchel from Cedar and soaked a cloth with the coca leaf tonic, then pressed that against his eye socket and did the same for the brand in his forehead. She quickly bandaged his head, and then wrapped his ribs, in hopes they weren't so broken that they were cutting up his insides.

She put his arm in a sling and soaked another cloth with the coca leaf to tie down tight over both sides of the hole in his leg.

He didn't wake. He didn't stir. But he was breathing.

"That's all," she said, trying to think through the call of the sisters, the incessant push for her to return to the coven, to walk, run, jump the ship if she had to. "That's all I can do for him. If the ship can be patched, any at all, it might help him."

"Bryn's working on it," Cedar said.

She looked up. Some time had passed. Miss Dupuis was sitting next to Mr. Theobald, holding his hand. She was very pale and silent, her eyes red as tears stained her face.

Mae knew that sorrow. Mr. Theobald had been more than a traveling companion to Miss Dupuis. He had been her love.

Wil and Cedar seemed oblivious to her pain, and stood squared off toward Alun Madder. From the set of their shoulders and grim expressions, it was clear they had been arguing.

"What?" Mae asked.

"You tell her, Mr. Hunt," Alun said. "It's your idea."

Cedar turned to her, and helped her stand. "Rose needs the Holder. Mr. Madder still thinks if we can find the tin piece of it, we can use it to draw out the key that is killing her."

"Yes," Mae said. "I remember."

"Mr. Shunt is down there. He was in the compound. I think he has the Holder with him," Cedar said.

"So you're going to go find him, right?" she asked. "You'll hunt him, find him, take the Holder from him, and bring it back for Rose."

"We don't have time."

His words were even, and without much emotion. But she could see the sorrow in his eyes.

Rose. It was Rose who didn't have the time.

"What can we do then? We can't just . . . Oh, Cedar, we can't just let her die."

"Can you save her?" he asked. "Your magic is vows and curses: bindings. Can you call to the Holder, Mae? Now that it is so near, can you cast a spell to bind the piece that's in her to the whole of it? It used to be one whole thing. It might respond to being one thing again at your urging. If you can bind it to itself, and to Rose, just like you bound the captain and his ship, you'd draw it here, right out of Shunt's hands. Rose might have a chance then. We could try to remove the piece once we have the chunk it came from."

"Bind it?" Mae's heart raced. "I don't . . . my magic. It's so hard to focus. To make magic do what I want. If I bound it to . . . to Rose. Made her a part of it like Captain Hink and the *Swift* . . ." She searched his face. "I could kill her."

Cedar nodded. "I can't think of any other way to save her, Mae. No time. No Holder. She'd want you to try. You know she would."

Mae looked away from him to his brother, Wil, who was watching her with the curious eyes of the wolf he once was. Then she looked at Alun. "You're against it?" she asked.

"Not entirely," he hedged. "If you think you can do it. Are you strong enough, Mrs. Lindson? Are you near enough the Holder to call it this far?"

Mae knew she was not. But she had to try. "I'll need a flame, a bowl of water, a stone or dirt, and smoke. And I'll need you all to give me and Rose space."

Alun lifted one eyebrow. "As you say."

Everyone on the ship moved away. Someone found the items she had asked for, and Cedar handed them to her.

A lantern for flame, a cup of water, a smooth stone out of Seldom's pocket, and a bundle of sage that would smoke once lit.

"Will these do?" Cedar asked.

"Yes." Mae took them and placed one at each compass point on the floor around Rose. Then she stood next to Rose.

It was as if all the color had washed out of her friend. Her skin was gray, her lips blue, and the fire of her hair dulled down to ash.

Her eyes were open, glossy as dull nickels, staring at the ceiling. Each breath stopped too soon, and the next began too late.

Mae took a deep breath. The sisters' chorus grew louder with her fear. She shouldn't be using magic, shouldn't whisper the spell, shouldn't utter the blessing, cast the binding. Magic turned dark in her hands. Magic turned wicked on her words.

The sisters did not want her to use magic.

Mae refused to listen to the voices. This was the only thing that might save Rose.

She took Rose's hand firmly in her own and closed her eyes.

The fragment to the whole, the Holder to the key. Two as one, joined, bound, forever. Come on the wind, come on the earth, come on the stars, come on the mist. Be bound, be whole, be healed once again.

She let the words of the spell reach out far and wide, singing it over the sound of the sisters' voices, singing it over the sound of the ships, the wind, the night.

But it was too much, impossible to think, to hear her own words, to guide the spell. The sisters were strong. Stronger than her.

And they intended to tear her mind apart.

CHAPTER THIRTY

Cedar balled his hands into fists. It was everything he could do to stand and watch Mae as she whispered over Rose.

He could smell Mae's fear, he could smell the sweat of her pain. Her entire body trembled with the effort of casting the spell to bind the Holder.

He didn't know how long she could endure. Didn't know how long before he grabbed her up in his arms, broke her spell, took her away from Rose. It's what the beast in him wanted to do—protect Mae at any cost.

And it would seal Rose's death.

Wil shifted and stood next to him, facing the opposite direction, watching the people in the ship and the door at Cedar's back where Miss Wright stood.

Cedar could look nowhere else other than at Mae.

Suddenly Mae stopped whispering.

The air became soft and burred, as if lightning were just about to strike. But it was not lightning. No, what Cedar tasted on the back of his tongue was the scent of the Strange. Of the Holder.

And then, like a star tearing through the sky, a piece of metal broke through the floor and hurtled into the ship. A song, huge and tempered by an otherworldly chorus, filled Cedar's ears.

The Holder ricocheted off the walls of the ship, scorching wood, bending metal.

The people in the ship each had their own reactions to it, but Cedar took scant note of Hink's crew's startled disbelief, the Madders' wild laughter, or Miss Dupuis's and Miss Wright's wonderment.

He was watching Mae. And Mae said one word, her lips trembling around it, nearly unable to give the word breath enough to form.

"One," she whispered.

And then the Holder shot toward Rose. Too fast for him to stop it. Too fast for Mae to block it. Too fast.

It struck her chest and spread out like liquid, bending to fit over her shoulder, flowing down to her collarbone, and up to her ear, like some kind of medieval armor.

Rose gasped, a huge, labored breath, her entire body arching.

And then she lay still in the hammock.

Cedar had run toward Rose as soon as the Holder entered the ship and only now reached the hammock. Everything had happened in a split second.

He caught Mae as she fainted.

Wil rushed up, half a step behind, and Alun and Miss Dupuis were on his heels.

"I'll be damned," Alun Madder said. "She did it! She called the Holder."

"Are they well?" Miss Wright asked from where she stood near the door. "Are they both well?"

Rose was still breathing, easier than she had been. Her color was better too, at least in her face, some of the natural pink and freckles appearing on her forehead, nose, cheeks.

The Holder looked like someone had melted it down to pour a liquid sheet of tin across Rose's shoulder and chest. He wondered if the key had gone liquid inside her body, if that was why her skin and eyes had been turning gray.

"Don't touch it," Alun Madder said. "It might take some time for the Holder to draw all of the key out of her blood and bones."

Cedar didn't wait around to watch. He carefully unclasped Mae's hand from Rose's and carried Mae over to one of the crew's cots toward the front of the ship, where he eased her down gently. He tucked a blanket up around her shoulders and brushed her hair away from her face.

She was breathing, but didn't stir.

A startled cry filled the room, and was quickly smothered out.

"Joonie!" Miss Dupuis said.

Cedar turned, but his nose, his ears told him what was happening before his eyes confirmed it.

Mr. Shunt stood in the doorway, Joonie Wright's back pressed hard against him. Three of his long, knobby fingers pressed over her mouth, the razor-sharp point of his index finger poised over her eye.

He must have climbed the anchor line, even though that was nearly an impossible thing.

But then, Mr. Shunt himself was a nearly impossible thing.

They had called the Holder, and Shunt had followed.

Cedar and Mae were the only two people at the head of the ship. Of the people toward the rear of the ship, Wil stood nearest Shunt, hands loose at his side, head bent, so he looked up through his hair at the monster. He might be standing in a man's skin, but it was wolf and rage that filled him now.

Cedar knew exactly what Wil was going to do. He was going to kill Shunt.

But not if Cedar killed Shunt first.

"Give the witch to me, Hunter," Shunt crooned. "Or this woman will die." He twitched his pinky and Joonie gasped as blood spilled down her neck.

Cedar didn't say anything. Didn't move. If he did, Shunt would slit her throat.

"The witch," Shunt hissed. "Now." He jerked his ring finger across Joonie's mouth.

She screamed as he sliced her lips open.

Miss Dupuis already had her hand on her gun. So did Ansell, Seldom, and Guffin.

But no one could shoot Shunt without hurting Joonie.

"You want the witch?" Cedar said, shifting his shoulders so that Shunt could better see Mae lying helpless and unconscious in the cot. "Come take her from me."

Shunt was fast.

So was everyone else on the ship.

Cedar felt like time wound down, slow, slow, slow.

Wil, faster even than Cedar, leaped at Shunt, gun already firing at his head.

Shunt flicked a silver blade from his cuff. The blade struck Wil in the chest.

Thread spooled out of Shunt's other hand to cinch around Joonie's neck. Then he shoved her at Wil.

Joonie, eyes wide, collided with Wil.

As Shunt ran for Mae.

Shunt yanked the thread. Joonie's head snapped back just as Wil caught her in his arms and they both went down.

The crew of the ship unloaded their guns. Into the doorframe, into the shelves, into the wall where Shunt had been just an instant before.

Shunt always one inch ahead of each shot.

The three Madders each pulled out devised weapons. Light blew through the ship. Sound rocked the sky and deafened. Lightning licked across metal lashing for Shunt. Any one of those weapons was enough to kill him. And not one of them could.

Shunt was too fast.

And besides, Shunt was Cedar's to kill.

Cedar ran straight at him.

He pulled his gun as Wil yelled his name. As the Madders reloaded their weapons. As the crew cursed and fired again.

Cedar caught the lapel of Shunt's coat. Yanked so hard, Shunt spun sideways toward him. Cedar muscled him into the gun in his fist.

Cedar was still running, pushing Shunt back toward the door. He shoved the barrel of the gun into Mr. Shunt's chest as far as it could go.

And pulled the trigger.

Shunt staggered back, too many arms, too many joints, too many blades and fingers and teeth cutting, digging, squirming to try to get away from Cedar.

But Cedar would not let go of the monster.

Shunt smashed his fist into Cedar's face, fingers digging for his eyes.

Cedar fired again. Shunt's hand jerked away from his face.

Wil was moving. Almost on his feet. He had no weapons.

Cedar glanced at him. He was bleeding, his arm hanging broken at his side. Cedar knew his brother had a plan. And he knew it would be suicide.

Shunt shoved his fingers up under Cedar's ribs, slicing, stabbing through muscle and scraping against bone.

Cedar yelled at the pain, but did not let go. He pushed. Ran. Pounded toward the door. Squeezed the trigger again, the gun slick with Shunt's blood and oil.

With his blood too.

Wil yelled something, a strangled cry. But Cedar would not let his brother die.

This was his fight.

Shunt threw a vicious kick at Cedar's leg.

Cedar felt bone crack.

Two more steps to the door.

One more.

Then there was no ground beneath his feet.

There was nothing but wind and night and the monster, Mr. Shunt, squirming and flailing beneath him, his eyes, his inhuman Strange face filled with fear.

Cedar laughed and fired every bullet in the gun.

Shunt screamed as bullet after bullet tore holes through him faster than he could stitch them up.

They fell. Together. Forever. The ships spun above them, the ground spun beneath them, the wind burned like frozen blades.

Cedar ran out of bullets. He let go of his gun and drew his knife instead.

Shunt sliced at him, biting, tearing at Cedar like a wild animal.

Shunt was very much not dead yet. But Cedar was going to make sure he accomplished that one thing before they both hit the ground.

He stabbed the knife into Shunt's chest, digging for something vital, something fatal he could cut off, pry loose, destroy.

The blade struck something in the center of his chest and Cedar jimmied it loose.

It popped free and metal wings, gold and crystal, like a clockwork bee or dragonfly zipped past his face.

Mr. Shunt stilled, stiffened. His eyes were no longer filled with fear. They were filled with hatred. "Die," he exhaled.

Cedar just kept stabbing, digging, pulling out cog, bone, and flesh.

Until Mr. Shunt suddenly lay into the wind, arms spread wide, head thrown back.

And even though Cedar was holding on to his coat, Mr. Shunt shattered, blowing apart into a thousand oily pieces that sifted like pebbles through his fingers.

Cedar yelled out his rage, wanting Shunt's blood, wanting to snap every bone in his damn body, wanting to feel him die again and again.

A cannon blast from high above him clapped across the mountains.

Then a thousand whips, no, ropes, flew past him. He heard the fans of the ship roar, as if the vessel were turning hard and fast. Then those ropes were right below him, forming a net with bolos weighting it. A net that pulled open and created a wall between him and the ground rushing up at him.

Cedar hit that net like a man striking stone. The ropes lashed around him, closed tight, and slammed his fall to a stop so quickly he heard his nose break, felt his ribs snap, heard his neck crack. And then he blacked out.

CHAPTER THIRTY-ONE

Daylight and the drone of fans woke Cedar from a deep sleep. That, and pain.

"Morning, Mr. Hunt." Alun Madder leaned forward in the chair, puffing on his pipe.

Cedar tried to moisten his mouth. Didn't work. "Mae?"

"Sleeping right over there in the cot you set her in. Rose is sleeping too. So are Captain Hink and Joonie Wright. All of them getting along well enough."

Wil, in wolf form now that it was daylight, lifted his head from where he was lying on the floor beside Cedar. His old copper eyes burned with accusation. There was no blood on him. That was the one good thing about the curse. Injuries healed quickly.

But from Wil's gaze Cedar knew he'd be spending the night apologizing to his brother for jumping out of the ship.

"I'm thinking those native gods should have given you wings instead of fur, Mr. Hunt, the way you dove into the night. For a second there, I supposed you thought you could fly."

Cedar pushed up, only made it halfway before his ribs sent hot licks of pain through him. His head felt heavy and his neck hurt. So did every other damn inch of him.

Wil growled.

Cedar lay back down and Wil stopped growling.

"We're under way?" he asked.

Alun reached into his voluminous overcoat, pulled out a flask and offered it to him. "Bryn's towing the *Swift*."

"Where?" Cedar asked.

Alun nodded to the flask and Cedar took a swig. Moonshine burned like lightning down to the soles of his feet.

He exhaled as the heat spread over his muscles and out to the tip of each finger. He took a second swallow, then handed it back to Alun.

"Kansas. I hear it's lovely this time of year," Alun said.

"Thank you," Cedar said.

"Oh, it is my pleasure, Mr. Hunt. My pleasure." Alun took a swallow of the hooch, then stood up. "Sleep yourself out. We've a while of sky ahead of us."

Cedar closed his eyes. He didn't think sleep would claim him, but the constant hum of the fans and the rocking of the *Swift* sent him down the path soon enough.

CHAPTER THIRTY-TWO

Mae sat in the rocking chair near the hearth of the coven's gathering hall. The familiar smells of her childhood surrounded her. She was home. And it was suddenly the last place she wanted to be.

Miss Adaline, the current matron of the coven, stood near the window with a cup of tea in her hand. "You have exposed us, Mae Rowan."

"Lindson," Mae said quietly. "Mrs. Lindson."

Miss Adaline was a wide woman, with gray hair pulled back tight and up into a bun on her head. She wore a soft shawl the color of wheat over her shoulders, and her modest day dress was deep forest green, seamed to give her figure the best advantage. She was unmarried, and monied by her father's investments in the wars.

She had been a force in Mae's life when she was younger. And she had not lost her command in the years that had passed.

Miss Adaline turned. She had the kind of beauty men would turn their heads for, even now at her age. But there was no kindness behind that beauty. Not for Mae.

"You have told outsiders we are witches. You have put our sisterhood in danger."

Mae waited. She didn't know what to say. It was true. But she could not change what had happened.

"Before you left the coven, it was suggested we cast you out. We knew you would bring trouble upon us. In these most unsettled times."

"I meant no harm," Mae said softly.

"And yet you have caused harm." Miss Adaline sighed. "It was my voice that raised on your behalf all those years ago. I thought your love of Mr. Lindson would keep you . . . far from us. And yet you return."

She made it sound like it was Mae's fault. Like Mae was some kind of bad penny she could not be rid of.

Mae prickled. "I was not the one who cast the spell to bind me to coven soil. I would not have come of my own volition."

Miss Adaline took a sip of tea, her brown eyes sharp. "That was sister Virginia's idea. She always worried you'd be alone and astray in the world. Of course, she thought that of any wild thing."

Mae stood out of the chair. "I am not a wild thing. You have made it clear I am no longer welcome here. I will leave as soon as my companions are recovered enough to travel. And," Mae said walking across the room to her elder, "I will break my ties to this coven. But only if the sisters assist me in breaking the curse on Mr. Hunt and his brother, and in healing Rose."

"We will want something in return."

Mae literally took half a step back, shocked. "Is that the way of the coven now? Bargaining for your advantage?"

"The war has changed us all, Mae Rowan. Time has changed us all. We adapt, and we survive."

"What do you want from me?"

"I want you to cast a spell for me."

Mae shook her head, but just then the front door opened and one of the younger sisters she didn't know stepped in. "Miss Adaline, the supplies from town have come and there is some mail for you. It looks official."

Adaline smiled and it seemed that warmth filled up the hard edges of her. "Thank you, Becky. Take it to my room, please. I'll be there shortly."

Becky shut the door.

"We will speak later." Adaline crossed the room to the other door, and left Mae standing with nothing but her doubts and anger.

The sisters had almost killed her trying to bring her home. Yes, she'd agreed to let them bind her blood to the soil of the coven, but she had never agreed that they could torture her as she tried to find her way home.

She could have died. Rose, Captain Cage, Wil, and Cedar, all could have died. She didn't know if the sisters intentions were to kill others, but they had clearly not cared if they killed her.

The travelers had spent the last week at the coven, resting. The sisters had left them mostly alone, though warm meals were provided.

She, however, was an outsider. Feared.

Mae had spent the last week trying to find forgiveness in her heart. But this place that she had always thought would be home to her was spoiled now. Closed. They did not want her here.

She didn't want to remain.

A woman's soft laughter and a man's low tone echoed from the hallway connecting the gathering hall to the guest rooms.

Rose and Captain Cage had been nearly inseparable.

Mae smiled despite her sour mood. She had to admit their courtship made her happy for both of them, but most especially for Rose.

"Mae," Rose said, walking into the room. "We hoped we'd find you here." Rose was moving slowly, as if her feet dragged a great weight behind them. But her color was better, the tin having faded from her face and neck, though there was still a sheen of silver to her skin and hair.

The sisters had very few guesses as to how to help Rose. It wasn't magic, exactly, that was plaguing her, nor exactly a physical ailment.

Strangeworked devices were well outside the realms of their spell craft.

"Where else would I be?" Mae meant it to be teasing, as she'd found herself here, by the fire at all hours of the day and night. But her words came out with the bitterness of someone sentenced to pace the same cell for the rest of her life.

"Well, it's a lovely place, and everyone has been so pleasant," Rose said. "You could be almost anywhere." She was leaning on Hink's arm pretty heavily as she made her way across the room.

Hink had recovered from most of his injuries to the point that he was moving smoothly. All, that is, except for his broken arm and missing eye. He wore a soft cloth over the eye, with a bandage messing up his hair a bit as it held the patch in place and covered the burn on his forehead. Once both the eye wound and the brand on his forehead were less sensitive, they'd fashion a patch, which he would wear for the rest of his life.

There was nothing they could do to hide the five-pointed star branded into his forehead, other than see it healed properly. He would carry that scar to his grave.

While he hadn't exactly taken his injuries gracefully, after spending three days drinking and coming up with new cuss words for Alabaster Saint's damned soul—an activity that his crew, and the Madder brothers, had joined in quite readily—he had shouldered the fact that he would never have his full eyesight again. Nor go unnoticed as the president's man.

As for having Rose at his side, leaning on him, well, he didn't look one bit upset about that.

"Are you sure you don't need me to support you a bit more, Rose?" he asked. "Perhaps my arm around your waist?"

"Like yesterday?" Rose asked.

"Yesterday?" he asked glibly.

"Yesterday. When you helped me," she said. "If you thought you were putting your hands on my waist, you need a refresher on body parts, Paisley."

He stopped cold and Rose was forced to stop too. "What?" she said, searching his face. "Are you all right? Your eye. Is it hurting again? The scar? Do you need the medicine?"

"Who," he bit off, "told you my name is Paisley?"

Rose's look of concern slid into one of wide-eyed innocence, though she was having a hard time keeping a smile off her face. "I'm not sure I recall. It must have been one of the crew."

"Seldom," Hink groused. "That man talks too much."

"It's a lovely name," Rose continued as they got back to walking. "And a lovely fabric. Why I've always admired paisley dresses, haven't you, Mae? They're so . . . frilly."

"Yes," Mae agreed. "Very pretty."

"My mother," he said through his teeth, "happened to like paisley. She had this one dress, given to her by a man who—" He shut his mouth.

"A man who what?" Rose asked.

"A man who—" Hink narrowed his eye as if just figuring her game. "Never mind what the man did, all right now? I prefer you use 'Lee' when you address me."

"What? Not 'Captain' or 'Marshal' or perhaps 'lord king of all the land'?"

"Well, I'd never stop a woman from calling me king."

"King Paisley," Rose mused. "Certainly has a ring to it."

"Forget it," he said, blowing out his breath. "You may call me Captain Hink. And not a syllable more."

"Didn't mean for you to get all flustered," Rose continued mercilessly. "It's just so difficult to sort through all your names. And you're sure there aren't some other things you'd like me to call you?"

"I can think of several things I'd like to hear on your lips," he said with a wicked grin, holding her gaze as he helped her sit in the other chair near the fire. "But not in polite company, my dear."

Rose's cheeks flamed red. "Oh," she managed.

Hink walked over to the fire, looking pleased as punch at securing Rose's silence.

"Were you looking for me?" Mae asked.

"Yes," Rose said, jumping on the change of subject. "We were. I know it hasn't been very long since we've been here, and the road was . . . hard."

Hink crouched down at the hearth and used the poker to rearrange the wood and ashes. Molly's death weighed heavily on him. He had refused to talk about it, or her.

"Hard on all of us," Rose amended. "This"—she waved toward her left side, where the Holder still capped her shoulder beneath her dress—"it's not the most worrisome thing that's happened, but I don't want to carry it all my life. It's a part of a weapon an awful lot of folk want their hands on. I'd rather be quit of it, if I can."

"We don't know what will happen if we try to remove it, Rose," Mae said. "Even the Madders aren't sure what will happen."

"I know," Rose said, pulling a small hook and yarn out of her pocket and stitching along the row to keep her fingers busy. It looked like she was crocheting a soft rope. Maybe an eye patch for the captain. "But I also know we won't find out what's going to happen unless we try. There isn't anyone in the world who's ever had a thing like this."

"So what are you asking, Rose?"

"I'm asking you to help remove it." She pulled on the yarn and rewound the thread through her fingers, stitching on again. "I don't know what else to do," she said softly. "You can bind things, join things. I was hoping you could unbind the Holder from me."

Mae wanted to tell her no. That asking the sisters for help with magic might come at too high a cost. But there simply wasn't anyone else, and certainly not anyone here, who could even attempt to unbind the Holder.

And it wasn't the only magic that Mae needed to do. She had bound Hink to his ship, so much so that the damage the ship received echoed through him. In a very real way, he shared the *Swift*'s pain. A condition she was sure he was eager to be done with.

She had also promised Cedar and Wil that she would try to break the curse the native gods had placed upon them.

She hadn't been strong enough to attempt that alone, back in Hallelujah. But now she was home, surrounded by twenty-five women skilled in magic. She would see that it was done, no matter what Miss Adaline wanted from her.

Rose waited, letting Mae think it through.

Hink leaned his good elbow on the mantel above the hearth, and let his gaze shift between Rose and the windows on the far side of the room, caught in his own thoughts. He was much quieter these days.

"I'll do what I can," Mae said. And at Rose's obvious relief she added, "We'll find a way to free you of it. There's no need for you to fret."

"Thank you," Rose said. "I wasn't sure if you'd be willing. And so soon. It will be soon, right?"

"Tonight, I think," Mae said. "I'll go talk to the sisters about it. Then we'll take care of this."

Mae stood. "I'll see about the preparations." As she left the room, the sound of Hink's voice, then Rose's laughter followed her.

Rose was brimming with hopefulness. She knew she had a second chance at life after coming so very close to death, and it looked like she intended to live it to the fullest.

Maybe Mae needed to start looking on the bright side herself. After all, she was a witch. A very powerful witch. And while it might have been her magic that had harmed her friends, it would be her magic that saved them as well.

CHAPTER THIRTY-THREE

Cedar stood out on the porch of the gathering hall, looking across the coven's fields to the orchards turning silver-orange in the setting sun. He still hurt if he moved too quickly, his ribs catching at simple movements. His neck and face were still so sore that he had a constant ache in his head.

The sisters had been surprised when the ships dropped anchor over their north field a week or so ago, but they had welcomed Mae and all the others in out of the rain and wind. They'd found a bed for everyone, and put their best healers to soothe the wounded.

The dead were wrapped in clean blankets and buried beneath the apple orchard with soft prayers. Miss Dupuis had stayed out by Theobald's grave for a day and night before coming back into the houses.

Tonight, Wil sat beside Cedar, silent as only a wolf can be, listening, just as Cedar was listening to the women who had been called from the surrounding acres, preparing for Mae to unbind the Holder.

He'd asked Mae if she was recovered enough to use magic again, and she'd avoided his eyes before answering him. He didn't know what it was about this place, but it made him uncomfortable.

Mae seemed uncomfortable too. Angry.

Alun Madder strolled up in front of the porch, the cherry-scented smoke from his pipe curling around his head. "You still owe us that promise, Mr. Hunt."

"Which promise, Mr. Madder?" Cedar asked. "That I hunt the Holder for you so long as our roads remained the same?"

"That's the one."

"Found it. The Holder's right back there in that room, attached to Miss Rose Small."

Alun leaned on the outside of the porch rail, his back to Cedar so he too could stare out at the sunset. "That's one piece of it. One out of seven. It's a good start, but it doesn't make your promise to us fulfilled."

"I killed Mr. Shunt," Cedar noted.

"That you did. But if you think his hands are the worst that the Holder can fall into, you are misunderstanding our problem."

Cedar crossed his arms carefully over his chest. "Why didn't you tell me about the others who were fighting the Strange, like Miss Dupuis, Mr. Theobald, and Miss Wright?"

Alun puffed on his pipe for a bit. The sun was nearly down, just a slight glow of deep red smudging the clouds at the horizon.

"Didn't think you'd believe me," Alun said. "Or my brothers. Didn't think you would join us. It's a select group, Mr. Hunt. Vowed to keep the land safe from the kinds of things you hunt. Strange things. All good people who would stand beside you, fight beside you."

"Die beside me."

"That too," Alun agreed.

"I've seen enough dying to last my years," Cedar said. "I'm not the man you need. Once this curse is off me, I won't feel the hunger to hunt any Strange thing. And I'll be glad for it."

Alun grunted in agreement. Then, "You recall that town we rode into a few weeks back? Vicinity, up Idaho way?"

"Yes."

"All those people dead. Unalives. Men and women and children.

Dead because just one piece of the Holder landed on their town. There's still six pieces of it out there. Stirring up six different hells."

Alun pushed off the porch rail and turned toward him as he started up the stairs. He walked past Cedar to the door, where he paused.

"People are going to die in great numbers while we track down the pieces of the Holder," he said. "That's just the facts of it. And not all of the people out looking for the Holder together can find those pieces as quickly as you and your brother can.

"The curse laid upon you, Mr. Hunt, might be seen as a blessing. Especially from the perspective of the people in the path of the Holder's destruction. People you could save."

Cedar heard the approach of footsteps from inside the building.

"Mr. Hunt? Oh, Mr. Madder," the elder sister, Miss Adaline, called out as she opened the door. "I didn't expect you on the threshold. Come in, please."

"Thank you, ma'am," Alun said.

"Are you coming, Mr. Hunt?" she asked. "The sisters have gathered and the sun's gone down. If you'd like to be present for Miss Small, now's the time. We'll be sealing the doors and windows shortly."

Cedar took a breath and looked over at Miss Adaline. She was old enough to be his mother, he supposed, and still held some beauty to her features. But there was something about her that sat wrong with him. A cunning to her eye he could not ignore.

She was the kind of woman he would not turn his back on for long.

Mae had said she and the sisters had agreed to try to break his curse. Could try to break Wil's curse too. It was what he had wanted. It was a part of why he had accompanied Mae to the coven.

Only a part of the reason, but still, he'd thought of nothing but being free of the curse since the day he'd woken up fevered, near dead, and covered in blood he thought was his brother's.

But Alun's words hung heavy on his mind.

If what he had said was true, then breaking the curse would be dooming hundreds, maybe thousands to suffer from the Holder.

"Mr. Hunt," Miss Adaline said, "are you well?"

"No," he said honestly, before he remembered his manners. He swallowed, and took his hat off his head, running his fingers along the brim as he pulled himself together. "Thank you, though," he said, "for your concern."

She gave him a tight smile. "Of course. Now come in from the cold. We'll all have something joyous to celebrate soon."

Wil stood, and pressed his head under Cedar's hand. He knew what Cedar was thinking, had heard and understood every word Alun had said.

And he knew what Cedar had decided.

"We deserve a little joy," Cedar said.

"Always, Mr. Hunt," she said. "And I've found there's not any dark circumstance that doesn't hold a glimmer of happiness."

He nodded, then he and Wil, together, walked into the gathering.

CHAPTER THIRTY-FOUR

One thing Rose had not expected was for magic to make her sneeze. But the sisters had set all sorts of herbs burning and sprinkled more in water, and even rubbed oil and herbs gently on her wrists, forehead and over her heart. All together the smoke and greenness made her eyes water and her nose tickle.

She tried not to sneeze, as she supposed it took away from what appeared to be a very serious ceremony. But holding her breath would go only so far, after all.

So when she thought no one was looking, she rubbed at her nose and wiped her eyes.

A muffled chuckle made her glance at Captain Hink. He, of course, had been staring at her the whole time.

She resisted the urge to stick her tongue out at him.

"Let us begin," Miss Adaline said.

Rose sat a little straighter in the chair situated in the middle of the gathering hall. The sisters, not all of whom lived here and tended the farm, surrounded her in a wide circle.

The rest of the people in attendance—Cedar Hunt, Wil, the Madders, Miss Dupuis, Miss Wright, and Mr. Seldom—were scattered about the room.

It made Rose nervous to be the center of attention of so much magic.

But it was also exciting. Here she was, Rose Small, in the middle of a circle of witches, about to get some strange device unstuck from her shoulder.

She should jot this all down in a letter to Mr. Gregor back in Hallelujah. He had wanted to hear about her travels and adventures. Maybe she'd leave out the almost dying part, but she thought he'd like to know where she had been. Airships, mountains, and now, Kansas.

She wanted to tell him she'd met Molly, and how wonderful and strong and kind she was and how bravely she'd died. She had known her so briefly, but was going to miss her keenly.

The sisters began singing. It was a soft, rising song. Rose didn't understand everything that was happening, but the song was nice, and when Mae walked behind her and placed her hand on the Holder, it was almost as if the entire song flowed through her hand.

Warmth rolled like a warm wind across her body. Rose had been told to just stay still and relax. But the warmth was heating up, becoming uncomfortable.

And then she must have fallen asleep for the blink of a moment.

White-hot pain raked through her like someone was pulling her naked over hot coals.

She opened her mouth to scream . . .

. . . and there was a cool cloth on her forehead, a soft bed beneath her.

Well, not quite a bed. She was lying in the gathering hall, near the fire, on a pile of soft blankets.

Miss Adaline placed the cool cloth over her forehead. "Back with us now?" she asked.

"Did I go somewhere?"

"You fainted, for a few minutes now. It must have hurt very much."

"It did," Rose said. "Is it done? Is it gone?"

"Mostly," Miss Adaline said. "Your shoulder is bare skin again." She gently drew her fingers over Rose's shoulder, and Rose flinched.

"Still aches," she said.

"I imagine it will for a while yet. When the metal fell free into Mae's hand a very small key was attached to it. How do you feel?"

"Better, I think," Rose said. "Can I talk to Mae?"

A shadow crossed Adaline's face, turning her features hard. But she nodded. "Of course."

Rose was getting the impression that the sisters were wary of Mae. Of her particular talents with magic.

And Mae had barely smiled in all the time they'd been here. She wondered if time would eventually make her happy to be home again.

Mae lowered herself next to Rose. She was pale, and looked tired, but she smiled. "How are you feeling?"

"I like having my skin back," Rose said. "Where is it? The Holder?"

"Bryn Madder had a very clever box to put it in." Mae looked over her shoulder. "He and the other Madders all made a big production that no one touch it, even though it was bare in my hands. Then the Madders put on thick gloves and carefully placed it, key and all, into the box. I think you'd have liked to have seen it, but Bryn's already taken it out to the airship and has said the box cannot be unsealed."

"Are they leaving?" Rose asked with a start. "Is everyone leaving?"

"No, they are arguing. Over who is going to take the piece of the Holder to safekeeping."

Now that Mae mentioned it, Rose could hear the lively discussion on the other side of the room. Alun Madder and Miss Dupuis were arguing with Captain Hink, of all people.

"The captain wants it?" Rose asked, surprised.

"He does. Apparently, it's part of what the president sent him out to find, and Cedar made a deal of some kind regarding it. But I'm not sure that the Madders, or Miss Dupuis, will let him have it."

"Let them store it, Cage." Cedar's voice was low, but rolled through the room like a wind closing a door. "You have no place to keep it, no way to transport it to the president, and no guarantee it won't harm you or others on the way."

"My mission—," Hink began.

"Was to find the Holder," Cedar finished for him. "And to keep it out of the wrong hands. You've found a piece of it. And these people will keep it out of everyone's hands. This is where it ends."

"You can't tell me what my orders are, Mr. Hunt."

"You want this piece of tin, you go through me to get it."

Everyone in the room was silent.

Finally, Miss Dupuis spoke up. "We are in contact with the president, Captain Cage. I give you my word. We will store it safely and contact him immediately. As Mr. Hunt says, we will keep this away from all living things."

"And if the president wants it?" Hink asked.

"He can ask for it, of course," Alun Madder said.

Rose knew the Madders well enough to know that just because they said you could do something, it didn't mean they would actually let you do it.

But she was on their side in this argument. She wanted the piece of the Holder locked up, locked away. The very idea of Captain Cage carrying it around with him as he made his way back to Washington put knots in her stomach.

"You know I'll hunt you down for it if I want it," Hink said with a friendliness that nonetheless carried a threat.

"Oh, we'd expect no less of you, Mr. Hink," Alun said cheerily. "Shall we drink on it, then?"

There was the passing of flasks, and then someone brought in wine. Mae sat silently with Rose, staring into the fire, seeming to smile slightly only when Cedar Hunt spoke.

Oh. Maybe that was the sadness that had taken her friend. Mae had come home, but Mr. Hunt might be moving on.

Rose was going to ask her, but the fire was warm, the sound of voices growing more and more friendly as the wine flowed, and eventually, without her consent, sleep took her to softer horizons.

She woke to someone whispering her name.

"Rose?"

She opened her eyes. It was dark in the room, the fire in the hearth banked down low. It took her a second or two to get her bearings. She was at the coven, in the great room, wrapped in blankets. Who was calling her name?

Captain Hink knelt down beside her. "Are you awake?"

"Is something wrong?"

"No. But it will be sunrise soon. I wanted to go out to the *Swift* and watch it rise. I thought . . ." He paused as if suddenly realizing he was waking her up out of bed and asking her to tromp off to his ship with him, alone in the dark.

"Hmm." He sat the rest of the way down on the floor. "Why is it," he said, "that every time I'm around you, I act like an idiot? Do you have some sort of magic that makes men turn dumb?"

"No. I think you just come by it in a natural sort of way, Captain."

He grinned at her. "I assure you, Rose, I am quite the suave buck around other women."

"Have you been around so many to test this theory of yours?" Rose asked sweetly. "Would you say dozens? Hundreds of women?"

Hink chuckled. "Oh, this is a conversation we are not about to undertake. So, never you mind, Rose Small. Go back to sleep. I'm sorry—"

"I'd love to see it," Rose said. "The sunrise. The ship. Help me up?"

"Be happy to." Hink stood, grunting a little from his own aches, then helped her up.

She wrapped the blankets tight around her and Hink wrapped his good arm firmly around her waist.

Walking was a little easier. No, everything was easier, including breathing. Being rid of the Holder made Rose feel like she was really well again.

They stepped outside into the still and silent pre-morning light.

There was something about the quiet of the day that she wanted to savor, the held breath of something new about to begin.

Captain Hink must have felt it too. He didn't say anything as they followed the trail out to the field where the airships had been towed and anchored. The strange blocky shape of the Madders' top-like ship took up more room than the *Swift*, and it at least appeared whole.

The *Swift* was a mess. Her envelope had been deflated, and now lay on the field like a blanket of tin that had been gently wrapped into a roll. The living space of the ship was missing part of the back end, and the glim trawling arms were both broken down to nubs.

She looked like a ship that had been torn apart by the seas and wrecked upon rocky shores.

A golden dragonfly buzzed down to land above the door to the ship, its wings like chips of crystal. The dragonfly looked almost like it was clockwork, but Rose was too far away to see it properly. And just before she got close enough, the dragonfly flew off, its wings ticking through the sky.

"The *Swift* served us well," Captain Hink said, drawing Rose from her thoughts.

"She did, poor thing," Rose said as they came up close enough to touch her. "She's been through a lot."

"She'll fly again," Captain Hink said. "Can't keep a girl like her out of the sky." He opened the door, and helped Rose step up into the ship.

Captain Hink stepped in behind her, blocking her escape, not that she wanted to escape. He took a deep breath and when he exhaled, his broad shoulders relaxed.

"What are you smiling about, Captain?" Rose asked.

He gestured for her to walk with him to the front of the ship, where there were two chairs, and a wide expanse of windows facing east.

"Pretty morning, pretty ship, pretty woman—why wouldn't I be smiling, Miss Small?"

"Look who's recovered his charm." Rose sat and Hink dropped down in the other chair.

"Just needed to get out under the sky," he said, "to clear my head."

"It's beautiful," Rose said as the brush of lavender light washed the sky, framed by the brass and tin and wood of the *Swift's* controls near the windows.

"It is. And out here, on the ship, it's like I can breathe again."

"You don't like being tied to the ground, do you, Captain?"

"It's never done me much good. And I thought you were going to call me Lee."

"Paisley."

He sighed. "You really going to keep at that?"

"Is it really your first name?"

"I could lie to you."

"I'd find out."

He paused, then, "She didn't know the name of one of her suitors. My mother. One of the men who might have been my father. But she was sweet on him. See, he'd bought her the prettiest thing she'd ever owned. A paisley dress." He stared out at the sky, as if he could still see his mother and her dress. "She thought it fine enough to remember him by. To name me by. It is my first name."

Rose turned and looked at him. He had a good profile, strong, wide features, and a mouth that couldn't seem to stay away from a smile for long. Even the bandage and scar beneath his yellow bangs gave him a little something, an aura of danger and adventure.

Just the look of him made her heart pound faster, and when he rankled under her teasing, she thought she'd melt away from the pleasure of it.

"You know she bound me to the ship, don't you?" he asked. "Your friend Mae?"

"Yes," Rose said. "I'm sure she can break that now. Here, with the . . . others helping her."

"I'm sure she can," he said. "But I've asked her not to."

"What? When? Why?"

"Yesterday before she took care of you and the Holder. And as for why"—he turned to look at her—"I can see when I'm on the *Swift*. Like I still have two eyes. Better than that. Being a part of the *Swift*, tied to her like this, means I can still fly her. Means I still have wings."

"But I thought when the ship is damaged, it harms you too."

"Contrary to the last few weeks you've known me," Hink said, "I do not make it a habit to crash my ship at every chance."

"You want to stay this way? All tied up and such?"

"For as long as it lasts. Mae isn't sure how long that will be. Said it could be years, or days. I'll take what I can get, as long as I can get it with the *Swift*."

"So I suppose you'll be leaving, then?" Rose asked.

"As soon as I can patch her up and catch a fair wind, which isn't looking likely until spring, but yes. I'll be burning sky the first chance I get."

"And your crew?"

"They're happy enough to stay here or in town so long as the wine and food hold out. Lazy nits. Figure they'll fly with me when I leave."

"Well," Rose said, her throat tight with a sadness she had not expected. "I wish you all the best with that, Captain."

Hink frowned. "You're going with me, Rose."

"What? Is that what you've decided?" Okay, now she was getting angry. Sure, she liked him, maybe was more than a little infatuated with him. But he couldn't just assume she was going to do anything he told her to do.

"No, it's what I'm asking you. I did ask you, didn't I?" His eye went wide, then he closed it. "No. I didn't. I practiced it so many times in my head, I meant to, it's just . . ." He opened his eye and spread his hand.

"Let me try this again. Proper. Rose Small, would you fly with me?"

Rose had always thought a marriage proposal would be the sweetest words she ever heard from a man. She was wrong. Every inch of her wanted to say yes. But she was a practical woman. She wasn't going to jump on a ship because some handsome pirate lawman airship captain sweet-talked her into it.

"And do what, Captain? Be your concubine?"

"Well, I was going to offer you to be my boilerman," he drawled, "but I could go with concubine if that's the job you'd rather take on."

"Boilerman?" Rose sat up straight and didn't even care that her blanket slid down off her shoulder, baring an awful lot of her skin.

Hink, however, seemed quite appreciative of the view.

"Since Molly is . . . gone," he said, trying his best not to stare at her chest, "I need someone who knows how to devise and keep the *Swift* running. The Madder brothers bragged you up as some kind of natural with wood and steam and gear, and Molly herself told me you were of fine Gregor teaching. I figured I'd give you a run at the sky. If you want it."

"Oh, I do," she said. "I do!" She reached over and before she had the sense to think it through, she kissed him.

Full on the mouth.

She froze, uncertain as to whether to go forward, or try to back out of this situation gracefully.

But Captain Hink did not freeze. His mouth accepted her, coaxing her to explore this predicament they'd suddenly fallen into. Then his hand joined in, and a short while after that, his tongue.

Rose sighed and melted into him. Captain Cage showed her some of the finer points of this particular sort of exploration. She let him do so with a willing heart, savoring the delicious sensations rolling through her body as dawn washed gold light over them, the airship, and the world.

CHAPTER THIRTY-FIVE

Cedar Hunt had taken his time to talk to the sisters about the binding on Mae. To explain to them how they had nearly killed her. Miss Adaline had not been amused nor surprised by his forthright manner.

She had told him that the ways of magic were between those of the coven. And that he and his were certainly not a voice to say otherwise.

He explained to her that when that magic involved Mae, he didn't give a damn about the coven's rules.

Then he said his good-byes to Miss Adaline and the other sisters, of kinder demeanors, who had taken them in. He'd said his good-byes to Captain Hink and his crew. Now he was saying his good-byes to Rose Small.

He'd been surprised that she'd decided to stay here at the coven for the winter as long as they'd have her and in town if her welcome wore out.

Of course, Captain Hink was staying with her. Cedar didn't know if Hink was going back to harvesting glim or riding as U.S. Marshal. That brand on his forehead would change the way he faced the world, the way he did his job.

Cedar hoped he stayed on the side of law, though with a Marshal's star burned into your head, it might make the proposition of staying undercover more difficult.

Still, Cedar knew Hink was the sort of a man who could be trusted. He'd done a lot for them, risked a lot, lost a lot. And he was sweet on Rose.

Cedar had never seen Rose happier than this last week. And with Hink promising her a place on his ship working the boiler, Cedar couldn't help but think that Rose was finally getting the adventure and life she had always longed for.

"You'll come back, won't you?" Rose asked when he'd gone out to the *Swift* to find her helping with what repairs they could tend to while the weather held. "If you can, before spring? And if not, you'll contact us, send a message, so I can see you again? Both of you," she added, with a gentle rub behind Wil's ears.

"I'll come back, I'll find you, I'll send messages," Cedar promised. "You know I'm a man of my word."

She smiled and it was like a new sun had broken the horizon. "Once she's flying again, I'll come find you. If you're traveling with the Madders, all I'll have to do is look for something blowing up and head that way."

Cedar chuckled but before he could reply, she threw her arms around him. "Thank you, Mr. Hunt. I'll miss you so." She gave him a warm hug, and Cedar put his arms around her gently.

He was fond of her and couldn't help but feel that saying good-bye meant he was losing someone very special.

"I'll miss you too, Rose," he said quietly.

Then he stepped back and Rose gave him a measuring look. "Have you spoken with Mae yet?"

"No. And don't give me that scowl, Miss Small. I'm on my way to see her now."

"Good," Rose said. "You shouldn't leave without talking to her first. Without . . . explaining."

Explaining. Why he had told her he didn't want her to break his curse or Wil's. Why he had decided to travel with the Madders. Why he had brought her to the coven and was leaving her behind while he and his brother hunted down the Holder.

Why he was putting his life on hold to chase down something that might be impossible to find.

"I'll do what I can," he said.

Cedar turned and walked back to the main gathering hall, where he knew he'd find Mae by the fire.

He walked up onto the porch and into the hall. One of the younger sisters was in the hall, humming as she swept the floor. Mae was not there.

"Hello, Mr. Hunt," she said. "Can I help you with something?"

"I'm looking for Mae. Do you know where she might be?"

"She's back in her cabin, I think."

"Thank you."

Cedar strolled out of the hall and headed to the small shack they had given Mae. All the other travelers had stayed in rooms in the great hall, but they had placed Mae in a cabin on her own, almost as if to keep her apart from any other person.

She had told him it wasn't that they didn't want her among them, but he knew even she didn't believe that.

Because it wasn't true. The sisterhood, while being generous, did not like having Mae there. They treated her with caution, with suspicion.

Cedar didn't like it. But this was Mae's home. These were her people. If she was happy here, then he was happy for her.

He knocked on the cabin door, and took off his hat.

"Come in," Mae said.

Cedar lifted the latch and pushed the door open.

Mae was standing next to the narrow bed in the only room of the house, packing a satchel.

"Mae?" Cedar said. "I need to speak to you." Then the meaning of her actions sank in. She was packing. "Where are you going?"

She latched the satchel and turned to face him. "With you."

Cedar held very still. "I don't understand."

"I . . . talked to Miss Adaline," Mae said, as she walked over to a hat stand, pulled a shawl off it, and wrapped it around her shoulders. "We came to an understanding. I am no longer tied to the coven."

"They broke the spell?" he asked, his mind still not working as quickly as her words.

"I broke the spell, with their help. But, well, breaking the spell means I am no longer welcome here. No longer part of the sisterhood."

"No," he said, "that can't be true. You are a witch, Mae. You told me it's something you're born into."

"Yes, I'm still a witch, but I have—it's hard to explain." Her voice shook a little and he knew it was also a thing of sorrow. "Time changes us all, Mr. Hunt. We adapt."

"Mae, you don't have to do this. You can change it. You can stay."

"Even if I wanted to? If things were different?" She shook her head. "I don't think I would. I've seen too much of the world. And still want to see a fair share more."

"Mae." He didn't know what else to say.

"It's fine. Truly." She put on her coat, then glanced around the room one last time and smiled. "I am happy . . . happier than I've been in a long while. Now, let's go."

Cedar finally gathered his wits. "You can't go with me, Mae. Wil and I, and the Madders will be looking for the other pieces of the Holder. You've seen what it can do. It won't be safe for you to travel with us."

"Can't?" Mae's eyebrows raised. "I don't believe you can tell me what I can and cannot do, Mr. Hunt. And as for danger, we came through the last few weeks still breathing. I'd like to point out that on several occasions I helped keep us safe, even without magic. And I was under great distress. Think of how much more useful I will be with a clear mind."

"Do you care so much about the Holder that you're willing to tramp across this country hunting it?" he asked.

"No," Mae said quietly. "I care that much about you."

Cedar felt like lightning had just struck him from out of a clear blue sky. He didn't know what to say, didn't want to say the wrong thing and break this fragile moment.

Mate, the beast whispered contentedly inside of his mind.

Should he tell her he felt the same? Would she understand that he more than cared for her? That he loved her?

Cedar held his breath. Then, "From the moment I first set eyes on you," he said, "I have cared for you a very great deal. I can't bear to leave you behind. But I can't bear to see you hurt either. It's safe here."

She crossed the room, her deep brown eyes searching his.

She stopped so close, he could feel the heat of her. But she was not touching him. Not yet.

"I'm not looking for safety." Mae reached up on tiptoe, her hand brushing his face. "I'm looking to live."

Cedar leaned down. He wrapped his arms around her and drew her close. He kissed her slowly, passionately, making promises with his touch that no words could convey.

"If you two are done sealing the deal," Alun Madder said from the door, "then we need to be leaving now."

Cedar pulled away and smiled at Mae, who smiled right back at him.

She stepped out of his arms and retrieved her luggage.

Cedar turned to Alun. Miss Dupuis stood beside him, wearing a lovely blue dress and politely studying the fingertips of her gloves as if they were the most fascinating thing in the world.

"Morning," Cedar said to Miss Dupuis.

"Good morning," she said, glancing up with a faint smile. "Will you and Mae be traveling with us, then?"

"Us?" Cedar asked.

"Miss Dupuis will accompany us for the first leg of the trip," Alun said. "See that the Holder gets stashed away safely."

"Where, exactly, are we headed?" Cedar asked.

"Exactly? Why, to find the Holder, Mr. Hunt," Alun said with a wide grin. "And to save the world." He spun on his heel and held out his arm for Miss Dupuis. "I thought you'd know that by now."

Cedar turned to Mae. She was smiling, her luggage in one hand, her satchel over her shoulder.

"Are you ready?" he asked.

"I am." Her smile grew wider. "Are you going to save the world, Mr. Hunt?"

Cedar glanced over his shoulder. Alun and Miss Dupuis were headed toward the brothers' airship, where Wil waited in the grass. Then he looked back at Mae.

"I certainly intend to do what I can," he said.

Cedar held his hand out for her, and she took it. Then he walked with Mae into the sunlight of a new day, the ship ready before him, his brother and Mae at his side, and his heart beating with newfound joy.

Devon Monk writes the Allie Beckstrom urban fantasy series, the Age of Steam steampunk series, and the occasional short story. She has one husband, two sons, and a dog named Mojo. Surrounded by numerous and colorful family members, she lives, writes, and knits in Oregon. For excerpts, information, and news, please visit her Web site at www.devonmonk.com.